THE NEWSMAKERS

Nigel Rees is a writer and broadcaster. On radio and television he has presented a large number of programmes ranging from news and current affairs to art and entertainment. His many best-selling books to date have dealt with aspects of the English language and, especially, the humour that derives from it. *THE NEWSMAKERS* is his first novel. Nigel Rees is married and lives in central London.

THE NEWSMAKERS

Nigel Rees

HEADLINE

First published in Great Britain in 1987
by HEADLINE BOOK PUBLISHING PLC

Reprinted 1987

British Library Cataloguing in Publication Data

Rees, Nigel.
The newsmakers.
I. Title
823'.914[F]   PR6068.E38/
ISBN 0-7472-0011-4

HEADLINE BOOK PUBLISHING PLC
Headline House
79 Great Titchfield Street
London W1P 7FN

Typeset by Alacrity Typesetters, Banwell Castle, Weston-super-Mare
Printed and bound in Great Britain by Billings, Worcester

To C.M.
who knows how it was

CHAPTER 1

It was when Jo threw the television at him that David briefly realized all was not well with their marriage.

'You're so stubborn,' she shouted. 'And you won't listen. It's impossible to shake you. And you never *say* anything.'

David indeed said nothing but waited, rather sheepishly, for his wife to stop.

'The only goddamn thing that matters to you is your work,' she raged on. 'The rest of your life, me, the boys, we're just extras. When *are* you going to grow up and behave like a normal human being?'

The American accent grated on David only when they were having a row. 'I'm sorry,' he said quietly. 'I have to pack. I'm already behind.'

'That's right. The news must come first. South Africa, Ireland, the tacky British economy – it always has to come first. Well, you can *take* your asshole news ...'

And picking up the portable TV she threw it at him.

The electric flex and the aerial cable conspired to spoil her aim. The TV fell far short of David, tumbling onto the armchair between them.

'For God's sake, Jo, not the television ...'

David grabbed at her hands as she made a lunge for him.

'Never, *never* do such a stupid thing again,' he shouted, suddenly roused.

As symbolic gestures go, however, it had been a good one. It seemed to him like an assault on his very existence.

Jo struggled to free her hands. But David was stronger and the fight was already going out of her. She was frankly surprised at the way he'd taken her impulsive gesture. She had stumbled by chance on the one action that could sting him.

'You don't do things like that to me, you bloody fool,' he said again, pressing harder on her frail, twig-like fingers. Then he pushed her onto the armchair where she fell in a bundle next to the discarded television set.

'Go to South Africa, then,' she cried. 'See if I care. You'll feel quite at home in a police state ...'

Jo made to scrabble in her handbag for cigarettes and a lighter.

This infuriated David all the more. Just as she was clumsily shaking one out, he swept the packet away and four or five fell into her lap. She picked them up. He made to grab them and, in so doing, crushed the cigarettes in her hand.

'Why the hell do you always have to reach for those things?' he demanded. 'Can't you deal with anything if you haven't got a fag in your mouth?'

Jo made no reply. Tears stained her face. Her shoulders heaved.

David paused for a moment, found her a packet of tissues to dry the tears, then left without another word.

Later that morning, after she'd repaired her face and clothes, Jo put the TV back in its proper place, tidied away the wires, and was quite surprised to find it still worked.

A cup of camomile tea, laced with honey, helped settle her nerves. She made a few, feeble attempts to get down to work. But she couldn't concentrate. The house felt oppressively empty. The children had been tidied away by the nanny when she'd heard the row. Life for Jo returned to being very bleak, as it always was when David was away – and as it was for a good deal of the time he was at home.

Mid-morning, she dialled him at the office.

'He's awfully tied up, Mrs K,' said a secretary, being diplomatic, 'but I'll see.'

There was a pause and music came on the line while Jo waited – middle-of-the-road, neutral, irritating, infuriating music.

'Hello,' David finally said, somewhere short of gruff.

Jo paused. 'I shouldn't have done that. I'm sorry,' she said. 'I went too far.'

'OK, thanks, forget it. Now I really must go. I'm in a meeting.'

What a wonderful voice he has, thought Jo. Intimate, rich, resonant. It still had the power to turn her on even after all this time, even over the telephone.

'Take care in South Africa,' she told him. 'Take real care.'

'OK.'

'Love you.'

'Love you, too,' said David, ritually. Then he hung up and went back to work.

The throwing of the TV set marked a climax in the stormy relationship he had with Jo. Nothing quite like it had happened before. Could he really remain in a marriage where such gestures

8

were made? He loved his children. He liked the idea of being married. But could he bear being married to that woman? Their marriage had long since ceased to be a pleasant affair.

Twelve hours later David Kenway was, as often, flying into trouble. He was aboard a South African Airways 747 nosing its way from London to Johannesburg. In his hand, as he sat in Gold Class, was a glass of Nederburg Riesling.

'It's good to be able to drink this stuff without having to clap my hand over the label,' he remarked provocatively to the even fairer-haired man in the seat next to him.

'You Brits, such two-faced bastards ...'

'No, honestly, I always said economic sanctions wouldn't work – even if there's an argument for imposing them. But cultural sanctions – I suppose wine is cultural? – I never had any faith in them.'

'It's very brave of you to come to South Africa,' the other man said, drily – but not totally without humour. 'You must know what a *dangerous* place it is to be. The Press paints such a terrifying picture.'

'I should know ... I'm kind of Press myself.'

'Oh, then you *are* a two-faced bastard, indeed.'

David joined in the other man's laughter. This was banter he could enjoy.

'And what sort of a bastard are you?' he inquired.

'I'm a karate instructor.'

'Goodness. What d'you do? Run classes?'

'Yes. At a school near Johannesburg. But tell me, do you write for a newspaper?'

'No. I'm with a TV news set-up.'

'BBC?'

'Used to be. Now I work for N-TV.'

'Have I seen you on the screen, then?'

'It's possible.'

'Yes, now I think I remember. What is your name?'

'David Kenway.'

'Mm. My name is Myburgh, by the way. N-TV is new?'

'Quite new. Round-the-clock news and current affairs from London. And by satellite to most of Western Europe. Started about three years ago.'

'So what brings you to South Africa? To look at our State of Emergency. Or to stir things up for us?'

'You haven't heard about Kobus, then?'

'What about him?'

'Shot dead.'

'The Information Minister? Christ! When was that?'

'I heard just before I left the office, mid-afternoon. I was coming anyway, but it gives more point to my visit.'

Myburgh slowly thought over what David had told him.

'So, they've started on the Government now . . . A black did it?'

'I suppose so.'

'Ominous.'

David took another sip of the wine. His curly blond hair pressed deep into the comfortable head-rest, his long jean-clad legs were ever restless. He had a pleasant, boyish face. He was happy in planes, where the world couldn't get at him.

He turned to look at the man on his right. Myburgh was so fair, his moustache and eyebrows melted into the skin. He looked as if he was in his late thirties, like David, though maybe a fraction younger. But his eyes were old. What had they seen to age him?

'Ah, well,' Myburgh concluded, after a lull. 'I imagine we can do without a Nationalist or two. We've managed pretty well so far with all that's been thrown at us . . .'

'Yes,' said David, non-committally. He was never sure how far to grill people he met on flights. You could end up with the most frightful bores. And their information was often unreliable.

He decided to go on, this once. 'Most of our reporting from Jo'burg is done by a bloke called Martin Ramsden. But he's having a spot of leave and I'm manning the fort while he's away.'

'Well, not too many lies, please . . .'

'It's always hard to tell the truth about your country. The Bureau for Information won't let us film an ant without permission.'

'You've been before, then?'

'First time was on my way to Rhodesia in '77 – and I've been back on and off since.'

'You have people to see?'

'Yes. Professionally – and otherwise.'

Myburgh didn't appear to notice his last two words, so David let the conversation lapse. In any case, one of the pleasures of being away from Britain was not being recognized and quizzed about his job in television. As far as he could, when he was abroad, David liked to behave anonymously.

*   *   *

The 747 droned on, southwards, into the night, towards the dark continent.

David took out two contact books, now well-thumbed and worn, and a file of newspaper cuttings with a few hastily stuffed-in pieces about Thys Kobus at the top.

The contact book, names and telephone numbers by the score, is a reporter's vital tool. Once a contact comes into a reporter's life, he could well be useful again and his whereabouts must be paintakingly recorded. There was scarcely a country in the world now where David couldn't turn up and immediately start telephoning well-placed people to find out what he wanted to know.

David's second contact book served a different purpose. It listed several score women on six continents.

In Washington, it was Kay with the legs; in Paris, Monique with the pixy breasts; in Bangkok, small but perfectly formed 'O'; in Sydney, talkative, toothsome Bobbie; in Tel Aviv, the beautiful Debbie; in Cairo, lissome Lorne ... Johannesburg meant Kay, initially, and failing her, Hennie or June. Maybe all three. But now this Kobus business had cropped up, he wasn't sure how much opportunity he would have for horizontal pleasures. Originally, he had intended to spill off the plane around breakfast time, spend the rest of the day collecting his impressions and getting organized, and wind up in bed with one of his women. As it was, he might have to buckle down and do a piece on the Kobus shooting.

David toyed with the cuttings, not really taking in what they said. Then he noticed the air stewardess working her way towards him, handing out dinner-trays. As he grew older, he felt less of an urge to pick up women casually. At one time, the stewardess would have been subjected to a chat-up in the famous Kenway voice, followed by a quick hotel seduction. Now, whoever she was, a new woman was less of a target for David's attentions. His global harem left him well catered for. He only grasped occasionally at unfamiliar flesh.

'Thinking what I'm thinking?' said the voice beside him. Myburgh had noticed David's residual interest in the handsome girl.

'I think she might break if you touched her,' came the dismissive reply.

Nonetheless, David had to admit that she wasn't at all bad. A blonde, she was tall, slim and well-tanned. But her make-up was too calculated and she'd had the natural spark trained out of her.

11

She leant over to pass a meal-tray to Myburgh. When she moved on, David admitted, 'I'd quite like to run my fingers through her hair, wouldn't you ... to ruffle it?'

'It's more the teeth I noticed.'

'A bit too toothy, if you ask me. Prominent.'

'I know,' said the South African. 'All the better for ... you know.'

David almost smiled. He preferred to keep his fantasies to himself. He wasn't a great talker at the best of times – except when he was getting paid for it – and the locker-room mode of sexual fantasizing was not one he favoured.

Before long, he'd finished the dregs of the small bottle of wine he had allowed himself. He unzipped his short boots, loosened the belt round his jeans, and soon dozed off into a state of half-waking, half-dreaming that lasted till morning.

One matter continued to disturb his contentment: that morning's row. Had Jo *broken* the TV? As for her jibes at his shortcomings and failings ... well, the memory of them grew steadily fainter as the 747 put more and more miles between him and his wife.

David and Jo's marriage became tolerable only when the partners were in different hemispheres, so how much longer could it possibly last?

CHAPTER 2

'Good grief,' exclaimed Sir Charles Craig, as March Stevens and Lynne Kimberley swept down the long staircase. 'What a magnificent sight! But I wonder who's minding the store?'

The two women, a good twenty years apart in age, managed to cut through the crowd of people wearing dinner jackets and evening gowns. Heads turned, necks craned. The barons of television, the sports commentators, the quiz-show hosts, the female personalities bursting out of their dresses, shrank away almost respectfully as the two famous faces proceeded on their way.

Sir Charles rose and beckoned them to him. After what seemed a long time, March and Lynne reached the large, circular table. Unbending rather more than he usually did, Sir Charles kissed the younger woman, March, by way of welcome. 'You look too beautiful,' he told her.

'Thank you,' she said, blushing, and hesitantly kissed him back.

Lynne bussed her boss twice.

Sir Charles exuded a proprietorial air, as well he might. He was the architect of their success.

As an afterthought, he turned to the small, severe woman at his side. 'You know these two, of course, Pam?'

Lady Craig greeted March in a motherly way, but it was the first time they had actually met.

'Hello, March ... and hello, Lynne, dear,' she said, turning to the other. 'Good to see you again ... and so glad you're both able to be here.'

March and Lynne went to look for their places at the dinner table. Lynne found herself seated between two worthy but dull members of the N-TV board of directors. She mumbled greetings and, unable to swap place-cards, took refuge in her cigarette packet. She fitted a long black cheroot into a holder, then busied herself with one of the champagne bottles already open on the table.

March had Michael Penn-Morrison, Sir Charles's deputy, on her left and Ben Brock, her fellow newscaster, on the right.

'March – more gorgeous than ever!' said Ben, giving her a

fatherly squeeze. He himself looked unspeakably distinguished in his dinner jacket. His bow-tie was large and just sufficiently uncontrolled to show that he'd tied it himself. A red carnation gleamed from his buttonhole.

'Hello, Van,' March greeted Ben's dark-haired companion. There was just a trace of unease in Vanessa's response as, indeed, there had been in March's initial greeting.

'I don't believe you've met Vanessa ...?' joked Ben. Vanessa, the one with the posh voice and the Laura Ashley wardrobe, worked for both of them.

Pre-dinner chatter filled the vast room. Almost at once, a posse of press photographers, most of them bearded and in leather jackets, made a direct assault on the N-TV table.

'Can we have Ben, Lynne and March?' was their immediate demand. Without a murmur, the two female newscasters dutifully clustered round Ben and hugged him for the benefit of the cameras.

Then, a little pointedly, they asked just to have Ben and March, followed by March on her own.

If Lynne noticed that the photographers were favouring her younger, slenderer colleague, she didn't show any irritation. Just because March had the sweetest face, dazzling white teeth, honey-coloured, shoulder-length hair and an English-rose complexion – just the sort of thing to obsess Fleet Street picture editors – that was no reason for Lynne to get upset. Lynne knew she had plenty of admirers who preferred the ampler charms of a mature woman. But March was rather pushing it, she thought, turning up at a do like this in a long silver-and-white dress, as though she were Cinderella come to the ball. Lynne was glad she'd chosen a purple grosgrain jacket and silk-satin trousers. It suited her mood, which was mellow. Only one thing really bothered her. Why did she always have to top up her own champagne glass?

As the photographers clicked on, filling the air with a curious retching sound as their cameras wound on, an outsider joined the scene. The Right Honourable Colin Lyon MP couldn't resist basking in the reflected glory of 'the First Family of TV News'.

For the Home Secretary, the combination of TV faces, especially female ones, and popping flash bulbs, was magnetic. He detached himself from his glamorous wife and went over towards the N-TV people.

Lyon didn't introduce himself. After all, if the journalists couldn't recognize him on sight, who could? The pressmen fell for Lyon's ploy and asked him to join the newscasting trio for a photograph. Ben Brock oozed charm and managed to conceal his irritation at the politician's pushiness. March smiled sweetly on. Lynne, already three sheets to the wind, was beyond caring.

Before heading back to his table, the Home Secretary allowed his hand to pat Sir Charles Craig on the back.

'I have it on good authority you've been bribing the judges again, Mr Editor, and you'll be collecting your award shortly ...'

Craig tried to assume the required bonhomie. It was hard, particularly given the anaesthetizing qualities of Lyon's aftershave. 'Rather like buying votes, Home Secretary ...'

'Ha, ha!' Lyon said, giving him a suspicious look. 'Ah, well, keep up the good work.' Then he went back to his table briskly.

'He's never forgiven us, you know,' Sir Charles murmured to Ben.

'Because he's not Prime Minister? Surely he's over that by now?'

'I'm not so sure. And to think he's our lord and master in Whitehall ...'

'I try very hard to forget it,' said Ben drily, and went back to his seat between Vanessa and March. The ceremony was about to begin.

It was the season of awards. That time of year when television people scratch each other's backs, sometimes playfully, sometimes painfully; when actors shufflingly read out nominations and actresses slide a finger along to release the contents of golden envelopes; when pride is swallowed or modesty assumed at the results; when lucky winners receive objects whose only possible use is to hold a door ajar or adorn a mantelpiece; when orchestras blare out versions of TV themes as familiar faces hurry between the dining tables to clutch their awards and mumble adequate or inadequate thanks; when Most Promising Newcomers begin to worry about becoming Most Forgotten Has-Beens.

The British Academy of Film and Television Arts was holding its annual awards ceremony in the Great Room at London's Grosvenor House hotel in Park Lane. A thousand diners watched under the TV lights as the long proceedings wound on. Cigar smoke coiled up into the dark above the dais where the Princess stood by the awards table. She possessed a good deal more poise than those who handed her the awards to present to the gawky recipients. Some of these winners, of course, were used to public exposure – though not on a stage; others, from behind the scenes, appeared ill at ease under the bright lights, on display before their colleagues and rivals.

As the presenters ploughed on through the minor awards – the one for the Best Cameraman in a Regional Documentary about a Left-handed Clergyman in Wales – Lynne Kimberley became ever the worse for wear. Dash it, she thought to herself, I'm not appearing on TV tonight, I don't have to make an acceptance speech, and I'm seated between two of the most wooden men ever to press their knees against me. So, what the hell.

It had been a mistake for her to come unescorted but that was how Sir Charles had issued the invitations.

March was in the same boat. She was oddly nervous – but, then, there was nothing unusual in that. She'd had butterflies more or less permanently ever since she started appearing on TV. It had all happened so suddenly, this newscasting, and everyone else appeared so much more experienced and assured. She turned for encouragement to Ben but he was busy being affable to Vanessa. March stared at the other tables and tried celebrity-spotting. All she could see, however, was people on the other tables celebrity-spotting her.

Eventually Derrick Bream, a chat-show host and the evening's master of ceremonies, peered once more at the teleprompter and announced: 'So we come to the award for the Best Television News Team. The nominations are ...'

Here Jacky Alexander, an actress better known for her performances in the gossip columns than for her nominal employment in a soap opera, read out from the back of an envelope: 'BBC Television for the *Nine O'Clock News*; ITN for *News at Ten*; and N-TV for the *Nightly News* ...

'And the winner is ... N-TV for the *Nightly News*!'

The audience, weary after applauding all evening, warmed noticeably to the result, liking the popular news programme which was the flagship of N-TV's coverage.

Derrick Bream spoke, still firmly locked into his teleprompter, his voice riding over the applause: 'Here to receive the award on behalf of N-TV is the man who, single-handed, has made the colour of his buttonhole a more burning issue than the doings of Presidents and Prime Ministers ... Ben Brock!'

From the N-TV table below the stage the tall distinguished figure rose with some grace, stubbed out his cigar, and glided up to receive the award. The orchestra played an unrecognizable version of the *Nightly News* theme. The Princess chatted inaudibly while Ben beamed down at her. She, too, seemed to be making a reference to the buttonhole which had become his trademark.

Then Ben walked to the microphone.

'Your Royal Highness, my Lords, Ladies and Gentlemen. John F. Kennedy once reminded us that "victory has a thousand fathers, but defeat is an orphan". When *we* at N-TV get it wrong, like any other television company, it's just like an orphanage. When we get it right – and by giving us this award, you seem to be saying we sometimes do – there are several hundred putative fathers who feel they should be accepting any awards that may be going.

'Any TV programme is a team effort but Sir Charles Craig, as Editor-in-Chief, decided that if the *Nightly News* did happen to win this award, it should be picked up by the newscaster with the least hair. That ruled out Lynne Kimberley and March Stevens, who are nevertheless here, as you may have noticed from their discreet entrance early on ... David Kenway has far too many blond curls, drat him, and besides, at this moment, he's on his way to South Africa. So that left me.

'There are, of course, yet more people back at N-TV House, putting out tonight's "Big News" (as we always call it), and working round the clock to provide our hourly headlines. Everybody at N-TV, in front of and behind the screen, shares in this award. And as relative newcomers to the game we're pretty pleased to have won. If I may use the little phrase with which I conclude the *Nightly News* whenever I'm presenting it, "Take another look at the world with us soon." Thank you ...'

The applause was warm and respectful. The presence of a news broadcaster always added a touch of grit to an awards ceremony devoted for much of its course to honouring the pursuit of froth and fantasy. As Ben threaded his way back to the N-TV table, hands stretched out to shake his or pat him on the back. He placed the award gently on the table between Sir Charles and his wife.

'You're only as good as your last acceptance speech, Ben!' It was typical of the Editor to want to puncture euphoria, however gently. Ben beamed back, unheeding, re-lit his cigar and stroked the glass of Cognac before him.

He wanted to savour the moment. March caught his eye and

gave him one of her shining smiles. Being such a new arrival at N-TV, she hardly felt entitled to share in the award, but she was pleased to see Ben looking so happy. When Lynne swayed over to give Ben a resounding kiss on the top of his head, March hardly liked to look. But seemingly nothing could bother Ben, so why should it worry her? Sir Charles noticed Lynne's behaviour, too, and pretended not to.

He preferred to dwell on his more positive achievement in creating N-TV. Ben had been floundering in radio after losing his editorship in Fleet Street, but Sir Charles had sensed a quality in him that no one else had spotted: a sound journalistic sense coupled with authority and warmth. His avuncularity, the slight fruitiness in his voice, might have been more obviously suited to a leading businessman or one of the older professions like the Law. Sir Charles had spotted how it could work wonders for the presentation of news.

The result was that Ben was now a household face, a British institution. He was trusted and respected out of all proportion – as he would be the first to admit – to what he actually did on the screen. If he ever stood for Parliament, he'd be in Downing Street before the year was out. But he had no ambitions in that direction. Indeed, he was rather bemused by his elevation to the status of national father-figure.

As for David Kenway – well, he showed formidable talent as a roving correspondent, even if he was much less at home in the studio. If he wanted to fritter away his spare time chasing everything in a skirt, that was his affair.

Lynne Kimberley, being a female newscaster still at work in her mid-forties, was something of a rarity. Feminine, yes, but with a firmness and authority that you'd be hard put to find anywhere else in the TV world. If only she could hold her drink, Sir Charles thought, his eyes narrowing as he heard her raucous laugh again, no one would have cause to doubt her place in the team.

March Stevens, although she'd only joined N-TV a few months before and had had little journalistic experience, was already knocking spots off the competition. She was just twenty-six and showed great promise. Besides, she only had to blink those innocent blue eyes in the middle of some tedious economic report for the whole nation to swoon. Cynics wondered whether newscasters had anything between their ears: with this line-up, you knew they had.

Yes, it was a good team, finely balanced, Sir Charles mused.

Whenever he caught a glimpse of N-TV publicity posters showing the four of them, on hoardings or the side of buses, he could hardly believe how like a family they looked. It was a gift to good public relations. What's more, it had produced the required results: ratings and respect.

Just then, Sir Charles's eyes met those of Colin Lyon, across the crowded Great Room. For all his enthusiasm to be photographed with the newscasters, if there was one person there that night who remained resolutely unimpressed by N-TV, it was the Home Secretary. And that mattered more than Sir Charles cared to admit.

Eventually, the TV lights dimmed as the live broadcast ended. Members of the Academy and their guests lingered, chewing the fat about winners and losers.

Ben picked up the N-TV award from the table and handed it to his boss. 'One for the foyer, I think, Charles . . . if you don't need it as a doorstop, of course.'

Ben kissed Lynne and March once more, bid Lady Craig a fulsome good night, and escorted Vanessa up the staircase.

The back-slapping and slightly artificial bonhomie continued as they made their way through the crowds of telly-folk queueing to get their coats.

In Park Lane, just as Ben held open the door of the Rolls for Vanessa to step inside, a press photographer pushed forward and snapped them together.

Ben tried hard not to show any anger or irritation. Why should he? He had a perfectly good reason for taking his secretary to the awards ceremony. Everyone knew that his wife was ill in hospital. The incident meant nothing.

But when the picture was developed, it would show Ben looking less than avuncular, downright shifty, in fact. Vanessa would appear simply embarrassed.

After he'd driven Vanessa home to her flat in Fulham that February night, Ben returned, alone, to his Kensington townhouse.

He took off his bow-tie and removed the carnation. He looked at the note from the hospital which Mrs Baldwin, his housekeeper, had left for him. Natalie had spent another 'comfortable' day. Her condition was 'stable'. Ben poured himself a brandy and glanced at the first editions of the papers which, as usual, had been delivered direct to his door. 'IVER THROWS CAMPAIGN

WIDE OPEN' was the headline over a report on the American Presidential primaries. 'HUNT FOR KOBUS ASSASSIN – More Arrests' was another, from South Africa.

He skimmed the papers into the small hours. Even after all these years, Ben couldn't see a paper without reading it cover to cover. Besides, there was no one to call him to bed. Poor Natalie. Ben knew that his wife would have been watching the awards show from her hospital bed. If only she'd been well enough to be at his side, to share his triumph.

Few who had seen the urbane, unflappable Ben that night would have guessed at the darker side to his customary charm. Nor would they have imagined the private grief which was starting to gnaw at him.

And the guilt. He kept thinking of the snatched photo of him and Vanessa. He could imagine the caption. Not that it mattered, but it did remind him how he had tended to take Natalie for granted over the years. It was only now she was seriously ill that he was paying her proper attention. He wanted nothing from his public life to intrude on this private concern.

Ben shrank from admitting that he wanted nothing from his private life to interfere with his public success, either.

He was going to have to put on a brave face. That came naturally to him: he knew no other way to behave. But would the old trick work for him again?

Ben drained his brandy glass, turned out the lights, and went wearily up to bed.

CHAPTER 3

The 747 caught the golden dawn on its wings as the flight approached Johannesburg. David Kenway felt the grubby stubble on his chin and rubbed his eyes. Most of the other passengers were still sprawled across seats or scrunched against each other, trying to catch a few more moments of sleep.

David went into the lavatory and splashed water on his face. He didn't shave unless he had to: it was always a relief for him not to have to look his best, and if he wasn't going to be in front of a TV camera for a day or two, he could afford the designer stubble. Myburgh woke up, dreaming of the stewardess with the teeth, or so he said.

As breakfast was served and the great bird came down over the veld towards Johannesburg, David said, 'There's something to be said for flying. You have your own seat, you're fed regularly, and all responsibility is taken from you. At 65,000 feet, you're released from the cares of planet earth.'

'You have those, too, huh?'

'Down there, people are always killing each other, fighting, involved in swindles and cheats. Up here, unless a hijacker does his stuff, you're above all that.'

'Enjoy it while you can,' the South African said, suspicious of David's little speech. Noticing the off-hand and noisy way David began to flip over the pages of *Time* and *Newsweek*, he added, 'All lies, of course.'

'Well, *they* can make up their stuff if they want to. We've got to get it on camera. So we've actually got to be on the spot when it happens.'

'TV's like writing on the wind, I've heard it said.'

'You seem to know a lot,' said David, shooting him a suspicious glance. What sort of karate instructor was Myburgh?

'Only what I've heard.'

The 747 touched down just before nine o'clock. David peered out of the small window in anticipation. He noted the languid blacks working near the airport perimeter. Johannesburg was a city of gold and gold managed to infuse the morning light.

David hadn't lost a sense of wonder at the world he reported, a world that was at once dangerous and exciting. Sometimes he even surprised himself by reacting emotionally with a lump in his throat at human folly. For the most part, though, he kept such feelings in check.

The Republic of South Africa was a country that never failed to produce conflicting emotions in him.

'Don't forget, man, it's a great country,' Myburgh said, shaking hands, as they prepared to leave the aircraft.

David had heard South Africans say this many times. He replied softly, 'It could be.' He thought of the rich earth and its beauty. And he thought of the wretched human problems on top of it. It seemed such a terrible waste.

Now, as he stepped from the aircraft into the terminal, he caught a whiff of African air. Mixed in with the smell of aero-engine fuel was just a trace of the distinctive smell of the veld.

'Good morning, sir.' The immigration official spoke evenly, courteously, and unsmilingly. 'May I ask what is the purpose of your visit?'

'Business,' David replied.

'And what is your business, sir?'

'Journalism.'

'In which case, sir, I must ask you to read these.' The official handed David a sheaf of coloured papers. They told him that he must register with the Bureau for Information. If he went about his work without official permission, he would be expelled from the country and reprisals would be taken against the news organization employing him.

'OK, OK, I know, I know,' David rattled back, adding to himself, 'Police state ...'

Then, seeing the immigration official about to do something to his passport below desk-level, David asked, 'Could you not stamp it, please? Thank you.'

He knew that a South African stamp on his passport would create problems when next he wanted to enter a black African state.

'I'm so sorry, I have already done so,' said the official without blinking. There indeed was the crimson stamp: '*Passportbeheer – Passport Control. Binnekoms. Entry. Jan Smutslughave/Airport.*'

So that was that. There was also documentation warning him, '*Purpose of entry may not be changed without permission.*' David felt his initial optimism ebbing away already. He hadn't even stepped out of the airport.

Still half-asleep, David was mildly irritated that Pieter Hart-mann, N-TV's fixer in South Africa, was not there to meet him. He rang Pieter's home number.

'Yes, master ... no, master,' the black servant replied to David's queries. He could never get used to this sort of talk, but it was as commonplace as the way African porters cupped their hands to receive tips. It made him feel uncomfortable.

Then Pieter himself came on the line, apologizing for being late and arranging to meet over lunch at David's hotel. 'I'm working on a little exclusive for you ...'

A journalistic visiting 'fireman' like David was supposed to travel from airport to city – wherever he was in the world – with a talkative taxi-driver to give him the conventional wisdom on events. But David hesitated with his luggage at the cab-rank and, on impulse, decided that he wasn't in the mood for stony-faced comments from an archetypal Van der Merwe. He decided to travel into Johannesburg city centre on the airport bus.

Quite casually, almost automatically, David pumped his fellow passengers for information. 'What do you think about the Kobus killing?' 'How about the terrorist attacks?' 'Are you nervous?' 'How has everyday life changed?' He always ended up interviewing people. As ever, David found the South Africans, whether Afrikaans- or English-speaking, hard to fathom. There was a strain of sadness to them all. No bubbly openness. Reserve. Or guilt?

But he enjoyed his brief chats, and it was a relief not to be recognized – as he was, remorselessly, at home – and be able to go about his work unhindered by the irrelevancies of fame.

As the bus was speeding along the highway into the city, there was a sudden screech of brakes. It wasn'nt immediately clear why. The traffic had piled up and was only slowly squeezing past a spot where police were standing over a body sprawled on the roadway.

One of the dead man's legs was twisted under him. His shoes and the contents of a parcel were scattered nearby. A pool of blood glistened at his head.

The English-speaking women sitting behind David peered briefly out of the window. Seeing the dead black on the road, one of them stated emphatically, 'He must have been drunk. They're all drunk.'

David winced. As the bus drove off, the women went back to

discussing a friend of theirs called Dulcie. As they passed a church hall, one remarked, 'That's where the flower show was held, wasn't it?'

He was back in the great country all right.

'David!' A familiar American voice hailed him. 'So it's true. If you're here, the balloon *is* about to go up!'

David had arrived at the Landdrost Hotel, on the corner of Plein and Twist streets. As he walked into the hotel foyer, he saw at once he wasn't the only TV journalist in South Africa. Surrounded by numerous pieces of video recording equipment and smart, but worn, travel bags, were American TV personnel he had encountered many times before, chief among them Aaron Rochester, a correspondent for the ABC network.

'I didn't see you on the plane, Aaron. You've not come from London?'

'No, we've been to Lusaka to talk to Tambo.'

'Tambo? What did he have to say for himself?'

'The usual rant about the racist state south of the border. At least he didn't give us any shit about not knowing how it's all financed. They're in it up to *here*.'

'The Moscow mercs?'

'You got it.'

'Are they behind the Kobus killing?'

'Didn't have time to ask,' said the American. 'That's why we scuttled down here. Got your minder yet?'

'Minder?'

'New rule. The Bureau for Information won't let you near the action unless you've got a smiling Afrikaner policeman holding your hand.'

'Does one have to cross his palm with silver?'

'Now don't go splashing it about,' said Aaron. 'We yankees aren't *made* of money, you know.'

It was a standing joke between them. Foreign trips cost the earth for any TV news organization to mount but whereas the Americans went about it in considerable style, the British always felt they were travelling steerage.

David and Aaron's paths had crossed numerous times in the past dozen years. Even though Aaron worked out of ABC's European office in London, they rarely met in the British capital; but it was inevitable they would meet when chasing the same news stories in Europe, Africa and the Middle East. They had developed a cagey respect for each other. They enjoyed chewing the fat over a beer at the end of a long day spent wrestling with devious politicians and stroppy camera crews.

'Fancy dinner tonight?' Aaron asked. 'I've heard of a little place just round the corner where they do very tasty *bobotie*.'

TV newsmen had a nose for the best restaurants. Their stomachs preceded them into trouble spots whether the bombs were going off in Belfast or Beirut. In Aaron's case, he did have something of an actual stomach to precede him. But then, he had written an occasional article for *Gourmet* magazine, so he had to keep up appearances.

'All right. Then we can catch up on the Bet,' David said knowingly.

'Ah, yes, the Bet. Have I got news for *you*!'

'Save it. See you later.'

David checked in, made a few quick calls to contacts, and dozed for an hour or two on the large double bed in a room heavy with dark brown panelling.

The morning sun was creeping between the blinds and the dull roar of the city's traffic meant that David couldn't really sleep. Besides, his mind was full of disturbing images. The dead black's body on the motorway, twisted. His shoes torn off ...

And a recurring image. A solitary black rider on a dark horse was coming towards him. He rode between high walls of sugar cane. He did not greet him, but nodded and rode past at a gallop.

At lunch, Pieter Hartmann, the bullet-headed fixer, came over and made up for his non-appearance at the airport by producing the proper accreditation papers David required for his visit.

'I've also got the makings of a scoopette for you, if you're interested, David.'

'I fear South Africans bearing gifts ...'

'Come on now, man,' Pieter protested, leaning over his beer in the Landdrost restaurant. 'How would you like to have an interview with the President, about the Kobus business?'

David was surprised at the offer but didn't jump at it. 'I don't want to seem ungrateful, Pieter ...'

'I know Van Der Linde's about as talkative as a dead snake, but he hasn't done any TV for some time and certainly not since Kobus was shot.'

'How far have you got with it?'

'I heard on the grapevine that the President came up from Cape Town yesterday.'

'To Pretoria?' During the Parliamentary session lasting from January to June, the State President lived in Cape Town but he maintained an office in the country's capital, forty-five minutes' drive from Johannesburg.

'Yes.'

'And?'

'And what?'

'What makes you think he'd want to talk to us?'

'Not to put too fine a point upon it, because the Bureau rang and offered him.'

'They rang and suggested we interview him? What are they up to?'

'No idea. Who can fathom the Afrikaner mind?' He laughed.

Piet could be ironic about his race, especially when helping overseas journalists of a 'Pro-Af' tinge – disposed, that is, more towards blacks than whites. When asked for his diagnosis of the country's ills, he would claim, 'Too much is being done to kiss the black man's arse.'

But David never quite felt that Pieter believed what he said. Not that what Pieter believed mattered a damn, anyway. He was just bloody good at his job, even if he did drink too much. But that was a common failing hereabouts and he indulged in ferocious physical activity both in and out of the bedroom to burn up the calories.

'We're not being set up, are we?' David wondered. 'I mean, I'm supposed to have to struggle a bit to get my stories, you know.'

'You should be grateful.'

'How do we nab him?'

'Just give the word. I've got a cousin in the Bureau. He's my contact. That's where the offer came from, actually. If you want to do him ... and I quite understand if you don't ...'

'Oh, piss off, Pieter, of course I do ...'

'Then we need to be in Pretoria at nine tomorrow morning.'

'All morning to package it, and get it on the satellite to London in the afternoon?'

'It's a standard booking.'

'OK, let's do him, but I still think it's fishy. I'd much rather get out and about in the country first.'

'That's the snag. It's impossible to go anywhere – the townships, the restricted territories, they're all no-go. It's changed a lot since you were last here. Tightened up.'

David pressed him. 'The Bureau won't allow us to shoot anything without their permission?'

'You know South Africa, David. When Van der Merwe says "no", he definitely means "no". They're like blocks of wood. And if you push them, you find yourself on the next plane out.'

'Or plummeting to your death from ground-floor windows, I suppose ... Are they really that twitchy?'

'Really twitchy. And now that Ministers are getting picked off, do you blame them? Whenever there was big trouble in the old days – Sharpeville, Soweto, Durban – they cracked down hard and knocked the stuffing right out of the blacks. With no regard for international opinion. They had the whip hand and they used it. Now they use it against whites, too. It's rigid, solid, immovable. Total blackout, if you'll pardon the expression.'

'But I must get a bit of bang-bang on tape ...'

'Look, David, I've got you the President. That'll have to do to be going on with. If you play your cards right, you could get more. It all depends.'

'OK, but they're counting their pennies as usual back in London. I can't stand around forever waiting for something to happen.'

'Like I said, let's wait and see. Meanwhile, London want you to do a package for tonight on the Kobus aftermath ...'

'Oh, shit. I've only just got here!'

'Don't worry. I've got all the material from SABC. It just needs a half-minute to-camera piece from you. Won't take half an hour to polish it off.'

'Thank God for that.'

'Oh, and by the way, I've got a message for you from someone else who wants to see you even more urgently than the President.'

'Who's that?'

'Remember Little Orphan Annie?'

'Oh, God! Hasn't she got herself fixed up yet?'

'Not to speak of. I suppose it's a bit odd for one with an arse like that. Anyway, she's panting for you.'

David frowned, then smiled. 'Where can I get her?'

Pieter scribbled down a telephone number and gave it to him.

'And don't forget,' he added, 'even if you're slaving over a hot little Annie tonight, we need to leave for Pretoria about eight tomorrow morning. At the latest.'

*   *   *

The restaurant Aaron took him to was called The Biltong, after the dish made from beef and venison. But *bobotie* was naturally on the menu and, despite the superb fish, fruit and vegetables to be had, this was what Aaron insisted they should eat.

Bobotie is a casserole of minced meat, flavoured with curry powder, lemon, almonds and sugar, and thickened with beaten egg. David chose a heavy red wine from the Groot Constantia estate on the Cape to go with it. He was rather more considerate dealing with the black wine waiter than he might have been with a white one. As the black poured the wine for him to taste, David noticed a skinny smell from the man, a smell speaking of a different culture far removed from restaurants and cutlery and starched white linen tablecloths.

David and Aaron were the same age. At thirty-seven, they'd seen more of the world's horrors than most of their generation. David, a roving correspondent with N-TV and before that with both BBC and Independent Television News, had reported on wars in the Middle East, South-East Asia, and Latin America. He had rubbed shoulders with presidents and kings, mercenaries and guerrillas, gangsters and frauds. He had been held hostage and shot at. He had witnessed massacres and any number of the smaller, callous cruelties of war.

Aaron's experience was broadly similar. Like David, he'd seen it all too early in life – but the good as well as the bad. For he had seen some of man's nobler achievements, the unforgettable sight of a spacecraft lifting off from Cape Canaveral, joy in the face of a heart-transplant survivor, the thrill of election victories for presidents and premiers who believed, for a moment, they'd be able to change the world.

'And how is the battlefield of N-TV?' Aaron asked, calling for a salad as a small token of respect towards his waistline.

'Where everyone walks with his back to the wall so no one can put the knife in? Actually, I've worked in worse. You know Charlie Craig – *Sir* Charles, as he now is – he may be sharp but he's quite a gent. If he thinks you've done a bum job he'll tell you to your face. You don't open a newspaper and find he's fired you.'

'That's happened to me in my time ...'

'The trouble with N-TV is it's on the crest of a wave. Since the launch, when money was running out of the door and staff were being fired every hour on the hour, it's made a remarkable recovery. We're making a profit, the ratings are up, and we've started collecting awards by the shelf-full. I had to miss another ceremony last night.'

'When the awards start coming, the writing's clearly on the wall,' said Aaron wiping his moustache. 'But I like your stuff. In London, I watch you in preference to the Corp or ITN. And in Europe. I was in Bonn the weekend before last and watched your satellite service. Liked it.'

'And how's ABC?' asked David. 'Still in the lead?'

'By the skin of our teeth. But we have our successes, like the Tripoli hijack, and we live to see another day.'

To add to the difficulty of getting as much food down his throat in the shortest possible time, Aaron now lit up a large Havana. Indeed, there was hardly a moment in the day when he wasn't to be seen waving a wand of Churchillian length before his face, or prising off small pieces of tobacco that had stuck to his lips. Or holding animated conversations with a small stoagy clamped to one side of his mouth.

'And how about you yourself?' Aaron managed to ask. 'Still in the shadow of the great Ben Brock?'

''Fraid so,' David answered. 'He's getting worse. Never gets out of the studio, has given up journalism for charm, and thinks drooling over the Royal Family is news. But there's no topping an act like that. He's got what you and I won't have for another twenty years.'

'A bald pate.'

'Yes, and he looks lived in. He's the nearest thing we've had to Cronkite, at least since Richard Dimbleby in the 'fifties. And Dimbleby wasn't a newscaster.'

'But you don't really want to be stuck behind a desk all day, reading a teleprompter. That's not *you*, David.'

'No, but think what you could do with a job like that . . . at the heart of things, pulling levers, exerting influence, ringmaster to the nation's affairs. Half the time, we're just glorified dogsbodies, waiting to be shot at. But Ben's had his day. He's living on borrowed time.'

'You could be right. I know being an anchor in the States is damned exposed. Look at Dan Rather, Tom Brokaw, Peter Jennings – sniped at all the time, and they hardly ever set foot outside the studio except on stupid junkets which set them up behind a desk in Red Square, Moscow, or some place. If you're a real writer or reporter, that's not a job for you. When I go old and grey, or old and bald, whichever, I'll get right out of the industry.

Go edit some broken-down local paper in Lockjaw, Missouri. Now that *would* be fun!'

The waitress came round to see if they wanted more to eat. '*Melktert*, twice,' Aaron ordered, without reference to David. And *melktert*, cinnamon-flavoured milk-pudding flan, it was.

Rubbishing their employers was what television men indulged in whenever they met. It was part of the job, almost more important than the job. In this case, though, it also served to prevent Aaron and David being too inquisitive about each other's current plans.

Buddies they might be but they still were professional rivals. David was bursting to brag to Aaron about his curiously-arranged interview with the President next morning but knew he had to keep quiet about it. Until it was safely in the can and on its way to London, Aaron could always scoop it.

Aaron helpfully provided another distraction by asking, 'And how's the Bet?'

David smiled the rare but glorious smile that could thrill women almost as much as his voice did.

'Very disappointing, I'm afraid. I expect you're ahead on points, as usual. Bachelor boy.'

'I'm not sure mine counts,' said Aaron, with merriment in his eye. 'Would you accept Namibia?'

'Namibia!' David mocked. 'Of course not. You know the rules. It's got to be a member state of the United Nations and – as even *your* limited knowledge of current events will tell you – Namibia, or South-West Africa, or whatever you like to call it, isn't that.'

'Anyway, she was good in the sack.'

The 'Bet' in question was not, strictly-speaking, a bet at all, in the sense that there was no possibility of it ever being finally settled. But it kept Aaron and David amused, like overgrown adolescents, whenever their paths crossed.

It had first arisen five years earlier, one drunken evening in Cairo, as they compared notes on women they'd known.

'And how *many* have you ever slept with?' Aaron had asked, abruptly. 'Come on, what's the total?'

'I've lost count,' David had replied.

'All right. How many different *nationalities* have you slept with? Women only, of course. I'm not interested in any slippage in pursuit of *la vice anglaise*.'

'Well, a US citizen, that's one,' David began.

'I believe on one occasion we slept with the *same* US citizen, though it wouldn't be polite to mention the fact.' Aaron was referring to Jo, at that moment about to become David's wife.

'And I've, let me see ... a Scotswoman, an Irishwoman and a Welshwoman ...'

'No, no, we can't be having that. The UK's your nation state, we can't be having all these minorities. Your own country doesn't count. Have another go.'

David pretended to find it difficult to remember, but then began to surprise even himself with the colourful list he dredged from his memory. 'An Australian ... a New Zealander ... a South African (white) ... a Rhodesian (pre-Independence, of course), a Frenchwoman, a German, an Italian, a Russian ... say, how many points do I get for *her*?'

Aaron countered with his conquests ... and so the idea of a competition between them was born. The more obscure the nationality, the greater the challenge of crossing it off the list.

In time, David boasted of such rarities as a Maldive Islander, a resident of San Marino ('She must've been the sister of the one I slept with,' Aaron thought), an Albanian and an Eskimo.

Aaron had been sidetracked into sleeping with Russian women from a number of the obscurer Soviet Socialist Republics – only achieved at great risk to his freedom – then a hot little number from Burma ('so difficult to get into these days'), a rare Falkland Islander, and a South Yemeni woman with whiskers and a quite hideous general mien.

At times, David and Aaron had tried to put the Bet on a more orderly footing.

'I think we should limit it to Europe,' David had proposed.

'That's what they said about World War Two,' replied Aaron, 'but it just kinda spread from there.'

Then they decided they would call it a day when either of them had slept his way through the member states of the United Nations. The only trouble was, whenever either started making progress towards reaching that distant goal, a host of new nations would take out membership.

'Well, for God's sake,' David warned now, 'don't cross the colour line while you're here in South Africa. They're still funny about it, despite the law-change. You'd get drummed out by the State President personally.'

Realizing he had unwittingly brought up a name he would rather have kept quiet, David created a distraction by waving for coffee and brandy.

'Not much chance of anything new on this trip,' Aaron said. 'Too much like hard work.'

'Me ditto,' said David, beginning to feel he'd rather be in female company at that very moment. 'Early start tomorrow. Got to do my homework.'

'Something cooking?'

'You'll find out soon enough.'

They walked slowly back from The Biltong to the Landdrost. Johannesburg's streets were as unnaturally clean and deserted as ever, though now there was more than a hint of curfew in the air.

Just as they stepped into the lobby of the hotel, they spotted a copper-haired girl checking in. Some go brown with the sun, others go pink. This girl was an unusually attractive pinky-brown. It was as if she was blushing under her tan – blushing evenly, all over.

'David!' Her voice leapt. Now she genuinely blushed with pleasure.

David had to think quickly to remember her name: 'Penny! Fancy meeting you here.'

Aaron, sensing the encounter would have nothing in it for him, begged a polite, 'Excuse me – goodnight' and collected his keys from the reception desk with a knowing look at his English friend.

'Business, business,' answered Penny, her brown eyes gleaming.

'Quick drink before bed?' David proposed, in what sounded like a format for quicker seduction than he'd intended.

'Sure.'

He took Penny to the bar. She ordered mineral water and he coffee, so they both felt like impostors.

The last time they'd met had been in Rome. Penny worked for an advertising agency and just happened to be in South Africa now visiting one of its affiliates. She knew David was married so wasn't too surprised when David told her, inconsequentially, 'Just before I left, Jo threw the telly at me.'

Penny didn't know whether to laugh or not, but the information cleared the way for what followed.

David didn't have to hold her, or touch her. He admired her steadily at a distance. Her skin was creamy, her hair well cut and full. The sleek turquoise dress slithered down her body without him doing anything to help.

Penny excused herself and slipped into the bathroom. David, left alone, was momentarily distracted by his notes for tomorrow. He even risked breaking the mood by phoning down to reception for an alarm call in the morning. Then, as Penny still hadn't come out of the bathroom, doing whatever it was that women did before lovemaking, he decided to undress himself. The white cotton jacket, the beige shirt, the jeans, the short boots – he slipped everything off and sat on the corner of the bed, not quite sure what to do with himself.

He looked at his watch, as usual noticed the odd inscription, 'Oyster Perpetual Day-Date', slipped that off, too, and propped it on the bedside table. But still there was no sign of Penny.

Without knocking, David went into the bathroom. She was simply standing there, as naked as he.

She whispered, 'I've been waiting for you. What have you been doing?'

He embraced her lightly, both of them gasping as he brushed against her.

'I forgot,' he murmured. 'I forgot this was how you liked it.'

She drew his lips towards hers. His body was taut, no loose flesh, and she pressed against it eagerly.

David ran his hands down her back, to the base of her spine. He might have forgotten Penny's penchant for bathroom lovemaking, but not this. Her skin was soft, cushiony. Her breasts were small but delicately up-tilted. Her eyes had to tilt up, too, to meet his.

They were standing just in front of the washbasin. He turned her so that she had her back to it and he stood in front of her. Catching sight of himself in the mirror, he glanced away, then noticed his reflection in the side mirror, and the multiple images reflecting away to infinity.

David reached for a towel and made to lay it on the edge of the washbasin.

'No, please,' said Penny.

Leaning backwards against the ice-cold marble of the wash-stand, she looked at her reflection on the long wall-mirror opposite. She saw David move slowly down until he was kneeling before her. Soon his tongue was inside, working rhythmically.

Her whole body turned a deeper shade of pink and brown. David stopped and stood up. With a brisk movement, he put his hands under her and lifted her so that she sat on the edge of the washbasin with her legs over the edge.

Steadying her with his arms, he began to press home. At first, Penny still studied the mirror, but then her eyes closed and she gave way to stifled sighing. Her hands reached out searching for colder surfaces.

'Oh, David, for God's sake,' she gasped.

When it was over, David picked her up, still at one with him, and carried her through to the bed.

Within seconds he was sound asleep, all passion spent, while Penny lay half-awake beside him.

CHAPTER 4

'How do you want me to answer these?'

Vanessa Sinclair handed March Stevens the sheaf of letters. Each running to some eight or more pages, they were all written with alternate lines in green and red ink. And they were all from the same person, a Mr Patel of Acton in West London.

Mr Patel apparently considered March to be the most beautiful person on his television screen. He worshipped her image. And he was not alone in his passionte enthusiasm.

'Oh, no, not him again,' said March, recognizing the writing.

Mr Patel of Acton would hardly have relished such short shrift from his goddess. March paused and read a sentence from the top letter.

'I suppose he's pretty harmless. I mean, he's not telling me what he does to himself when he sees me on the box, or asking for my used knickers, or anything ...'

'Well, do you want me to acknowledge it or not?'

Vanessa was sounding at her most Sloane Rangerish. She never quite managed to avoid giving the impression that working for a television company was, for a girl of her background, tantamount to slumming – as though she were doing social work before marrying and having the children. As March was a recent arrival at N-TV and, indeed, a comparatively recent arrival in the world of work, all Vanessa's organizing and mothering instincts were channelled into her.

'Mr Patel's a bit of a twit, if you ask me. And Acton *is* rather close for comfort. You thank him for me,' March suggested gently.

'I'm not even sure I should do that. The more you thank these loonies, the more it encourages them.'

N-TV had decreed from the start that all fan mail was to be answered as part of its public relations effort. Sir Charles Craig's only known view on the subject was that viewers who wrote to newscasters should be encouraged, gently, to appreciate that they were there to do a journalistic job. They were not entertainers.

'Well, I don't know,' March wavered. 'You know best. Perhaps you could acknowledge every *sixth* letter he sends. And enclose a boring booklet on how the N-TV elections computer works. Anything . . .'

'So, no photograph?'

'Does he ask for one?'

'Yes, but I don't think so, do you? That *would* only encourage him.'

Vanessa's job was to take some of the burden off N-TV's newscasters by answering their mail. Ben Brock treated it all as a huge joke, kindly but firmly refusing all offers to open supermarkets or address ladies' luncheon clubs. If someone wrote to criticize him for what he had said, he would more than likely crumple up the letter and toss it in the wastepaper basket from which Vanessa would have to retrieve it.

David Kenway – when he was in the country, that is – took this approach one stage further. He was inclined to pick up his accumulated mail and dump it out of Vanessa's reach. Not that this had always been David's way. When he worked for Yorkshire TV he took delight in saving up letters from female viewers who wrote asking him to 'drop in for a cup of tea when you're down our way'. It was said he took the first opportunity to claim his cup of tea, and more – but no one had been able to substantiate the rumour.

The male newscasters found it easy to treat their letters lightly. Most of the critical letters were written, they presumed, by cranks. Letters of undying passion and proposals of marriage from women viewers were no more than a source of amusement.

'Ben and David are hopeless. You've got to tread a middle path,' Vanessa began to lecture March, hooking her lanky dark hair behind her ears as she did so, and resting hands on hips. 'Now Lynne, you see, takes it too seriously. I don't mean when she's being told to get her ugly mug off the screen, or getting invites to bondage parties in Princes Risborough . . .

'I mean, if a viewer writes in seeking advice, however obscure the subject, Lynne tries to give it. If I didn't stop her, she'd dictate an individual reply to every letter she got. Even she needs to see that's not her job. She's a newscaster, not an agony aunt.'

'I'm still feeling my way,' March said quietly, in that steady, contained way which was known to reduce grown men to jelly. 'I mustn't let those letters *get* to me.'

Vanessa softened. At thirty-eight, she was much older than March. Wearing her Sloane regalia of Gucci loafers, sensible skirts, scarves and hair-bands, she was attractive to men who liked that kind of thing. She had a bright smile when she wanted to use it and a horse-face when she didn't.

'That's right, March. Sorry if I sound bossy, but I'm only here to protect you.'

'Thanks, I know. It's just odd becoming a piece of public property. I feel more like a piece of *lost* property. I've never known it quite like this before. When I started in TV, down in Plymouth, it was all very cosy and friendly.'

March's blessing – or curse, depending on how one looked at it – was that the camera loved her. True, she had certain winning features even before she stepped into the studio. She had the most remarkable hair. Yellowy-red, golden, no words quite described it. It was like honey held up to sunlight. And it fell to her shoulders, framing a soft face, a few freckles, doll-like features, and a turned-up nose. Even with all this going for her, March could – and did – pass unnoticed in the crowd. It took the peculiar alchemy of television to turn her into a small, but potent, goddess.

'MARCH STORMS IN LIKE A LION,' was a typical headline from the *Sun*, as soon as her initial impact began to be felt. 'GOLDEN MARCH!' the *Daily Star* chimed in. 'MARCH SENSATION,' claimed the *Daily Mirror* when one of her earrings fell off during the *Nightly News* and she had continued reading as though nothing had happened.

This had all been during the past four months. Promoted to N-TV in London from appearing on TSW's local magazine programme in the West Country, March instantly became flavour of the month. Her peaches-and-cream Englishness, her apparent lack of private life, her novelty, gave a number of ageing hacks the chance to wax lyrical over her.

Where the newspapers and magazines led, their readers followed. There was a March Stevens fan club, even a March Stevens Lusting Society, established by Leicestershire rugby players. Quite what they did at their meetings, and what their long-term objectives were, was mercifully unclear.

Seeing the kind of pressure she was under, Sir Charles had tried to reassure her. 'I'm going to make sure you do your share of reporting duties outside the studio as well as presenting the *Nightly*,' he had told her. This way he thought she might escape being just a glamorous front person. He made sure March wasn't shielded from criticism either, but advised how to handle herself.

The truth was that Sir Charles hadn't been altogether convinced she was ideal for the job. She was too young, too inexperienced. Yet, equally, he soon realized that selecting her was one of the best decisions he'd ever made.

On the nights March was not on the screen, a disappointed sigh could be heard going up from the nation's male viewing population. When she *was* appearing, there was a collective gasp of desire.

'You've seen this?' said Vanessa, handing March a cutting from the *Daily Express*. Vanessa took no pleasure in the knocks that 'her' newscasters took, but she drew their attention to them just the same.

'What is it?'

Vanessa pointed to a paragraph by one of Fleet Street's more opinionated female columnists.

'The cow,' March murmured – an unusually strong word, almost an expletive, in *her* mouth.

The article said:

Newscasterine March Stevens, 26, may set male hearts a-flutter as she broadcasts news of fresh disasters on land, sea and air, but when did she last set foot in a frock shop?

Two nights running last week, she wore the same dowdy off-the-peg little number that wouldn't have offended Queen Victoria.

Come on, March, you are what you wear – and fashion is 'news' just as much as the earth-tremors you're always telling us about these days!

'I can't win, can I?' March looked put out. 'If I wear a different outfit every night, I'm told I'm extravagant – "What about the unemployed?" and all that. And she's got a nerve, going at me like that. She was all over me when I saw her in the Caprice last week. Old cow!'

'Quite agree,' Vanessa said, supportively. She was only acting on Sir Charles's instructions. His newscasters were not to be pampered.

'Anyway,' March quietly countered by saying, 'I see you've had your picture in the paper, too.'

The picture of Ben Brock ushering Vanessa into his Rolls after the awards dinner had appeared in two newspapers. The caption to one had insinuated he was dallying with Vanessa while his wife lay dangerously ill in hospital. The other had wrongly identified Vanessa as Ben's daughter.

'I could have done without it. Mummy was on the phone like pronto. The cleaner had arrived from the village and shoved it under her nose, otherwise she would never have seen it. Ben's more annoyed about it than I am, the old love. As if he hadn't got better things to worry about.'

'How is his wife?'

'No change as far as I know. Everyone seems to think it's not looking good.'

'Do you know what she's got?'

'Ben won't say. It's anyone's guess. He's taking it wonderfully, but there's a limit to what you can do to cheer up another woman's husband, wouldn't you say?'

'I suppose he just busies himself with work to keep his mind off it,' said March.

'He's a news-freak, anyhow. Even before Natalie's trouble blew up. He lives and breathes it. You don't, do you?'

March glanced at Vanessa to see what she was driving at and replied, honestly, 'Well, I'm *interested*, but I don't think it's the be-all and end-all of existence.'

'I suppose you've got to, though, if you're in Ben's position,' Vanessa went on. 'If you didn't, you'd begin to wonder what all the fuss was about. You'd find it hard to put up with all the frenetic activity and people going off their rocker all over the place.'

'David's the same, isn't he?' said March. 'Seems to *live* for scoops and exclusives. Lynne and I aren't like that.'

'Lynne has other interests,' Vanessa said. 'She has her music and painting and lots of friends in the real world. She's very *professional*, but being on the telly's not the most important thing in her life, if you know what I mean. But if you're David, say, and you're going to be shot at and have to drag yourself round the world's trouble spots the way he does, you've got to believe that it's what life's all about, haven't you?'

'Is it true what they say about David's love-life?' March asked with unusual directness. 'That he's got a girl in every port?'

'Yes, and not just *one* in every port – about a dozen more like. I think he behaves very shittily, actually. I don't know why his wife puts up with it.'

'I've never met her. What's she like?'

'She's American, you know. Journalist, apparently, though I've never read anything she's written. She never shows her face round here. Perhaps as well. I wouldn't give their marriage another five minutes, frankly.'

'Oh, dear,' said March.

Vanessa looked at her. 'Fancy him a bit, do you?'

March looked away.

'Well, you're not the only one. So be careful.' She took Mr Patel's letters out of March's hands.

March looked at her watch. 'I'd better be going. Time for the three o'clock meeting.'

She walked towards the door. Then, remembering, she turned to Vanessa and said, as casually as she could: 'Oh, that man from Acton. Send him a photo. What do I care?'

CHAPTER 5

'Your alarm call, Mr Kenway.'

'Thank you, yes, good morning.' David checked with his watch. It was indeed seven-thirty. The southern African sun was licking round the hotel blinds. Penny, now rolled up in a foetal position, was lost to the world. She'd been unable to sleep at first with David still inside her. It was only when he rolled away about 1:30 a.m., rolled away with all the selfishness of the sleeper and the satisfied lover, that she'd been able to settle herself.

David glanced at her. He liked her because she was uncomplicated. No, not quite that, for all women, in his view, were complicated. It was just that there were no obvious complications between him and her. No bonds, no ties, hardly any obligations. She represented a freer world he was supposed to have abandoned when he got married.

Hardly a day went by without his yearning for the simpler ways of the single man. Aaron's ways, in fact. Surely it was preferable to his present lot?

Now David was showering, removing the stickiness of lovemaking from his body and the sleep from his eyes. He shaved, washed his hair, and dressed in the smart fawn safari suit he'd carried separately from his luggage all the way from London.

There had been an edict at N-TV about the clothes worn by newsmen on the road. Editor Craig wouldn't tolerate any scruffiness among his on-screen reporters, even if they were in the middle of a desert among famine victims or in a Lebanese foxhole with bullets zinging over their heads. Not that David had to try very hard to look good. His height, his boyish mass of cream-coloured curls, his chiselled features, all made him look far too dashing for any worries in the costume and make-up departments.

He slipped on the Rolex, picked up his notes and, with barely a glance at Penny's still-sleeping form, left the room and went down to the lobby. In a few minutes, Pieter Hartmann pulled up in the camera car. With him were Sammy Stalker, a freelance Canadian cameraman who'd been operating in South Africa for ten years, and Brian Watkins, a freelance sound recordist, originally from England.

David greeted them like old comrades-in-arms. Sammy was known as 'One-Eye' because he'd managed to lose one of his eyes covering a riot in Bogota. Brian, though still intact, had once ended up in hospital after being badly stoned – and having his recording equipment destroyed – during a race riot back home in Brixton.

Like David, they were rather like mercenaries, going wherever the action was, exposing themselves to considerable risk, and being well paid for it. They never thought of putting their slippers on and retiring. While they still had their health and sufficient working bodily parts, they would continue with their rootless existence.

'Tough assignment today,' David said mockingly.

'That's why I've put on a clean eye-patch,' replied Sammy. 'Must look our best to meet the President.'

'Just a straight interview, an establishing shot, and perhaps a little bit of him and me walking about in deep and meaningful conversation. Shot mute.'

'We've got extra lights if we need them,' Pieter added. 'But his office is pretty bright – over by the window it is, anyhow. Don't you think we ought to get him away from his desk, if we can?'

'Yes, sure,' David agreed. 'I want to see his legs twisting and turning in agony.'

Brian whooped with delight.

In Pretoria, they drove up to the State President's office in the east wing of the old, mellow, browny-yellow Union Buildings. The orange-white-and-blue flag of the Republic fluttered over-head in the breeze of the morning.

Security men gave the TV crew a surly looking-over, but David noticed there was nothing like the thorough search they'd have been subjected to in other trouble-spots. Perhaps if they were white they were deemed to be friendly.

Two quietly-spoken officials from the Bureau for Information greeted them and even helped carry their camera equipment along the quiet, clean corridors. Lining the walls were sedate oil paintings of the country's earlier Prime Ministers and Presidents.

They were told that the interview must be conducted in the President's outer office. This was so he wouldn't have to be disturbed until absolutely necessary. One of the Bureau officials, an Afrikaner called Swartz, took David to one side.

'And what are you going to ask the President?'

'Oh, very soft stuff. You know, how he sees the present situation, his reaction to Kobus's death, are sanctions biting? how long can SA hold out? when is he going to open up the restricted territories to the media? – that sort of thing.'

It doesn't matter what you *say* you're going to ask, he always thought. Once you're in there and rolling, you can ask what you bloody well like.

Swartz ponderously wrote down in long-hand the questions David had rattled off. David noticed he translated them into Afrikaans, so he wouldn't have been any the wiser if Swartz had been making them up.

Politicians generally were a good deal less worried about the questions they were going to be asked than were the press officers and acolytes who were paid to worry on their behalf.

Only a few would resort to the walking-out technique, which always made them look worse than if they had stayed; and only the Australian Bob Hawke, in David's experience, had ever resorted to shouting, 'Fuck, fuck, fuck!' if he was asked a question he didn't like. He reckoned no responsible organization would ever dare broadcast the obscenities.

Swartz glided away and was admitted to the President's inner office to brief him. When the video camera had been set up on its tripod and a little extra lighting positioned to give a lift to the interview area, David signalled to the President's secretary that they were ready.

A moment or two later, Dr Van Der Linde came out with Swartz leading the way and performing the introductions.

'How do you do, sir.' David had been told long ago that 'sir' could apply to any man, whatever his rank, whatever his creed or race. It wasn't necessarily an indication of respect.

'It is very good of you to spare the time to see me,' President Van Der Linde said carefully in heavily accented English.

'No, no. It's *your* time we're grateful for,' David said, the charm not exactly flowing.

'I think I know what you want to ask me, in broad terms,' the President went on. 'Now where do you wish for me to sit?'

'In the big chair, if you'd be so kind.'

'Thank you. Do I get to have a microphone?'

'Yes, if I may ...' Brian leapt forward. 'Do you mind having this small one clipped to your tie?'

'Now can you tell me, Mr Kenway,' the President asked,

beginning to enjoy the warm glow of lights on his face, 'what your first question is going to be?'

'I'll ask what your reaction is to the death of Mr Kobus. All right?'

'I see,' said the President. 'Yes.'

Once they were off, President Van Der Linde maintained his rigidly formal demeanour. David tried all the tricks of smiling, beaming acknowledgement and agreement, but clearly nothing was going to soften the formidable block of manhood in front of him.

If presidents were supposed to represent the spirit of their countrymen, this was one well cast in the role. He didn't seem ill-at-ease but he was clipped and largely uninformative, however hard David pressed him. He was impressive up to a point, but, as his lack of small-talk before the interview had shown, he was of the icily-courteous type. Like many Afrikaans-speakers, when he turned to English he talked almost in slow motion.

'The loss of Thys Kobus is a grievous one for this country. His murderers will gain nothing from their activities,' he warned. 'We will not flinch. We will drive out these disruptive elements, whoever they may be and wherever they may come from.'

'But, if I understand you, Mr President,' David had to think fast, 'you seem to be making a connection between the killers of Mr Kobus and the instigators of wider unrest. I thought that no one had yet been charged with the murder?'

'No, that is not the case. You misunderstand me. I was talking about attacks in general against this country. Now, as it happens, a person has just been arrested and charged with Mr Kobus's murder.'

'And are you at liberty to say what the motive might have been?'

'No, I am not. All I can tell you is that the accused is a thirty-five-year-old white man.'

'A white man ...?'

The surprise was evident in David's voice. It was a sharp move, not to reveal this devastating piece of information until they'd started recording.

'That is correct.'

Not for the first time when interviewing a senior politician, David suddenly felt he was up against Goliath.

With an effort, he heard himself launch into the unrelated questions he had worked out in advance.

'But, Mr President ...' – he was afraid he'd begun *every* question with the phrase – 'for the first time it seems that South Africa is becoming ungovernable. There is a breakdown in the ordered running of society ...'

'I reject that idea totally,' the President bristled. 'There is no breakdown. Life goes on. We have our difficulties but they are being contained. You can see for yourself.'

David seized his chance.

'The world has been unable to see for itself for quite some time, Mr President. While you deny the media access to the restricted territories, it's surely wrong to give the impression that you have a normal, open society, or anything like it. If you say "Life goes on", I hope you'll have no objection, Mr President, to a television correspondent visiting the restricted territories and seeing for himself.'

The President gave an imperial wave.

'With proper regard for security and with the agreement of the appropriate agencies, you may see for yourself, Mr Kenway. You only had to ask. These matters can be arranged.'

David paused, then turned to Sammy behind the camera. 'That'll do. Did you get all that?'

'Yes, fine.'

'Brian?'

The sound recordist nodded. Pieter Hartmann, hovering outside the brightly-lit area of the interview, came forward and asserted himself. 'Thank you, Mr President. We hope that you will communicate your view to the appropriate agency. We would very much like to take Mr Kenway to the restricted territories.'

'It shall be arranged,' said the President and made to stand up. Brian briskly moved forward to unclip the small microphone from Van Der Linde's tie.

'I hope you found that satisfactory, Mr Kenway?'

'Yes, indeed, Mr President.'

'Thank you for making it so painless.'

This was the nearest the President seemed likely to get to making a joke. But David had heard it said after so many interviews. He wondered when someone would actually admit an interview *had* been painful.

In another moment, the President had gone. David then recorded all his questions with the camera pointed at him. He managed to re-phrase his questions about the killer of Kobus so that he didn't appear quite so ignorant. Then he did a few 'noddies', nodding gestures which could come in useful when editing the interview.

'All right, Pieter?' David turned for reassurance to Hartmann.

'Good strong interview, not too much bullshitting, eh?' Pieter kept his voice low. 'And I liked the last bit. A "you may go", in as many words, and we even have them on tape if he tries to go back on it!'

'Fancy the whites starting to kill each other,' David mused. 'I wonder what his motive was?'

Pieter had no answer, but simply noted, 'For a while the whites put down the blacks. Then the blacks put down the blacks. And now the whites are putting down the whites.'

Swartz was as good as his word. He rang the N-TV office in Jo'burg within the hour. Taking the call, Pieter turned to David and announced: 'We have a sightseeing trip for tomorrow.'

'Where to?'

'Oudtshoorn.'

'But that's miles away.'

'I know it's a most unlikely place, but that's where the Bureau says we can go.'

'Isn't it risky leaving town? What happens if something comes up on the Kobus story?'

'That's your decision, David. I'm not sure there will be anything.'

'So how do we get to Oudtshoorn? And has anything ever happened there? It's on the Cape, isn't it?'

'Yes, quite a long way. About four hundred miles. Too far to drive. We could take a small plane and fly direct.'

'But the money, Pieter ...'

Which is why the following morning, at dawn, the Hawker Siddeley jet bearing David, Sammy and Brian southwards also contained Aaron Rochester and his five-man team. A need to share the extravagant costs of news-gathering had triumphed over any desire for exclusivity on N-TV's part.

Soon after breakfast-time, the plane touched down at the small airfield of Oudtshoorn – a small, quiet town not far from the dry tableland of the Klein Karoo.

A truck had been ordered up to carry all the video equipment. An official called Eyles from the Bureau for Information met the two teams off the plane and frostily greeted them.

'A charming guide for our journey into the unknown,' Aaron murmured, spitting out a morsel of tobacco from his unlit stoagy.

'Gentlemen,' Eyles said (ignoring the fact that one of the Americans was all too obviously female – a sassy Texan production assistant called Jerry, in designer jeans), 'gentlemen, I have received instructions to take you into an area where there has been some hitherto unreported, er, unrest. You may film the damage and do your reports. I will give you a statement of what happened. You must not film any military installation or, indeed, anything without my approval, otherwise your film will be confiscated and you will be ordered to leave the country.'

Under his breath again, Aaron muttered, 'I've a horrible feeling we're being set up.'

'Sold a pup,' David agreed. 'But what can we do?'

The truck, with all aboard, set off preceded by an army jeep.

At least the scenery was worth coming all this way for. Heat-hazed pastures full of brightly-coloured flowers stretched away as far as the eye could see. Here and there, ostriches poked their long necks over metal fences.

'Ever had ostrich steak?' Aaron inquired.

Jerry pulled a face.

'Tough as old boots,' Sammy Stalker piped up, speaking from experience.

'Like eating someone's armpits.'

'You should try springbok steak. That's very tasty. You can get that in Oudtshoorn.' This was Eyles attempting to be less frosty.

'Show us the way to some good footage,' Aaron said, 'and we'll buy you one before we leave.'

'That would be most tasty and agreeable,' Eyles replied, with something approaching a smile.

They drove nearly twenty miles towards the hills.

'It's the old story,' muttered David. 'The nastiest things happen in the nicest places.'

'I'm not convinced that anything nasty *has* happened here,' Aaron replied.

Another mile or two and, just where the veld met the hills, Eyles showed them a burnt-out hut where he claimed a cache of arms had been discovered recently. 'A number of terrorist suspects were arrested nearby.'

'How many?' David asked.

'I'm not at liberty to say.'

Aaron briefly took the stoagy from his lips and spat. 'Call that evidence?'

'Communist-backed ANC, of course,' said the Bureau official.

'Why do you say that?'

'I am not at liberty to say.'

Next they drove to see a mobile headquarters vehicle, from which the security organizations monitored suspicious activity in the area. They were not allowed to look at the markings on the wall-maps.

'Who can I kick for getting us into this pickle?' David said, exasperatedly.

Finally, in the late afternoon, they drove back into Oudtshoorn itself. Desperate to salvage something from the trip, David told Sammy and Brian to set up their equipment in the main street.

'I'll do a "sit rep" about how nothing's happening – and that'll have to do.'

Turning to Eyles who was hovering at his side, David said, 'Frankly, I don't think you deserve a springbok steak after this wanker's day out.'

Eyles raised his hands and shoulders with a shrug as if to say, 'Don't blame me.'

The light was failing, to Sammy Stalker's concern as he set up his camera. David stood with his back to the skyline, the saucer-rim of hills beyond the town, and tried to gather his thoughts before recording the piece. He had never found it easy to remember his lines, even when he was doing these short bursts to camera. He was forbidden to refer to a notebook – that was only allowed to court reporters when they were quoting evidence – and he usually needed two or three takes before he got it right.

Now he was aware that he was hot and dusty. His fawn safari suit was badly creased and he had to keep his arms close to his sides lest damp patches under the arms show on camera. After a minute or two pacing up and down, he said to Sammy, 'OK, let's have a go.'

'Rolling,' Brian Watkins shouted, poring over the video re-corder and monitoring the sound.

'When you come to a quiet provincial town like Oudtshoorn,' David began, 'it's easy to believe Government claims that the State of Emergency has made little impression on South African life. But the number and frequency of terrorist attacks is hard to judge as the Government is putting a virtual blackout on information ...'

Brian looked up at Eyles who was standing just within earshot, but he hadn't reacted perceptibly to these words.

'Evidence of unrest is hard to come by in this area even when, on the personal instructions of the State President, N-TV was allowed into one of the so-called restricted territories ...'

A short distance down the street, Aaron Rochester was going through similar paces for American viewers. The camera turned as he walked slowly towards it. 'Oudtshoorn is a homely little town in the back of beyond and the riots and bombings in the big cities are just so much foreign news to its inhabitants ...'

At that moment there was a yellow flash and a deafening, ear-splitting bang. Aaron, momentarily stunned, felt his ears buzz. An acrid smell filled the air. Aaron choked on his words and turned in the direction of the explosion.

A black cloud of smoke was coiling up above the shattered remains of a car while sheets of corrugated metal and planks of wood flew through the air. A number of black women were screaming. No one appeared to be injured, just shocked.

Then, as the dust and smoke cleared, Aaron saw a body lying on the ground.

It was dressed in a fawn safari suit.

David Kenway.

CHAPTER 6

Lynne Kimberley was one of those who had benefitted from positive discrimination in television. She'd been twenty-eight in 1970, just as the first waves of Women's Liberation washed against Britain's media.

Before then, her talents had not been put to much use. After leaving college she had tried, briefly, to be an actress, worked as a secretary in publishing, and by a zig-zag route ended up as researcher on a BBC Current Affairs programme.

Then she crossed over to ITN as a reporter. She was just right for the role: capable, tough, and neither too obviously feminine to look out of place covering a picket line nor too butch to alienate the viewer, of whatever sex.

She made her mark.

Having despatched two husbands, Lynne was living from affair to affair. She tended to avoid entanglements with male colleagues, not as a matter of policy or from any dislike of TV journalists. Rather she was drawn to more artistic types, so she lived with and loved a succession of future novelists currently working in advertising, pop musicians, classical violinists, and the like. She herself liked to paint and regretted every minute of the day when she couldn't be listening to music. It didn't matter what. Her tastes were catholic.

This was not a side of Lynne most people were aware of. They knew her best for crisp, efficient reports on a whole range of topics, delivered in a distinctive style, occasionally bordering on the eccentric. Following ITN's policy of not restricting female reporters to fashion shows and Royal babies, Lynne had covered her share of sectarian killings in Northern Ireland and shoot-ups in Lebanon.

When Charles Craig was setting up N-TV he invited her to join the team with the suggestion that she do more studio work.

Now in her mid-forties, Lynne was no stanger to criticism. Some thought she presented too unsmiling an image for popular TV, while others preferred women newscasters to be younger and 'less touched by time', as one TV critic tactfully put it.

Another way of putting it was that Lynne was erratic in her looks and behaviour. On good days she could look stunning. The russet hair would be beautifully swept back into a bun with curls dangling by her ears. She would be dressed in an expensive purple silk blouse, and – even if unseen under the studio desk – would be wearing jodhpurs and buttoned-up boots below.

At other times, she looked as if she had just fallen out of bed. And she would stumble over her words.

The fact was that Lynne suffered from bouts of depression which made it extremely difficult for her to be one hundred per cent reliable. When she was good, she was very, very good, but when she was off-form, she made it hard even for friends and supporters to justify her continued employment. It was then that cattiness would reach its peak behind the scenes. People would call her a cow and a bitch. They even hinted that she was a lesbian.

They didn't even have to hint that she drank too much; she readily confessed she did. Her favourite pose – or, at least, her most frequent – was with be-ringed fingers encircling a rapidly-emptying glass of gin and orange.

That was exactly her position the night after the BAFTA awards. She and Ben Brock had presented the *Nightly News* together and were now having a quiet nightcap.

'That was a bugger, wasn't it?' Lynne said.

'Yes, it was,' he agreed, unconvincingly, for Ben himself had been as smoothly in command as ever. Lynne had stumbled several times over her words or lost track of what she'd been saying.

'I find it's getting harder, not easier, the more live TV I do,' she said. 'Perhaps it's middle age?'

'Of course not, Lynne. Middle aged! You?'

'I always feel out of practice. I need to do it every day, otherwise the muscles seize up.'

'Don't let the *News of the World* hear you say that!'

They had come to the roof-top bar of the St George's Hotel, which overlooks Broadcasting House.

'I always like to come up here,' Ben said. 'It enables me to look down on the BBC!'

'Surely you don't need to come up here to do that?' Lynne laughed. She was glad they had come away from N-TV for their drink. She would have felt uncomfortable there, fearful that people would be on at her for messing up the programme. Besides, at the St George's she could have a drink in relative privacy and not fuel any jokes about her boozy leanings.

She was on her third gin by now while Ben was still on his first large brandy.

'How's Natalie?' she asked, solicitously.

'So-so,' Ben replied, on his guard.

'You're very good the way you're always popping off to see her.'

'Well, it's the least I can do, isn't it?'

'What is she in for?'

Ben paused, then answered blandly: 'Oh ... tests. You know what doctors are like. Always doing tests, or waiting for results of tests ...'

'Will she be all right?'

'I should think so.'

'Come on, you can tell me ...'

Ben had to be firm. 'Lynne, stop interviewing me. The programme's over.'

''Nother drink?'

'Not just yet, thanks.'

'Mind if I press ahead?'

Lynne always made a point of paying for her rounds, if only because it left her free to suggest the next one.

Ben puffed his cigar and noted the glances from other drinkers in the bar. The dark February night, bitterly cold, beat against the wide plate-glass windows. In Broadcasting House, down below, lights burned on. Someone else was keeping the wheels of communication turning even if Ben and Lynne had done their bit for the day.

The BBC's television news would be over now, as it was just half-past nine. ITN, round the corner, would be starting up at ten. One thing to be said about N-TV's eight o'clock programme was that it didn't completely ruin your evening.

Lynne came back with her fourth large gin.

'I know they're trying to get rid of me,' she burst out.

'Who are, Lynne? What on earth are you talking about?'

'*Them* – not Sir Charles necessarily, but people like Michael Penn-Morrison. They've really got it in for me. I can see it in their eyes and the little things they say.'

'Nonsense, woman. What on earth gives you that idea?'

'At my age, Ben, if you're a woman, you're finished on TV. Can you think of any other woman in her mid-forties who's still on TV news?'

'There's Barbara Walters.'

'She's in the States. So, there you are. All they want is fresh-faced little things like March, and once you're over thirty, let alone forty, you're living on borrowed time.'

'In that case,' Ben said, with a smile, 'you've borrowed a heck of a lot of it.'

'Ben!'

'Now listen, you only started at N-TV four years ago, like the rest of us. You were over forty, then. So, if what you say is true, you'de never have got the job.'

'But it *is* true, Ben, really. If you're a man, the older you get the better you look, the more "right" you are for doing the news. Nobody wants to look at a frump, particularly when there's somebody like March to look at instead. I could strangle her sometimes, the way she comes on with that virginal look, as if butter wouldn't melt in her mouth.'

'For a start, Lynne, you're *not* a frump. There are many people who appreciate you. You must know that. And as for March, yes, she *is* very beautiful, and a great asset, but she can't do, yet, what you can do so well.'

'Like what?'

'Interviewing, reporting, and giving a bit of authority to the news. Those qualities only come with time.'

'Well, I don't know. I feel the ground shaking beneath my feet. And people at N-TV are being plain nasty and difficult.'

'N-TV is on the crest of a wave, yes, and we're about due for a spot of trouble. But I haven't heard a single whisper about you from anyone. And I would have done if there had been any.'

Lynne didn't seem very reassured by Ben's words.

'Ah, well, time for bobos,' she said, draining her glass. 'Back to our lonely cells. We both seem a bit that way at the moment, don't we?'

They collected their coats and wrapped up against the cold and windy night. Taking the lift down to the ground floor, Ben again asked Lynne if he could run her home.

'No, no, I'll be all right. Don't you worry. 'Night, Ben.'

On impulse, she gave him a hug and walked off into the dark. Ben climbed into his Rolls, parked half on, half off the pavement, and set off homewards in the direction of the Royal Borough.

Lynne located her red BMW – her 'fire engine' as she called it – and spent a long time trying to fit the key in the ignition. She only had to drive to Maida Vale but for some reason soon found herself travelling up Haverstock Hill in the direction of Hampstead.

She couldn't understand why other drivers kept flashing their lights at her. Had she forgotten to put her lights on? Was she driving down a bus lane? Surely that didn't matter at this time of night.

Indeed, it wouldn't have mattered had Lynne been driving in the right direction down the bus lane. She discovered her error when she came to a set of traffic lights. She chose to brazen it out and make a dash for it when the lights changed.

It was just her luck that a police patrol car was coming the other way. She hoped it hadn't spotted her, and was so busy checking that she went clean through a second set of traffic lights. The police had reversed now and were pursuing her. She looked in her rear-view mirror to check on their progress.

The next thing she knew was that her BMW had nudged up against a concrete lamp-post. There was no getting out of it now.

Lynne sobered up rapidly on the way to the police station. She treated what had happened as confirmation of the imminent misfortunes Ben had pooh-poohed.

She was breath-tested and found to have almost twice the legal limit of alcohol in her system.

At least he doesn't know who I am, she thought, as the policeman gravely took down her particulars.

He did know who she was, in fact, and by the early hours of the following morning the news was on the agency tapes.

CHAPTER 7

At eleven o'clock the next morning Ben stood in a bleak Oxford meadow. He was well-lagged and muffled against the February cold. With him was an American, equally tall and broad, whose sturdy head was topped by a full, but greying, mop of hair.

Inside Magdalen College, undergraduates could be seen poring over their books in the warm light. For a moment, the private world of academic study seemed an enviable place.

Soon the cameraman arrived with a lighting man, carrying portable lights and a rechargeable battery between them. When the lights were switched on, they cast an artificially warm glow over the two men and the damp grass, but made the figures stand out against the college background as intended.

The sound man crouched below them, out of camera range, and tilted up a microphone enclosed in a long muffler. The cameraman nodded, and the set-up was complete.

'Mr Mann,' Ben addressed the American. 'Many people in Britain are deeply concerned about the basing here of American nuclear weapons. Can you give them any assurance that a greater degree of shared control could be worked out between our two countries?'

Winston Mann outlined his position to Ben who then took him over such matters as American attitudes to Europe and the Soviet Union, the threat of another recession, and his hopes for a negotiated settlement in South Africa.

Finally, Ben asked: 'Mr Mann, do you think you have the slightest chance of becoming the next President of the United States?'

Winston seemed to brighten at this most difficult of questions because it was the one he was most prepared for.

'You know and I know, Mr Brock, that every candidate for the Presidency must have an outsized sense of his own worth even to stand up and declare himself. It has always seemed the most presumptuous thing for any man, or woman, to range himself along with the best his party has to offer – and this time around it seems there's an awful lot of that best – to challenge an incumbent President. But all I would say at this time is, and you know I haven't declared myself as a candidate, nor am I participating in

55

the Iowa caucus or the New Hampshire primary ... all I would say is, in the short history of my country, elections have happened every four years. And at slightly longer intervals challengers, one way and another, have ended up in the White House. I think that my present best efforts in that regard will not be wasted, should it come to that. But as of this hour, I am not a candidate.'

Ben was not going to let him get away with it: 'But will you be a candidate, if you don't leave it too late?'

Winston broke into a grin. Wisps of frozen breath departed over his shoulder. 'I'm sorry, but I'll just have to say it, Mr Brock – "No comment".'

Ben left a pause, then led the small TV crew in chuckles of relief. 'Quite good, quite good, Winston! Rather you than me.'

Winston laughed engagingly, 'But it wasn't what I *meant* to say at all!'

'Well, you can't have another go. It's too cold out here.'

The cameraman did a spot-check to make sure the interview was safely on tape and the group broke up.

'Say what,' Winston declared, 'time for a beer before we leave? Is the Turf still open?'

Ben despatched the camera crew back to London. The broadcaster and the politician stepped out of Magdalen, walked up the High Street and then turned into Queen's Lane.

Ben's friendship with Winston dated back to their time together at Oxford in the 1950s. Winston arrived as a Rhodes Scholar in 1952, the year after Ben had gone up to Magdalen. Winston was given rooms on the same college staircase and that is how he and Ben had come to know each other. Any newsman depends on keeping up his contacts, and on a hefty portion of good luck in them, but back in those days it would have taken the sharpest Nostradamus to predict how their television and political careers would eventually bring the two men together again.

Now Ben hoped that maintaining contact with Winston over the years, however casually, would pay off. The chances of his ever becoming President were infinitesimal, but Ben could muse fruitfully about the possibility.

The two men disappeared down the dark crack known as Hell's Passage. Few remarked on their progress from Magdalen, though they were imposing figures and spoke expansively. They also had the walk of the famous, a rolling gait, confident and steady, as though ready to acknowledge plaudits and recognition.

Few recognized them this day. It might have been because the Oxford shoppers were intent on scurrying back to their warm firesides. Then again, it might have been because the two men were out of context. Or because of that Oxford superiority towards those who made it in the real world beyond the university walls. The Englishman and the American were celebrities of a kind, but to the university they were a touch frivolous merely for being *in* the real world.

'I'm glad to see it's still here,' said Winston, as they ducked through the door of the Turf Tavern.

'It's about the only thing that is. Do you remember the Kemp in the Broad, the Kardomah in Cornmarket? All gone. And, worst of all, do you remember Kingston Bagpuize ...?'

'Kingston Bagpuize – now, that's a name I haven't heard for thirty years, Ben. What was it called, the pub there? The Black Swan, the Dirty Duck...?'

'The Lamb and Flag. It was later known as Dudley's. Do you remember cadging a ride out there in '52 or '53 with two girls, and having hare ... or was it pheasant?'

'I remember the food and the beer, but not the women. I wonder where they are now? Grandmothers, I expect.'

'I went looking for it a year or two back,' said Ben. 'It'd break your heart, Winston.'

'Kentucky Fried Chicken?'

'Almost. Some Berni Inn or other, with little pink lampshades.'

'What you going to have to drink, Ben? A beer?'

'Yes, something strong and Oxfordy.' Ben took off his hat and the barman gave a flicker of recognition.

'Two pints of that one there,' said Winston. When the black, muddy liquid had been poured, he said, 'Cheers, Ben. Here's to us!'

Even though Winston Mann hadn't declared himself as a Democratic hopeful, he was being treated in Britain – and not just by Ben Brock – as though he might be in with a chance.

The Republican President, Henry Carson, had been in the White House for three years and such was the ineptitude he had displayed in domestic and international affairs there was a very real chance he could be ousted by a strong Democratic challenger. Consequently, the field was a big one. Some twelve Democratic candidates were now gathering their strength – and their funds. By March – when President Carson would announce whether he would run again – the field might swell to sixteen, an unprecedented number. It was the customary mixture of ageing heroes making their last flag-waving stand, middle-of-the-road senators and governors, often with one major axe to grind, and fortyish hopefuls trying to emulate President Kennedy, with more charm and *chutzpah* than experience or sound policies.

Winston fell clearly into the second group though he had no major axe to grind except his own ambition. He was approaching fifty-eight and was largely unknown outside Ohio, his native state, where he had served, competently rather than memorably, two terms as Governor.

He had come to Britain on the visit paid sooner or later by most Presidential hopefuls, the chief purpose of which is to establish potential candidates in the eyes of the American electorate as people who know where 'abroad' is, and who are on nodding terms with leaders in other countries.

Nodding terms was as far as it went, though. Winston had managed to be photographed shaking hands with Trevor Ross, the Prime Minister, and Harry Marchant, Leader of the Opposition, but their 'substantive discussions' had gone no further.

A group of undergraduates burst noisily into the pub, laughing and talking loudly. One of them recognized Ben instantly and said, 'Good evening, *sir*!' in a way that managed to be at once polite and cheeky. He ignored Winston.

'Savour the moment,' Ben said, noticing, as if to reassure Winston. 'If you do decide to run, you'll never again be able to sit unnoticed in an English pub or walk unrecognized down an Oxford street, or go anywhere in the world without attracting attention. Is it a price worth paying?'

'Stop asking questions, Ben! It *is* a price worth paying if there's an ambition you have.'

'I wish I could be as sure as you, Winston.'

'Faint heart! You're too old to be having a mid-life crisis, Ben. So, shape up! Is there something the matter?'

Ben looked glum and fiddled for a second with the white buttonhole which was in danger of being squashed by his overcoat.

'Forgive me for having to tell you like this. I've not told anyone else ...'

'What, Ben? Shoot.'

'It's Natalie. She ... she's in hospital and it's serious – very serious.'

Winston put down his beer. 'I'm sorry, Ben, truly sorry. Heck, I don't know what to say. I had no idea ... but I thought something was up.'

'Cancer's not something you shout about. I suppose I've bottled it up.'

'Don't let it get you down, Ben. I know it's hard to hold your head up in public when you've got some private burden like that. But it's the ultimate test. Hell, I'm sorry.'

'Thank you, Winston. Talking about it at least has helped.'

'Now, forgive me, Ben, I'd better get back to my people. It was a good idea to do the interview here at Oxford rather than London. I appreciate it.'

'Yes, I've got to get back, too,' said Ben, looking at his watch. 'I'm on tonight.'

'You'll run our interview?'

'I hope so.'

The two men made to leave the Turf and walk back up Hell's Passage.

'Tell you what, I'll do a deal with you,' Winston announced. 'You can be the first person to interview me when I get to the White House.'

'I'd expect nothing less,' Ben grinned, quickly regaining his usual composure. 'The future suddenly seems pregnant with possibilities!'

'That's the spirit!' Winston clapped Ben, rather manfully and presidentially, on the back. 'And remember what JFK used to quote ... those lines of Robert Frost: "The woods are lovely, dark and deep, but I have promises to keep and miles to go before I sleep ..."'

'Winston, you must be careful not to overdo this Kennedy stuff. I'm not your media adviser, but *someone* ought to tell you.'

'OK, OK.'

'And you make the news, remember. I report it.'

'Nonsense,' said Winston. 'You're as much of a newsmaker as any politician. You're always making it up!'

Roused by this, Ben asked his old friend: 'You don't *really* expect to get anywhere with this bid of yours, do you?'

'Not a cat's chance. But I'm going to have one helluva lot of fun before I withdraw. You see.'

CHAPTER 8

Before Ben Brock arrived back in London for the three o'clock meeting, the Editor-in-Chief had already set it in motion. Sir Charles Craig never moved, if he could help it, from behind his large desk. It was free of clutter and spoke of an orderly mind and perhaps, too, of a desire to impose that order on the world beyond.

Sir Charles remained seated because, if he stood up, he would have been revealed as the smallest man in the room. He was nicknamed 'The Shrimp' but he was only really shrimp-like in comparison with the big men he chose to employ. Why did such a small person surround himself with people built like rugby-players and policemen?

It was a question few would dare to raise with the man himself. He had little small-talk, his voice was clipped, and he was teetotal – the exact opposite of almost everyone else in the room.

His secretary, Celia, circulated copies of the news 'prospects' which would form the basis for discussion of that night's Big News, and exited, leaving March Stevens the only woman in the room. In a mint-green jumpsuit, she glowed among the beards, shirtsleeves, greying heads of hair, and beer-bellies of the men.

Sir Charles stared at the list and said, 'All quiet on the Potomac.' This was his coded way of saying, 'It's a dull news day.'

'HNE,' he went on, turning to George Lee, 'what's the best among your lot?'

The Home News Editor ducked the implied criticism. 'The PM may have something to say on the SA killing at Question Time.'

'Jack,' Sir Charles turned, more warmly, to the Foreign News Editor, Jack Somerset. 'Can we repeat the clip from David's SA piece where he got the quote about the white? I felt we didn't slug it enough through the night.'

To an outsider, the jargon was near impenetrable, but it was a familiar scene to insiders, with the Editor-in-Chief gently prodding those who had to deliver the goods into making the best of what the world had to offer.

'News doesn't grow on trees,' was one of Sir Charles's maxims, by which he meant you shouldn't wait for it to happen. If you

60

pointed at the tree for long enough, it might even turn into news.

Ben strode in, apologizing for his late arrival. There was a slight hint of resistance to the on-screen star, perceptible in the lack of interest shown by the assembled producers and editors. Ben sat next to March, gravitating naturally towards the other performer in the room.

'How was Governor Mann?' Sir Charles asked. 'Has he made up his mind to run?'

'Not in so many words,' said Ben, 'but I think it's a safe bet.'

'He really is going about it in the most odd way. Your interview all right? Not too much of the "old buddy" touch, I trust?'

Ben pretended to frown.

'We've got room for it tonight,' said Jack Somerset, coming to his rescue, 'but can we dress it up a bit? Call him the Undecided Candidate or the Dithering Democrat or Johnny Come Lately, or something like that?'

'Any of those,' intoned Ben solemnly, 'would perfectly well describe Winston at the moment.'

One of the scriptwriters whose job it was to turn agency tape into punchy prose started doodling alliterative combinations with the word 'Democrat' – docile, delaying, decrepit, decoy, dead . . .'

'FNE,' Sir Charles went on, 'what more are we getting out of David in Jo'burg? Have you heard from him?'

'Pieter Hartmann telexed to say they've been given a facility trip. He wanted to share the costs with ABC, so I OK'd it.'

Sir Charles grunted, but he knew that the economic arguments for cooperation with N-TV's American rival were unanswerable.

'Anything on the People front?'

The Entertainment Editor ran down possible gossip items from a list to be packaged in a special 'People' section of the programme – a new musical from Lloyd Webber, a Soviet dancer defecting in France, a pop star on a drugs charge. But if there was any real gossip among it, Sir Charles would insist it be labelled as something else.

March sat through the meeting without saying a word. She was going to be co-presenting with Ben but her lack of participation at this stage was not unusual. She knew how to steer things her way, items that she wanted to present herself, a little later in the afternoon. These meetings were a formality she had to sit through.

Sir Charles never formally closed the proceedings. That wasn't his style. They just dissolved when those with work to do went off to do it. As always, the newscasters were the last to leave.

'I did get one little nugget out of Winston,' Ben told Sir Charles.

'What was that?'

'He says if he gets to the White House, I can have the first interview.'

'So he's going to run?'

'As I said, not yet in as many words!'

'Good, good.'

Ben looked at March and they departed together.

Sir Charles turned to his tidy desk, reached for the control which operated six TV screens on the other side of the room, and faded up the sound on the N-TV monitor.

Although the *Nightly News* was the lynch-pin of N-TV's 24-hour service, Sir Charles had to keep an eye on the rolling news format which took up the rest of the day. In any one hour, there was a package of hourly headlines lasting twenty minutes (though part of that time was commercials), followed by two twenty-minute programmes on a variety of themes – business, sport, fashion, entertainment, science.

On the screen now was N-TV's Arts Correspondent. Sir Charles listened to what he had to say for a minute and then wrote something on a pad in front of him. In the fullness of time, the Arts Correspondent would have to answer one of the Editor-in-Chief's curt memos. Why was he wearing a striped shirt with a striped tie? Why hadn't he asked the really key question? Why was he boring everyone with all this flatulent stuff about modern art?

Well, after all, those were the questions editors were *there* to ask.

The hospital room was in shade and smelling sweetly of freesias when Ben Brock entered quietly just after five o'clock in the afternoon. Natalie was sitting propped up on the pillows, a delicate pink shawl on her shoulders, a copy of *Watership Down* held unread between finger and thumb.

'Ben ...?' Her eyes opened as soon as she was aware of her husband. 'I must have dozed off.'

Ben leant forward and kissed her lightly on the forehead, picked up the book and laid it on the bedside table crowded with other books and cards and photographs of Drew and Heather, their two children.

'It's a quiet day,' Ben said gently, 'so I was able to slip away for five minutes. Sorry about yesterday but it all got rather hectic.'

Conveniently, the hospital was only a short step round the corner from N-TV House. Ben had been given a bleeper for just such occasions but he couldn't quite get over the feeling of playing truant. If anything happened in the real world, he'd have to hot-foot it back.

'You gave a lovely speech at the awards,' his wife said. She hadn't always been so complimentary about Ben's public efforts in the past.

'I wish you could have been there. Mind you, it's rather a marathon. Goes on for hours. Everyone was asking after you.'

'How did the Shrimp enjoy it?'

'Charles? Cock-a-hoop, not that you'd have noticed. He was only a fraction less tight-lipped than usual.'

'What's he had to say about Lynne Kimberley's latest escapade?'

'What escapade?'

'It says in the *Post* she ran into a lamp-post last night and got breathalysed.'

Ben clapped a hand to his head. 'So that's why I'm on with March tonight. That's terrible! We went for a drink at the St George's after the programme. I knew she'd been knocking it back, but she wouldn't let me run her home. Nobody said anything about it in the office just now, but I've been in Oxford all morning. Winston sends his love, by the way. Poor Lynne! That's not going to go down at all well with the Shrimp.'

Natalie tried to change the subject. 'I had a letter from Heather. She said she'd try and come up at the weekend. I know it's hard for her to get away . . .'

'Yes, yes – oh, that's good . . .' said Ben.

All their life together Natalie had tried to stop him talking about his work but Ben talked family only with reluctance.

'I'm beginning to wonder if he's going to chuck it in,' he said.

'Who, darling?'

'The Shrimp. He's got his gong. He's won the approbation of the world. It might be time-to-make-way-for-a-younger-man time.'

'Not really?'

'Quite possible. And I've a good mind to jump with him, too, if he goes.'

'Oh, not that again, lovey! You could go on at N-TV til you drop. In that job, you're like the sovereign. You don't give up. There'd be a revolution if you did.'

'That, my darling, is piddle, and you know it.' Ben playfully took his wife's hand and squeezed the fingers one by one. 'If I resigned tomorrow, there'd be a temporary fuss and I'd be forgotten within the month. It's the nature of the beast.'

'But you do it so well! I can't understand why you have these repeated attacks of the droops.'

Ben couldn't tell Natalie the real reason.

When Ben had been told how ill his wife was, he hadn't felt able to break the news to her. The great communicator to the nation couldn't find it in himself to tell his partner of twenty-eight years what her fate must be. For months now, in consequence, he had had to play along with the charade that Natalie had kidney trouble, that she was in hospital for tests, and had to be kept there under supervision.

It wasn't hard for Ben to put on a show for the rest of the world. His unruffled charm, his panache, his benign image, all effectively disguised his real feelings. But he had never, in all their years of marriage, succeeded in keeping anything from Natalie, nor she from him.

So, in order to explain his own, inner discomfort, Ben pretended to be more dissatisfied with his work than he in fact was. He tended to harp on about the hollowness of his role at N-TV. 'What can I tell the children I've achieved?' he would ask. 'It's a cosmetic job, reading an autocue, writing two-minute essays any cub reporter could toss off on his first day at a local paper.'

Natalie would listen to these outbursts and smile. 'You're an odd one, Ben. On the box, you seem to carry all the cares of the world on your shoulders. You tell people about disasters in space, or motorway crashes, you look concerned and sad, but philosophical about it. You're reassuring to people. Only *I* have to hear *this*. If you said one half of this on the box, you *would* have to chuck it in. Because it's not what people want to hear.'

'I know, my darling. That's why I have to be such a ruddy *actor* most of the time ...'

'Well, promise me one thing. No more thoughts of chucking it in. You're marvellous at it. You may not think it's much of a gift, but people out there thank you for it. Please ...'

'I must be getting back.' Ben looked at his watch.

'You haven't told me about Winston,' Natalie said. 'How was he?'

'Very much the same old Winston. A little hard to fathom. I think he *is* going to declare himself. But out of a misplaced sense of honour he seems to think that he must wait for Carson to announce he isn't going to stand before jumping in. That's the only reason I can think of.'

'Perhaps he's worried about the cost of it all?'

'Winston? Never. He's got lots of backing lined up. Fat cats from Ohio and beyond will flock to help him rather than that Gerry Iver – who's a piece of cardboard if ever I saw one.'

'But there are so many candidates ...'

'I know. He said he hasn't got a hope in hell's chance but he's doing it for the *fun*!'

'Good for him. You ought to take the same attitude, darling.'

''Nuff said,' Ben winked. It was his usual way of rounding off a marital discussion, especially one he wasn't winning. 'And now I really *must* get back.'

He leant forward to kiss his wife once more.

She removed one of her hairs from his lapel and touched his buttonhole.

He put *Watership Down* back into her hands and left without another word.

CHAPTER 9

It was just as well the television still worked after Jo's rough treatment, because the set provided her with much-needed companionship and was often her only source of information as to David's whereabouts.

Since marrying him five years ago and having the two children – Bill, soon to be four, and Harry, who was two – she had found herself increasingly cut off.

She was, in any case, a stranger in the land. Born Jo Lake, daughter of a Ne York stockbroker and an actress, she had been to Columbia University and to journalism college before doing social work in Manhattan.

The departure lounge at Kennedy Airport was where David and she had first met as they both waited to catch a flight to London. When they reached England, in a sudden rush of romanticism, David had dined her every night for two weeks and they were married within three months of their first meeting.

Settled into the strange domestic environment of a media wife in England, Jo found her natural talents and enthusiasms oddly stifled. David was not so much obsessed with work as too busy ever to think of anything else. As far as Jo could judge, every other marriage at N-TV was in a similarly rocky state, but the English wives she encountered in Islington, where the Kenways had their house, failed to understand how anyone married to so dashing a man in so glamorous a job could end up so depressed.

Soon after Bill was born, an *au pair* was engaged, theoretically to free Jo from her domestic chores. But that was not how it turned out. Una, the Finnish *au pair*, had started dating a West Indian she'd picked up at a Meatloaf concert and if she wasn't audibly being seen to by him at the Kenways' house, she was off in darkest Brixton being attended to similarly.

Jo spent more time worrying over the *au pair* than the *au pair* did over the children. David, to give him his due, laid not a finger on the Finnish temptress, but he was abroad most of the time anyway. At the end of a year, Jo was so tired of the sight and sound of Una that she was sent back to Finland amid tearful scenes.

An English nanny, also called Jo, was then engaged and

dubbed Nanny Jo to avoid confusion. So a new regime was inaugurated. Harry was born, and Jo attempted to freelance, doing odds and ends of magazine writing.

She hadn't been able to make any real friends in London. She liked the place well enough, but worked herself into considerable outrage at the British workman's lack of efficiency. She complained volubly if telephonists didn't pick up the phone after three rings. But she enjoyed another side of London – the literary associations, the parks, the old buildings, the theatre, and the television. It was just that, for most of the time, she had to enjoy these things on her own.

There was no question that Little Bill was his father's son. He had the same mop of cream-coloured thatch and the same noble nose. He was keenly intelligent and kept Jo on her toes with sharp questions about the state of her marriage and David's role in the world.

'Mummy,' he would say, looking at her steadily, 'wouldn't you rather Daddy was at home? I don't like him on the TV, do you? Why isn't he a musician?'

While Jo selected which of these difficult points to answer fist, Harry, the younger boy, would simply point at David on the screen and beam with delight. Whether he really knew who it was, Jo wasn't sure, but at least he wasn't as disappointed as his brother. 'Da, da!' he would often squeak as he managed, with unnerving accuracy, to splash the screen with puréed carrot.

'Why is South Africa?' was Bill's current talking point. Jo couldn't be sure whether to dismiss the question as being of the intended-to-annoy 'Why is the sky blue, Mummy?' variety or whether to attempt a serious answer, as she thought she was supposed to do.

'How do you mean, "Why is South Africa?"'

'Why is Daddy go there?'

'Because there are lots of unhappy people in South Africa,' Jo began, taking a deep breath. 'The white people aren't very kind to the black people – some of them – so Daddy's job is to explain to everybody in the world why that is.'

Jo herself was quite impressed with the clearly pivotal role she had discovered for her husband.

'Why does he do that?'

'Because – because that's his job, Billy. He helps people to find out what's happening. That's what a television reporter does. He brings them the news.'

'Why is news?' Bill asked bluntly.

It was a question that older minds than Bill's had wrestled with unsuccessfully. Why news, indeed? Jo couldn't help feeling there was too much news these days, that people were being given more information than they knew what to do with. They were also made to feel guilty about events which fifty or a hundred years ago they wouldn't have worried about because they simply wouldn't have heard of them.

'Why news, Mummy?' Bill persisted.

'Oh, Billy. It's Daddy's job, that's why. People like to have the news, that's why ...'

Jo felt her argument sagging. She would have to create a diversion.

'Soon be time for bed.'

'When's Daddy coming home?'

'Soon, Bill, soon ... I think.'

'Da, da!' said Harry, pointing at a pretty actress on the screen.

Jo looked at her watch, saw that she had half an hour before the *Nightly News* came on, poured herself a glass of Chablis and told Nanny Jo to get the boys to bed.

It was seven-thirty in the evening. At N-TV, Studio B was in the middle of a 'stagger through' the *Nightly News*. Ben and March read out whatever parts of the script were available on the teleprompter.

The director, Paul Whitehall, with his lighter-than-air manner, called up reports that had already been boiled down into packages on videotape and topped and tailed them so he knew where to cut them off if time were short.

He also ran throuh pictures stored in a caption generator so that they came up on screen at the touch of a button.

Occasionally Paul would demand a better picture. 'Haven't we got a less serious one of Trevor Ross? He's supposed to be happy for once.' A researcher would run off to find a more suitable slide of the Prime Minister from the stock available and prepare it for transmission.

The programme editor of the day, Liz Hastings, talked direct to Ben or March over the small ear-piece each had hidden. 'Ben, can't you say "uninterested", not "disinterested". There is a difference, you know ...'

If Ben could be bothered, he'd tell the teleprompter operator to make the emendation.

It was chaotic. March felt her mouth and tongue get dry with nerves. Surely no one actually *enjoyed* rehearsals like this?

At 7:48, Paul Whitehall demanded everyone's attention and gave what was likely to be the final running order for the first eighteen-minute segment of the one-hour show. It went:

1A LAB REACTION
2   M6 CRASH
2A SAFETY WRAP
3   HOSPITALS
3A NURSE STRIKE ...

'No, we've got an update on that. As you were, loves. First, M6 CRASH, add live insert Manchester – script on its way, Ben. March, you take ROSS SPEECH. Then LAB REACTION. Then HOSPITALS, NURSE STRIKE ...'

'That's too heavy, Paul,' Ben said. 'Can't we pull up something from the second half?'

'Like what?'

'Well, I'd like to put in that 17A obit for Eddie Walker. It's a bit more, you know, sexy than salmonella poisoning.'

'No can do, love. 17A is on the same VT machine as the Labour 1A stuff and there isn't time to get from one to the other.'

'Couldn't we promote the America package 35A?' Ben suggested this a little tentatively, realizing he'd be accused of pushing his own interview with Winston Mann.

'No,' Liz Hastings told him sharply, 'I want to keep the foreign stuff to Part Two.'

The problem soon resolved itself. The M6 motorway crash material from Manchester wouldn't be ready until they were six minutes into the programme, so it couldn't be the first item. Back to square one ...

'But we must have a taster for the headlines,' Liz barked down the phone at Manchester. 'What do you mean we can't, you fuck-wit ...'

'OK, folks,' Paul said soothingly, 'back to where we were ... ROSS SPEECH, LAB REACTION, M6 CRASH, SAFETY WRAP ...'

Down on the studio floor, Serena Hardie, the make-up girl, couldn't wait any longer. It was always the same. There was supposed to be fifteen minutes' break before the programme went out, but they never got it. So she repaired the light make-up Ben and March wore for the cameras, toning down a shining patch on Ben's head, quietening the blusher on March's exquisite cheek-bones, while the two newscasters had their minds on other matters.

'Three minutes, studio,' yelped Patricia, the production assistant, and the information was absorbed almost subliminally by people who were too busy talking and thinking with the adrenalin pumping through them.

'Er, Ben,' the director suddenly announced. 'We've a problem with Archie Tuke. We're not going to be able to get to him till Part Three.'

'Messy,' was Ben's only comment. Archie Tuke, the leader of the Alliance Party, was due to come into the studio to be interviewed live by Ben on the dramatic drop in unemployment figures – the lead item.

'He's got stuck at the airport. Can't be helped.'

Ben scribbled a few lines of recap to put on the autocue before he interviewed Tuke.

'Oh, Adrian,' he whispered to a figure in the shadows just out of camera range, 'Give me a couple of back-up questions for Archie in case I have to spin it out at the end of the prog.'

'Will do,' said the invisible Adrian.

'Two minutes,' barked Patricia.

'March, love' – Paul was putting on the coolness now – 'when you do item 17A, the Walker obit, you may have to re-voice it live. I know you pre-recorded it, but we may have to cut it down a frac. You'll get it on the autocue. Sorry about that.'

'It's OK.'

'And can I ask you to take it slowly through that sequence of film pics. It's tricky for us unless you breathe between each one.'

'I'll try.'

'One minute.'

Sir Charles Craig turned on the television at his home in Gerrard's Cross and sat attentively in his armchair, a glass of water at his side. The previous hour's cycle on N-TV had been due to end with a very lightweight fashion series which he knew he wouldn't enjoy, so he'd made a point of missing it. With a twenty-four-hour-station, he couldn't be expected to watch *everything*.

The commercial break ended.

'It's eight o'clock,' said an off-screen voice.

With a burst of colour, the screen exploded into the familiar tapestry of people and events. At any moment there were twenty-four smaller pictures all moving on the screen. The N-TV theme hummed out. It was an impressive package. As it had cost Sir Charles £85,000 for twenty-five seconds' screen time, he had a vested interest in believing it had been worth it.

'We are N-TV, the Newsmakers,' another sonorous voice boomed. 'And this is the N-TV Nightly News, with Ben Brock and March Stevens.'

And there they were, seated before a vast revolving globe which slowed to a halt as Ben began to speak. The two of them sitting side by side – father and daughter, experience and youth, male and female ... what was the winning combination? Sir Charles felt good.

The two newscasters batted alternately through the six headlines. In a rapid-fire package, big close-ups of Ben and March were interspersed with clips from the upcoming stories.

It was very punchy. Sir Charles, for all his personal reserve, was quite well aware that it was as thrusting an opening as any film thriller or pop show. But such fireworks were especially necessary tonight when the news was on the dull side.

Ben intoned, 'Unemployment is *down* for the first time in over twenty years.' Not by an inflection could he hint that he had a view on the subject, or whether he believed it. What he had to do was show that he thought it was important.

'The Prime Minister, Trevor Ross, said: "The tide has turned, as we always said it would." Labour leader, Harry Marchant, commented, "Well, he would say that, wouldn't he? But where's the proof?" ...'

March took up the multiple crash on the M6 motorway. 'Seven people are feared dead after a pile-up on the M6 late this afternoon. The accident occurred south of Congleton in Cheshire ...'

Despite her regretful voice, she looked ravishing. Her hair shone above a light blue tartan jacket, silk blouse and gold chains. She had chosen to wear a darker lipstick than usual.

On to Part Two, and mostly foreign news. A massive bank robbery in Rome which might well turn out to be the world's largest. A report from Johannesburg. Said March: 'The South African President, Dr Van Der Linde, has told Parliament in Cape Town that he totally rejects calls from the American

Secretary of State, Arthur S. Willenden, for the United Nations to take over mediation attempts ...'

While the reports played on videotape, Ben hastily pencilled alterations to his script for the next item, a report on the US primaries.

'The crowded field of candidates in pursuit of the Democratic presidential nomination,' he said, 'has undergone something of a shake-out. Of the fifteen who started out in January, a mere five retain any credibility after yesterday's voting in the Iowa caucuses. Top of the poll, as widely predicted, was front-runner Senator Gerry Iver with 42% of the vote; second, Senator David Hike with 19%; third, Gloria Stanton, with 16%; fourth, Senator Bob Brown of Florida with 9%; and fifth, the Reverend Bill Montega with 5%. N-TV's Washington correspondent, Graham Johnson, was with Senator Iver as the news of his win came through ...'

There was a touch of pleasure in Ben's voice as he led into Graham Johnson's report from New Hampshire. After it would come his own small package on Winston Mann including two minutes from the interview recorded in Oxford that morning.

Again, while the American tape played, there was frantic activity in the studio. March was told through her ear-piece to stand by for an extra item.

Paul Whitehall told Ben and March simultaneously, 'We've got to drop 16B. MANN/BROCK is killed.'

Ben tried his hardest not to look irritated by this change and didn't entirely succeed.

'We've got an update from South Africa. David Kenway's been in a bomb attack. March, back-announce the Johnson piece, and take the new link off autocue.'

March looked across at Ben. Her eyes widened in puzzlement. His brows furrowed, but he said nothing and simply reached for a sheet of paper and jotted down notes with a pencil.

The director came back to both newscasters. 'Right, everybody, just to recap. Drop 16B and 17. We've got a new 17A which we're calling BOMB. We're very tight for time, March, love, in this part. If you don't get autocue, say it's a special report from Aaron Rochester of ABC in South Africa – don't say Pretoria. Ben, we'll see if we can find you ten seconds, to back-cue it and go into the break. It may be less.'

The American primaries report was coming to an end.

March read sight unseen from the teleprompter:

News just in from South Africa. N-TV special correspondent David Kenway was wounded earlier today when a terrorist mine exploded during a visit he was making to Cape Province. Following his interview with President Van Der Linde, which we showed in last night's *Nightly News*, David Kenway had gone to Oudtshoorn – until now well away from the scene of known unrest. He'd requested President Van Der Linde to be allowed to visit areas where access has been denied newsmen and had travelled to the town at the suggestion of government officials. The same officials now say that the Soviet-made limpet mine was of the type formerly used by the African National Congress.

Aaron Rochester of ABC News, who travelled with David Kenway, has just sent us this report ...

The package combined material shot by both David's and Aaron's crews. David was shown examining the alleged traces of terrorist activity while Aaron's voice explained: 'Kenway and this reporter had not been entirely convinced that Oudtshoorn was in any way a centre, or even the scene, of any terrorist activity in recent weeks. The evidence we were shown by a Bureau for Information official was scanty to say the least. The real action seemed a long way distant. Then towards the end of the day, Kenway prepared to conclude his visit to the area with an in-vision report. This is what happened when he did ...'

David was shown speaking to camera in the main street of Oudtshoorn with a row of cars behind him. Then, as he came to the words, 'Evidence of unrest is hard to come by in this area,' the camera shook and David was visibly blown off screen, to be replaced by a cloud of dust ... amid signs that the camerman was having difficulty in keeping upright.

Aaron's calm voice continued: 'David Kenway was badly concussed and suffered severe cuts from flying glass and debris. He was flown to a hospital in Cape Town for treatment and his condition is presently described as "serious". Just one question remains: how was it that two foreign newsmen were taken to an area where there have been no major incidents reported – only to walk straight into the middle of one? This is Aaron Rochester, for N-TV, in South Africa.'

It fell to Ben to close the section. He ad-libbed around the terse sentences that appeared for him on the autocue. 'We have just heard from Pretoria that the South African President has expressed regret at the incident involving David Kenway and has promised a full investigation.

'For our part, we wish David a speedy recovery, as we are reminded that a reporter's life is not something apart from the events he observes.'

Then Ben positively beamed reassurance. 'We'll have an update on that story later. In Part Three, Archie Tuke, leader of the Alliance Party questions the unemployment breakthrough ...'

CHAPTER 10

Jo stood in front of the television set, shaking, wineglass unheeded in her hand. Tears came into her eyes. They were talking about David ...

There was her husband being blown up.

How could they let her find out this way?

She had an irrational fear that the two boys, despite being tucked up in bed, might come into the room and learn about their father's accident. So she pressed against the door while continuing to cry and listening to Ben Brock.

But now they were into the commercials. Stupid, silly commercials, all jollity and froth. Good God, didn't they know what had happened to her husband? Why had the show got to go on?

At N-TV, too, it was a chore getting through Part Three, after the commercials. Fortunately, the contents were mostly recorded 'slugs', as they were called, about people in the news, sport, arts, and entertainment. Then Ben had to conduct his interview with Archie Tuke who was his usual slightly difficult self, an interview Ben hadn't much fancied doing even before the upheaval.

But Ben was a pro and so the show went on. At the end, he and March indulged in the routine gathering up of papers, putting away of pens, and unheard small-talk, as the closing credits rolled.

Anyone who could lip-read would have heard Ben say, 'I could do with a large brandy after that' – while March replied, '*Poor David. I felt quite sick.*'

Ben disentangled himself from his ear-piece.

'I could do with a drink, too,' March added, sounding more one of the boys than usual. The studio lights were quickly extinguished in blocks and the cameras parked forlornly in a corner with hoods over them.

Ben turned to Tuke who was still sitting like a trapped bird in his interview seat. A sound man unclipped the small microphone which threatened to leave a mark on the politician's pastel-striped tie.

'I'm sorry we were a bit rushed,' said Ben, in his most bedside of manners, 'but we were all a bit of a jitter, I'm afraid.'

'Didn't notice anything,' Tuke said, brightly, eager to be pleased. 'Thank you for making it so painless.' Then he added: '... as usual,' to give the impression he was an old hand. 'I'm sorry I couldn't get here earlier.'

'Oh, not at all, not at all,' Ben continued to steamroller him with good humour. 'Can you stay for a drink? Good.'

Ben gestured to March, downing an invisible glass.

'I'll be right with you,' she said and went off to slip out of her studio clothes.

Ben steered Tuke between the cameras, over the cables, and into the make-up room.

'A slice of cucumber, if you'd be so kind.'

Ben ritually made this little remark when he came into Make-Up after a programme. Serena Hardie had ready the small damp Fresh'n Up pads he used to remove the light tan off his face.

Tuke, unwisely, chose the more heroic method of soap and water. That way he managed to get the make-up into his eyes, which would smart for hours afterwards, and onto his shirt-collar.

Apparently oblivious of these after-effects, he then allowed himself to be ushered along to the hospitality room which N-TV provided for guests and for programme staff *after* they'd finished their work for the day.

'I was sorry to hear about your man in South Africa,' Tuke said. 'Sounded serious.'

'Yes,' Ben said quietly. He was having more than his share of intimations of mortality at the moment. 'If you ask me, it has all the makings of a put-up job. I mean, why cart him and that ABC chap off to the middle of nowhere, only to have him blown up?'

'Might have been coincidence ...'

Already, the hospitality room was crowded. George Lee, the HNE, was busy making himself a lethal concoction. Ben couldn't resist asking, 'Are you sure you remembered to put some gin in that? Archie, what would you like?'

'A spot of white wine, if you have it ...'

'Of course.'

Paul Whitehall sidled up in light white gear and sneakers. 'Sorry about the panic, Ben, love.'

'There wasn't any panic, Paul. Oh, Archie, this is Paul Whitehall, the studio director. Archie Tuke, Paul Whitehall.'

'Yes, we've met, Mr Tuke, at last year's Alliance conference, you remember?'

'Of course, yes,' said Tuke, clearly nonplussed.

'There wasn't any panic, as far as *I* was concerned,' Ben boomed on. 'It was just that I felt the programme was rather messy, dotting backwards and forwards between South Africa and unemployment, unemployment and South Africa.'

'Oh, that was my fault,' Tuke piped up. 'I really should've been here for the start of the programme.'

'Not at all, not at all, I didn't mean that ...'

What an egocentric lot politicians were, thought Ben.

'What *I* don't understand,' said Paul, 'is why we didn't know in advance about David Kenway. Jo'burg gave us no warning. It just came off the satellite.'

Ben thought for a moment. 'Perhaps that ground man in Johannesburg, what's he called ...?'

'Hartmann.'

'Pieter Hartmann, yes. Perhaps he was too busy looking after David to let us know.'

At that moment, Michael Penn-Morrison came in, clutching his clipboard and looking harassed. He made the most perfunctory of apologies to Tuke and pulled Ben over to speak to him.

'I've just been getting my ear chewed off by Sir Charles. He wanted to know why we hadn't told him about David K.'

'But we didn't know ourselves ...'

'That's what I said. It just fell off the satellite.'

'It must have come as a shock to him. It came as a bit of a shock to *me*, frankly.'

'I do wish he wouldn't ring up as soon as we're off the air like that.'

'You should be glad he's not here in the studio of an evening, Michael. He used to be in the early days, you know.'

March arrived having changed back into her jumpsuit.

'Oh, Michael,' she said, 'there was a call for you in the newsroom. I think it was Johannesburg.'

'Better go and chase it up. 'Scuse me, Ben.'

Ben struck a match and lit his usual post-programme cigar.

'Any objections to my smoking?' he asked. A small chorus cried, 'Yes!' emphatically, and he ignored it as usual.

Rescuing Archie Tuke from the clutches of Paul Whitehall, Ben attempted to indulge in parliamentary small-talk. Tuke, on the other hand, having noticed the arrival of March, showed a marked lack of interest in the topic.

In a moment, he had effected an introduction and was doing the sincerity bit all over her. She found it hard to concentrate on what he was saying and overheard instead the cutting remarks some of the team were making about David's accident. Only half in jest, Adrian, the researcher, said, 'Well, that'll put a damper on his screwing for a while ...'

March felt quite angry.

Then she heard the Leader of the Alliance Party ask her if she'd like to join him for dinner.

CHAPTER 11

Tuke was clearly on a high when he arrived with March at Soho's L'Escargot. Elena, the warm-hearted manageress, greeted them at the top of the stairs and wafted the two celebrities to a corner table under a signed photograph of Vincent Price. Here their well-known profiles could be observed by the rest of the clientele without them being bothered by too much eye-contact.

'What's it to be, then?' Tuke asked, prompted by a waiter. 'A small aperitif?'

'Just a glass of Badoit for me,' March replied.

'Oh.' Archie was thrown by her response, but then, rejecting caution and sobriety, he asked for a *kir*.

'They do a very good *kir*, here,' he told March. 'Not too much *cassis*. Just enough to tint the colour of the white wine. Doesn't end up looking like Ribena.'

Tuke looked wonderfully rumpled, especially in these sur-roundings. His clothes were hardly what politicians normally wore. They'd have been happier sitting on a farmer or the more eccentric type of vet. And his beard ... why was there such a disparity between its ginger and the auburn hair on his head? March itched to give it all a trim with a pair of scissors. Tuke's appearance was unique, to be sure, in both Houses of Parliament. No wonder he was the darling of the cartoonists.

Relations between TV organizations and political parties were cautious at the best of times and March knew that the invitation to dinner hadn't been a straightforward one. If she'd refused him, Tuke might have felt snubbed by N-TV.

Equally the sight of March in public with one political leader might be misinterpreted. It was all very difficult.

'Takes time, I expect, settling down after your broadcasts,' Tuke continued, breaking one of the rolls and buttering it lavishly. Belatedly, he offered her the basket, but she declined it anyway.

'Yes, it does. Ben always says you have to scrape him off the ceiling after a busy Big News.'

'Well, fancy that! Ben always seems sto calm and confident, I'd never have guessed. Of course, you look the same. Very cool and collected. Must be very demanding?'

'It's taken a bit of getting used to. I've only been on for about four months. I find the words go round and round in my head till I get to sleep.'

Tuke was on the verge of asking all the questions that arose in his mind at this point – 'So you sleep alone, do you?', 'Don't you have a lover?', 'If not, why not?' and so on. But he refrained, not least because he didn't want to attract questions from March about his own domestic arrangements.

March must know, he reasoned, about Molly, his stout and frumpy wife, whom he kept tucked away in his Midlands constituency most of the time. It was hard for a political leader whom it suited to trade, when necessary, on being a family man, to draw a veil over that domestic side at other times.

But it did get in the way of the little fantasy he was playing out with March. Provided he did not make a fool of himself, it would be safe enough.

'Does your wife come to London much?' March had clearly read his thoughts.

'No, she's a political "widow", I'm afraid. It's one of the penalties of life at Westminster,' Tuke explained. 'No MP's wife can really hope to see much of her other half when the House is sitting. That's why Parliament is littered with divorces and broken marriages and squalid little affairs.'

Tuke hoped he wasn't going too far with this last observation. But it gave him a small thrill even to mention such matters in conversation with a girl as ravishing as March.

'They tell me that television is just as bad in that respect,' Tuke pushed on. 'It's a marriage-wrecker. How about N-TV?'

'Seems to be,' replied March, wondering where this was leading them. 'Of course, some people have been married for years. Ben and his wife, for instance. They've stuck together, you know. Sir Charles Craig – I think he's been married for a good long time. But everyone else – you're right. The pressures of the work, the odd hours, the travelling, mean that nobody seems to stay married for long.'

This is the moment, thought Tuke.

'So you've never been tempted in that direction, yourself?'

'To get married?'

'Yes.'

'Not yet. But I rather think that if I *did* get married, it would be to someone *not* in television.'

'But would that be any better? If your husband wasn't in TV, he'd have no idea what the pressures were.'

'I hadn't thought of it that way.' March took another sip of her Badoit and asked innocently, 'You have children?'

She isn't letting up, is she? Tuke thought. 'Two. Catriona's at university; Simon's in the sixth form.' There, he really had ruined his image.

The waiter brought their food. March nibbled and crunched her way through an oakleaf salad while Tuke slurped his crab bisque.

'You know . . .' Tuke was off on another tack. March began to study the green walls with their photos of regular celebrity diners, and then the snail trails woven into the carpet. 'I'm a great admirer of N-TV. You always seem to treat everybody fairly. There's never any of the trouble we're having at the BBC. A third party, like the Alliance, has a running battle to get its fair share of air-time. And they're always very hostile at the BBC.'

'I'm surprised you say that, Mr Tuke.'

'"Archie", please. No, I mean it – I appreciate what N-TV does for us. It's just that . . . it's just that I think you ought to be very careful where the Government is concerned. They seem to have a bit of a thing about you. I don't know why it is. It may be a residue from the Thatcher years. She certainly blamed you for her downfall. I think that resentment was passed on, like a torch, to Trevor Ross.'

'I've never met him,' said March. 'At least, not to speak to. I've never interviewed him.'

'Ross is all right, but some of his team are dubious to say the least. And there's a particular animosity towards N-TV. I'm surprised you're not aware of it.'

March wondered why Tuke had chosen to make this little speech to her. She carried no weight.

'Well, I don't see what anyone can do about it,' she said, gamely. 'I should have thought it quite *healthy* for the media not to be on too good terms with the Prime Minister.'

'Yes, I know, but you have to be careful. If the Government really took against a company like yours, it could scupper it.'

Tuke wondered whether he had gone too far with March, again. It was a little hobby-horse of his. On the other hand, if she wasn't influential at N-TV, his view would go no further.

A great fuss over the wine list resulted in Tuke plumping for half-bottles of Nuits St Georges and Sancerre of which March, well-disciplined in looking after her body, was not going to drink more than a thimbleful. Tuke, not one to let good wine go to waste, succeeded in putting most of it into himself.

March ate her grilled sea bass, Archie made quick work of his plate of Barbary duck breast with honey and peaches.

Conversation was difficult as Archie filled his face, but it gave him the opportunity to study the girl sitting opposite him.

'How do you like being the leader of the Alliance?' she asked, firmly reintroducing general matters.

'It's the best of jobs and the worst of jobs,' he replied in a voice that suggested he had made the remark several times before. 'Technically, since the Social Democrats and the Liberals amalgamated into this one, proper party, and we killed off the two-headed monster, it should have been easier, but it's like so many ferrets fighting in a sack. A party of individuals, however fine a concept, is unfortunately a recipe for in-fighting ...'

Tuke was getting nicely into another of his monologues when he realized they were being watched from a nearby table. 'Who is that man who's looking at us?'

'Tim Rathbone,' March replied softly. 'He's from the *Express* diary.'

'Ah, yes. I suppose we'll merit a paragraph as a result?'

'If that's what you want ...'

Tuke was stung by March's pointed comment. He tried to laugh it off. 'All part of the price of fame, I suppose ...'

March declined a pudding, but Tuke ordered whisky-and-chocolate cake and, in addition, demolished the chocolate snails which came with the coffee. He looked more and more intently at March. The repressed desires of a lifetime of faithful marriage welled towards the surface. Why must he be so well behaved? Other men got away with it.

He couldn't even be bothered to answer his own question. He couldn't afford a scandal. He hadn't the dash to carry it off. He must be content with having taken March out to dinner.

At last, the bill was paid and Tuke organized a cab to take them home. It would proceed to March's Primrose Hill flat and then all the way down to Pimlico where he maintained a pied-à-terre.

If he hoped for anything more, he didn't get it. He had to take the long ride down to Pimlico on his own and put up with the taxi-driver's predictable comments on current events.

Tuke was able to take with him one small consolation, however. As he had said goodbye to March at her door, he made to kiss her in a fatherly sort of way upon the cheek. Just a peck. But their lips had met.

Tuke felt he had stumbled on banked fires. It had made the whole evening worthwhile. And he had warned her about the Government and N-TV. And he had been interviewed on the *Nightly News*. He was very pleased with himself.

CHAPTER 12

It was no secret that David Kenway was not Sir Charles's favourite person. In fact, the Editor could barely stand being in the same room with him. It would've had to be the size of a football stadium, anyway, to accommodate two such formidable egos. Nevertheless, Sir Charles wasn't one to underestimate David's qualities as a reporter. After all, it was he who had poached David from ITN. So he had a certain proprietorial interest in seeing David live up to expectations.

It was significant, too, now that David had been injured in the line of duty, that the Editor's first reaction was to get in touch with David's long-suffering wife. He wanted to apologize profusely to Jo for the way news of the accident had been handled, realizing that his staff and their relatives must be treated with consideration at times such as these.

'Get me Mrs Kenway, please,' he said to his secretary, Celia.

'Yes, Sir Charles.'

The Editor noted the expressions on the faces of the two producers who were sitting with him. He indicated by a slight gesture of the hand that they should leave.

'Mrs Kenway,' Celia intoned, 'I have Sir Charles Craig for you.'

'Jo? I wanted to let you know what's being done about David. I take it you've already heard from one of the people here.'

'No. The first I heard was when it came up on the news.'

'Dear, dear. I can't apologize enough,' Sir Charles went on. 'We had no notice, you see. The Americans just put it on the satellite. We didn't have time to warn you.'

'How is he?'

'He's in Cape Town, you know that, in hospital. Aaron Rochester evidently took it into his head to fly David to where he *knew* there was a hospital, and Cape Town was nearest. Then he flew back to Johannesburg and put the report over to us.'

'Can David come home?'

'Yes, of course. He could stay in Cape Town; they're pretty used to dealing with that sort of thing by now and, as you know, they've some of the best medical people in the world. But I thought you'd agree it would be more diplomatic ... and more comfortable ... if he came home to recuperate. Oh, and we're paying for everything, so you don't have to worry about that.'

'Thank you.'

Jo's American accent was warm, clear and bell-like. It was hard for Sir Charles to tell what she really felt. Perhaps she had worked out a way to deal with the freewheeling behaviour of her husband.

He went on: 'His injuries are much less serious than we thought at first. Chiefly cuts from flying glass and a little bit of burning, not to the skin but to the hair. Some bruising, too, but above all it's the shock. I think you can say he had a lucky escape. He can have as much leave as is necessary to get fully recovered. I have in mind putting him on newscasting in a nice safe studio for a month or two. That's if he feels up to it.'

'I'm sure you're right.'

Sir Charles gave her David's number in Cape Town and told her to route her call through the N-TV switchboard if she wanted to save money.

Having dealt with that problem, Sir Charles ruminated quietly and reached for the presenters' rota for the month of March. There were not that many newscasters on the payroll and he didn't like promoting ordinary reporters to the job if he could help it. Reporters lacked the performing polish necessary for studio presentation.

If David could be well enough for more or less immediate action he could be slotted into the main evening news where his own newsworthiness wouldn't go amiss either. Sir Charles toyed with various combinations: Ben and March, March and David, David and Lynne Kimberley ... ah, yes, Lynne. There was a bit of a question-mark hanging over Lynne. He must speak to her urgently about this drink/driving charge.

'Groote Schuur?' David had exclaimed when they told him where the plane was taking him. 'They're not going to give me a fucking heart transplant, are they?'

It was not as bad as that. Aaron Rochester, in an impulsive gesture, had just wanted to put as much distance as possible between Oudtshoorn and themselves. Defying attempts by the town's police to make them stay, Aaron had insisted on the little plane flying David to Cape Town and then took it back with the two TV crews to Jo'burg.

One result was that David was now very much on his own in

Cape Town. He was bandaged and bored. The nurses were too busy to be flirted with and David hadn't felt much of a sexual urge since the explosion. There had been delayed shock. At the moment of the blast, he'd felt exhilarated. His body had been lifted up and thrown against an empty vehicle. He hadn't even felt the impact at the time. Then he had passed out.

It was only when he was on the plane flying southwards that his wounds really began to hurt, compounded by an anger and exasperation at what had happened to him.

'What was it?' he asked plaintively of Aaron.

'Oudtshoorn's first bomb, or so the police assured me. They claim it was an ANC job. They said it bore all the marks.'

'But why *me*?' David, like most television reporters who strayed into the firing line, found it hard to understand that he didn't have neutral status. He was just an observer. He was not supposed to be drawn into events. Unfortunately, the other side didn't know this.

'You were the poor guy who happened to be standing there when the bomb went off. Nothing more sinister.'

'I find that hard to believe. In this country.'

David had gone painfully white and was sweating. His hair was singed and his safari suit was torn and blackened beyond repair.

Two days later he was surprised by a warble from the telephone by his hospital bed.

'David,' said a soft voice. 'It's Penny.'

'Oh, Penny ... how did you find me?'

'I heard from a friend in London. The news of your ... accident ... was on TV there.'

'It's not in the paper here.'

'Right. Anyway, I hope you don't mind. I got in touch with your office here in Johannesburg. They told me where you were.'

David shifted off his side, which was painful, and lay on his back with the telephone lying by, rather than against, his ear. A lot had happened since they'd made love at the Landdrost.

'It's just as well you can't see me,' he told her. 'I'm not a lot of good to woman or beast in my present condition.'

'Nothing too serious?' asked Penny, in her innocent way.

'Of course it's fucking serious!' David sounded unduly harsh. He could imagine the pink-brown blush he must have produced in her. 'I can't even get a hard on!'

'I'm sorry, David. I didn't mean that. I don't understand what happened.'

'Old Van Der Linde suddenly relented and let us go to one of the restricted territories. We arrived and found that next to nothing had ever happened there. Next thing, I'm flattened by a ruddy mine. Teaching the media a lesson is what I call it. I bet they're laughing up their sleeves in Pretoria ...'

At that moment the line went dead.

David lay for a moment before replacing the receiver. Almost as soon as he did so, the phone rang again.

He picked it up. 'Penny?'

At once, he knew it wasn't her. There was a pause and on the line he could hear the metallic atmosphere that indicated the call was coming from a distance.

A voice said, 'No, David. It's Jo.'

'Oh, hello ... I thought it was someone else ...'

'Evidently ...' There was another silence and space yawned between husband and wife.

'How are you getting on?' Jo resumed.

'So-so. I'll just be glad to get out of this god-awful country.'

'Sir Charles says they're flying you home.'

'Does he? The sooner the better. I think you could say I've lost my appetite for disasters just now.'

'He wants to put you on to newscasting, for as long as you like.'

'Just as well I don't need plastic surgery then.'

'You're all right, aren't you?'

'Shaken but not stirred.'

'That's better. I'm real sorry. Particularly after, you know, the way we parted.'

'Forget it, Jo. How are the boys?'

'Harry thinks you're more of a hero than ever. He's going round saying, "My Dad got blown up and lived!"'

'Well, tell him to shut up.'

'I could fly out and meet you.'

'No, really, Jo, there's no need. Pieter Hartmann can collect my bits and bobs from Jo'burg and he'll post me back to you in one piece.'

'Promise me no more wars after this one?'

'No more wars after this one ...'

*　　*　　*

David felt curiously comforted by this stiff exchange with his wife.

At least now, he could go home without foreboding. Jo's sympathy might even make his enforced domesticity bearable.

He'd quite forgotten about the interrupted call he'd been having with the blushing Penny. If she'd tried to ring back after the line went dead, the number would have been engaged.

Never mind. It was Jo's turn once more to be the focus of his attention.

CHAPTER 13

'Never a dull moment . . .' remarked Sir Charles Craig, drolly. 'If I ever write my memoirs, perhaps I'll call them that.'

The Shrimp was a deceptively shy man for an editor. He spoke quietly, operated quietly, and thus surprised people with occasional outbursts of energy and decisiveness. No one moved more quickly, when he had to, than Sir Charles.

He had fought hard for the establishment of N-TV as a separate news-gathering organization, had almost singlehandedly put the consortium together which had been awarded the franchise for the station, and he ran it, as was said, with a whim of iron.

Or, that was the way he told it. He wasn't short on modesty. And there were those at N-TV who resented the way he was always interfering, ringing up from home to ask why such and such a story hadn't been included in the programmes or why BBC or ITN had obtained better pictures than N-TV.

The morning after Lynne's 'accident', he picked up the story from the agency tapes and immediately gave instructions that she mustn't front that night's Big News. March would have to be brought in on her off-day to do it – which was how she'd come to be teamed with Ben when the news of David Kenway's troubles came through.

When Lynne received a call telling her of the Editor's decision, she felt like a schoolgirl who'd been made to stand in a corner. She was quite unable to do anything for the rest of the day. And so she comforted herself with a bottle of Gordon's.

Now, the following morning, she was having to face what the national press was making of the incident through a colossal hangover. She was even fuller of remorse. In some cases, her story was front-page news. 'LYNNE DRINK RAP' was one of the more straightforward headlines. 'TRAFFIC NEWS', was the predictable dry comment over the *Guardian*'s piece. Whatever the treatment, the news was splashed all over the papers.

Knowing his strong views on publicity, Lynne decided to seize the bull by the horns and rang Sir Charles, asking for a chat. He sounded understanding. He asked her to come in that afternoon and she did so. there had been a query in his mind about Lynne's erratic performance for several months, but he didn't want to over-react if he could help it.

'Things like this, Lynne, only last in the public mind for as long as the tabloids are prepared to play them. You'll find yourself given a thorough going-over for a few days, then they'll turn on someone else. So if you can possibly lie low for that time, I'll put you back on the screen next week.'

'Yes. Thank you. I agree.'

'Drink's a tricky thing.'

Lynne swallowed, dreading whatever it was Sir Charles was going to say next.

'You won't mind me putting it bluntly like this. What you do in your own time is your own affair – up to a point. I'm glad to say there's never been the slightest hint that you've had too much to drink before appearing on camera ...'

Lynne swallowed again. As she heard it, that was a none-too-subtle way of saying there *had* been such hints.

'When – or rather, if – the police proceed with your case, there's bound to be more publicity, but we'll do the same and you can stay off screen for a week.'

'Yes, yes, thank you.'

Lynne was utterly touched by the quiet way her boss had dealt with the matter. When she'd left his office she felt a sudden wave of relief, as if a burden had been lifted from her. If her immediate reaction was to think of having another drink to celebrate, she hesitated and lit up one of her long black cigarettes instead.

'Celia, sorry to keep everyone waiting,' Sir Charles intoned to the intercom. 'I'm ready for the conference now ...'

The duty editors, producers and newscasters trooped into Sir Charles's office.

Quite lightly he said, as if in parody of broadcasters' style, 'And now let's turn from the newscasters to the news itself ...'

CHAPTER 14

On the last day of February that year, what was the real news around the world?

As the Editor-in-Chief always took pains to point out to N-TV's visitors, a surprising proportion of 'news' events was predictable. The debates in Parliament, publication of official reports and opinion polls, Royal comings and goings, embargoed announcements – all these took organization to deal with, but they didn't come as any surprise.

What the viewing public thought of as 'news', however, lay in the unpredictable. The sudden earthquakes, plane crashes, terrorist attacks, deaths of the famous. Here there was a good deal of luck in whether your cameraman or reporter was in the right place at the right time. You were lucky if you pulled it off on fifty per cent of newsmaking occasions.

There was a third type of news: the predictable that turned into the unpredictable. Even here, 'nous' and good judgement should have ensured that N-TV wasn't caught too often with its trousers down ...

For most of his term, Henry Carson had lived up to the epithet 'The Do-Nothing President'. He didn't even have the saving grace of personal charm. His standing in the opinion polls was even lower than President Carter's at the end of *his* presidency. Indeed, it was said that 'Carson makes Carter look like George Washington.'

As another presidential election hove into view, few commentators believed that Carson would dare stand again. For another thing, he wouldn't have the energy. He would simply fade from the scene and go back to his rocking chair in Montana.

Graham Johnson, N-TV's Washington correspondent, was amid the snows of New Hampshire covering the primaries when routine chatting with his media colleagues threw up the information that Carson was poised to make a TV address to the nation. On a call to London, Johnson relayed to his bosses that this was the 'word', stateside, and they duly began to absorb the notion and allowed it to colour their thinking. The teams who were responsible for readying back-up material started dusting down their 'obituaries'. One producer set to work making a punchy round-up of Carson's docile years. Another did a feature on Republican hopefuls. Yet another tackled the Democrats.

Hearing of this activity, Ben Brock told the producer of 'The Democrat File', 'You won't forget that interview I did with Winston Mann, will you? It never went out. It's probably one of the greatest interviews ever done. It'd be a pity for it to go to waste.'

'Ben,' came the firm answer, 'Mann only gets a look in if he declares himself. He's pretty much a long-shot.'

'Yes, I know,' said Ben. 'But he's an old friend of mine ...'

As February turned into March, Senator Gerry Iver, the youthful, thrusting Democrat, came out on top in New Hampshire. A few days later, the Republicans held *their* primaries and Henry Carson only just benefitted from the traditional loyalty accorded to an incumbent President. But the obvious Republican candidate he would remain ... until he indicated he was going to step down.

All this was faithfully relayed by Graham Johnson to N-TV. He returned to Washington after the New Hampshire results and soon, on a tip from the White House, sent a telex to London stating: 'CARSON TO BROADCAST 20:00 EST. EXPECTED TO ANNOUNCE NOT RE-STANDING. SUGGEST LIVE FEED AND PUNDITRY FROM HERE.'

Live coverage of the President's broadcast would mean that it would be seen in Britain at one o'clock in the morning. But as N-TV was a twenty-four-hour service, the speech would be a natural thing for it to relay direct. Never mind if only a handful of insomniacs and news-junkies was watching. Clips from the broadcast could be used hourly thereafter, probably for the rest of the day.

President Carson approached his 'farewell address' to the nation with a realistic impression of sloth. 'I want something or other,' he told his trio of speechwriters, 'that summarizes my period in office, lists the achievements, binds the wounds, that kinda thing.' The speechwriters went off into a huddle and did what they could.

When the time came for the broadcast from the Oval Office, Carson fretted that it would delay his dinner. 'Keep it hot for me, Ellie,' he told his wife.

'Yes, I sure will,' she replied, with the unquestioning devotion which had become her hallmark.

'It won't take me long. Then we can relax a little.'

Wayne, the President's black valet, dusted the dandruff off his collar and straightened his tie. With a weary look, Carson kissed his wife on each cheek and walked over to the Oval Office which had briskly been fitted with cameras, lights and microphones.

'I've never gotten used to that goddamn roller,' said Carson, gesturing at the teleprompter.

'I know, Mr President,' said Peterson, the network representative, soothingly, 'but this is the best there is available. State of the art. Hold on to your manuscript notes and try and mix the two for a more natural effect.'

'Sure, sure. I know. Pity I can't smoke,' the President mused.

No answer came, so he busied himself rustling the manuscript of his speech.

'Er, Mr President, can I just ask you not to rustle the paper too audibly? It makes a very loud noise when the mikes pick it up.'

'Oh, sure, sure.'

The rehearsal began.

'Cue, Mr President ...'

'My fellow Americans, it is now three years and two months since I took the oath of office as your President. While it has been my proud privilege ...'

The rehearsal ended with the words as scripted.

'And so, my fellow Americans, I believe in all humility that I have carried the burden of the Presidency for long enough. I have tried to the best of my ability to justify the faith and hope you have entrusted to me. I have accomplished so far as is possible the goals and aims I took on to accomplish in this office. I thought it only right to make my position clear, to give my party the time to choose a new candidate, and for you to decide on his fitness to hold this great office.

'I thank you for your support over this most interesting of times. God bless you all. Goodnight.'

The network executive and the technicians in the Oval Office tried not to be too conscious of what the President was doing. It was an historic moment in its way, even if it seemed odd to be rehearsing it. They might well have felt for the President. They could equally well have exploded with mirth at some of the things he had to say.

As the minutes slipped towards eight o'clock in the American capital, a mile or so away from the White House, in a small studio linked by satellite to N-TV in London, Graham Johnson was filing a background report. His main argument was that this was going to be Carson's swansong. It would also signal a real hotting up of the race to the White House.

A minute before the President's broadcast, his wife Ellie slipped into the Oval Office to sit and watch.

'The President of the United States.' A blue caption bearing the Presidential seal appeared on TV screens. After five seconds it mixed to a shot of the warm glow from the Oval Office window spilling out into the black night.

Then, there was Henry Carson looking, it had to be said, very Presidential. 'My fellow Americans, it is now three years and two months since I took the oath of office ...'

Graham Johnson watched, still seated in his small Washington studio, notepad on knee. With him he had a Washington pundit ready to discuss the President's speech as soon as it was over. They had more or less worked out the questions between them in advance.

As the President spoke on, they occasionally muttered grunts of acknowledgement as he made the kind of claims they had anticipated.

Finally, it was time for the peroration.

Petersen, the network executive, was the first to notice that something was different.

'And so my fellow Americans, I believe in all humility that ...'

The President's eyes dropped from the camera to the papers in front of him for the first time. Petersen heard the President audibly shuffling forward his manuscript notes. He faltered and repeated himself.

'I believe in all humility that ... it is my duty ... to offer myself once more for my party's nomination to serve as your President. I look forward to holding this great office in trust once more to the American people.

'God bless you and good night.'

As soon as the TV lights were dimmed in the Oval Office, Ellie Carson rushed forward and embraced the President. She hadn't been sure he would substitute the last paragraph until he actually began to speak it. They had discussed the move, of course, but Henry had prevaricated and said he would act as the mood took him. And so he had.

'Now,' he said, 'where's my dinner, Ellie?'

Graham Johnson looked mildly shell-shocked as he stumbled through his interview with the Washington pundit. They'd had to chuck away their carefully-planned questions and answers.

While the United States slept on the President's surprise announcement, across the Atlantic, as a new day began, the British Prime Minister was talking with his Press Secretary.

'So, the old bugger's staying on after all ...' Trevor Ross glanced through the front pages of the national newspapers which led, without exception, on the Presidential news. 'Ah, well. Better the devil, you know, I suppose ...'

Ross then turned to the neat file of edited extracts from the papers that Norman Heathcliffe, the Press Secretary, had compiled for him before breakfast. He affected not to be terribly interested in what the columnists and editorial writers had to say about him.

'And where's the media file?'

'Here, Prime Minister.'

Heathcliffe produced a slimmer file of cuttings and statistics surveying the supposed bias against the Government exhibited by certain sections of the media. Belief in this bias was something almost every government had; it was a particular obsession of the present Conservative Government.

Even though Ross had been re-elected the previous October with a comfortable majority, he appeared to enjoy hearing particularly juicy examples of media bias. This was what the daily list was supposed to supply him with: details of a soft interview with an Opposition MP on Radio 4's *Today* programme, a blatantly biased edition of *Panorama* on the BBC, a routinely Trotskyite political programme on Channel 4. It was all in the eye or ear of the beholder, of course.

'What's this?' he said, as he caught sight of a small paragraph and picture from that morning's gossip column in the *Daily Express*. '"NEW ALLIANCE" – that's the headline ...'

'Oh, that ...'

'"Tatty-suited Alliance leader, Archie Tuke, 52, has succeeded where other more glamorous suitors have failed. Family-man Tuke, who usually puts two hundred miles between his frumpy wife, Molly, and his Westminster affairs, was seen gazing into the limpid eyes of N-TV's golden-haired newscasterette, March

Stevens, 26, the other night. The scene of their political discussions was a cosy *table à deux* at L'Escargot, the favourite media person's nosherie in Soho ..."'

'Gossip,' declared Heathcliffe.

'I know,' said the Prime Minister. 'But I don't like that sort of fraternizing with the media, as you know. Arm's length is where they should be kept.'

'Oh, Prime Minister ...'

'I don't like it. It just confirms what I've always said about N-TV and us. If their interviewers canoodle with the Alliance in public, it's not surprising they give them an easy ride on the screen. Something's got to be done about N-TV. They're too damn smug at the moment. Need taking down a peg.'

'Yes.'

'Thank you, Norman. That'll be all. I'll see you later, for the lobby meeting.'

Heathcliffe picked up the clippings and left the Prime Minister's study. He had been given the clearest of signals. Something must be done about N-TV. Who could he talk to about it? The Home Secretary was the minister responsible for broadcasting. He had better arrange a meeting through official channels. Or perhaps it would be better if he didn't do it direct?

CHAPTER 15

David Kenway hobbled off the flight from Cape Town to Johannesburg wearing a loud yellow-and-red check shirt and a new pair of jeans about two sizes too big for him. Prior to his discharge from Groote Schuur, the hospital had presented him with these replacement clothes 'with the compliments of the South African Government'.

It was partly to collect the rest of his belongings from the Landdrost that he'd broken his journey home to London. Pieter Hartmann met him at Jan Smuts airport with them all in a bag.

'I'm not flying home in this shirt *or* in these jeans,' David said as he checked through the bag to make sure nothing had been left at the hotel. 'My own jeans may stink but they're what I wear to fly in, and that's that.'

'Something missing?' Pieter Harmann asked knowingly, as David continued his hunt round the bag.

'Christ, yes – where are they?'

'Your contact books ...'

'Yes, where the hell are they? They're worth their weight in gold.'

'Thereby hangs a tale, I'm afraid.'

'Give,' demanded David, heatedly.

'Confiscated by the security service – as a temporary measure, so they said.'

'But that's outrageous!'

'You know which country you're in, David ...'

'What happened?'

'The management at the Landdrost cleared your room as soon as they heard of your accident. Next thing, an agent from the security services was round and commandeered your books. Here's the receipt.'

David shifted about restlessly, his leg still painful. 'God, you know those books are my life-blood. There's bound to be telephone numbers of ANC people – and whites – they can go and harass. Not to mention the women ...'

'I'm sorry, David. It was just unlucky that you left them at the hotel. They'll send them to you in London.'

'God! It's like having your fucking arms chopped off. And I don't like the idea of spooks sniffing all over them ... Anyway, what about Oudtshoorn? Have they discovered who did it?'

'Well, no word yet. They're working on the assumption it was an ANC mine and you were the accidental, totally innocent victim.'

'Hmm ...'

It was only three weeks since David had flown into South Africa and all its woes. Now it was high time he jetted out again.

'With all respect to your *grrreat* country, Pieter, I have to report that, as usual, it's ended up giving me the creeps.'

'I know, I know. I hope they find you something less adventurous to do back in London.'

'You bet. I'll be sitting in a nice warm studio every night, reading the autocue. That's what I've been told, anyway.'

'You'll miss life on the road *then* ...'

'Yep. But it'll make a change and flatter my ego.'

'You said it!'

David stalked off to the airport rest-room and slipped into one of his own clean shirts and his own far from clean jeans. Refreshed, he ceremoniously presented the hospital gear to a bemused black attendant.

Rejoining Pieter, he said, 'Thanks for everything else, by the way. I'm sorry about the messy ending.'

'Well, it was quite a good story while it lasted,' said Pieter, wrily, '... and you got to make a little news yourself!'

'I don't see that as my job, if you don't mind.'

'Still, good luck, and maybe we'll see you back before too long. Oh, just one thing, before you go ...' Pieter handed him a newspaper. 'You see the headline, "KOBUS MURDER TRIAL"?'

'That's bloody quick.'

'It hasn't started yet, but what's interesting is that this man Olivier who's the defendant is a member of the *Weerstandsbeweging* – you know, the Afrikaner Resistance movement, Storm Falcons and all that.'

'Those lunatics?'

'Yes. It's being suggested he killed Kobus because of the mess he was making of South Africa's image in the media! Far too soft, they thought. They wanted a total blackout!'

'Rather an extreme measure against a glorified PR guy!'

'That's the theory.'

'Rum do, if you ask me. Well, look after yourself, Pieter. Don't let them take it out on *you* just because you work for the dreaded foreign media.'

'Perhaps, in a way, they already have ...'

David didn't have time to ask Pieter what he meant. With a wave, he hobbled off to catch his flight to London.

It was a considerable relief when the plane hauled itself away from God's own country and journeyed north to colder climes.

The more so as David found himself, in his dirty jeans, reclining in a First Class seat, courtesy of N-TV.

Annie Friedman was that day's programme editor for the *Nightly News* and she was about to let March Stevens loose as a reporter.

The story in question was far removed from bank interest rates, terrorism, world affairs, and macho stuff like that. Predictably, March was to cut her teeth in the traditionally 'soft' area of Royalty, and now found herself setting off for the Victoria and Albert Museum in the company of Mike Feather, a bright young scriptwriter who worked mainly on the *Nightly News* and was much the same age.

'I'm awfully glad you're with me,' March confided as they bounced along to the V & A in a taxi. 'I'm scared stiff.'

'Safety in numbers,' Mike agreed. 'And if you're with me, there's less chance of *my* screwing it up.'

'Surely, that should be the other way round?'

'No, they've never forgiven me for one or two blunders I made when I was a reporter.'

Mike's candour was refreshing. So many people at N-TV whistled, deafeningly, to keep their spirits up.

'Once I came back from an interview I'd done with some teachers' union leader and got torn off a strip by Michael Penn-Morrison.'

'What for? He's nice enough, isn't he?'

'Well, I suppose he was right, but he told me I hadn't asked the key question and sent me back to do it again. Talk about eating crow ...'

'What was the question?'

'Well, it was whether they should strike or not. They hadn't struck before. The mention he'd made of industrial action in his speech was rather vague, but I failed to spot it and shove it up the front. So that was that. Then there was the time I let David Kenway beat me to a story,' Mike went on, obviously enjoying these cathartic confessions.

March was always interested to pick up whatever she could about the famous David Kenway. 'I haven't much chance to get to know him. What's he like? A bit formidable, isn't he?'

'You can say that again,' said Mike, edging back into the taxi seat and taking off his fancy glasses to give them a clean. 'In fact, *shit* is more accurate. He really seems to believe in all that stuff about scoops and exclusives ... which is why he's a high-flying reporter and I'm not, I suppose.' Certainly Mike didn't seem like a journalist himself. With his baggy, speckled suit and unruly hair he looked more like an advertising copywriter. 'I've never been able to get very worked up over that side of things. A scoop is like sex. Once you've got it, there's nothing there. Getting there is everything.'

'Tell me about him beating you to the story.' March was curious about Mike's animosity.

'It was the Christmas before last. Some woman had abandoned her baby in the wilds of Essex. Being Christmas, you know, it was a natural. No room at the inn, that sort of angle. Anyway, come the New Year, she'd been identified and the massed bands of the media were outside a cottage she'd holed up in out on the Essex marshes.

'She wasn't talking to anyone. She wasn't even showing her face. So the papers got up to their usual tricks. At one point, the *News of the World* blocked off the road so no one else could get at her. Anyway, I was sent down with a crew and, of course, being TV, it was hard to do anything. I tried to speak to the woman through the letter-box but she just told me to fuck off. Now, if I'd been a press hack, I could've made quite a good piece out of that and invented the quotes. But for telly, you've got to have the person in vision, properly lit, and talking whole sentences.'

'So what did you do?'

'Nothing. That was the trouble. After camping about in the cold for most of the day, I went home, saying the story was a dead duck. Blow me, if I didn't get home and turn on the Big News and it was the lead story with David-bloody-Kenway chatting to the woman, all hearts and flowers and weeping violins!'

'How had he done it?'

'Dunno. But I'm pretty sure he had the secret weapon I didn't have: bundles of fivers. He probably kept shoving 'em under the door until she caved in.'

'Poor you! Not exactly a glorious victory for David, though ...'

'If he got the story, good for him; never mind *how* he got it. Anyway, that's David Kenway for you. And that's why you've got me, not him, to hold your hand today.'

'I think I'd rather have you.' She said it with a delightful smile and Mike was pleased. But nothing of what he told her about David had lessened March's interest in the man she secretly admired and longed to know better.

For his part, Mike had so far shared the conventional view of March as a beautiful pea-brain, but perhaps she had other qualities. She didn't have to be a tough-as-nails reporter like Delia Steele, all iron knickers and brittle voice.

'Leave this to me, kid,' Mike bantered on. 'Together we'll make a great team.'

At the V & A, they had to get out of the taxi a short way from the entrance, as it was cordoned off, and a small crowd had already gathered.

March was soon spotted and her autograph sought. Mike found himself ignored, hopping from one foot to another, while she obliged.

'Sorry about that,' she said, breaking away from the mob.

'Rather you than me, any day,' Mike countered.

Fishing out their invitations, March and Mike went into the museum where they soon ran into the BBC TV crew which was the sole unit allowed to follow the Royal family about on public appearances that year. The TV networks took it in turn to perform this duty, then pooled the same pictures, so as not to overwhelm the Royals with cameras. Each network was then entitled to put whatever commentary it liked to go with the pictures and to edit them however it wished.

Precisely at noon, March and Mike stood in the little press pen as Her Royal Highness the Princess of Wales, accompanied by Sir Anthony Wardlaw, Director of the V & A, swept into the Dress Collection. The Department of Textiles and Dress had refurbished it for a special exhibition devoted to Royal fashion in the twentieth century.

The Princess – who had launched so many fashion trends herself – was today wearing a blue spotted dress and wide-brimmed white hat, with court shoes and matching handbag. Wardlaw, dapper as ever, sported a black suit with bold white stripes and wide lapels, topped by a vermilion tie.

Opening the exhibition, the Princess read a few sentences from a card, barely taking her eyes off it. But what she said didn't matter. She had star quality enough.

Then she began to tour the exhibits. They included some of her own clothes, dating from 1981, the year of her marriage to the Prince of Wales. There was the wedding dress designed by the Emanuels, a strapless evening gown, an outfit with a sailor collar, and even one of her woolly jumpers with sheep on it.

'I wonder what she feels like, seeing her old clothes in a museum already?' March whispered to Mike.

'Good point,' he replied. 'Put it in your script.'

'I mean ... she's only a year older than me.'

'Yes, it's not exactly what you think of as museum-fodder, is it – when they take the clothes right off your back and shove 'em in a glass case?'

The Princess seemed to find the idea amusing, too, but it was hard to catch what she was saying to Sir Anthony. There was a slight flush on her cheeks, her eyes still tended to lower, and her feet naturally formed a ballet position whenever she had to stand in one place for a few seconds.

Soon they were heading off to lunch. As the Princess walked out, she passed within a yard or two of March and momentarily they exchanged glances. Was there a flicker of mutual recognition?

Then the Press flocked round the exhibits and Mike had a word with the BBC cameraman to make sure he took pictures of the particular dresses they needed for March's report.

'Seen enough?' Mike asked her.

March nodded. 'I think so. But I haven't a clue what to say.'

'Remember the golden rule of reporting: say the first thing that comes into your head. It's usually the best.'

They took a taxi back to N-TV and viewed the recording of the morning's ceremony as soon as it had been sent over by the BBC.

'Shouldn't I have done a piece to camera?' March asked. 'You know, standing in front of the frocks?'

'You can't do that when we're using pooled video. Anyway, you'll be introducing the item yourself in the studio, so that's much the same thing. And that's what we have to start with.'

'How do you mean?'

'We need to write what you're going to say in the introduction *first*. Most reporters leave that till *last* and don't leave the newscaster in the studio with anything to say.'

Mike turned up a file on the VDU on his desk. 'What was your overall reaction?'

'Like I said, that it must be a bit odd for her finding her cast-offs in a museum.'

'There you are then.' Mike's fingers clicked over the keys and the words sprayed up on the screen. ' "*The Princess of Wales came face to face with some of her old cast-offs earlier today when she went to the Victoria and Albert Museum in London.*" New sentence. Got to keep it snappy. Er ... "*The clothes that have made her a trend-setter all over the world are now part of an exhibition that traces the story of Royal fashion from the 1900s to the 1980s . . .*" Now we need to get *you* into it, to show you were there.'

'Doesn't that make me sound a bit pushy?'

'OK, OK. So we'll scrap that. Let's have an "Andy" instead.'

'A what?'

'An "Andy" – a sentence beginning with "And". It always helps things along. I know ... "*And, needless to say, she was wearing another stunning creation for the occasion, just to show she hasn't lost any of her famous flair.*" Sorry, that sounds a bit flabby. Let's come back to that. We go to pictures now, starting with the Princess arriving with old Wardlaw, so we need to say who he is.'

'Can we say that she looked a touch embarrassed at becoming a museum piece?'

'Well, *you* can say it,' Mike teased, 'but I hate putting thoughts in their heads. But I like the idea of her being a "museum piece". Save it up to the end. It'd make a good punch line.'

March was grateful for Mike's help. He didn't show the slightest resentment and avoided the patronizing tone she detected in everyone else she had to deal with at N-TV.

They completed the package and added March's commentary. It lasted three and a half minutes. Annie Friedman said, 'That'll make a nice ender for the programme, though I might put it higher up. Well done, March. We'll have you covering riots yet.'

The day hummed on in the newsroom. March was miffed when she saw clips of the Princess of Wales being used in earlier bulletins. But the *Nightly News* would have *her* report – and at greater length. She felt bucked at the prospect. She was presenting with Hamish Treleaven that night. He wasn't nearly so rock-like as Ben Brock and she never knew when she was going to have to pick up the pieces, or deal with some awful ad-lib he threw at her.

Eventually, near the end of the programme, she found herself saying, 'The Princess of Wales came face-to-face with some of her old cast-offs today ...' The item ran its allotted length, and finished: 'So, once again, the Princess showed that, though the clothes she wore yesterday are now in a museum, she's anything but a museum piece herself.'

She still felt the last sentence sounded contrived. What really spoiled it, though, was Hamish ad-libbing, 'And that piece, er, report was by March Stevens, who's a match for the Princess any day.'

March had to smile, but she could have strangled him.

Ben Brock would never have said anything trite like that.

'Thanks for your help,' March said to Mike in the hospitality room afterwards.

'Pleasure's mine,' he said. 'Pity about that creep, Hamish.'

'Yes, I *know,*' March dropped her voice. 'But there you go.'

'If only he'd stick to the script ...'

March had viewed her modest collaboration with Mike as a purely professional encounter, which was why she was rather taken aback when, topping up their glasses with white wine from the drinks trolley, he asked her, 'You wouldn't like to go out for a bite, would you?'

March hesitated. Why couldn't he leave things as they were?

'Er ... no, Mike ... I can't. Perhaps ... another night.'

'OK, OK. Fine ... fine,' Mike said, trying not to seem crestfallen. March sensed what pluck it had taken to make the suggestion. And now there would only be awkwardness between them. She said her goodnights to the room in general and returned, alone, to her flat.

CHAPTER 16

Was it significant that Women in Media had chosen to hold its annual get-together at the London Zoo? If any male chauvinist pigs were within spitting distance, they'd be safely behind bars. Women from the press, broadcasting, advertising, publishing and public relations were gathered – together with the odd, token male – to pour scorn on those who had offended them in the sex wars.

The producer of a TV commercial that portrayed housewives as idiots swooning at the thought of a super-new lavatory cleanser had been invited along to receive an award in the shape of a pink pig. It was a measure of the relaxed nature of the event that she – yes, she – had turned up in person to be booed and jeered at. Other awards went to designers of sexist book-jackets and producers of TV series portraying women as sex objects.

When the formal part of the evening was over guests lingered to chat. It was an occasion when women who toiled in one media vineyard had an opportunity to mingle and gossip with those who toiled in another. Geraldine Botolph was a feature-writer on *Woman* and she found herself talking to a woman with a helmet of jet-black curls in the approved female-astronaut feminist-playwright mould. She had an American accent. It was Jo Lake Kenway.

'And what do you do?' Geraldine asked her, innocently.

Jo wanted to respond, 'I'm a world-famous magazine writer, I expect you've heard of me ...' But she shrank from that. 'Oh, I'm Jo Lake. I dabble in magazines, mostly American ones, so I'm interested in what the group stands for ...'

'Of course you write,' Geraldine tried to come in with a late save. 'I'm sure I've read some of your ...' She was going to say 'stuff' but that sounded impolite so she substituted 'material'. 'I'm Geraldine Botolph, *Woman* ...'

Jo wasn't sure what she meant at first. 'Oh, I see, *Woman* magazine ...!' She leant on the first syllable of *magazine*.

They talked of the difficulties of being a freelance.

'Do you *have* to work?' asked Geraldine, pointedly.

'How d'you mean?'

'Are you married?'

'What if I am? You're not supposed to ask questions like that, least of all at Women in Media ...'

'Sorry.'

Jo looked away to where a group of women were noisily talking and laughing, their voices obviously raised by alcohol.

'Mmm,' murmured Geraldine, noticing Jo's line of sight. 'I might have guessed. That's Lynne Kimberley.'

'Yes, I know. My husband works for N-TV, but I've never met her.'

'Should I *know* your husband?'

'He's David Kenway.'

'Yes, of course. The one who was injured in South Africa. That was terrible.'

'Uh-huh.'

'You ought to meet Lynne. She's a good sort, even if she does put it away rather.'

'OK.'

They moved over to where Lynne was holding court and Geraldine introduced Jo. It was apparent immediately that she had made a mistake.

'Ah,' slurred Lynne, 'David's little wifey ...'

The other women tittered.

'It's odd,' said Jo, 'our paths have never crossed before. But David never lets me near N-TV.'

Lynne topped up her glass without offering any of the wine to Jo. Then Jo made things worse by saying, 'I was sorry to hear about your accident.'

Lynne gave her a look. 'In the Gordon's Gin Grand Prix?'

'Well, yeah, if that's what you want to call it ...'

'You know, Sarah' – Lynne turned abruptly to one of her cronies – 'next year Women in Media ought to have a special prize for the most sexist thing said about a woman newscaster. I'll donate the prize myself. The *stuff* I've had to put up with about my little misdemeanour ...'

'How do you mean?' asked Jo, innocently.

'"Red-haired news-screamer, Lynne Kimberley, 45" ... "Tired and emotional newscaster, Lynne Kimberley ..." They just don't say that sort of thing about men when they get done by the police ...'

'Never mind,' said Jo. 'Worse things happen at sea.'

'You reckon?'

Lynne gave Jo another look and then stared into her glass.

Why had Lynne taken such an instant dislike to Jo? Because she was from the States? Usually Lynne got on very well with Americans. Because she was married to David?

That must be it. Lynne felt David was a ruthless, unlikeable operator, however good he might be at his job. He never seemed able to pass the time of day with her. He was much too busy polishing up his ego. And, as for the way he carried on with women, Lynne had encountered far too many men of that type in her time. His reputed lovemaking skills didn't impress her.

Given that Jo was a victim of David's behaviour, it was somewhat irrational of Lynne to extend dislike of the man to his wife, but alcohol hadn't improved her grasp of logic.

'I gather he's joining us as a newscaster,' Lynne said, a little less than graciously.

'If he's well enough,' said Jo, now desperately looking for a way of escape from this embarrassing encounter.

'Never did like South Africa myself. Give me Belfast or Beirut any day.'

'I saw you at the BAFTA awards,' said Jo, gamely struggling against Lynne's oppressive mood.

'Oh, were you there?' Lynne asked, snootily.

'No, I mean, I saw you on TV. I never get to go to dos like that.'

'Doesn't hubby approve?'

'He doesn't think wives and work mix.'

'I wonder why ever not?'

Geraldine Botolph noted the knowing look in Lynne's eye. She couldn't understand why these sparks were flying. She wouldn't have introduced them if she'd known.

Lynne had never been the recipient of any of David's attentions. I expect he looks upon me as a *difficult* woman, Lynne thought. He prefers them young and witless.

But she wasn't going to spell any of this out to Jo. And yet, why not? Just because David had had a nasty accident there was no reason to change her view of him.

'I expect you'll be glad to have him back where you can keep an eye on him,' Lynne went on, dangerously. 'Stop him from falling into the wrong hands.'

The innuendo wasn't lost on Jo.

She said nothing, but looked faintly martyred in a way that she'd practised for some time. She only needed the two boys dragging at her skirts for a full portrayal of the wronged wife.

'None of my business, of course,' said Lynne. 'But he does

seem to ... play the field, if you know what I mean?'

Jo felt her colour rising. There was no one with a lower view of David's infidelities than herself, but the cheek of this woman to rub her nose in it ...

'I don't know what you mean,' Jo stuttered, giving Lynne the chance to tell her.

'Oh, come on, dear ...'

That 'dear' was a red rag to Jo, and on such a sisterly occasion, too ...

'The whole world knows what Foreign Affairs means to David. We call him "Our Foreign Co-respondent" in the office!'

'You bitch!' Jo exploded. She stood up, clumsily knocking her chair over. Women in Media stragglers turned to look, Lynne's cronies shrank in embarrassment.

Jo slapped Lynne sharply in the face.

'You mind your own goddam business, you bitch! He's *my* husband and I don't need *you* to tell me what he gets up to. You're too *drunk* to know what you're saying, I suppose?'

With this, Jo picked up her bag and shawl and shot out of the restaurant, leaving a gaggle of amused, appalled, and sympathetic faces gawping after her.

Geraldine made to go with her, and then thought better of it.

Jo rushed away from the Zoo as quickly as she could.

If this was how Women in Media behaved among themselves, what hope was there in the wider world beyond ...?

Half a mile away, a car drew up. March Stevens said goodnight to the driver and walked down the flight of stone steps to her garden flat. In the dark she fumbled for the outside light switch. Then she froze. There was someone in the shadows behind her.

In terror, she dropped her briefcase, half-expecting to be grabbed from behind, a hand to come over her mouth.

She lashed out, her door keys held like a knuckle-duster. But there was nothing for the keys to hit, so they fell to the ground.

She kicked out, finally making contact with the human shape in the shadows. The man groaned, then dashed up the stone steps to streetlevel as quickly as he could, slamming the iron gate behind him and running off down the street.

March's heart was pounding so violently she couldn't stand still.

At last she found the switch, turned on the light and picked up her keys. Her briefcase lay where she'd dropped it. She hadn't been robbed. She hadn't been molested. It was all right.

Letting herself into the flat, still breathless, she bolted the door behind her.

She put one hand on the phone and thought about ringing the police. But they'd only make a fuss and come round to gawp. It'd get in the papers. She would have to keep it to herself.

Next day, March decided she had to tell someone. She confided in Vanessa, who could always be relied on for practical advice.

'Simple. Ask your driver to see you into the house, or at least wait until you're inside. They're fabulously good like that. They usually hang on a bit, anyway, making a note of the journey, so it's no hardship. I'm sure they'd do it for you, especially.'

'All right, I'll try that,' March said. 'You don't think I should tell the police?'

'Probably only encourage them to lurk in the shadows, too.'

'Thanks, Van. It gave me quite a turn, I can tell you. I could hardly sleep.'

'I bet. Now,' she went on briskly, 'do you fancy signing letters for me? A few sensible ones this week. Unusual, eh? Five garden fêtes – the season is approaching – which I turned down as you said. One supermarket opening, but you know Sir Charles doesn't like you doing those. Three proposals of marriage, thirty-seven requests for a photograph, sixteen lunatics and one sweet old dear.'

'Mrs Simpson again?'

'Even she.'

'She writes *every* time I'm on ...'

'Nothing from your ghastly fan, Mr Patel.'

'That's a relief. Perhaps his ardour has cooled.'

'Probably had a heart attack when he got your photo.'

For all her brisk manner, Vanessa *was* becoming a person March could turn to, despite their differences.

'*I* don't know,' Ben said to no one in particular as he sat in the newsroom. 'You can't blow your nose round here without some-body writing about it in the papers.'

'Who is it now?' March inquired, glancing up from the scripts she was skimming through.

'Lynne ... most unpleasant. Probably a pack of lies. In the *Standard*.'

Ben stared at the offending note in the paper's Diary, with his big thick reading glasses perched on the end of his nose, glasses he'd never dream of wearing on the box for as long as he could read the Autocue without them. He was in classic newshound pose, crouched over an old-fashioned typewriter that seemed minuscule in relation to his size. The sleeves of his crisp white James Meade shirt were rolled up and he sported a brilliant pair of red braces. He bashed the *Standard* with his fist, as though ready to eat it.

'Let's see ...'

March moved over and stood looking over his shoulder.

'Oh, no ...'

That walking international incident, N-TV's Lynne Kimberley, has been at it again. The sisterly calm of Women in Media's shindig at the London Zoo last night was rudely shattered when the red-haired newscasterette was set upon by another harpy. Inspired by the zoological locale, the claws were out, in a manner of speaking, and Ms Kimberley received a slap across the kisser.

   Her assailant was Jo Kenway, wife of N-TV's other accident-prone newsman, David.

   Lynne Kimberley is due to face drink-driving charges at Hampstead Magistrates' Court shortly.

   And that is the end of the news.

'Poor Lynne,' said March. 'It's just not her lucky month, is it?'

Ben hesitated. 'She certainly seems to attract the lightning, does our Lynne,' he said, taking off his glasses and looking at March. 'Promise me you'll never let it happen to you.'

For a moment, March wondered whether Ben knew about her own experiences that night. But no, he couldn't possibly.

'I wonder what the argument was about?'

'You'll have to ask Lynne,' Ben chuckled. 'Go on. I dare you.'

The *Nightly News* that evening passed off almost without incident.   Sir Charles Craig was absolutely insistent that his news presenters should not betray their views on topical matters. A raised eyebrow, a frown, could so easily colour an item.

   And yet when Ben Brock was presenting a news item about a girl aged eight who had died of a particularly virulent form of cancer, his voice had actually *broken*. A desperate, bleak look filled his eyes. It was so rare for Ben to show his feelings like that. Sir Charles made a mental note to raise it with him at the first opportunity.

Sir Charles hoped it was not a straw in the wind. Watching at home as usual, he nudged his wife.

'How terrible,' Lady Pam said, not knowing what her husband meant by the gesture.

'Yes, it is,' he agreed. 'A very sad story.'

CHAPTER 17

Ben's momentary lapse on the *Nightly News* wasn't noticed only by his editor.

The *London Post*'s television columnist was a man called Gabriel Monk who wrote a daily half-page of tittle-tattle about the industry and laced it with spiky remarks about programmes and the people who made or appeared in them. His own appearance didn't lift the spirits of those who met him. According to Vanessa, he looked as if he'd crawled out from under a stone. It was true that his suits were creased, that what hair he had needed washing, and that a fall of dandruff ringed his shoulders. Maybe this was because he spent so much of his time in the dark, watching television, and starved of the life-giving qualities of daylight.

Ben, as a former Fleet Street editor who'd made good in the more glamorous world of television, was everything Monk was not. Monk was apprehensive on the few occasions he managed to snatch a few words with Ben, then became over-matey on the basis that they were all hacks together.

Ben, as ever, was courteous, even to such an unappetizing specimen. If Ben had still been in Fleet Street he might have taken a different attitude to Monk but, as it was, he felt that politeness, even to TV critics, was part of the job.

'Could I have a word, Mr Brock?', said Monk, sidling up to Ben as he came out from visiting Natalie in hospital.

'Gabriel Monk, the *Post*,' the journalist introduced himself, wisely not assuming that Ben would know who he was.

'Yes, we've met before. And how is "Britain's Most Knowledgeable TV Writer"?'

'Oh, please ...'

Ben continued to his Rolls and when they reached it, invited Monk to sit inside with him.

'Just happened to be passing the hospital and saw you coming out...'

'Yes, well ... what can I help you with?'

'Oh, nothing, really. Everything all right, is it? Your wife's in there, isn't she?'

'Yes, she's having some tests, you know. It's quite close to N-TV, happily. So I can pop in most days.'

'Nothing serious, then?'

Ben's bleak look returned.

'You have to keep on working and put such matters out of your mind. Are you married?'

'Not yet,' Monk replied weakly.

There was a pause, and Monk found himself admiring the dashboard of the Rolls. He felt small and insignificant in the handsome leather seats. He changed topics.

'Is everything all right at N-TV?' he asked, fishing for more.

'Of course,' Ben replied blandly. 'Why shouldn't it be?'

'Just gossip. There's a feeling that you're not in Downing Street's good books, that Ross has it in for you ... Not you personally, I mean, the company ...'

'I don't think there's anything in that. We've certainly not been aware of any lack of cooperation. All governments dislike criticism and I suppose we can't be flavour of the month all the time.'

'Um. Do you think it's the Prime Minister in particular who feels most strongly about it?'

'I can't see why he should bother. He's got a safe majority now. And, besides, Charlie Craig got a knighthood in the New Year honours. I hardly feel the PM would let that through if he'd got a down on us.'

'Lots of people felt he shouldn't have accepted that until he retired,' Monk went on, wrenching the conversation in yet another direction.

'I don't think it matters either way.'

'Um,' said Monk. 'I agree it's a bit rum. But the rumours are there.'

'Yes. I know.'

'Well, nice to talk to you. Hope I haven't kept you.'

'Don't quote me direct. Off the record, all that.'

'Sure, sure.'

Monk fussed and fiddled before finding the right knob to open the door of the Rolls and then climbed out. Before he closed it and departed, he leant back in and asked Ben:

'Not cancer, is it?'

Ben pretended not to have followed the shift in conversation.

'Is what?'

'It was just ... Last night, I saw you doing that story about the little girl who died of it. You looked very upset.'

Ben was disconcerted.

'Get in again for a moment.'

Monk plopped back on the front seat.

'Yes, since you ask, my wife has got cancer. I regret what happened last night: usually I try to be detached, professional. But that story about the little girl really got to me.'

'I'm really very sorry, Mr Brock. I'm sure people'd be very sympathetic, if they knew.'

'But Natalie doesn't know, you see. I decided not to tell her.'

'Well, I'm very sorry.'

Suitably embarrassed, Monk shook Ben by the hand and made away.

Ben sat for a long time staring through the windscreen before he drove off home.

The world kept on turning, with N-TV in hot pursuit. The slogan 'N-TV – We are the Newsmakers' was uttered on the hour, every hour, every day, every week, every month. Working for the company was like being at the hub of the universe.

When David Kenway returned home from South Africa he went straight to Jo. She was waiting with some apprehension to see what state he'd be in.

'Dammit, David, there's nothing the matter with you at all!' she exclaimed after a quick inspection for surface damage.

'You haven't seen me with my clothes off.'

'Hold on a sec!' she grinned, friskily, her eyes gleaming.

Her look was not wasted on David.

'No, you're right. The wounded hero is not a stretcher-case. Just a little shell-shocked, and one or two aches and pains that won't go away.'

If it took a bomb to bring him back to me, Jo thought to herself, it must have been a blessing in disguise. She was glad to have him back. She'd been falling apart.

'Where are my boys?' David demanded.

Bill and Harry were rounded up by Nanny Jo and greeted their father tentatively. Jo had warned them that Daddy was 'not very well' and had had 'a terrible experience' in Africa.

They were surprised when he swept them off their feet and hugged them fiercely.

He clearly adored the boys and they, however much or little they understood, obviously adored him. David would never have expressed it so frankly but they were what made him tick. Much of what he did in his working life was so that they could look up to him as a man who did a worthwhile job, something useful, almost heroic.

His own father had died when David was Harry's age, so there had never been a figure to look up to or react against. He was determined that, whatever his failings might be in other respects, he would at least be a good father to his sons. They, much more than Jo, were why David came home. When he strayed, the boys were what brought him back on course.

'And now, upstairs ...' he said to Jo.

The boys were tidied out of the way by Nanny Jo.

Husband and wife ran upstairs to their bedroom – or, at least, as fast as David's shaky legs could carry him – and made love while they still had their clothes on.

'My lord returned from the wars today, and pleasured me twice in his top boots,' Jo murmured.

'I know,' said David, 'the Duchess of Marlborough. But I'm not sure about twice. My back's hurting like hell.'

Jo stroked the abrasions on his skin and tried not to disturb the bandages. She felt no guilt at the raunchiness of their love-making.

'Oh, it's so wonderful to have you back. You've no idea how much I've missed you, how frightened I was when I saw you being blown up. It was the worst thing that's happened to us. It really brought it home to me, the mad way you earn your living, everything ...'

'I didn't enjoy it much myself, to be honest ... But, haven't you noticed, I have to go away in order to come back to you? When I come back it's always so much better between us. If I stayed here, we'd always be fighting ...'

'You promised me, though – no more wars, no more trouble-spots. It's just not worth it. And if you really love the boys, you must never risk your neck like that again.'

David didn't answer.

Then, despite his back, David did manage it again, and, passion spent, fell asleep half on top of Jo.

She didn't mind. She hoped he was home for good this time.

Mike Feather had convinced himself that March was exactly the kind of woman he ought to be getting involved with, and knew from experience that a good way of making advances was to do so indirectly. A girl was often very intrigued if a friend passed on the view that 'I think so-and-so fancies you.' It gave times for the seeds of affection to grow.

But how was the seed to be planted in March's golden head? Who would play the go-between?

He decided to try Vanessa and began ingratiating himself, casually dropping in to disturb her in the office. Vanessa, naturally, didn't for a moment consider that *she* was the target of the scriptwriter's attentions. She already had a steady called Eric who worked in the City. So it was quite a pally relationship that grew up between then, totally devoid of sexual content.

Vanessa was opening the latest sack of newscasters' mail when Mike breezed in one morning.

'Ah,' he said, noticing the bumper bundle, 'and what is it that they want this time? David Kenway's underwear? A lock of March's hair?'

'Actually, they're mostly letters of sympathy for David,' Vanessa replied, truthfully. 'There's been quite a run of them. It's nice to know people care.'

This was not a subject close to Mike's heart.

'What sort of letters does Lynne get?' he asked.

'Hands off, naughty,' Vanessa chided, her manner positively gym-mistressy. 'They're supposed to be private.'

'Sorrreee, sorrreee. But does Lynne, you know, get 'em going?'

'She's very popular,' said Vanessa loyally. 'Nobody has written the smallest criticism of her drink-driving thing. They tell her they love it when she makes a cock-up on the news. And a lot of men find her a turn-on. So there.'

'Amazing. And what about the latest incident?'

'When she was slapped by Jo Kenway?'

'Yes. What was that all about?'

'I haven't a clue. She's not said anything about it.'

'There's not anything going on there?'

'How d'you mean?'

'Between David and Lynne?'

'Mike, dear boy, you know nothing! The chances of David being the slightest bit interested in Lynne are quite, quite remote. He's into younger flesh, as you very well know. I expect Lynne said something Jo Kenway took exception to. So she got slapped. Quite a volatile lady is Mrs K ... She threw a telly at David not long ago. It's one of those physical marriages.'

Deceptively casual, Mike went on: 'And how's March getting on?'

'Why don't you ask her yourself? I gather you two had a productive collaboration over the POW's clothes the other day?'

'The POW ...? Ah, I see, yes. Did she mention that?' Mike asked hopefully.

'No, I saw your name on the script, that's all ... and detected the Feather touch.'

'Oh, I've got a "touch" now, have I?'

'Fancy her, do you?'

Vanessa was doing all the driving, and Mike wasn't happy at being drawn.

'Yes,' he replied, not looking at her. 'Well, no. You know ...'

'So you do.'

'Don't you go saying anything now ...'

Although this was the reverse of the instruction Mike intended to give, he realized as he was saying it that it would probably have the desired effect.

'Hands off March,' Vanessa said firmly. 'She could do without people pressing their attentions on her.'

'How do you mean?'

'She had a nasty experience the other night. Someone followed her home or something.'

As soon as she'd said this, Vanessa realized she might have broken a confidence.

But she had Mike really hooked now.

'Oh,' he said, thoughtfully.

Perhaps March was really in need of protection; perhaps Mike Feather was just the man to provide her with it. He would have to find out more.

117

CHAPTER 18

Super Tuesday, when eight primaries were held, was the next stage in the race to the White House. If Winston Mann was to stand a chance of taking the Democratic nomination, he would have to stop prevaricating and declare himself before then. So, on the Friday before the Tuesday, he was at last ready.

As he stood before the American flag in his old school hall in Ohio, he found himself addressing an array of cameras and microphones outnumbering the real people in the room. With him was his wife and a small campaign team – a professor from Harvard, a TV quiz-show producer who'd handle his media appearances, half a dozen young interns, and a business manager. That was it. It was hardly a mighty political machine.

Winston spoke sincerely and movingly. He was photographed clasping his wife Lorraine's upraised hand and standing with his grown-up children. The photographs went round the world.

Most of them were spiked. He wasn't an important candidate. There were so many others. He'd left it too late. There was other news that day ...

But at N-TV a short video clip of the declaration was worked into the hourly bulletins, and even half a minute from the interview Winston had given to Ben at Oxford those few weeks before. Ben was pleased. He hated to see any work wasted, especially his own. He sent a cable to Winston wishing him all the luck in the world.

When David returned to the office, his wounds healing and no perceptible damage to his spirits, he found he wasn't greeted there as a returning hero. Sir Charles had him in, offered words of encouragement, and confirmed that David should spend several weeks, if not months, as a newscaster on the *Nightly News* before going back on the road.

Sir Charles was quite open about it. 'You're a newsworthy fellow yourself,' he told David. 'You'll bring a touch of the real world to the studio. Hone up your presenting skills a touch, and enjoy yourself.'

David knew he'd feel constrained, sitting at a desk and reading the autocue. It was a treadmill sort of a job compared to being out in the field and he'd have to get used to it. But at least he'd have time to give to other things. Marital bliss having worn off already, he immediately began to wonder what those things might be ...

His eyes fell, almost at once, on the interesting form of Nikki Brennan. He'd never paid much attention to Nikki before, though they'd spoken often on the phone as he rang in from foreign parts or made his travel arrangements. She was the assistant to N-TV's Foreign Editor.

'Wotcher, knickers,' he hailed her. It had always been a prime tactic in David's seduction policy that if you treated a woman as though you'd slept with her, you very soon would.

'I see you haven't improved, darling,' Nikki replied, leaning back in her chair and resting on the arm so that her long blonde hair fell down below her breasts.

'Not strictly true,' David said. 'In fact, a very important part of me was blown off in the late unpleasantness, but through the amazing skill of South Africa's top surgeons, they managed to sew another one on.'

'I hope they didn't pick the wrong colour.'

Others in the newsroom, reading newspapers, poring over VDUs, looked up to see who was holding forth. When they saw it was only David, they looked down again.

'I wish someone had told me you were coming in today, darling. You could have saved me lots of stamps.'

'Meaning?'

'A parcel came for you from South Africa yesterday and I re-directed it.

'Oh, Christ! Just something the authorities "borrowed" from me when my back was turned. My contact books.'

'Oh, I see. Don't want them falling into the wrong hands?'

'They've *already* fallen into the wrong hands, but if you must know, I don't particularly want my wife thumbing through the more personal pages ...'

'Got it, darling. Well, I'm sorry. How was I to know?'

Nikki was saved by the arrival of her boss, Jack Somerset.

'Oh, God, look what the tide's brought in,' Somerset said wearily from behind half-moon spectacles. 'Come into the office ... good to have you back.'

David declined the offer of a chair and sat perched on Jack's desk. This enabled him to keep an eye on Nikki outside as she stretched out her leather-clad legs.

'Well, my boy, are you glad to be back home?'

'No,' replied David flatly. 'You know I've never liked being nailed to the studio floor and made to read other people's crap. I think I'm fit enough to go back on the road.'

'Sir Charles's orders, I'm afraid. He has an idea that having a newscaster with the dust of battle still on him lends enchantment to the viewers.'

'I know, he told me.'

'You'll soon be back on the road. We need you there – and I mean that. We're pretty stretched at the moment. The stringers we have to rely on are sending really scruffy stuff and you usually deliver the goods. So get well soon.'

David was only half-listening. He was busy scrutinizing Nikki. Without being overweight, she was a big girl. She was a bit scraggy at the edges, though. David noted the baggy sweater and the odd broken fingernail. Still, under the sweater there was obviously much to fondle and he had already decided that he would do just that.

'We haven't had any joy out of the Bureau yet,' said Jack.

'Sorry?' David took a moment to bring his thoughts back to foreign rather than domestic affairs.

'The Bureau for Information. We've put in an official complaint to the South Africans about what happened to you. N-TV thought it should. But I don't suppose there's much they can do.'

'Are you fishing for compensation?'

'No, I don't think we'd have a leg to stand on – if you'll pardon the expression – but there was a feeling that Pretoria had quite clearly got you into a situation where you were at risk and they should've looked after you.'

'Wouldn't wash, though I admit that was my first reaction when I came round. I felt sure they'd set me up. I'm not saying they wanted to kill me, but perhaps they wanted to warn off the media. And not for the first time. Then when I saw Pieter in Jo'burg on the way back, he told me something interesting. The man they've charged with the Kobus killing was one of these Storm Falcon twits, from the loony Right.'

'Indeed, yes.'

'Pieter sort of suggested that perhaps the Government *had* been acting in good faith when they shipped us out to Oudtshoorn – but that the mine that got me wasn't some bungled ANC job. Perhaps it had been planted by a white fanatic with a bee in his bonnet about foreign media.'

'But how would *they* know you were going to be in Oudtshoorn, doing a report on the very spot where the mine or bomb was?'

'They could've had a tip-off – but, yes, I guess you're right. The chance of my being in the line of fire was a million to one.'

'Hmmm.' Jack Somerset took off his half-moons and sucked the ends. He looked the very image of the desk-bound executive, a million miles away from the trouble-spots, with a quiet life in Dorking, walking and drinking beer in the Surrey hills at weekends. Almost an academic who had strayed into the frantic world of television news.

'I'll give Pieter a gentle hint. Tell him to feed back anything he hears. Are you happy to leave it like that?'

'Sure.'

'Well, take it easy now,' Jack advised, as David slid off the desk and made to go. 'Everything else all right?'

'The occasional twinge, but nothing worse.'

'Good, good ... and good luck with the newscasting. It needs a shot in the arm. Ben's a bit morose at the moment – his wife's none too well. And you heard about Lynne's drinking case?'

'It had to happen some day, and my wife says there was a spot of bother between them the other night. What's wrong with Lynne? The menopause?'

'David! You're not supposed to say things like that. She's not *that* old ...'

David laughed and went out of the room to where Nikki was attending to one of her broken fingernails. David noticed the quite unmistakable aura of sex about her. But he didn't say anything. He was in no hurry. He went off to fish out copies of his South African reports from the videotape library.

CHAPTER 19

Two things decided N-TV to make the short trip to Whitehall to interview Colin Lyon. George Lee, the Home News Editor, had a news crew available and Sir Charles thought it might be more diplomatic if the mountain went to Mahomet this time rather than the other way round.

The Home Secretary was a prickly fish and appeared to have a well-established grudge against N-TV. In addition, the Editor-in-Chief had picked up the Government's rumblings about N-TV being a nest of Trotskyite vipers. Rather than irritate the sore, he felt that a spot of soothing balm should be applied.

The subject of the interview was the case of two chief constables recently relieved of their duties, one for having fraternized to quite an exceptional extent with a well-known criminal, and the other for getting caught with his hand in the till. Besides which, the statistics on crime in the Metropolitan Police area had shown that, in almost every category, criminals were modelling their standards on those of the two dismissed chief constables.

'A quick trot round the course, then,' Michael Penn-Morrison had told Ben. 'And don't let him blather on. Find out what he's really trying to do about the mess.'

'Yes, yes,' said Ben. 'But he's a slippery bugger. Hard to nail.'

'I know you can cope.'

Sir Charles added to Ben's slight unease before the interview by telling Ben quite the reverse. 'Mind how you go. We don't want to upset the Home Secretary more than we have to, just at the moment. Understand?'

The Right Honourable Colin Lyon, the present broadcasting watchdog, was typical of a new breed of Conservative high-fliers. Not for him a privileged background of old money and public-school education. He had little idea of what a grouse moor even looked like.

Lyon was one of the grammar-school educated, computer-literate generation of Tories who'd come to prominence under Margaret Thatcher. To be exact, Lyon went to a minor public school rather than to a grammar school, but he managed to conceal it quite successfully. As for computers, he was good at singing their praises but equally adept at getting other people to work them for him.

Like many British politicians, on the Left *and* Right of the House of Commons, he had an exaggerated regard for people who had made money through business. He hadn't done so himself, having only pottered around the foothills of property management before entering Parliament as one of the youngest MPs, more or less straight down from Oxbridge.

By being diligent, conscientious and not exhibiting over-much flair for anything, he had loyally served Margaret Thatcher and then been promited to Cabinet rank by Trevor Ross.

'Ben Brock!' the Home Secretary exclaimed with a gleam in his eye. 'Come on in, come on in. It really is most kind of you to come here to see me.' With a squeeze of the hand and shoulder, then a sincere look, he added: 'I really do appreciate it. I know how busy *you* are, but it does save *me* a little bit of time.'

Ben was bemused by this welcome, and by the wave of after-shave smelling like floor-polish which floated in his direction. He stepped out of his own more sullen mood and started laying on the charm with equal aplomb. 'No trouble, no trouble. Anything to get out of the studio ... We won't be long setting up, I promise.'

True to this, 'Nosmo' King, the cameraman, and 'Jelly' Bean, the sound recordist, soon organized themselves. The room was high and wide and about the only problem it created was a slight 'boominess' in the acoustics. But with clip-on microphones this was reduced to a minimum.

The Home Secretary watched the furniture being re-arranged and reflected on the efficiency of the two men from N-TV. He was almost disappointed that, including Ben, it was possible for just three people to record the interview. When the BBC came, there were always armies of people and he was able to give them a little speech on the need for lean, slick organizations and on the over-manning which was the curse of so much British industry today.

On this occasion, any over-manning was all on his side, with no fewer than three people from the Press Office dancing attend-ance.

'So, what can I do for you?' asked Lyon, like a dog sitting up to beg.

'I think we sent a note of the questions in advance ...' said Ben.

'Oh, I don't need to know the questions,' he announced flatly. 'Fire away, anything you like. I can deal with it.'

'Good,' said Ben, puzzled again by the curious display the Home Secretary was putting on.

'Crime figures, first. Then the two chief constables,' Ben said by way of summary.

'Yes, fine. Ready when you are.'

They took their seats before the camera and Ben prompted Lyon to give a spot of voice level before proceeding to tape the interview. Ben managed to be firm without being aggressive, no one lost his temper; and despite smiling almost without a break, the Home Secretary seemed not to be playing down the seriousness of the crime figures or the fall of the chief constables. He admitted the gravity of the situation, promised Government investigation and action; in other words he did all that could be hoped of him in such an interview.

'Like a drink at all?' he said to Ben, when it was all over.

'Not when I'm on duty, thanks all the same,' Ben smiled. 'Mustn't be sloshed in charge of a television programme.'

The press officers tittered dutifully.

The group of them now hovered near Lyon's desk. The Home Secretary stood with his back to the window. On this March day there were some very slight hints that Spring was approaching. Ben decided that the view out of the window over St James's Park was infinitely preferable to the view in, with its amalgam of oil paintings and Civil Service furniture.

'Of course, there are people who don't have a high regard for N-TV,' Lyon suddenly declared.

'Forgive me,' said Ben, 'but I'd always understood that you were one of them!'

Lyon contrived to beam and frown simultaneously.

'I read somewhere,' Ben went on, 'that you blamed one of our programmes for single-handedly losing you to the Party leadership ...'

'Well, there may've been some suggestions along those lines.' Lyon was now all of a twitch. A hand ran over his crinkly hair and he tugged the lobe of one ear. 'But that's all so much water under the bridge, as far as I'm concerned. What I meant to tell you was that someone, not very far from here, is pretty irate with you people. You're not exactly "on our side", as he puts it.'

'Thank heavens for that,' Ben answered, breezily. 'We're not supposed to be on anyone's side, least of all the Prime Minister's, if that's who you mean ...'

'Far be it from me ...'

To change the subject, Lyon leant forward over his desk and revealed a copy of the *London Post* which had been folded to show a particular half-page. He turned a concerned and caring face to Ben.

'I was sad to read about your wife. I had no idea. You have considerable courage, if I may say so.'

'What?' Ben asked, puzzled.

'Until I read the piece in this evening's *Post*, I had no idea that your wife's condition was so serious.'

Ben's charm vanished and he peremptorily held out his hand to take the paper. When he looked, it didn't totally surprise him to find Gabriel Monk's TV page. The small headline said, 'BROCK'S SADNESS' and the story underneath detailed the highly confidential information that he'd given Monk about Natalie's illness.

Ben could hardly speak. The paper shook in his hands. He felt he'd been betrayed quite shamelessly. And what if Natalie should see it?

He could lynch Monk. If Ben had still been an editor he knew what he'd have done to a reporter who'd ratted on a source like that.

'I'm extremely angry this has appeared.'

Ben was trembling. No one in the room had ever seen him lose his cool to such a degree. His face was white and he choked on his words. 'I told the reporter about my wife in order to explain a point, and he's betrayed a confidence. You see, my wife doesn't know ... She might well read about it in the paper ...'

Lyon hesitated. 'I'm very sorry to hear this, Ben,' he said, soothingly. 'We've all been bruised by the Press at one time or other. I feel for you. If there's anything I can do ...'

'No, no ...'

'The Press does behave abominably at times ...'

Ben realized the Home Secretary was about to make another of his points. He didn't want to listen and, making a fumbling farewell, he threw the paper down on the desk and with a half-wave made to go. The two junior press officers ran after him, colliding as they did so with Nosmo who was carrying out the camera.

Lyon turned to the Principal Press Officer, raised his hands with a gesture as if to say, 'Well, fancy that ...' and sat down at his desk.

The PPO hovered, sensing there was more to be said.

'There's no honour among thieves,' Lyon added, rather coldly.

'Thank you for pointing that article out to me. I wouldn't have spotted it myself. I try to avoid reading the *Post* if I possibly can.'

'Yes.'

'Well, how was I – in the interview?'

'Very good, if I may say so. Of course, Brock is pretty straight.'

'Better than some people at N-TV one could mention,' Lyon spluttered.

'Ah, yes. Norman Heathcliffe told me of an extraordinary plan they've hatched at the Number 10 Press Office to take N-TV down a peg. It was all HMV, of course – what the PM had told him. They seem to think we should make things difficult for N-TV. Perhaps we missed an opportunity this afternoon ...'

The PPO prepared to leave.

'Never mind,' Lyon murmured. 'We upset Ben Brock quite enough as it is ...'

CHAPTER 20

March hesitated when Lynne asked her if she'd like to have a drink after the *Nightly News*. Her hesitation was the greater because the invitation was coupled with another to ride back in Lynne's car to her maisonette in Maida Vale. But quickly deciding to postpone her return to an empty flat and the possible attentions of her mystery assailant, March said, 'Yes, I'd love to.'

When they reached Lynne's place, part of an old mansion block, March was surprised to find how warm and comfortable it was. Unlike her own flat, it had a lived-in feel, it was a real home.

The walls were covered with paintings and drawings which announced instantly that they'd been chosen because of a special meaning they had for the owner. Perhaps she knew the artist or they'd been given her by a lover. What was certain was they hadn't been part of an interior designer's job lot.

March's own flat never quite escaped having that air. The rooms were functional and not very homely. They'd been painted in a uniform light colour because, being a garden flat in a basement, the rooms tended to be dark.

Lynne's, being at the top of a block, didn't lack light. And so the walls could be painted in darker colours, wine-red for the dining room, a dark blue, almost purple, for the bedroom, and dark green for the kitchen.

March was also impressed by the long shelves lining the hall, shelves filled with books on every conceivable subject. Did Lynne never throw any away? There were art books, hundreds of biographies, quite possibly thousands of novels. All this spoke of a rounded character, a woman of experience, everything that March herself couldn't yet claim to be.

'What would you like to eat?' Lynne asked, handing March a glass of Vin Sauvage, a bubbly white wine which March would have turned down in favour of Perrier if she'd been given the choice.

'Oh, nothing much. A salad would be fine.'

'A salad it'll be then,' replied Lynne. 'And you won't mind a steak to go with it?'

'Oh ...' March's resolve crumbled and she said, no, she'd love one.

127

As Lynne prepared the supper, she conducted a disjointed conversation through the doorway with March, who remained in the sitting room.

It was the usual chatter from Lynne, unwinding after a programme. What a shit the programme editor had been, 'fussing about like an old woman'; what a wet hen the director, Paul Whitehall, was. 'Why should *we* always have to rescue *them* from their mistakes? Why is everyone so incompetent?'

In time, the older woman emerged from the kitchen with an attractively-laid tray and they ate their steaks and salads seated at a polished refectory table. Lynne lit the silver candelabra and she kept on topping up March's glass in a way that was hard to resist. Consequently, March became more relaxed than usual. She warmed to Lynne, who seemed much more of a real person now that she was away from the studios.

'Oh, God, yes,' was Lynne's reply when March plucked up the courage to ask if she'd ever been married. 'Twice, would you believe? But not at the moment, as you can see. And I'm inclined to say "Never again".'

'Who were they? What sort of person, I mean?'

'I first got married when I was twenty-three. It seemed like a good idea at the time. I was working on a local paper south of the river, then. That was in the mid 'sixties – 1965, actually. Simon was this terribly clever literary bloke. I thought he was a genius, perhaps because I was rather in awe of university graduates, not being one myself. Anyway, he was also a bloody good fuck, so I married him.'

March's eyes widened. 'How long did it last?'

'Rather hard to say, really. I kept on working and he drifted about doing 'sixties things – you know, writing for underground magazines, smoking pot, and such. And we drifted apart. He's now on a *kibbutz* in Israel. He's been there for years.'

'Oh. So he's Jewish?'

'No. You don't have to be Jewish to live in a *kibbutz*.'

'Then I got married to Jack Phillips, have you heard of him? No. Well, he was quite a big-name TV producer in the early 'seventies, just when I was making the switch from papers to TV.'

'What was he like?'

'They say that when you re-marry you make the same mistake twice, but Jack wasn't a bit like Simon. He was bright and clever in his own way. Very pushy. When he was in the studio, he really would snap his fingers and tell people to be "zingy" and "zippy".

Rather a caricature, if truth be told.'

'So why did you marry him?'

'He asked me. I was quite presentable in those days and I suppose he thought I was the coming thing. Unfortunately, I wasn't. Perhaps he did it for a dare – I don't know. Anyway, within a year he was dead of a heart attack. The usual TV producer's way out. It's either that, or a car-smash. Or they get kicked out, or they become executives. Nobody seems to last very long.'

'Yes, I've noticed there aren't many over forty. What happens to the ones who don't collapse on the job?'

'Search me. They just disappear into a black hole.'

'So you're ... a widow.'

March almost enjoyed saying this. She'd never been in a position to say it to anyone before.

'Yes!' said Lynne, positively brightening. 'Though I imagine most people think I'm a divorcee – and I suppose I am that, too.'

March started to wonder whether Lynne was lonely. She even felt quite sorry for her.

'You're dead against remarrying then?'

'Yes, not that I've been short of offers. You'd be amazed how men are drawn to divorcees and widows. They know you've been opened up, so to speak, so they don't have to worry about breaking you in. Men also love to feel they're doing you a good turn, especially those who're married already. Oh, I have my little flings. I have constant companions and "walkers", if you know what they are. So I'm kitted out. I expect you were worried I was lonely?'

'Well, yes, I was, because ...'

'Because I'm not obviously attached to anyone? That's only because since Jack died I've always avoided entanglements with people in the business. All my friends, of both sexes – and I have quite a circle – are from outside television. Real people, you know. I find it better that way.'

'I can understand.'

'And what about you?'

March had been dreading this bit. She didn't know quite what to say.

Lynne prompted her. 'I know you're not married but I'm not even sure you've got a fellah.'

'I had, when I was down in Plymouth,' March admitted. 'But I'm afraid he *was* in TV – on the same programme as me. Since I came to London we've hardly been in touch. I expect he thinks I'm a bit grand for him now.'

'So, at the moment, you're on your own-io?'

'Yes. But I don't mind.'

'I bet they're all after you at the Big N?'

'Not that I've noticed.'

'Bunch of rabbits they are. You can hardly hear yourself speak for the noise of marriages breaking up and people banging each other. They say when there's a war on, people lose their inhibitions and carry on like there's no tomorrow. Well, I think working in news has the same effect. A sort of desperation. A need to live for the moment.'

'Oh, well . . .'

'I can't believe you've been with us for – what is it? – six months, and not had any approaches.'

'One of the scriptwriters sort of asked me out.'

'Which one?'

'Mike Feather.'

'Oh, him . . . You turned him down, I trust? Very wise. He's pretty hopeless. He was a reporter, you know. But he was taken off it.'

'Yes, I know. He told me.'

'Did he now? At least he admits to that, then. He's a very cocky scriptwriter. You can't tell him anything.'

There was a pause. March declined Lynne's offer of more Vin Sauvage, which enabled Lynne to polish off the second bottle herself, and sat pondering. Lynne clucked inwardly to herself; all this had confirmed what she expected, that March had no private life to speak of. It made her looks and the fuss made over her easier to bear.

'And what do you make of David K?' Lynne asked mischievously.

March lowered her eyes. 'Oh, I don't know. I've hardly ever met him. He always seems to be away.'

'You'll have plenty of time to get to know him now.'

'Yes, I know. We'll be doing the *Nightly* together. Do you like him?'

'Good God, no! Can't stand the brat. Full of himself. About as likeable as a polecat. Fortunately, he just ignores me. I suppose I'm too old for the likes of him. You'd better watch out, March. He'd scalp you given half the chance, I bet.'

March was intrigued at the possibility. 'But he's married . . .'

'So what? Hasn't stopped him yet. Yes, you give him half an inch and he'll have you up against the wall.'

'Well, I'm not sure I'd mind,' March admitted, her tongue loosened by the wine. 'He's pretty sexy.'

'Just be careful, love. He's a shit and everyone knows it.'

The more Lynne spoke against David, the more March liked the idea of finding out for herself.

Then sleepiness came over her. Lynne rapidly organized a mini-cab to take her the short distance from Maida Vale to Primrose Hill. March was too tired to worry now about any admirer haunting her doorway, and in no time, she was sound asleep, alone in her bed.

And so, a little more restlessly, was Lynne in hers.

The object of March's dreams had enjoyed a less satisfactory evening. It began with him studiously avoiding the *Nightly News*. David always found an excuse not to watch what his colleagues did and this evening the excuse was that, as it was a rare night at home, he should take Jo out to a Greek restaurant.

Settled upstairs at Lemonia, on Regent's Park Road, David stuffed himself with meze, followed by souvla, while Jo fiddled with a small moussaka and salad. They both enthusiastically shared more than one bottle of retsina.

'At least you didn't throw a TV at Lynne,' said David cheerfully. 'But fancy slapping the old bag, among all those feminists. What a place to choose!'

'I just couldn't help it, David. I was so angry with her. She seemed determined to be as unpleasant as she could – insinuating cow! And after your accident, too. What's the matter with her? Frustrated?'

'I think she feels the skids are under her,' David replied, secretly rather proud that Jo had taken it out on Lynne. 'People have been on about her erratic performance on screen, and her drinking, for a while now. Then along came that trouble with the police and, bingo, it confirmed what everyone'd been saying. I know she can look very good at times – and she's a bloody good reporter if only she'd get down to it more often – but I think she knows she's getting on. In TV terms, she's a very old lady indeed.'

David waited for Jo to get on her inevitable feminist soapbox.

'It won't do, you know,' she said, 'judging a woman by her age. If this was the States, the lawyers'd be out by now.'

'In the States, the lawyers are out at the first hint of anything,' said David. 'But you're wrong if you think it does them any good. There was that case about a woman called Craft. She thought she'd been sacked because she wouldn't do herself up like a dolly bird.'

'Yeah, right,' Jo countered sharply, 'and she won her case.'

'No, she didn't. She won it, then lost on appeal. Besides,' David went on, 'Lynne hasn't been sacked. I was only saying things don't look too good for her.'

Torn between her feminism and her dislike for the woman in question, Jo suddenly plumped for the latter. 'Well, I hope she gets what she deserves.'

'Ho, ho,' said David, with some glee. 'So much for female solidarity.'

But really he was pleased with Jo. He admired her fighting spirit, despite the occasional disadvantages on the domestic front, which probably explained why the other women in his life were of a more compliant nature.

Back from Lemonia, they crept past Nanny Jo who'd fallen asleep in front of the television, looked in on the boys, and then went up to bed, early. David was first in, leaning back against the pillows expectantly.

Jo seemed to be taking her time, but when she came in to the bedroom she was already naked. David kicked back the sheets and covers.

'Come here.'

Jo shook her head. It was her way of saying they were going to do it her way. David wouldn't take this from other women, but was prepared to with Jo. Expertly, Jo licked him all over. There was little he had to do but relax and enjoy it. Finally, she lowered herself astride him and rode him desperately to orgasm.

Despite her sign of satisfaction, Jo was still distant, and David was determined to find out what it was.

'Nothing,' she answered, tired now.

'Yes, there is. What is it?'

Jo said nothing and reached down to one of the drawers at the bedside. She handed David his two contact books.

'How the hell did these get here?' he demanded.

'The postman tried to shove them through the letter box. The parcel got torn, so I took them out ...'

'Well, I hope you had a good snoop,' David murmured frostily.

He put out the light on his side of the bed, turned over and went to sleep.

They might just as well not have made love. Whatever temporary truce had been signalled by David's return from South Africa had lasted barely a week.

CHAPTER 21

N-TV never slept. It remained on the screen throughout the hours of darkness. It was a punishing burden for those who carried any kind of responsibility for the programmes.

And in that April, when N-TV rode high in the ratings and cherished its awards and the good words that people wrote about it, there was one person who suddenly decided he'd had enough.

At the morning meeting with his senior editors, Sir Charles let out word of his decision so quietly that few, at first, realized what he had said.

'You'll be interested to hear,' he remarked drily, 'that I've decided to call it a day ...'

The editorial group with their pot-bellies and greying temples seemed not to register. Only Michael Penn-Morrison asked for clarification, not least because as Deputy he might be expected to succeed Sir Charles.

'I've decided to call it a day, it's as simple as that ...'

'But why, chief? This place is unthinkable without you. We expected you to be here for ever.'

'No one is irreplaceable, Michael. First rule of television. I'm fifty-five, we're on the crest of a wave, and I'd rather bow out gracefully than wait to be kicked out.'

'How far have you got with this?' Jack Somerset inquired. 'I agree with Michael. It's unthinkable. Have you told the Board?'

'The Board is being told. I'll stay on until they appoint a replacement.'

'Who's that going to be?' asked George Lee, Home News Editor, another concerned voice. Penn-Morrison looked sheepish.

'Who can say? I don't have a view on the matter, except that someone from the inside would obviously know how we do things. But they might feel an outsider could freshen things up.'

Penn-Morrison suddenly sensed he'd lost the battle.

Stifled ambitions immediately took root in many a breast in the Editor's office that morning. The work of the day would take second place to thoughts of, 'If only ...'

'Frankly,' Sir Charles went on, 'youth counts for a lot in this game and I'm running out of it. I want to go while I can still do other things, perhaps in independent production or some totally different sphere. I feel it's right to go when the ship is on a steady course.'

'If you do go now,' said Somerset, forcefully, 'it'll give ammunition to our critics. You've heard the rumours that Ross has got it in for us. You might appear as a scapegoat.'

'Well, Jack, the fact is, I'm not. And if there's speculation to that end, then I'd be grateful if you could tell people that it's entirely my decision. I know it's hard for people to believe that anybody in his right mind might *want* to resign from a job in TV. Or that anything could happen in this world *without* there being a conspiracy or plot behind it. But I assure you, in my case, there's nothing whatsoever mysterious about my going.'

The prospects for N-TV were upheaval and discomfort as the familiar was replaced by the unknown.

Among those who had no hope of getting the job, there grew a bubbling resentment that the tried and tested routines, the comfortable assumptions would go into the melting pot.

Merely by signalling his intention, the Shrimp had ensured that N-TV would never be the same again.

CHAPTER 22

David Kenway heard the news of Sir Charles's departure with less concern than most. Jack Somerset had paused before going into his office and said to Nikki Brennan, 'The chief says he's going. The lights are going out all over Europe.'

Nikki had only a vague idea what her boss was alluding to and took the first opportunity to ask David. He was still haunting the office, and particularly her, before joining the *Nightly News* as a newscaster. Theoretically, he was supposed to be briefing himself, all ready for the big day. In effect, this meant he sat around chatting most of the time, interrupting others as they went about their work, and treating any women he encountered to suggestive banter which wouldn't have gone down well in a sexual harassment case.

David could have worked from home, but there was no question of that since the rapid demise of his relations with Jo. He seemed to rely increasingly on Nikki as a confidante. He couldn't keep his hands off her. She, in so far as this was possible, began to bloom under his attentions. Her clothes became less slutty, her broken fingernails began to be the subject of continuous attention, and she didn't seem to mind when David went on at her about the fact that she smoked. Once, he actually pulled a cigarette out of her mouth and threw it away.

'I don't want you killing yourself,' he was kind enough to say. 'Aren't you getting enough oral gratification, is that it?'

'Look, darling,' she replied, 'I know what you're after, but if you want to get between my thighs, I think you should know there's a waiting list.'

David found such directness both daunting and a turn-on. He liked to set the pace with women. If they were too forward, he froze. He didn't like assertive women ever since he'd married one.

'Would you like the Editor's job?'

Nikki was letting him off the hook.

David had his answer ready. 'No, sir. I'm a reporter, plain and simple. I'd hate all that paper work, kow-towing to the Chairman and the Board, agonizing over who to give jobs to. I'd rather be blown up any day than endure that. A kind of living death, if you ask me.'

Nikki crossed her long legs, revealing an expanse of thigh covered with fishnet stockings. David noticed the stockings were laddered. She leant back in her secretary's posture chair and happened to moisten her lips. All this was quite unconscious on her part but it still produced the inevitable reaction.

'I've got to watch the Big News go out tonight,' David told her. 'Orders from above so I know what's expected of me on Monday. Feel like staying on?'

Nikki shot him a hard glance but didn't bother to wonder whether this was a proposition. She responded with careless, fresh-faced enthusiasm. 'OK, since you ask.'

David touched her arm and the deal was made.

Ben and Lynne were fronting the *Nightly News*. David was intrigued to see how they operated. Ben was the same off-screen as on. TV personalities were usually either taller or shorter in the flesh than could be guessed from their screen appearance, or they were older or younger, or they were more or less charming than was supposed. Ben was resolutely the same.

Lynne was different from her screen image and David spent a moment, as he sat across the newscasters' table from her, trying to work out *how* she was different. She was less sexy off than on, for a start. Older men might find her a turn-on but David had never sensed it. She was formless off-screen; the camera pulled her together. That was when she was sober, of course. When she was pissed, all the king's horses and men wouldn't have been able to do that.

She was unaware of David's scrutiny. On this occasion, abstemious to the point of dehydration before the broadcast, Lynne exhibited a fiendish concentration on the job in hand. She seemed quite capable of writing her scripts on a VDU while people talked and gossiped around her. This was a skill David himself had yet to acquire.

He suspected that Ben was the same. He kept the video screen at arm's length. It was a question of age. Reared in the old traditions of Fleet Street, where the typewriter was king and a spike the best discipline for bad copy, Ben had dutifully retrained when he entered TV. But with computers, he'd never thrown off the air of a man gingerly learning to ride a bicycle rather late in life.

'I gather you're going to put in for the chief's job ...'

David fabricated this gossip deliberately to see how Ben would react to it.

'Who on earth fed you that load of cock?' Ben turned to look at David, a mini-second of steel in his eyes, before the benign twinkle replaced it.

'Suit you down to the ground.'

'Kick me upstairs, more like. That's what you're after, isn't it? Get me out of the way, so you can take over the Big News? I wasn't born yesterday, you know. I bet you fixed that little business in Africa just so you could weasel your way on to my patch!'

'Ben, Ben, this isn't like you! No, seriously, you've got better editorial credentials than most people round here. You've been editor of a national paper. You're adored and respected from Land's End to John O'Groats. You'd be an inspired choice.'

'Only one snag,' said Lynne, joining in. 'He doesn't want the job and he's indispensable at what he does. So, for heaven's sake, don't put any ideas in his head. They'll bring in an outsider, anyway.'

'I think she's right,' said Ben, in an attempt to close the discussion.

'Well, God help all of us,' David commented. 'I'd be happier if you were my boss, rather than some jumped-up hack or some grey man in a suit from the BBC.'

'Only time will tell,' said Ben with another twinkle, using one of the clichés proscribed at N-TV.

'Is hospitality open yet?' asked David.

'No, it's not,' said Lynne knowledgeably, and went back to work.

Ben looked at David as though he were about to make some comment and then turned wordlessly back to his video screen.

David felt at a loose end and wandered off to buy a cup of tea.

'Oh dear,' Ben said to Lynne. 'There'll be lots more conversations like that before we're finished ... The trouble is I *am* bored with newscasting. I *would* like to have more of an editorial role, but my real impulse is to chuck it all in and do something quite different.'

'You must be mad. You're too old to be having a mid-life crisis. If anyone's due to have one of those, it's me ...'

Lynne paused and then spoke softly to Ben so no one could hear. She rested her hand on his arm.

'Ben, promise me one thing, and don't think I'm being a busybody: don't let your worries over Natalie affect your judgement. I know it's almost inevitable with all that hanging over you, but try not to let it. Please.'

Ben swallowed, touched. To be sure, he'd forgotten what it was like to have a woman's sympathy and it gave him quite a charge. He felt his eyes fill with tears and looked away. Then he murmured:

'You know what it's like, don't you, Lynne?'

'Yes, I do.'

Ben talked slowly, willing his voice not to break.

'Do you think everyone knows about Natalie now . . . after the *Post* piece?'

'Probably. It was a dirty trick.'

'Trouble is, I can't honestly say we wouldn't do the same thing here. That's what makes me feel I'd like to get out of this business altogether. It's that callous milking of other people's lives that makes me despair.'

'D'you know whether Natalie saw it?'

'The nurses said not. Bless them, they'd kept the offending edition out of sight. But I suspect she knows without having been told. She'll guess from the way people behave towards her. It makes me mad, the whole business.'

'Don't let it get you down, Ben.'

'No . . .'

Lynne came over warmly and well that night. David watched the programme go out from the control gallery and was impressed. He knew what standard he had to achieve when he joined the team. He even allowed himself a nerve or two at the prospect.

'God, I'm getting bored with this subject already,' Lynne exclaimed as she poured out more wine to make up for lost time. The topic after the show was again Sir Charles's departure.

David smiled, nodded and turned to where Nikki was standing. She'd lit up a Gauloise which immediately attracted his displeasure. It also provoked his interest. Nikki was wearing a big shirt over her woollen pullover and skirt, with shiny black boots below. It was a plain but striking outfit, made more interesting by the voluptuous form that filled it.

'Did I hear you'd been to the Sorbonne?' David asked her, a touch gruffly, as if this would explain her Left Bank air.

'No, Nantes,' she replied, looking up from under her dark eyebrows and ejecting a cloud of thick smoke sideways from her mouth.

'Did it do you any good?'

'Not really. I had a good time, though.' Nikki laughed apologetically. 'I got a First in Having a Good Time. No, actually, I didn't finish my degree.'

'How did you get mixed up in this racket?'

'They advertised for someone who could speak German and French. You need it for fixing circuits, sometimes.'

David barely listened to her answers. He was keen just to keep open the line of communication.

'Fancy a bite?'

The propositioning was becoming more outspoken. Nikki knew she would go along with it.

'Come on, let's go. I know somewhere.'

Making no attempt to disguise how and with whom he was leaving, David called out a generalized farewell and guided Nikki from the room.

One or two knowing looks were exchanged. Having collected his bag and her coat from the newsroom the pair was heading for the reception area when David suggested they pop down to the studio from which the *Nightly News* was transmitted. He wanted to check something.

'OK, suits me,' said Nikki with bland indifference.

Studio B was deserted, not needed now till next morning. A plain working light remained on. The banks of strong programme lamps had long been extinguished, but a faint aroma of hot equipment still lingered, despite the chill efficiency of air conditioning. Four cameras, pushed to one side, looked like abandoned dinosaurs.

David went over to the newscasters' desk to which he would regularly be chained from the following Monday. From the front it looked stylish; from the side on which he would sit, it was a jumble of wires, unfinished wood, discarded scripts, things taped to other things.

They were alone. Nikki didn't seem curious about David's need to come to the studio.

'Now aren't you going to stub that awful thing out?'

Nikki made no move, so David himself took the cigarette and ground it into an ashtray. He pulled her upright and then lowered her to the desk and stood between her legs. She clasped her boots round the back of his legs and noticed him stir. She put her hands round the back of his jeans, then slid them to the front, pressing her head against his chest.

David gave a sigh and fondled her hair. He bent and kissed the top of her head.

'Are we all right here? Will anyone see us?' Nikki asked, her voice muffled.

'No one'll come,' David replied quietly but confidently.

'I do hope you're wrong about that . . .' she said lasciviously.

David started teasing and moulding Nikki's breasts through her pullover.

They did not know how their lovemaking would develop. She was content to leave it to David. But as the sharp stabs of pleasure sank deeper and deeper into her body and her gasps began to fall into a regular pattern, Nikki dimly realized the unusual position in which she was about to be laid.

David pushed up her shirt and unhooked her skirt. It slid to the floor. She flicked it to one side with her boot. Then he knelt before her, licking her eagerly until she was incapable of standing.

He picked her up and laid her on the desk. The design of the set meant that the same carpeting on the floor and walls also swept up and over the top of the desk, so it didn't feel hard to naked flesh.

He had soon slipped inside her. Again she pinned him to her by locking his legs with hers. She squeezed with her strong thighs and dug her fingernails through his shirt back. She shifted and found her head close to the edge of the desk.

Wordlessly, they continued, David moving in a measured way until he detected another change of tone in Nikki's sighs and felt himself rising. He tried to resist it, to prolong the coming. He raised himself to make more dramatic, exhibitionist strokes, but Nikki pulled him back deeper, in the mutual selfishness of those bidding for orgasm.

Nikki was neither a shouter nor a screamer. She was a breather. Heavy breaths, gasping, burst from her lips, as David raced and juddered to a climax. She herself came more quietly as she felt the warm, sticky fluid soaking her innermost parts. Then she melted into silent space.

They lay gasping for several minutes. Then they lay longer in silence. Then there was a bustle of activity as they prepared to leave and adjusted their clothes.

'Just as well they're pointing the other way . . .'Nikki nodded at the cameras.

'Natural modesty, I expect.'

'You've got what it takes,' Nikki said, in a forgivably obvious turn of phrase.

If David minded the cliché, he didn't show it. His mind was already working on the next opportunity.

CHAPTER 23

By the time of the three o'clock editorial meeting that Monday, a telephone call had already been made to March's home to find out why she hadn't turned up for work. There was no reply. It was most unusual. It was not unknown for people to forget what day they were supposed to be at N-TV – but they could usually be tracked down soon enough.

Liz Hastings, programme editor of the day, began asking around, but drew a blank. She asked Vanessa whether March had been due to go away for the weekend.

'Not as far as I know,' Vanessa replied. 'She keeps herself to herself at the best of times. You sort of expect her to show up and she always does.'

Liz Hastings then had an 'I've-got-better-things-to-be-bothering-about-than-missing-newscasters' tantrum and went back to worrying over the list of 'probables' and 'possibles' for that evening's programme, now less than five hours away.

The Managing Editor, Tony Sharpe, took over the problem and the afternoon meeting went ahead without March's participation. David Kenway was twitchy at the prospect of doing his first studio programme in almost a year and ratty that March wasn't in her proper place.

At four o'clock there was still no sign of her and Delia Steele was told she'd have to deputize.

All phone calls to March's home remained unanswered. There was not even an answering machine to annoy the callers. Mike Feather was aware of the crisis and, not entirely without self-interest, suggested he taxi up to Primrose Hill and see what he could find out. Perhaps a neighbour would have seen her.

At the flat, he rang the doorbell. The venetian blinds by the front window were down and he couldn't see in. Mike tried peering through the letter-box but that gave no view of the flat's interior, just of the box, which was empty.

He rang a few doorbells of neighbouring houses and flats but, even when there was a reply, the occupants hadn't seen March. Indeed, Mike wondered whether they even knew she existed, let alone who she was.

'I think I may have seen a light on last night,' said one old woman, 'but, honest, I can't be sure ...'

'Thank you, never mind,' said Mike, and realized he would have to go back to N-TV without accomplishing his mission.

'Is it time to call in the police?' he asked.

'I don't think so,' said Tony Sharpe. 'It's not *that* serious, is it? She's probably got the day wrong. Pity she doesn't have an agent we could shout at. Just one of those things. And we don't want to make too much of it otherwise it'll look bad for her and for us. Especially if the papers get on to it.'

'I'll keep ringing her number, if you like.'

'Yes, Mike, you do that.' The Managing Editor wondered quite why Mike Feather had taken it upon himself to join the search for March with such gusto.

David Kenway's first TV appearance since returning from South Africa was, as a result, accompanied by a certain jitteriness in the production team. It was odd of March to let them down. Her replacement, Delia Steele, though tough enough as a reporter, didn't possess the flair March had for presenting in the rather special way they encouraged on the *Nightly News*. Delia and David didn't make a team. There was no chemistry between them.

The programme itself was a shambles. One still photograph needed at the start only reached the studio fifteen seconds beforehand. Videotape and film didn't always come up when needed and David, still rusty in his studio technique, was left with egg on his face.

Liz Hastings was furious. 'What a bloody dog's dinner!' was all she could say once the final credits had faded. She wished her name hadn't been on them.

'You win some, you lose some,' daid David, in a not very successful attempt at imitating Ben Brock's sang-froid.

The team shuffled into the hospitality room for drinks, waiting for a bad-tempered call from Sir Charles Craig – a call which never came.

Having picked over the bones of the disaster, everyone – as if on cue – decided that the real reason for their collective jitters was the mystery surrounding March. They fell once more to worrying about her.

'Yes, I think it *is* a mystery,' urged Mike Feather. 'We've done umpteen stories in the past about kids who go missing from home – who disappear off the face of the earth – and here we have a case on our very own doorstep.'

'You've been to her flat, haven't you, Mike?' asked Delia. 'So what else is there we can do?'

'Bring in the cops?' he suggested.

'I'm reluctant,' said Liz Hastings. 'We all know what bloody PC Plod is like once he gets the bit between his teeth. Before you can say "'Evenin' all", he'll be walking one of his policewomen round the streets, dressed up as March, in a bid to jog people's memories about her last hours ...'

'Come on, Liz,' David said. 'Aren't you jumping the gun a bit? I'm sure there's a perfectly simple explanation. I don't get the feeling there's anything odd about it, really.'

'But there is ...' It was Mike Feather speaking now. David looked at him coolly and thought of making a sharp remark about Mike's newly assumed role as the missing girl's protector. 'I heard that someone jumped on March outside her front door one night recently. He got away, though.'

'I didn't know that,' Liz Hastings began, trying to draw a line under a discussion which was getting edgy. 'But can I just suggest we leave it till tomorrow? If there's no sign of her in the morning, we'll tell the police.'

A murmur of agreement went round and the drift homeward began, more promptly than usual. Mike Feather was not putting March out of his mind, however. Just to make sure, he thought, he'd make one more visit to her flat in Primrose Hill.

Ben felt very alone on the planet. In most people's view a man of achievement, and surrounded by all the luxuries money could buy, he now knew that he would one day soon lose his dearest possession.

Edmund Cook was the cancer specialist who had handled Natalie's case for over a year. Marginally younger than Ben, he had similar qualities, a smooth manner enhanced by the medical man's air of thinking he held the key to life's mysteries.

'I hope you didn't mind my asking you here?' he said, gesturing Ben to an antique window-seat where the April sunshine streamed into his Harley Street consulting rooms.

'Not at all, not at all,' murmured Ben, with only a slight hint of apprehension.

'I'll come straight to the point ...'

Ben listened to the specialist's phrases as they emerged from his mouth with polite little thuds. He had heard them before. He might have imagined that one day they would be said to him. He tried, in vain, to lessen their impact by hearing them as though they were not real, as though they were being addressed to someone else.

'You've known all along that Natalie's condition was ... not one we could do very much about.'

'I've understood that.'

'Well, I'm afraid the cancer has spread so far in her stomach that ... it's only a matter of time now.'

Ben swallowed. Edmund Cook looked at him, but Ben's eyes were fixed on the trees beyond the window, in Cavendish Square. Trees that he couldn't really see, however intensely he stared at them. Cook felt an impulse to put a hand on Ben's shoulder, but resisted it.

How odd it was for him to know that this immensely famous man could be deflated or demolished by whatever he had to say.

'I'm afraid, Mr Brock, you're going to lose her.'

The tears rolled down Ben's face. He made no move to wipe them away, but continued to stare fixedly at the trees.

Cook said nothing. Nor did he move. He had had to give this news to hundreds of people during his career, but this time it was particularly poignant as, for all the wrong reasons, he felt that he *knew* Ben – that he was more than just the husband of a patient.

For his part, Ben had no shame about showing his emotion. He must concentrate upon his grief at this moment.

Before today, he had gradually been coming to terms with the fact that he would one day lose his wife. From the earliest years of his marriage he had wondered what that would be like. When Natalie's illness was diagnosed, he had had to face the realization that she would be the first to go, and much sooner than he had ever imagined. The old age they had joked about spending together would now be denied them.

But Edmund Cook's words were so final. Before this, there had always been a chance that something would intervene to save her.

The silence between the two men lengthened. Then Ben reached for his handkerchief and dried his tears, without making any reference to them.

'Can you say when?' he asked.

'No, I'm afraid I can't. It could be soon or in six months. It's really impossible to say.'

Ben wondered if he could believe Cook. He felt a welter of questions. Could he bear to keep on working? How would he tell the children? How could he talk to Natalie, knowing what he did?

Cook tried to make Ben open up: 'I gather you were worried Natalie might have seen about her condition in the press?'

'Yes. I have been.'

'I have respected your wish not to tell her ...'

'I know.'

'... even though, on the whole, I recommend that patients and relatives *should* be open about it ...'

'Yes, indeed.'

'The hospital sister tells me she is sure your wife is still in the dark. The paper in question didn't reach her. I can appreciate your anxiety.'

Ben started stoking up his spirits in order to be able to leave the Harley Street doctor's rooms.

'This is a bloody piece of news to tell a man!' he exclaimed.

Cook gestured airily, not knowing what to reply.

'Can she come home from hospital? That'd make it more bearable for *me*.'

'I think it's best not to disturb her now. And if she's in the hospital, she can get the attention she needs. Why don't you visit her again as soon as you can. I think that would help – you as well as her.'

'I'll certainly do that,' said Ben. 'But don't blame me if she drowns in my blubbing ...'

'Don't brood, Mr Brock.'

'All right, I'll take your advice,' said Ben with a sudden grin.

A shake of the hand, a goodbye, and he was walking out past the receptionist who glanced up at the familiar figure. If she had any hint of his plight, she concealed it.

Ben's professional manner concealed his feelings, too. If anyone had glimpsed him now in the street, they would never have guessed he had just lost a part of himself. Part of his reason for being. It would have taken someone very close to Ben to have pierced that smiling armour and found out what was really biting him.

As he crossed Cavendish Square mulling over his thoughts, a small boy approached him and hesitantly asked for an autograph. Ben, unfailingly professional, obliged and chatted cheerily for a moment. Then he walked on.

Sir Charles had been out to dinner the night of the débâcle and only caught up when he flicked through the videotape later.

When he came into the office next morning, the production team braced itself for criticism.

Sir Charles reserved his anger, though, for the lack of action over March's disappearance. He couldn't understand why more hadn't been done to locate the girl. A call to the liaison officer at New Scotland Yard soon set the police machinery in motion, and towards the end of the morning, a detective sergeant turned up at N-TV.

His name was Evans and, as the jokes about 'PC Plod' had anticipated, he seemed more inclined to enjoy his visit to the TV studios than get on with the dull job of locating March. He interviewed all the obvious people, obtained names of relatives from the personnel office, took a photograph of March for circulating if necessary, and grilled Mike Feather on his amateur sleuthing.

'Do you think she's all right?' said Mike anxiously.

'I always look on the bright side myself, Mr Feather, and I suggest you do the same.'

The detective sergeant's expression somewhat belied his words but Mike allowed himself to be reassured. At least the policeman hadn't mentioned murder or rape.

'And what do *you* think has happened to Miss Stevens?' This was the cue Mike had been waiting for.

'Well,' he began, 'you can rule out all the usual things. She's not in a drug-induced haze, she's got into that sort of thing. Far from it. If she'd been kidnapped – and it's not beyond the bounds, is it? – we'd surely have heard from her captors by now. And I don't think anything worse has happened because ... well, I just don't. Mind you, I did hear she was almost mugged or something outside her flat quite recently.'

'Was she now?'

'She must have mentioned it and it got about the office.'

'I'm afraid that isn't very much help, Mr Feather. Is there anyone else I could talk to? Anyone on the staff she's been chummy with?'

'Not "chummy" to speak of ...'

'You aren't her boyfriend, are you?'

'No. Whatever made you think that?' Mike responded edgily. 'Just good colleagues, you know.'

'How about a girlfriend?'

'She's only been here a short while. But you could try talking to Vanessa Sinclair, the newscasters' secretary.'

148

'I'd like to do that. Could you take me to her?'

'Certainly.'

Vanessa, as it turned out, was more worked up about March's disappearance than anyone else.

'I'll tell you what's bothering *me* about all this,' she began. 'A couple of weeks ago, March told me when she got back home, there'd been someone hanging about outside her door. He bolted, but it gave her a nasty turn.'

'Did she say what sort of person it was? A man, presumably?'

'Yes – no, she didn't describe him or anything. I suggested she ask her driver to hang on until she was well inside her flat in future. I don't know whether that sank in.'

'Well, thank you, Miss Sinclair. Tell me, has Miss Stevens ever been bothered at all by admirers?'

'She's started to get a lot of fan-mail over the past few weeks. Usually four or five hundred letters or so.'

'What sort of letters?'

'Quite nice on the whole. I tend to winkle out the mucky ones, anyway, before I show them to her. Otherwise it's chaps mostly telling her how wonderful she is. Rather wet really. Then there's an old lady from Bristol who writes her a rambling letter every time she's on, discussing every item in the news, though it's hard to be sure because her writing's so bad.'

'I see. No threats of any kind?'

'Not really – unless you count marriage proposals.'

'Would it be possible for me to see any letters?'

'Take your pick.'

'Thank you.'

The detective sergeant slowly began to read them, rather as though he wasn't used to such matters. He made an occasional mark in his notebook.

Vanessa wondered when on earth he'd go away. The chances of his ever solving the mystery seemed very slim.

Ben walked straight from Harley Street to the hospital. He was not on that night and knew that he would be unable to work at home either.

He was shown in to see Natalie who seemed to be asleep. This surprised him as it was near lunchtime. The room was lightly shaded and the distant noise of taxi-brakes squealing and car-horns tooting was the only mild intrusion from the outside world.

Ben sat by his wife's side and waited a full five minutes before she woke. He held her hand, stared at the blue lace nightdress she wore, and felt a lump in his throat when he saw her profile outlined against the vases full of white flowers. She'd always insisted on white flowers, whatever the occasion.

With the heightened perception of her mortality, Ben began to discover more signs of weakness in her than he had allowed himself to acknowledge before. It was apparent that Natalie's body was almost separate from her spirit. The body he had known for a quarter of a century was now that of a stranger. But through Natalie's eyes, her spirit shone. She was alive in them.

'Hello,' she said, attempting to squeeze his hand. There was hardly any strength in her grasp. Barely a sound escaped her mouth.

Ben was determined not to cry, not to betray by one word or gesture the terrible secret he held. It made him feel powerful, but pointlessly so. The easiest thing would be to avoid meeting her eyes. And yet if he failed to do that, she would know he was hiding from her.

'Love you, Ben,' she spoke in a whisper.

'Love you, too, old thing,' Ben replied in the ritual exchange, his heart blank with sadness. He looked her in the eyes at last and she returned his gaze, knowingly.

No more was said the entire time he spent with her. They sat together hand in hand, as they had done so many times in their life together. Now Ben could make no connection with her. What he knew prevented that. The agony of it ...

He tried blotting out thoughts and feelings as the only way to see him through the ordeal. One moment, he convinced himself she was dead already. Her eyes closed and she became still as marble. Even her frail hands felt cold as death in his.

Then she opened her eyes. Ben, caught out, grinned nervously.

Her eyes were calm. What would come, would come.

At last, too heavy-hearted to pretend further, too shattered to disguise his feelings he wept by her side.

Natalie said nothing. But from her look, Ben was certain she understood.

He didn't try to explain his tears to her. Rather ineptly, he worked his way out of the room. He didn't turn back, but kept on walking until he was out of the hospital. Then he walked and walked, until he was almost home in Kensington.

CHAPTER 24

'NEWSGIRL GOES MISSING' declared a headline on page two of the *London Post*.

With a look of distaste, Sir Charles glanced at the report and muttered, 'At least it's not on the front page.'

Michael Penn-Morrison remarked, 'It makes you wonder, doesn't it, about the police? You'd think 999 calls passed through the Press Association, the speed they let out information.'

'Odd lot, the police,' commented Sir Charles. 'If *they* want *our* help, to solve crimes, they're all over us. But if *we* want something from *them*, you'd be hard put to believe they were the same people. Shut up like clams. 'Twas ever thus.'

'Do we mention it in the bulletins? Now that it's out about March, I mean.'

'I'd say not. It won't help find the girl. If the papers get on to you, tell them where to get off.'

Penn-Morrison was surprised at such language coming from Sir Charles, normally the most reserved of men. Was he demob happy? Or irritated, now his intention to leave had been announced, that problems were starting to pile up?

It proved hard to tell the Press where to get off. They soon sensed a story at N-TV and bombarded everyone they could get through to with calls to elicit an angle on March's disappearance.

The other TV news organizations showed no interest, however. They weren't going to give publicity to N-TV. Not yet, anyway.

By the early evening of the second day, a small posse of photographers and reporters had camped outside March's flat in Primrose Hill – with a view to what, no one was quite sure, except that back in the office their editors could rest content that there was 'a man on the job' and, if anything occurred, they'd be 'covered'.

Kentish Town police soon heard about this and relayed the news back to N-TV. Sir Charles changed his mind about N-TV mentioning it. Consequently, at the end of the *Nightly News*, David Kenway stared coolly at the camera as a publicity shot of March reared up on the screen behind him.

'And finally,' he intoned, 'a search of special concern to all of us at N-TV. The whereabouts of March Stevens are unknown. She was unable to present last night's edition of the *Nightly News*. She is not at her London home and all other moves to contact her have failed. The police have been informed. So, get in touch, March. We're worried about you.'

Lynne Kimberley closed the show with the headlines and her own word to March, and that was that.

After the bumpy ride of the night before, the *Nightly News* had passed off without a hitch. It often took a disastrous edition to get everyone back on form. The news about March likewise jolted the team into a new seriousness. Except for David, that is. 'I bet the little minx is having us all on,' he muttered to Lynne as the closing theme played. 'I mean, it's not as if the Yorkshire Ripper's still at large, is it?'

Lynne looked askance at him for his cheap remark.

A phone call from Sir Charles did come after this show. 'I thought the mention of March was just right,' he told Liz Hastings. 'No news from the police, I suppose?'

Sir Charles had scarcely put down the phone at his home in Gerrard's Cross when it rang again.

'Charles? It's Ben.'

'Yes, Ben. What can I do for you?'

'Sorry to add to your troubles. I'm afraid Natalie died earlier this evening, and I was wondering if ...'

'Oh, poor Ben, I'm so sorry. How are you taking it?'

This struck Ben as an odd question, but a good one. 'I suppose it's a relief. I knew it would happen. I only heard this morning that she'd taken a turn for the worse. I saw her before lunch. She seemed quite peaceful. It could've taken another six weeks or even six months ...'

'You'll need time, Ben. Don't worry about us. Come back when you're able ...'

'I'm down to do tomorrow night ...'

'No question of that. We can cope.'

'I'm sorry this had to come on top of the March business.'

'Don't worry, Ben.'

Sir Charles reflected that, in spite of what he'd said, N-TV did seem to be going through a difficult patch. March and Ben now out of the running, Lynne's court-case coming up at any moment, David still not into the swing of things. It was all very inconvenient – and not good for the ratings to have to rely so much on substitutes.

'I'd like to attend the funeral,' he said, 'if that's all right. Will it be a family one or ...'

'Mostly family, yes, but do please come. I'd like that. I'll let you know the date. If you can count me out of the rota for a day or two, I'd be most grateful.'

'Make it a week or two, Ben,' Sir Charles said grandly, 'then we'll see ...'

After the phone call, Sir Charles uttered a rare expletive. Lady Pam heard it and asked for the reason.

He told her.

A policeman pushed his way through the journalists outside March's flat. He peered through the letter-box. As before, he could see nothing suspicious. In fact, he couldn't see anything at all. The Venetian blinds on the front window cut out most of the light. To peer into the rear of the flat would have meant climbing over garden fences. But at this stage in the hunt, there really was no reason to do that. It was assumed March was elsewhere. As for breaking down the door, it was simply not what the police did at that stage in their routine.

Which was unfortunate because, on this occasion, the instinct of the Press to congregate outside the obvious place, and the only place they could think of, was the right one.

March had reached London in her Volkswagen at about nine o' clock on the Sunday night. She had wanted to be back a little earlier in order to read the papers to set her up for a stint on the *Nightly News* next day. But hold-ups on the M4, the usual jam of drivers returning from weekends in the country, had delayed her return from visiting her parents in Dartmouth.

So she didn't reach her flat until it was dark. She carried an overnight case and a plastic bag full of vegetables and fruit her mother had pressed on her. She went down the stone steps to the flat, rather awkwardly carrying both bags and banging them against the iron bannisters.

Just as she slotted her key in the lock, turned it and moved forward with her bags, she felt a push from behind.

She fell sharply forward, letting the bags drop, so that vegetables and fruit spilled over the carpet. The door slammed behind her and March felt a man kneeling on her back. Her heart pounded, her mouth went dry. She felt the sharp prick of a knife pressing at her waist.

'You're March Steven, aren't you?' said a voice. 'Well, I've found you now.'

March, petrified, said nothing. She was still shaking.

She sensed that he was as nervous as she.

'What on earth do you want?' she managed to hiss, her face still pressed uncomfortably against an earthy potato.

The man pushed harder on the knife. If this was what being stabbed was like, March found herself thinking, it was oddly painless.

'Please, don't be angry. I'll explain ...'

They were still in the dark. He held March so that she couldn't move. Her pulse began to settle down and calmness of a sort returned, though she could hardly hear herself think for the pounding of her heart.

'I wanted to tell you ...' the man began.

'What do you *want*?' she interrupted, surprised by her rage. 'Get out. Who do you think you are?'

'But, March ...'

At least he knows who I am, March thought, as if that would make any difference.

'Was it you ... the other time?' she asked.

'Yes, it was, but this time I've got you.'

'Look,' she said. 'I don't know who you are, but just go. Get out.'

'No. Let me talk with you. That's what I want, just to talk with you.'

'But why? What is this?'

'You got my letters?'

March missed a beat. 'What letters?'

'Yes, every week, every day, I am writing to you. You never replied. Always a letter from your secretary. Then, recently, you sent me a photograph. I had to meet you.'

'Look,' said March, 'I've heard of autograph-hunters, but this is ridiculous.'

'Just let me talk. Don't send me away.'

March felt less pressure on the knife that the man still held to her side.

'OK,' she said. 'Put on the light.'

'No!' There was a note of hysteria in the man's voice.

'Let us talk here, in the dark,' he went on, huskily. 'I like especially your voice. It is soft and sexy.'

'Oh, yes?' March took the hint. So that's what he was after. 'Can't we get up? I'm so uncomfortable.'

'OK, but move slowly, or I'll ...'

March shifted slightly until she was sitting with her back against the wall. The man sat right beside her, his knife dimly glinting in the dark room. He kicked the vegetables and fruit away from them.

'What's your name?' March asked him, resigned now to a prolonged encounter.

'But you know it,' replied the man, 'for I've written to you. You must know it now. It is not important.'

'I get lots of letters. What is it you want?'

'Nothing. Just to talk with you. You have the most beautiful voice to listen to. As well as being most beautiful to look at, if I may say so.'

'Well, you can't see much of that, if we don't have the light on.'

She dimly saw the knife turn away from her, but there was nothing she could do. She couldn't wrestle it from the man. He would be stronger than she.

'I am a great admirer.'

March suddenly twigged.

'I know who you are,' she said. 'I've suddenly realized. It's your voice. It all connects. Aren't you from Ealing or somewhere?'

'Acton, yes. See, you know who I am! You remember!'

'Mr Patel, I suppose?'

The man was so pleased at being recognized that he threw caution to the winds. 'Yes, Beni Patel. You *do* know me. I am your greatest admirer, probably in the world. That is why I had to talk to you.'

'Well, Mr Patel, you're very foolish ...'

'No, I am not. I found out your address. I followed you many times. I knew you would never agree to see me at the studios of N-TV. So I had to find your home. That is what I have done.'

'But don't you realize you could go to prison for this?'

'Oh, no, surely not ...'

March concluded he was a nutter, but that made it no easier. If she was his goddess, then heaven knew where that left them. It was going to be a job to get rid of him. He had the strange oppressive power of the enthusiast. And he had a knife.

What did he really want? she kept on wondering. If it was sex, he had made no obvious move. Did not touch her. Said nothing. But March couldn't be sure.

And so they talked. They talked for much of the first night. March had never talked so much in her life before. She knew that she mustn't give him a moment to brood.

Towards dawn, Beni eventually allowed her to move to the back of the flat, overlooking the garden, allowed her to make tea and food, even allowed her to sleep. He himself didn't sleep. He just wanted to stare at her, asleep or awake.

He had some guile, too. But although he unplugged the telephone, it was the sort that would still ring even when disconnected. He made sure no light appeared at the front of the flat. And that the curtains were well drawn at the back. To the outside world it looked as though the flat was empty.

A trick which, as became apparent, worked all too well.

CHAPTER 25

On the first morning, March managed an hour or two of sleep altogether, but it was not nearly enough. It was clear that Beni wasn't going to let her go to work, even to present the *Nightly News* which he claimed to watch every time she was on it.

When the telephone started to ring, March imagined it was N-TV trying to contact her.

Beni admitted he was laying siege to her, but his aim was still obscure. It was not a kidnap for money. So far he hadn't made any sexual advances. He seemed just to want to be with March. To have her to talk to, all by himself. But still he had the knife and the power of his unpredictable, unsettled personality.

March tried to find out what she could about him, and he was eager to talk.

He had come to England as a tiny boy when his Asian parents were expelled from Uganda. He was now twenty-two and worked in his father's post office and general store in Acton. He had all his own gadgets, including his own TV and video recorder. As he admitted, he doted on TV stars, though none could compare with March since first she came before his eyes. She was his obsession. So beautiful, so young, his goddess.

'Do you have any girlfriends?' asked March, still making the running in conversation, as the hours crawled by.

'Oh, no,' was the reply. 'Only you.'

'But I'm not yours. I'm just someone who appears on your TV.'

'That is enough.'

'No, it's not. Otherwise you wouldn't be holding me prisoner like this.'

Beni flinched at the word 'prisoner'.

'No, it is not true, please. You are not prisoner. I am your visitor. Your special visitor.'

March realized that she was getting nowhere with this man.

He was not unattractive. He had dark good looks, occasionally illuminated by a flash of white teeth when he smiled. His clothes were quite smart. In another setting she could well have fancied him.

At 8:00 p.m. on the second full day, March suggested they watch the *Nightly News*. The television had already been turned on from time to time during her captivity, mostly so that Beni could watch N-TV's headline bulletins. He kept the sound down low.

'I suspect you're hoping there'll be some mention of us,' March challenged him.

'No, no, not at all,' was all he would say.

But then, at the close of the programme, March saw her picture flash up on the screen. This had a noticeable effect on Beni, a mixture of agitation at the mention of police and satisfaction at having precipitated a media event. If nothing else, the mention proved to him that he had made his mark.

'Well, are you satisfied now? You see, they miss me. How much longer do you want to drag this out?'

Beni was silent. But March sensed his mood had changed. He even put down his knife, though she knew that made no difference. She was sure he wouldn't hesitate to use it if pushed too far.

Although the tension had sapped her energy, she managed to keep up a continuous stream of provoking remarks at Beni. She hadn't considered whether this was the right strategy, or whether it might make her captor more hostile. It stemmed from real anger at her position. March, never the most positive of people – one who had let things happen to her rather than tried to make them happen – felt herself becoming harder, much more inclined to fight for herself.

'I have a boss, you know – an Editor-in-Chief, actually,' she said, as the *Nightly News* faded from the screen. 'He's called Sir Charles Craig. And the one thing he can't stand is when his newscasters make news themselves. It's not cricket, he says. He'll be furious.'

'I'm truly sorry.' That was Beni's first hint of contrition.

'Look,' she said. 'I'll do a deal with you. It's very sweet, this admiring me and being a fan and all that, but you *can't* go around pestering people like this. I tell you what, if you leave me now, you can walk out of here. I won't call the police. I won't even say what has happened. I'll make out that it was all a misunder-standing ... I'd got my dates wrong, or something ... to explain why I didn't turn up for work. I won't say who you are, but you'll have to promise never, ever to do anything like this again, or to contact me, or treat anyone else like this, ever again.'

Beni said nothing but was clearly unhappy as he thought very hard about his position. He was even more tired than March after two days and nights of watching her.

'OK,' he said suddenly. 'If you'll do that, then I'll go. But there's one last thing. I must love you.'

March presumed she knew what he meant. He didn't mean love at all. Dimly she began to rehearse the arguments. If she consented, it wouldn't be rape, would it? She didn't know. She was prepared to do it, if only it would lead to her freedom.

'What d'you mean. You want to go to bed with me? As long as you've got that knife, that'd be rape. Don't you see?'

Beni fingered the knife, nervously.

Then he laid it down.

'There ...'

She let him hold her very gently, and then she gave him her mouth.

CHAPTER 26

They emerged for the first time in two days from the rooms at the rear of the flat. They came into the front room, and stood by the door. Hearing the hubbub outside, Beni suddenly panicked.

He hadn't realized the reporters were there, chatting, smoking, idly filling the time. Neither of them had been aware of this, holed up at the back.

Beni's escape was blocked. They had to retreat and think of another way out for him.

'Can I get out through the garden?' he asked.

March felt herself being made an accomplice and resented it. 'You'd be seen, even if you could find your way. We'll have to get rid of the reporters. Call them off somehow. I'll have to make a phone call. Is that all right? The bargain still holds ...'

'I trust you,' said Beni, his eyes liquid with devotion. 'Here, let me plug the phone back in, please.'

He did so. He no longer bothered with his knife. March looked in her briefcase and found a booklet containing a list of N-TV staff, together with their addresses and telephone numbers. It was freely circulated round the office and, although it had been compiled so that people could be contacted quickly if there was an emergency, it was not without its social uses, too, especially among the unattached members of the company.

March dialled Mike Feather's home.

He was there.

'Mike ... it's March ...'

'Good God, where are you? We've been looking everywhere for you?'

'I know, I know. I'll explain everything, but it's just a little fraught. I'm ringing because there's something you can do for me.'

'Where are you?'

'I can't tell you. I can't tell you anything.'

Beni listened in intently.

'All right,' said Mike, catching the note of nervousness in March's voice. 'I understand. What is it then?'

'There's a group of reporters outside my flat. Do you know where it is?'

'Yes, of course I do. I've been there a couple of times while we've been searching for you.'

'Well, they must go. I can't explain. Can you get rid of them? Tell them I've been found. Tell them anything. It's important.'

'I understand. Get rid of the reporters, that's all?'

'Yes. I'll ring and tell you where I am. When I'm safe.'

Mike, however, hardly needed to be told where she was.

'All right. I'll do what I can. I'll go back to N-TV. Ring me again on my extension there, if you need to.'

Mike went into town in a state of high nervousness but with some satisfaction that March had come to him for help. He grabbed a taxi and headed for N-TV while trying hard to think of a solution. Gradually, it came to him. It might not work, but it was all he could come up with.

First, he spoke to the night-duty editor who was much too wrapped up in producing the hourly bulletins to worry about March – and said so. Then he rang Tony Sharpe, the Managing Editor, at home and told him that March was safe but needed help. Would it be all right if he put out a statement to the Press Association?

'Check it out with the Press Office,' said Sharpe.

Mike's heart sank, not wanting to bring in more people than he needed to. But he had to agree.

He dictated a brief story to the PA newsdesk. The March Stevens disappearance mystery had been solved. She had been found safe and well. Then he added – and Mike was not sure whether March would go along with the next bit – she would talk to the Press at N-TV at 11:15 that night. This seemed the only way to get news editors to recall their men from outside March's flat.

It worked.

Within an hour of March's call to Mike, news had filtered through to the group of reporters and they drifted away.

Beni, peering out from the darkened front room of March's flat, finally felt confident the way was clear. He looked at his watch. It was 10:07.

'I'll go, then, Miss Steven – March. I am truly grateful to you. You have made me so happy. But, now I must ask you to help me. Keep your word. Don't tell on me. I will never trouble you more. I promise. I am very sorry for this. Thank you. Goodbye.'

'Goodbye ... Beni,' said March quietly. 'I'll keep your secret. That's a promise. Just go away now, and never ever trouble anyone like this again. I'll just have to fib my way out as best I can.'

'Thank you. You are a woman in a million.'

March sighed – with exhaustion and at the foolishness of the man. 'Have you enough money to get home?'

'Yes, I have.'

March opened the front door and let him slip out. Beni furtively crept up the steps from the basement to the street. There was nobody about and he began to walk quickly away into the night.

Abruptly, the doors of a parked car swung open and two plainclothes police officers leapt out and chased him a short distance before, bewildered, he was caught and bundled off to Kentish Town police station.

March wasn't aware of this until – still numb and confused – she heard heavy footsteps coming down the steps to her door. There were muffled shouts from the street.

At once she knew it was the police. It was a distinctive sound, almost a distinctive atmosphere they carried about with them.

'March Stevens?' a voice called out at the same time as her doorbell rang.

'Yes, yes, here I am,' said March, opening up.

'So you've been here all along?' said the policeman.

'That's right. But how did you ...?'

'Tip-off from one of your colleagues. Said everything would be all right when the Press had gone away.'

March realized the police must have been lying in wait for Beni. He had been betrayed.

'We caught him,' said the policeman. 'They've got him in the car outside.'

'Oh ...'

March crumpled up, and started to cry. Relief, unhappiness, betrayal ... she was torn several ways. 'But I didn't mean ... not ...'

'Never mind, miss.'

A policewoman was now at the door. March saw that it was all over for Beni. She would have to tell the truth now.

She sank in a heap on a chair and the policewoman moved over to comfort her.

CHAPTER 27

The Houses of Parliament glowed in the April sunshine as Lynne stepped from her taxi at the St Stephen's entrance and paid the driver. For a moment, she stood on the pavement looking over towards the lofty square Victoria Tower over which a vast Union Jack flew, showing that both Houses were in session. Then she turned and looked the other way to where the tower of Big Ben rose up. The clock had just struck the quarter hour after noon. Lynne knew she must hurry or be late for her appointment.

Just inside the entrance, the police sergeant from the courteous corps who work at Westminster asked what her business was.

'Lord Almley's expecting me.'

'Right you are, madam.' He seemed unsure whether to let on he knew who she was. 'Go through to the Central Lobby and they'll find him for you.'

Lynne, looking at her most stately in a brown velvet suit with a huge yellow silk bow at the neck, passed through the security kiosk and walked up a flight of stone steps. She glanced left to look into the Great Hall where so many scenes from English history had been played out: the trial of Charles I, the lying-in-state of kings and heroes, the speeches made by Churchill and visiting statesmen. She thrilled to the echoes of all that.

Once in the Central Lobby, she wasn't sure of the procedure, but a frock-coated attendant disappeared and eventually located Lord Almley in the Guests' Bar and brought him out to meet her.

Plummond Almley had a fine Roman nose, rampant grey lamb-chop whiskers, and a booming voice. He clutched a file of notes and new copies of *Hansard* to his dark blue Savile Row suit.

'Lynne, my dear,' he greeted her. 'What a pleasure this is.'

He kissed her on the cheek and took her by the hand, as if rather pleased to be exhibiting his guest to his colleagues from the Upper Chamber, who staggered along the corridors, most of them the worse for age.

They went into the bar overlooking the Terrace and the River Thames. Lynne immediately recognized some of the peers, and struggled to recognize others. There were several politicians she'd vaguely assumed dead.

'What are you drinking?' Lord Almley asked her.

'Oh, God, can you believe, orange juice?'

'But I was expecting to crack a bottle of champagne ...'

'I know, I hate myself, but I've got to be a good little girl. I'm doing the Big News tonight, and you know my reputation.'

'I thought you were having the day off?'

'I was going to, and I was looking forward to our lunch and writing off the rest of the day, but you've probably heard ...'

'They can't manage without you?'

'Not quite. There's hardly anyone left. Ben Brock's wife has died.'

'Oh, I'm so sorry ...'

'It had been coming. Anyway, he's had to disappear until after the funeral. Then there's been the drama over March Stevens.'

'The pretty girl? Yes, quite extraordinary. The *Telegraph* says she's been found. Kidnapped by a fan!'

'I feel terribly guilty about it. She told me she was frightened of going home. And blow me if this Asian bloke doesn't kidnap her for a couple of days. I hope we're not getting accident-prone.'

'But you, my dear, are all right? Looking the picture of health, if I may say so.'

'Sweet of you, Plum. But I'll be in the dog-house again next week. That's when my case comes up.'

Lynne enjoyed the attentions of Lord Almley. He was flirtatious in the least offensive way. And he was, after all, a Lord. It was odd how a title made the most sober and boring people that little bit special.

In fact, Plummond Almley was a Conservative Life Peer. It was said that he'd been given his peerage for donating considerable sums to Party funds. He had made millions from an immensely successful food empire. But he had also figured in local politics and on certain statutory bodies.

Like many members of the House of Lords, he found its atmosphere of an exclusive gentlemen's club addictive and liked to use its cachet to lure guests to lunch there.

Lynne had noticed that actresses in particular were always trooping through, seduced and flattered by the attentions of elderly peers.

'Plum' first met Lynne when she had interviewed him and this invitation to lunch had been a long-standing one only recently finalized.

'Of course, I'll get sent to the Tower for being seen with the likes of *you*, you know,' he said with a laugh, when they'd settled down to their plates of quails' eggs and smoked salmon.

'Why do you say that?'

'Well, I mean with you being an N-TV personality! The gods are angry, you know. No wonder all these terrible things are happening to you and your colleagues ...'

'Which particular gods have you in mind?'

'Oh, d'you mind terribly if I have a glass of champagne? Are you sure you won't join me?'

'No, I really mustn't ...'

'Waiter, a glass of champagne, if you'd be so kind, and *another* orange juice for Miss Kimberley ... No, what I mean is, your Editor's leaving. Am I right?'

'Yes, he is.'

'What reason has he given?'

'That he's done all he can at N-TV. He wants to establish himself as an independent before he reaches retirement age. Nothing sinister in that.'

'Don't you believe it, my dear. People make up excuses like that after they've been *pushed*.'

'Who's pushing him then?'

'I could guess. Now I'm not a member of the Government. I'm just a Tory, with no hot-line to the PM or anybody, but mark my words, Ross and the Cabinet have got it in for you lot. They don't like the kind of things you say about them.'

'But that's childish ...'

'Maybe, Lynne, but that is the way of the world. Whoever's in office, Conservative or Labour, it doesn't take long before they've convinced themselves that sections of the media are against them.'

Lynne sipped her orange juice and Lord Almley welcomed the chilled glass of champagne the waiter brought him.

'All right, then – how does a Government get rid of an editor it doesn't like?'

'Easy as pie, my dear.'

'Even when he's protected by a board of directors, approved by the IBA, and got a knighthood in the New Year Honours ... come on!'

'You'd be amazed at the power of official persuasion. A Government with a good majority barely has to raise a finger to remove an irritant. And N-TV is seen by this Government, and the PM especially, as an irritant.'

'But you haven't told me how it's done.'

'Not by direct action. Just by gently tapping people on the shoulder. Putting the word around. I bet some of your Board have already been tipped the wink. The franchise won't be renewed if they don't mend their ways, that sort of thing. It's always been done. Always will be, I suppose.'

'But surely a little nitpicking doesn't matter to the Government?
Ross's got a majority of 76, he's in for another five years if he wants to be. What's he worried about?'

'The vanity of politicians knows no bounds. The more secure they seem, the more insecurely they behave. There's also the itch to interfere. The role of government is to be bossy. Mark my words.'

'I say, this lunch isn't to tip me the wink, is it?' Lynne tried to make her inquiry as friendly as she could. "Cos I have to tell you I've not got one iota of infuence at N-TV. I'm just a hack.'

'Oh, come now, my dear. I've told you, I'm not part of the Government. I'm just passing on scraps of what I hear. But I'd watch very closely who's appointed to succeed Craig.'

'He'll be Government-approved?'

'No, not really.'

'So who'll it be?'

'I'd predict a foreigner with no axe to grind.'

'A foreigner?'

'Well, in a manner of speaking ...'

'You mean you *know*?'

'Really, Lynne, I've no idea. I'm just joking.'

Lynne wasn't so sure. If Lord Almley had wanted to seduce her over lunch, she could have coped with that. But she didn't like being lobbied.

'God, I could do with a stiff drink,' she exclaimed.

'Well, why not have one, then?'

'Oh, what the hell ...!'

The rest of lunch, consequently, passed in discussion of lighter topics. Almley continued in his booming way and gradually calmed Lynne's suspicions. They parted with many kisses and protestations of undying affection: they must have lunch together more often.

Lynne took a taxi to N-TV and managed to arrive in time for the three o'clock meeting only moderately the worse for wear.

'Well, who is it then?'

'He comes to us with a very good reputation from Australia ...'

'Australia, for heaven's sake! As if there aren't enough of them over here already ...'

'That's as may be, Ben, but he's one of the top TV news people down under. It'll be announced, as I say, very shortly.'

'And he's called?'

'Patrick Ritchie.'

'Never heard of him, but thank God he's not some twenty-one-year-old. You had me quite worried for a moment. Do you think I'll get on with him?'

'I don't know the man, either. But, all I can say is, it's probably better to have someone brought in from outside – and Australia's pretty outside, isn't it? – rather than promote from within. There're always petty, lingering jealousies when that happens. And, anyhow, if you don't like it, you can always come running to me.'

'Meaning?'

'They're putting me on the Board. I'll still be around.'

'Thank God for that, and congratulations. Another glass of champagne?'

It was amazing what a good host Ben was, even on a difficult occasion like this. He radiated spirit and affected everybody who came within its spell. Ben dreaded any of his guests leaving.

Lynne was one of the first to signal that she must be getting back to town.

'You're not on tonight, are you?'

'Yes, 'fraid so. And I've drunk too much of your delicious bubbly. Anyway, lots of love, Ben. You'll be all right. And if you ever need someone to cook your supper, I'll be only too pleased.'

'Bless you, Lynne. And take care. Get that court case out of the way. Then we'll all be back to where we were.'

'By the way,' Lynne asked slyly. 'Any news yet about who's getting Charlie-boy's job?'

Ben wasn't going to let on what he'd just heard, especially as Lynne was leaky as a sieve, and Gabriel Monk would have it out of her and into his TV column before you could say Jack Robinson.

'Not as far as I know,' he lied.

'Um, well, I'll tell you a funny thing, Ben. I was having lunch with Plummond Almley at the Lords the other day ...'

'My, you do move in elevated circles ...'

'He told me – and you know what an old gossip he is – that the Government would contrive to have us accept a "foreigner with no axe to grind".'

'As the new Editor, you mean? Ah, well,' Ben replied, a curious look on his face, 'then that explains everything ...'

'What do you mean?'

'Nothing, dear, nothing ...'

CHAPTER 29

For the fourth evening in a row, David found himself fronting the *Nightly News* with Lynne. He already felt he was getting better at the job, though he didn't take too kindly to being a workhorse. He resented March's adventure because it distracted attention from him. He resented Ben's absence, although he understood the reason why. And he was irritated by Lynne's chaotic approach to her work.

Given the chance – and very *sotto voce* – he could be extremely waspish about all of them.

As for March, she'd been whisked off and settled in an anonymous Central London hotel until the fuss over her abduction died down. She hadn't sold her story to a Sunday newspaper, and she had refused to go along with Mike Feather's diversionary press conference after her release. She had even refused to be interviewed for N-TV. There was some sympathy with her on this score from above, as Sir Charles wasn't sure it was the kind of publicity N-TV needed anyway.

But Fleet Street said the inevitable: 'TV likes publicity when it wants it, but not otherwise' – and there were several editors and disgruntled reporters who took to thinking of March as 'that little madam from N-TV'.

It was hard for Mike Feather not to do the same. It was to him March had turned for help, yet when she gained her freedom, he found himself ignored, victim of her guilt about Patel's arrest.

Mike was not alone in feeling rejected.

David had been avoiding Nikki ever since they'd made it on the newscasters' desk, and one evening Mike and Nikki found themselves consoling each other in a heart-to-heart at Greeley's wine bar, just across the road from N-TV.

Nikki had finished for the day but Mike was on call for the *Nightly News*. If he was needed before 7:30, they could always find him through his bleeper. Nikki couldn't resist indulging her preoccupation.

'What do you make of David K?'

'Do you mean do I like him? No, I don't. He's a shit of the first order.'

'Go on.' Nikki rested her chin on her knuckles, and her elbows on the table, so as to give her full attention to Mike.

Mike thought for a moment and then said, 'Well, I can see he's very glam in a sort of way, and he's a good reporter. Better than I could ever be. But he's just a shit.'

'I've just discovered he's a one-hit wonder.'

'You what?'

'What I said. It was all very casual. I lingered on after the *Nightly* because he obviously wanted me to. And we made it on the desk in Studio B. Now he's ignoring me.'

Mike could hardly restrain his amusement at the idea of a desk-trembler and what N-TV's viewers might make of it if only they knew.

'God help you, Nikki. You do like living dangerously. Serve you right if someone had caught you at it.'

'I wasn't in the mood for worrying. It just seemed, you know, a fun thing to do. He's pretty irresistible once his cock's up. Trouble is he doesn't want to know you when it's down.'

Mike wasn't sure how to handle this confidence. Whatever he thought of saying sounded either prim or sour grapes. 'Of course, he's married. I expect it all depends how he's getting on with his missus.'

'I know,' Nikki nodded. 'I knew what I was getting into, but I'd never heard of him getting involved with anyone at N-TV before. I thought he kept his prick pretty clean round the office. Only messed about when he was abroad.'

'You could be right,' said Mike. 'I haven't heard of him bonking anyone here. Thought he was mostly into air hostesses.'

'Well, it's tricky,' mused Nikki. 'I half feel I've been *used*. Trouble is, he's a bloody good screw. It might be easier if he wasn't.'

'You're hoping for more!'

'I don't know what to think. I expect that's the end of it. 'Nother glass of wine?'

'Sure. Why not? Drown your sorrows, Nikki. Tomorrow is another day.'

David was summoned by Vanessa and made to sit down while she went through his mail with him. Almost nightly appearances on the news had reminded viewers of David's charms in a way that no amount of solid four-minute reports from around the globe could have done. The bomb which had driven him into a studio role had done less for his public image than the solid – and to him rather boring – grind of reading the teleprompter night after night.

Vanessa encouraged him to sign a stack of colour photos of himself and asked several questions from viewers' letters that she could answer for him.

David put on an air of being above all this showbiz stuff and amused himself by flirting with her. He'd never fancied Sloane women much. He considered their minds, such as they were, boring and their sexual appetites best serviced by drunken Hooray Henrys after hunt balls. In fact, he imagined that sex to them was like riding a hunter over a series of difficult fences.

Still, perhaps he'd been wrong about Vanessa. With her clothes off and flat on her back, she might lose her severity. She might be inclined to be bossy but a little work with the snaffle and bit would probably bring her round.

As she droned on about the mail, David's interest waned. She's probably engaged to some stuffy, over-paid nerd in the City, he thought. So David abandoned plans to seduce her . . . for the time being.

'Here you are, I've kept the nice bone till last,' Vanessa told him. Clearly, she enjoyed exercising her small degree of control. 'You'd better read it yourself.'

David took the embossed card and studied it without saying a word.

'Well?'

'Has everyone else got one?' David asked.

'No, not as far as I know. It's specially for you.'

'How very curious. Why me? Why not Ben?'

'Ben's been before. Long time ago. When Maggie Thatcher was still there. But this is the first invite I've heard of since Ross went to Number 10.'

'What sort of do will it be, d'you think?'

'A gathering of the great and the good, I expect, with a smattering of show business and media, which is not to say that *they* aren't great and good in their own way, of course . . .'

'It's addressed to me and Jo.'

'Yes, well, you see, they do things properly at Downing Street.' Vanessa gave him a meaningful look, which he chose to ignore.

'Are you going to go, then?' she asked.

'Of course, I'll go – but I thought N-TV was supposed to be *persona non grata* with Downing Street these days.'

'Perhaps he's going to nobble you.'

'Um. Hold on – before you reply to the invite, I'd better ask Jo whether she really wants to go. She's not a great one for socializing as the company wife. She hates Ross, anyway.'

'You ask her then and let me know.'

CHAPTER 30

'Why don't you open a bottle of wine? After all, this is a special occasion,' said Jo. David was at home with his wife, which meant he was restless, eager to be elsewhere.

Jo made a point of parading the boys in front of their father until it was time for them to go to bed. She had been promised an evening alone with David and had even said she'd cook for him.

He opened a bottle of burgundy and tried to make himself mellow. But he had caught the hint of danger. He didn't try to find out what was getting at Jo, but she was giving off vibes. Then, unable to contain herself any longer, she came out with it.

'I've had a little surprise in the post.'

David was bemused.

'Shall I show it to you? Or rather, *play* it?'

David could tell by her tone that it wasn't going to be a pleasant surprise, whatever it was.

'What is it, Jo?'

'*This.*'

She produced a tape cassette from behind a cornflake packet in the kitchen.

'Magical Mystery Tour. Put it on the cassette-player, you dumb-head.'

'You mean ...'

'Yes. *Play* it!'

There was to be no getting out of it. David took the tape to the player and slotted it in. He turned on the amplifier and put up the volume.

For a long time, nothing happened. Just the occasional sound of people moving about. Not a word.

Then, very loudly, and perfectly recorded, as though the microphone was professionally positioned, he heard Nikki's voice say, 'Are we all right here? Will anyone see us?'

Then he heard his own voice murmur, quietly but confidently, 'No one will come.'

'I do hope you're wrong about that.'

There were sounds of clothes rustling and muffled excitement, followed by the unmistakable sounds of lovemaking.

At this, David moved towards the cassette-player and ejected the tape.

'Where the hell did you get that from?' he asked icily, not bothering to pretend he didn't know what it was.

Jo seethed. 'It came in the post at lunchtime. Nice of someone. One of your likable workmates, I suppose. Probably that Kimberley bitch. As if I had no idea about all the balling and screwing you get up to, they have to send a tacky tape of you doing it.'

David was seething, too. It was a million-to-one chance that somebody had been lingering in the sound booth of Studio B and recorded his session with Nikki.

But to send it to his wife! That was sleazy. There must be someone at N-TV who really had it in for him.

'Mischief-makers!' David tried hard to brazen it out. 'Believe nothing that you hear and only half of what you see. Old motto.'

'You can't wriggle out of it like that,' Jo told him, reaching for her cigarettes. 'I get the picture. There's no smoke without fire.'

'Jo, forget it. That tape is just someone stirring it up between us. I've no idea what it's about.'

There was a long silence between them. David continued to knock back the burgundy. Jo allowed the dinner to spoil itself.

After a time, David attempted to talk Jo round by telling her of the Prime Minister's invitation.

'Of course, I'll bloody well go!' was her unequivocal response.

'But I thought you couldn't stand Ross?'

'So? What's that got to do with it? I want to see inside the place. Besides, I'm your wife, remember? I'm not having you waltz off there with some floozy.'

'I'll accept then.'

'Yes. You do that. Come on, we'd best eat.'

David casually picked up the tape and dropped it in the bin.

CHAPTER 31

The hand-over of power at N-TV happened more quickly than anyone had anticipated. One week, Sir Charles Craig was still presiding over his self-created empire, in an autocratic but reasonably benign way; the next week, a portly Australian bull had taken over the china shop. There was no denying that the management style of Patrick Ritchie would be different. It was a considerable shock to everyone at N-TV to discover just *how* different.

Nobody knew very much about him, except that he was 'spoken of very highly in Australian TV' and had also 'been in newspapers with Rupert Murdoch in the 'Seventies'. Then he erupted into the office. He might have been in his mid-forties but he looked ten years older. He had greying auburn hair, lugubrious eyes with bags under them, and a paunch. His skin was pale, apparently untouched even by the Australian sun. But he could quickly turn the colour of beetroot when he was shooting his mouth off, which was most of the time.

Even before Sir Charles was out of the building, Ritchie started making his presence felt. After a quick meeting with senior staff, he decided not to retain Michael Penn-Morrison as Deputy Editor-in-Chief. 'He's as thin as a streak of pelican shit,' he pronounced. 'There's something wrong with a guy like that.' Adam Ravenscroft was summoned from the Features Department and given the job on the grounds that he had once worked for Rupert Murdoch, and survived. Penn-Morrison meekly went over to programme editing in order to stay on the payroll, remarking waspishly of Ritchie as he went, 'He's like Hobbes' definition of life. Nasty, brutish and short.'

On the other hand, 'He's not so bad, after all,' muttered Jack Somerset to Nikki. Coming from him, this was a compliment. 'I might actually manage to work with him. He's nothing if not straightforward.'

Ritchie's next executive action was to dispense with the services of Sir Charles's secretary, Celia, declaring her to be 'uglier than a cobbler's dog'. He brought in Sharon, a peroxide blonde with her roots showing, who'd worked in London for an Australian-owned newspaper. She soon made herself at home and took to saying, 'Well, *we* thought it would be better to do it *this* way,' when passing on the thoughts of her boss – which endeared her to everyone.

Ritchie made one particular error – in the etiquette of N-TV at least – by inviting himself to the modest farewell lunch given for Sir Charles. This was held at Lockets in Westminster and was a slightly strained affair, if only because the exigencies of a twenty-four-hour, seven-days-a-week station meant that it wasn't possible for many people at N-TV to attend.

Ben was there, naturally, having accepted Sir Charles's blandishments about throwing himself back into work. March sat next to him, seemingly recovered from her recent trauma. Lynne turned up, £250 the poorer and banned from driving for a year. And David was there, not accompanied by his wife, but only because spouses hadn't been invited.

Penn-Morrison made a short speech in praise of Sir Charles, successfully disguising his own misgivings about the changes under way, and bravely sounding optimistic about the new era N-TV was moving into.

Sir Charles replied in a speech also projecting optimism that a corner had been turned, a sunlit plateau reached, and thanked all present for their help in raising N-TV to its present pinnacle of excellence.

For Patrick Ritchie, this was too much to take on board. Without actually staggering to his feet and making a formal speech, he freely distributed his liquor-flavoured remarks to anyone who cared to listen to them. It was hard not to.

His general thrust was that N-TV's programming had been so bad, so inept, that even 'Blind Freddie could have seen it'. The *Nightly News* he dismissed as 'arthritic crap'. Ben Brock was 'an ageing matinee idol, always licking the Royal Family's arse'. Lynne Kimberley, 'clearly a dipso dyke'. March Stevens? 'Aw, c'mon, who wants bloody virgins reading the news? She looks as though she's never had it, and wouldn't know what to do with it if she had.' And David Kenway: 'A crypto-pinko ... without a teleprompter he'd be up the creek in a barbed wire canoe without a paddle.'

Sir Charles tried to block his ears to this ominous diatribe. 'He must be drunk,' he said to Penn-Morrison who winced and wished he'd had the guts to resign from N-TV altogether.

Only Adam Ravenscroft sat quietly by Ritchie's side, seemingly unappalled by the new Editor-in-Chief's performance.

CHAPTER 32

It began to rain at six o'clock that May evening and poured down steadily from then on. The sky was black as doom. Jo was frazzled athe very thought of getting dressed up to go to the Prime Minister's reception.

'We'll never be able to park the car,' she started on David who all too simply was slipping into his dinner jacket and efficiently tying his black bow.

'If we can find a parking space in Whitehall we'll only have a couple of hundred yards to walk,' David said. 'We certainly can't park in Downing Street.'

'But in this rainstorm!' Jo moaned. 'My feet'll get soaked. We'll arrive looking like a couple of drowned ducks.'

'So, we'll get a cab.' David went off to organize one on the phone, which he did with difficulty. It was almost worth it, though, for him to be able to reply, '10 Downing Street,' when asked what his destination would be.

The girl who took the booking asked, 'Downing Street ... where's that?'

'SW1,' said David, smiling to himself.

When Jo was ready, David had to admit she was looking more glamorous than he'd seen her in years. Her face positively shone, her hair was up, and she exuded Osiris perfume, a particular favourite of his – worn, he felt sure, in some way to spite him. Her dress was a Ralph Lauren evening gown in dark blue wool, the back slashed to the waist, a simple black belt the only adornment.

David tried to compliment her, but to no avail, given the deep frost that had descended since the cassette incident. In fact, they'd hardly spoken since then and were only doing it now so that Jo could get to visit Number 10 and so that David would have an approved partner for the occasion.

Where Downing Street joins Whitehall, a damp policeman stuck his head in the cab and asked to see the Kenways' invitation before allowing them to proceed to the famous front door.

'This is not quite how I imagined it.' said David. 'I was expecting a perfect summer evening. How wrong can you be!'

Jo ignored his remark and stepped in a puddle as she got out of the cab. Her first entrance into the Prime Minister's residence was thus not quite as stylish as she might have wished.

Security was tight. Guests were not actually body-searched, but the most scrupulous attempts were made to match the bodies to the guest list.

David and Jo ascended the main staircase to the first floor. It was lined with photographs of immediate past Prime Ministers – Macmillan, Douglas-Home, Wilson, Heath, Callaghan, Thatcher ... A queue stretched from the top of the stairs into the Pillared Reception Room.

'Mr and Mrs David Kenway,' David told the toastmaster, to Jo's annoyance. She would have preferred 'Mr David Kenway and Ms Jo Lake Kenway'. 'Much shorter, my way,' he said to forestall argument as they walked forward and had their pictures taken shaking hands with the Prime Minister and his wife.

Trevor Ross greeted them warmly, though David wasn't totally sure he knew who they were. A glazed charm enabled Ross to shake them by the hand, while an aide whispered information in his ear. There was no real contact.

The Kenways were thrust into the body of the reception and at last received a cold glass of white wine. They then looked for people they knew. All they seemed able to see were half-familiar actors and actresses. Jo proved much better at identifying them than David who was largely ignorant of the soap triumphs in that part of television he ignored.

The invitation was – rather oddly, thought David – for nine o'clock, which seemed to suggest that guests were supposed to have eaten before they arrived. But in the event there was a large buffet, which was a relief to Jo who'd failed to eat in the scramble to leave home on time.

Despite the crowd, they felt isolated and David was about to launch into his usual 'How I hate parties and how soon can we leave?' speech when a familiar figure ploughed through the crowd to greet him.

'Hi, Dave, fancy seeing you here. All the best people, eh? And how's our studio boy?'

It was Aaron Rochester looking bronzed and well and, as David immediately noted, no less tubby. He did, of course, have a cigar in his hand.

'Hi, Jo. Good to see you.'

David was a little annoyed that Aaron was present and that Jo should have to meet him again here. Aaron and Jo were in separate compartments of David's life and he'd have liked to keep them that way.

In fact, Aaron hadn't seen David since the Oudtshoorn incident three months earlier. Once Aaron and his crew had deposited David at the Groote Schuur Hospital and were satisfied he was going to survive, they had returned to Johannesburg in order to put their videotape on the satellite.

Aaron duly asked after David's health.

'All parts in good working order,' he replied, in a way that made Jo wince.

'Good, good.'

'Where've you been lately?'

'Just back from Sicily, looking at the Mafia. As you know, that's a subject of great interest to certain minority audiences in the States. Got some great stuff. Interesting place. The pasta's out of this world ...'

Jo examined Aaron as he chatted on. They had had a one-night stand just before she married David, but it hadn't left much of an impression. She knew that her husband sometimes bumped into Aaron abroad and went out on the town together, but that was really all she knew. Tonight, in the unlikely setting of the Prime Minister's reception, she found herself discovering him afresh. He, likewise, seemed keenly drawn to her.

It was inevitable that Aaron's mental image of Jo had been coloured for a long while now by David's sour descriptions of her moods. Now that he could see Jo for himself, he wondered why David took quite so much trouble to do her down.

She was radiantly sexual. She had an allure and a warmth that he didn't really recall from their liaison of long ago. Of course, she was maturer now, another man's wife and a mother. Whatever it was, he felt a beguiling urge to be near her. She too felt herself responding to him, opening up in a way she hadn't done for years. Her initial impression was of someone kinder than David. Or maybe it was because they were both Americans they could talk the same language.

When David wandered off to talk to a BBC nabob, Jo asked Aaron directly, 'You haven't brought a partner? When are you going to get married?'

'Why buy a cow when you can steal a bottle of milk?' Aaron joshed her. Remarks like that were supposed to be taboo with feminist card-carriers like Jo. But she didn't seem to mind and was rather taken with his laugh and with his old-style, stoagy-waving personality.

'No,' he went on. 'Never fallen for marriage. Doesn't really go with the job, saving your husband's presence. And, as to why I'm here on my own tonight. Simple. I was all that got asked. And how do *you* like having your roving correspondent back in the bosom of the family?'

Jo didn't answer directly.

'Put it this way,' she said. 'We get on much better when there's at least a thousand miles between us.'

'Ah.' Aaron looked to where David was staring down the *décolletage* of an actress who had recently starred in a series of TV dramas about the lives of Prime Ministers. Aaron moved nearer to Jo and, aided perhaps by the wine, felt stirrings within him.

He fancied Jo, and so he flirted.

'What's that perfume you're wearing,' he asked. 'It's incredible. It reminds me of, well, I'd rather not say ...'

'Osiris. It's David's favourite, too. There was a time when he wouldn't make love to me unless I had it on. I got through a lot of bottles in those days ...'

'Figures ... And now?'

'Don't pry.'

'Well, if you ever find yourself alone with your bottle of Osiris, you know where to find me ...'

Jo laughed and her eyes lit up. 'Aaron, what are you saying?'

Jo hadn't thought about what might happen. She wanted to be taken in Aaron's arms and kissed. Here was a man who was interested in her and showed it. She also wanted to bring home to David that she wouldn't be messed about any longer.

Heart beating wildly, she followed him down to the ground floor where attendants and policemen were thin on the ground, now the reception was under way. They just wanted a room where they could be alone together.

When the door of the Cabinet Room closed behind them, Aaron held her. Then Jo knew what would happen. She hadn't been with another man since marrying David, and she had rather forgotten that it could be a new, exciting, thrilling experience, even if you were thirty-six.

'No, for heaven's sake, Aaron, not here,' she ritually protested, in a whisper.

As for the location, it was certainly daring: the room where the

Cabinet met. It was probably the first time ever the historic table had been used for the purpose, with the possible exception of a few heroic couplings by David Lloyd George and his secretary.

No words were spoken now between Aaron and Jo, lest the noise give them away. There was a slight agitation between them because of the urgency. Someone would come in. Someone would observe them come out. So it was quickly and passionately that it happened. Slightly flushed from the wine but more excited by the very daringness of the act, Aaron held Jo steady enough, delighting in her warmth beneath the wool dress as he mounted to a climax.

They both came quickly. Then they walked back upstairs, as nonchalantly as they could, to re-join the party.

The Prime Minister was standing in an odd pose, holding his whisky glass from above, by the rim. After a quick swish to agitate the ice-cubes, he transferred it to his other hand and took a sip.

From his immense height, he looked down over his half-moon spectacles at David Kenway.

'You must have mixed feelings towards the South Africans. You wouldn't be human if you didn't feel angry.'

David waited a moment before attempting a reply.

'Well, put it this way. I didn't think much of the system before they tried to blow me up, and I didn't feel any better about it afterwards ...'

'Of course, none of us *likes* apartheid but, little by little, I think we're wearing them down.'

David felt like saying, If you believe that, you'll believe anything, but wisely refrained.

'D'you know, David, there's a clear connection between the bomb that nearly killed you and the shooting of the Information Minister? Neither had anything to do with ANC extremists, as they said originally. That was what you'd call official disinformation.'

'I beg your pardon?'

'It was the Storm Petrels who were responsible for both.'

'Don't you mean Storm Falcons?'

'Yes, Storm Falcons. They've a fairly hysterical view of the foreign media. They feel the Republic's being sold short and the Bureau for Information is incompetent.'

'I know that's why they shot Thys Kobus. The killer was found guilty. But where do I fit in?'

'They also plotted to kill a foreign reporter or correspondent. You drew the short straw.'

David said nothing. He was angry at the casual way he was being fed this startling information in the middle of a party.

'I may say,' Prime Minister Ross added with a treacly smile, 'that there are those in *this* country who'd do much the same to reporters here!'

David swallowed hard, but couldn't hold back.

'We're talking about my bloody life!'

'Come, come, David, let's not spoil an enjoyable evening. I can understand your anger but can I just ask you to think about it – coolly, if you can? You escaped with your life. It's never going to be possible to establish precisely who plotted to kill you. Even if it was, there's nothing we could do about it. Such things can't be investigated and brought to a proper conclusion as they might be nearer home under normal conditions.'

David felt patronized.

'I thought it only right to tell you what I'd learned, but I must ask you to leave it there. It really wouldn't be in anybody's interests to take the matter further.'

David remained speechless with anger. The Prime Minister abruptly changed tack.

'You've a new Editor, I gather?'

'Yes, er, yes. Patrick Ritchie. From Australia.'

'Good. I was pleased to hear of his appointment.'

Not for the first time, David felt it had been wrong for a reporter to socialize with his subjects. He was being leant on, and it hurt.

The Prime Minister had perfected the technique of terminating a conversation when he wanted to and David found himself standing before an empty space. He looked for Jo and Aaron, so he could unburden his anger.

He couldn't quite locate them just at that moment.

CHAPTER 33

Michael Penn-Morrison braced himself. Having meekly acquiesced in his demotion, he was one of the first to be summoned for an ear-wigging from the new Editor-in-Chief.

'I tell you what's wrong with this station,' Ritchie bawled. 'It's the TOV. Know what that is? It's the tone of voice. Everybody speaks as if they're *frightened* of the news, as if it might bite them on the bum. Too reserved. Like eating cucumber sandwiches. What I want is more *involvement*.'

Penn-Morrison shifted uneasily in his seat, not sure how to respond to this kind of theorizing. 'Are you thinking of anyone in particular, when you say that?' he asked, cautiously.

'You bet I am. Take a look at this – ' Ritchie scrabbled around on his cluttered desk for a videotape of a recent *Nightly news* that he'd stopped in fury when first he played it through. He slotted it in the Sony U-Matic machine, rewound a short length, and then pressed the 'play' button.

'Now look at this broad ...'

Lynne Kimberley's familiar features bounced into focus. She was reading a news item, quite a complicated piece about Latin-American politics, straight to the camera. Unfortunately, it was not one of her better performances.

'About as gripping as the Queen's Christmas Broadcast, isn't it?' Ritchie suggested.

Lynne stumbled several times and said what sounded like 'Grazilian buverment' instead of 'Brazilian government'.

'She's always doing that! Now, in my humble view, the first thing a newscaster's got to be able to do is to *read* the news without falling about like an Abo at breakfast-time.'

'I'm afraid that's always been a problem with Lynne,' Penn-Morrison said soothingly. 'I don't mean the drink. She tends to fudge her words even when she's stone sober.'

'Maybe,' said Ritchie, 'but why the fuck do we have to put up with it?'

'Because she's got this background of being a good reporter and correspondent. Besides, viewers like her.'

'Bloody peculiar, if you ask me. I mean, look at her ...' Ritchie froze the frame. Lynne's face filled the screen like a rabbit caught in a trap. 'Her hair's a sight. Does she cut it herself with the kitchen scissors? You can *hear* the patter of crow's feet up the side of her face. She's a middle-aged trollop.'

'You're being rather hard on her.'

'You think she's a good reporter, huh?'

'Absolutely. You're not thinking of dropping her?'

'I'm not thinking anything – just yet. I'll announce any changes in due course. I certainly think she needs help. A lot of it. She's got to clean up her act. She's not got the image I want for this station.'

Penn-Morrison sighed inwardly. Same old thing. New brooms always had to sweep clean and were witheringly unsentimental about the human furniture they inherited. A good track-record counted for nothing. He feared Lynne was in for a rough ride.

'Is she a women's libber?' Ritchie asked. 'I expect she is. Look at her. Doesn't she give off that smell? That "Wouldn't it be better if we ruled the world?" attitude? Sticks out a mile.'

'I wouldn't say she was a card-carrying feminist,' Penn-Morrison said supportively.

'I gather she had a fight at some feminist bash?'

'Oh, Women in Media. You've heard about that?'

'Yep. You'd be surprised what I pick up, Penn-Morrison. I'm a fast learner.'

It spread through N-TV quickly that Ritchie was planning radical changes. A collective nervousness was established. Some people started wondering whether they should make the break they'd long promised themselves and go and work elsewhere. Or they took comfort in liquid reassurance. Or they spent hours in little groups slagging off the Editor-in-Chief.

'He's a monster,' said Vanessa, concluding a long diatribe. 'I can't imagine why they let him in. He's a major disaster. Got it written all over him.'

'Like everyone else, you're over-reacting' replied David, pulling the bedclothes over his naked haunches. 'He may be a shit, but he's Australian, so what do you expect? And maybe a shit is what N-TV needs just now.'

'I simply must have a ciggy,' Vanessa trilled. 'And you won't have to get hysterical.'

David duly said nothing and watched as Vanessa strode purposefully away from the bed to rummage in her handbag for a packet and lighter. Her bottom was more apple-shaped than pear-shaped, he observed, but it didn't matter now. He had bedded his secretary. It wasn't an experience he was likely to repeat.

Unselfconsciously, Vanessa plopped back beside him and rearranged the pillows so she could sit up and smoke. She balanced a small glass ashtray on her stomach and briskly flicked ash into it with a steady rhythm.

'At least *you're* not in the firing line,' David told her, resuming their post-coital discussion of the N-TV villain. 'He's not going to bother you.'

'No, but he may bother my newscasters, and that rubs off on me, if they get totally twitchy.'

'So we're *your* newscasters, are we?'

'Yes, I take a certain proprietorial interest.'

Vanessa said all this in a very correct, rather bossy tone, which David disliked.

'Oh, is that what you call it?' David imagined she talked like this to all her Hooray menfriends in Fulham. She probably regarded them as labradors who had to be fed, watered and taken for walkies, not out of real affection but because that was what women were supposed to do. Vanessa had certainly made David feel like a labrador when they were making love.

David wondered whether he was losing his touch. His enforced sojourn as a newscaster was the cause of it. If he hadn't been trapped in London, he would have been able to carry on abroad as he always did. As it was, he was having to grab whatever was passing at N-TV, and he didn't usually like to shit on his own doorstep.

'I don't know what Eric will say if he finds out about us. Throw an absolutely ghastly fit, I expect ...'

'Who the hell's Eric?'

'He's my bloke, sort of. He has ideas of marrying me. Wouldn't say no. He's got pots of money, works in the City, and both our families know each other.'

'Oh, good,' said David, quietly sarcastic.

'Anyway, I don't make a habit of being an easy lay,' Vanessa assured him. 'I was simply curious about your reputation. So I thought I'd see how you were.'

'And how was I?' asked David, a touch bemused by the clinically detached way in which Vanessa was assessing their moment of passion in her flat near the Hurlingham Club.

'Quite amusing. But you're all the same. Dip it in, take it out and wipe it. Men are always on such an ego trip with their gigantic thrusts and groans and making your titties sore. What about the poor woman on the receiving end? Honestly, the number of times I've had to go and finish myself off in the bathroom, it's *amazing*.'

David tried not to listen.

'And I don't know,' Vanessa went on, in full flood, 'why men can't enjoy straightforward sex. These days it's all, "Can I tie you up, or can we do it in the bath, or up the back?" What's wrong with the old-fashioned way? It was good enough for our parents otherwise we wouldn't be here.'

'You're a conservative, Van – a true conservative.'

'What if I am? It doesn't stop me wanting to get laid properly.'

'But you came. What more do you want?'

'And so did you, so we're even. Hold on, I'm dribbling on the sheets. Heigh ho, they were due for the laundry anyway.'

David shrank even smaller and wondered which would be worse, now his Rolex showed 11:05 p.m. – staying with Vanessa for the night or going home to Jo. Since the Downing Street party Jo had been in a curiously good mood, though he was still made to feel unwelcome in the marital bed. In the end, there was no choice. Vanessa kicked him out.

'Caroline will be back soon. We have a pact not to clutter up the house with boyfriends, so I'm afraid you'll have to go. She'd only recognize you, anyway, and ask for your autograph.'

So that was that, thought David. At least he'd satisfied his curiosity as to what Vanessa was like in bed. He wasn't altogether pleased with the answer. She threw on a dressing gown to show him to the door. She even allowed him to give her a peck.

'I wouldn't rule out a second go,' she said, rather to David's dismay, as he walked down the path.

He stumbled off to look for a taxi, thinking of excuses to give to Jo.

Beni Patel was charged in June with falsely imprisoning March Stevens. March wasn't called to give evidence but a statement from her was read out in court. Patel was found guilty and given a two-year prison sentence.

The question of sex, with or without consent, was not made an issue and neither March nor Beni made any mention of the matter.

March breathed a sigh of relief that the whole episode was over. As if to draw a line under it, she put her Primrose Hill flat up for sale and looked for an apartment in a more anonymous block nearer to the centre of London.

Vanessa was surprised when March agreed to talk to a journalist from *Woman*. She hadn't been giving interviews since the Patel affair because of the impending trial. Now that was out of the way, she wanted to clear up one or two misconceptions. Patrick Ritchie's approval was sought and readily given. It was arranged that March would see the journalist at N-TV, not on her home ground, and that N-TV's press officer would sit in just to hold her hand. March even insisted that the journalist send in cuttings of her previous work so the press officer could be sure she was acceptable.

Geraldine Botolph duly arrived with notebooks, pencils and portable tape recorder and set about trying to prize some quotable remarks from March. Beni Patel was soon dealt with as March had given some thought to what she would say.

'I bear him no ill-will, I really don't. Of course, it was a shock – an unpleasant ordeal – but I was lucky, I suppose, that he did me no harm. He was a touch confused but it was clear that what he did was the result of misguided admiration rather than anything more sinister.'

'Are you aware,' Geraldine asked, 'of a great mass of people like him out there, waiting to get at you?'

'It *is* a little unsettling. The fact is, though, that you usually only meet the nice ones. Most people are rather shy, or simply friendly.'

'So you get recognized a lot?'

'No, I don't, actually. I don't consider I've got very recognizable features. And women can easily alter their appearance by putting their hair up or down. Some recognize the voice, when I go into shops, but that's different. And some notice my name.'

'I was going to ask you about that. Were you born in March?'

March lowered her eyes. 'No, I was born in December.'

'Ah,' said the journalist. 'Who are your parents? Did they have anything to do with the media?'

'Not at all. My father's a GP in Dartmouth, which is where I come from. And my mother isn't, if you see what I mean. She likes the theatre and used to do amateur dramatics, but really neither of them had anything to do with this mad world I've come into.'

'Do they approve?'

'They weren't terribly keen at first. They thought that television was full of people leading immoral lives and best avoided. I
suppose recent events might have confirmed that view. But,
secretly, I think they're rather proud when their friends tell them
they've seen me on the box.'

Geraldine Botolph maintained a starry-eyed manner in her
interviewing. Her rapt attention seemed to convey that she
thought every word falling from March's lips was a gem and the
girl herself was every bit the glamorous TV star she wanted to
write her up as being.

The press officer sat smiling and put in the odd word or
suggestion, but he didn't have to intervene to protect March from
any tricky questions.

'You're not married, are you, March?'

'No.'

'Never have been? No one tucked away?'

'No skeletons, if that's what you mean ...'

'No one special?'

'Now, that's a leading question, isn't it?' March glanced at the
press officer, but didn't bring him into the conversation. She
could handle this. 'Put it this way. There are various men in my
life – you know, that I see – but no one's talking about marriage.'

'And how d'you get on with the other newscasters? Ben Brock,
for instance?'

'Oh, Ben's a dream. Terribly supportive, terribly professional.
I always feel wonderfully safe when I'm on with him.'

'You've also appeared a lot recently with David Kenway ...'

The journalist at once detected a change in March's demeanour. Her eyes softened for a moment before she blinked.

'Oh, he's a dream, too. Terribly professional. A really wonderful reporter. We all get on terribly well. It's boring, but it's true
...'

Geraldine wasn't taken in by March's bland expressions of
respect for David. The girl clearly felt something more personal
for him. She squiggled a shorthand note to remind herself,
continued to beam at her subject, nodding with concern when
appropriate.

'Do you get any dubious fan-mail?'

'I don't get to see it if I do. No, what's more worrying is the
other type. There are a lot of unhappy people who write in and
expect me to be able to help them. They think I'm Superwoman
or something.'

'Finally, March, dear, what are your ambitions?'

'Just to continue with what I'm doing. I don't want to be some fantastic TV star with managers and agents and things. I'm not like that. I'm quite happy doing what I'm doing and letting the future take care of itself.'

Geraldine beamed her thanks all the way out of the N-TV building. The press officer congratulated March and told her she had handled the interview well. He hadn't noticed how much March had given away of her feelings for David Kenway. But then, that would have surprised March herself.

CHAPTER 34

Ben Brock was taking the day off. In the morning, someone was coming to take away all Natalie's clothes, shoes and accessories. When she died, Ben had gathered them up and thrown them into a box-room, even though this meant bedroom cupboards were left gaping bare. Natalie's dressing table stood unused, accusingly, until Ben dragged it out of the room and hid it in a spare bedroom. Wherever Ben turned, he kept finding reminders of his late wife, though bit by bit, a kind of bachelor scruffiness began to take over the house instead.

Ben reviewed his position endlessly. Every possibility was considered: selling the townhouse, selling Brantholme. The townhouse was ridiculously large now for one person to live in alone, even with the housekeeper and her husband down in the basement. Drew and Heather were barely at home any more. It echoed with the past and Ben felt like a squatter. As bravely as he could, he told himself not to take any hasty action and to sit it out until the future was clearer.

It emerged, though, that he wasn't the only person concerned for his welfare. Within a couple of weeks of Natalie's funeral, Ben received through the post a handwritten letter with 'Personal' firmly written across the top of the envelope. Inside was a note from the man in charge of television news at the BBC. Would Ben agree to have lunch so they could discuss matters of 'mutual interest'?

Ben wondered whether such 'matters' might be his escape route from N-TV. The prospect was appealing, though he knew that any move to the BBC would be for less money. He didn't relish the arm-twisting and haggling needed if he was to make a move. Still, it was nice to be asked, if that was what the lunch betokened, and Ben said he'd be pleased to talk.

Harrison Edgar, the BBC's Controller of News, had booked a table for the two of them at the White Tower. Ben was instantly encouraged by this signal that the BBC was not economizing. He debated whether to take his Roller along, just to let Edgar know what was what, but knew he'd never be able to park it in Charlotte Street at lunchtime, and settled for a taxi instead.

Arriving at the White Tower, Ben asked for Mr Edgar's table and was shown through into the downstairs part of the restaurant, and there, rising and beckoning, was the BBC man.

The only trouble was that Ben's gaze was drawn irresistibly to the man sitting and waiting for *his* guest at the table immediately to the left of Harry Edgar.

Patrick Ritchie was impossible to miss. Ben almost did a 360° turn, not knowing where to put himself, but eventually steadied and brazened it out.

Before clutching Harrison Edgar's still outstretched hand, Ben paused to have a word with Ritchie. He murmured, at his fruitiest, 'Hasn't taken you long to discover the works' canteen, eh?'

Ben debated introducing Ritchie to his opposite number at the BBC, but thought better of it, working on the assumption that Ritchie wouldn't know who the BBC man was.

He sat down beside Edgar, separated from the other table by a glass screen.

'This is an honour, Harry,' Ben said, 'but I fear we may have to keep our voices down if you're going to tell me any BBC gossip.'

'Why's that?'

'Do you know who that is? The man I said hello to?'

'No.'

'Well, he's my new boss! Patrick Ritchie.'

'The Australian?' The BBC man blanched. 'I had no idea.'

'It doesn't matter. By the end of lunch, we'll have all our rivals in here. Sir Alastair usually sits over there. It's like a club.'

Over taramosalata, duck and copious flagons of wine, Harrison Edgar eventually came round to the point of the lunch:

'Ben, we want you. Simple as that. We'll do anything to get you to come over.'

'Defect, you mean?'

'Put it how you like. We're great admirers of you and, indeed, N-TV in general. Under Charles Craig it really put the rest of us to shame. In the old days, as you know, we used to have newsreaders. People like Kenneth Kendall and Richard Baker and Robert Dougall. Excellent chaps in their way, but basically they were radio voices, reading out what was written for them. Then ITN showed what a difference it made if you had news presenters who were people with authority. Whether they'd actually written the bulletins or not didn't matter.

'Then you came along,' the BBC man said ingratiatingly, 'and topped the lot. They say you're like Walter Cronkite used to be in the States and they're right. Without you, I doubt whether N-TV would be where it is today. But we were wondering ...'

Ben was amused by Edgar's use of the 'We were wondering' ploy and, in turn, he was wondering how the BBC, in all its labyrinthine workings, had managed to pull its wonderings together and get to the stage of approaching him.

'That's very flattering,' said Ben, reaching for one of his cigars. 'But I'm very happy where I am, you know. The BBC didn't exactly fall over itself to employ me when I was kicked out of Fleet Street.'

'Ah, well ...'

'What could you let me have that I don't have at N-TV? More money? More editorial control?'

'That's something we could talk about, Ben ... but, can I ask you, what is your contractual position? Is there any daylight in it?'

'Um.' Ben breathed out a small cloud of cigar smoke, aiming courteously past Edgar's left ear. 'Come to think of it, you've chosen rather a good time to come fishing. I'm up for renewal in two months. It's a rolling contract more or less but both sides are supposed to put it through the sheep dip every twelve months.'

Now it was the BBC man's turn to say, 'Um.' Then: 'You don't have any fears over what the newcomer might do?'

'What keyholes have *you* been listening at? No, and frankly, I don't really care. When you've been around as long as I have, you've been buggered about from pillar to post, so there's not much even an Australian can do to embarrass you. I suppose I could be made to front the news wearing a hat with corks round it, but I don't expect so.'

Brandies and coffees were called for. 'Ben, are you telling me we can't dangle anything more enticing before you?'

Ben thought before answering, 'Of course, the BBC *is* the BBC and that's not to be sniffed at but, to be blunt, I just *know* you'd never top what N-TV pays me. Still, you never know, Harrison, in this business. I may have to come crying to you tomorrow if anything changes.'

'Let me say, then, that the door will be as wide open as we can push it.'

As they made to depart, Ben fished in his pocket to find the wherewithal to tip the cloakroom attendant handsomely, then he realized he had neglected to acknowledge Patrick Ritchie on the way out. He went back into the restaurant, thinking it best to do so.

To his considerable amazement he now saw who Ritchie's fellow luncher had been. None other than the Right Honourable Colin Lyon MP, Home Secretary.

Ben wondered whether he oughtn't to say something to them. It might seem rude to ignore Lyon. Then he remembered the awkward circumstances of their last meeting. If he spoke to Lyon, the subject of Natalie was bound to come up, and he didn't want to go through any more of *those* conversations than he had to.

So Ben said goodbye neither to the Home Secretary nor to Patrick Ritchie. Outside, he told Harrison Edgar about the odd twosome and added, 'Ritchie's obviously not slow when it comes to making contacts.'

Harrison Edgar laughed. 'Perhaps I'm lunching the wrong people!'

Ben thanked him, clapped him on the back, and strode off until he was lost in the Oxford Street crowds.

Nothing had been settled.

'Right, g'day to you,' said Patrick Ritchie standing small, stumpy and swaying slightly in front of his chaotic desk. His office was crowded to the door with as many senior N-TV staff as could be spared from their daily duties. Ben and David were the only two newscasters present, as they were in together for the *Nightly News*.

'Thank you all for coming here this arvo. I know it's difficult putting over plans like this when not everyone can gather round at the same time but I hope that you'll pass on what you hear. Where my decisions directly affect individuals who aren't here today, I'll see them personally over the next few days.'

Sounds ominous, thought Jack Somerset.

'What I've decided,' Richie went on, 'and you're at liberty to think I'm up the creek on this, is that I'm not putting all this down on paper. I know that'd be a way of reaching everyone in the organization but' – here he swivelled round, giving a piercing look to all and sundry – 'I'd rather not have it splashed all over *The Guardian*'s Media page before I tell you. This is a leaky joint we all work for and I'm not going to make it any easier for the bastards by writing it all down for them.'

There was laughter and a murmur of what might have been approval at Ritchie's methods.

'What I've tried to do is to retain and strengthen those elements in N-TV's programming which I think are beaut . . . and to torpedo the rest. Generally, I'll tell you, it does a pretty good job, but you can't sit on your arse in this business. What was winning awards three months ago could be what's driving away viewers today. So we have to keep on polishing the kettle . . .

'I'll tell you the worst thing about our output: it's too bloody flabby. The other day I heard a reporter asking a tax inspector if tax wasn't a "personal" problem. Well, of course, it's a bloody "personal" problem. What else could it be? I want grittier questions, grittier reporting.'

Most of Ritchie's audience spent the next few moments trying to remember which twit of a reporter had asked the question in question.

'The other side to our treatment is that it's too grey for my taste. Too earnest. I want to see a damn sight more excitement and colour. "Info-tainment" is what they call it in the States. And I want to expand much more into the area of people-reporting, entertainment, and that whole scene. This is an exciting and dangerous world we live in. I want N-TV to reflect that.'

More than one person in the room reflected quietly to himself that it was OK for newsgatherers to regard it as an exciting and dangerous world, provided it wasn't happening to them . . .

'Above all, I want everyone to pitch in a bit more,' Ritchie continued. 'It's all too *hands-off* at the moment. I want to see, for example, newscasters getting about more.'

Ben looked impassive but groaned inwardly at the inevitability of the proposal.

'I don't think there should be a division between newscasters and reporters. Everyone should be capable of doing the other man's job. And, more than that, they should actually *do* it.'

David Kenway took this calmly – after all, he had just about survived the transition from war-scarred veteran to studio smoothy, so it would be no skin off his fine nose if the philosophy became general. But it did occur to him to wonder how March Stevens, to think of the most notorious example, would look in combat gear.

The meeting broke up after half an hour. It sounded dynamic coming from Ritchie, garnished with Australianisms, but at bottom no one was quite sure how they were to bring about the changes he was proposing. How did you add grit, anyway?

The only member of staff privileged to be told more precise details of Ritchie's plans was Adam Ravenscroft, his quietly-spoken deputy in the shiny blue suit. In fact, he was now the only person at N-TV in whom Ritchie confided at all.

'That Ben Brock, he's treading water. I don't care if his wife has just croaked. That's nothing to do with me. It's like having bloody Royalty having him on the payroll. I feel I've to tug my forelock when I meet him. Do you know I saw him dining at the White Tower with some BBC-wallah. At least that's who I'm told it was. I was having lunch with Colin Lyon – you know, the Home Secretary ...'

'Yes, I know,' said Ravenscroft, a little drily.

'And he told me. Edgar Harrison or somebody.'

'Harrison Edgar.'

'Yer. Maybe. Head of BBC News or some such. Perhaps old Ben is thinking of moving over?'

'I very much doubt whether the BBC could afford him. He gets two-two-five grand from us, which is a helluva lot by anybody's standards.'

'Anyway, that's him. David Kenway has a lot going for him. I'm warming to him. He seems real, though he needs to go to TV school. Has some irritating mannerisms. March Stevens – well, I don't know what we're going to do with her. There's a limit to the usefulness of the sheila-factor, in my opinion. Even if half the audience sits there wanting to give her one, her value is debatable. If you can prove to me that our ratings would fall if she got permanently kidnapped, I'd believe yer. As it is, I think we've really got to get her off her sweet little bum and doing some reporting. I don't like news being presented by actresses.'

'But she's not an actress.'

'She's a body. Same thing. And, as for Lynne Kimberley, she's a walking disaster area. She'll be the first to go.'

'You can't sack everyone and start from scratch, you know.'

'That, mate, is precisely what I intend to do. How else can I give this place some balls?'

CHAPTER 35

Lynne remained ignorant of the force moving against her. She was not on N-TV screens that week, nor had she been able to attend Patrick Ritchie's meeting, or listen to the rumours that began to circulate after it. And why? Because she and Nikki Brennan had teamed up and were batting down to Italy by car for a short holiday together.

As Lynne was prevented from driving, she'd talked Nikki into driving her old fire engine for her.

'I'm glad to get out of England for a while,' Lynne said, as they drove southwards from Calais. 'I feel like forgetting the last few months. It's been hellish. The atmosphere at N-TV's been pretty poisonous.'

'Know what you mean,' said Nikki, as she forced the red BMW on, faster and faster.

'There's a word for a period like the one we've just been through.'

'Cathartic ... um, transitional ... bloody awful?'

'Bloody awful, that'll do. And I don't expect it'll get any better with that evil little Aussie sticking his nose into everything.'

'Oh, don't say that, Lynne. You don't *know* that he's going to be that bad. A change of boss is always difficult.'

'Yes, but why's it got to coincide with my bloody menopausal behaviour? Not good timing. But do stop me, if I go moaning on.'

'All girls together!'

'In a manner of speaking. And why not? There's a lot to be said for consigning men to the back burner once in a while.'

They spent their first night en route at the Grand Hôtel de L'Europe inside the old walled town of Langres. It was not as grand as it sounded but Lynne, for one, was deliriously happy after she'd mopped up delicious *quenelles* dripping in prawn sauce and divine chicken in tarragon.

Next morning they awoke as the sun crept through half-open shutters. They drove across the Franche Comté, glistening in the morning dew, ravishing in its June foliage. Lynne absorbed a timelessness from the villages that made any preoccupation with work seem very footling indeed.

*   *   *

After crossing the Swiss border and skirting Lake Geneva, Lynne and Nikki took the Mont Blanc road tunnel through the Alps into northern Italy. They hammered down the *autostrada* until the towers, domes and cypress trees of Tuscany began to fill the landscape. They picked their way through Florence and then drove up the hill to Fiesole. They were staying, largely at Lynne's expense, at the Villa San Michele, a Renaissance villa which was originally a Franciscan monastery, with a façade said to have been designed by Michelangelo. It was now a truly grand hotel, filled with flowers.

Nikki toyed with her campari and soda and looked out over Florence from the terrace of the hotel as the evening light faded. She had just told Lynne of her fling with David Kenway.

'Oh, Nikki, you poor fool. I'd no idea. I must have been going round with my eyes shut not to have noticed anything. Wrapped up in my own little problems.'

'I'm not surprised you didn't notice. It was only a cough and a spit. Over in no time at all.'

Lynne drank deep of her very dry martini. 'Fancy you falling for him, though,' she said. 'He's a Casanova of the first water. It stands out a mile.'

'Well,' smiled Nikki ruefully. 'Not quite a mile, but near enough.'

Lynne ignored her innuendo. 'So he loved you and left you?'

'Yes, after the show one night. Next day he cut me dead. How do people get to be like that? It's so ... sort of obvious, isn't it?'

'He's the one with the problem, darling. I sometimes wonder if he doesn't look upon sex like a scoop. He's into all that, isn't he? Getting the big story, screwing whatever takes his fancy. As soon as he's got it, he loses interest.'

'So I'm yesterday's newspaper? Only fit for wrapping fish and chips?'

'Well, though there's nothing deader than yesterday's papers, they do become interesting again in time. Perhaps he'll be back.'

'If he likes archaeology.'

'Poor Nikki. He's an A-Number-One bastard. I told his wife so, and she sloshed me.'

'You mean she hit you because you were rude about David?'

'Yes, you bet. I gently alluded to the fact that he's always poking about. Hit a raw nerve I did. But, I mean, why should she feign ignorance when all the world knows? I'm too honest, that's my trouble. I can't stand bullshit. It was at a Women in Media dinner.'

'*Quel* scene!' exclaimed Nikki. 'I heard she threw a TV set at David. In fact, *he* told me. But I didn't know this ...'

'Oh, yes. Jo Lake Kenway is an emotional spasm just waiting to happen. I don't know why they stick together.

'Well, he's very attractive, you know ...'

'But everyone else's marriage is always a mystery, like that Swiss proverb, "Marriage is a covered dish".'

Nikki felt nicely warm having revealed her secret to Lynne. She would have to begin getting over it soon.

'Come on,' said Lynne, briskly. 'Time to put our nosebags on. After all that driving today you must be whacked. I just sat there while you did all the work, and *I'm* exhausted. Early night tonight.'

If David's ears were burning, it didn't show, as he was pre-occupied with a minor discomfort of a different sort.

March, ever more confident since her ordeal in the Spring, had decided to set her cap at him. Married David might be, but that didn't seem to affect the way he carried on, so what was to stop her pursuing him? She had to find out what he was really like.

'David,' she approached him after they'd fronted the *Nightly News*, 'fancy coming home for a nightcap?'

It was as blatant an invitation as any, but David's instinctive reaction was evasive. He liked to make the first move and he'd always considered March out of bounds.

'Oh,' he said, nonplussed. 'You mean tonight?'

'Yes. Only if you've got nothing else on.' She could hear herself back-tracking.

'Well, all right, yes. I've forgotten where you live now. Haven't you moved?'

'Yes, I've got a new apartment in Bayswater. Overlooking Hyde Park. Shall we share the driver?'

'Mmm. OK. Whatever you like.'

David maintained his air of bemused curiosity all the way back to March's flat. Every detail of their departure together had been noted by people standing around in the N-TV foyer.

'You moved out of your old flat after that, um, business with young Mr Patel?' David asked, once he'd been ushered into March's palatial new home.

'Yes. I loved my old flat and its little garden, but after what happened I couldn't go back to it. Not once the Press knew where I lived. This block is nicely anonymous. The security people at the door virtually frisk anyone who calls. And in the daytime it's got a ravishing view over the trees. It's lovely. Let me fix you a drink. Something bubbly?'

'Yes, OK. Perrier'll do.'

'Oh, come on! I've got a bottle of Lanson Black Label sent by a fan. You open it for me. I'll just slip out of these clothes. They're terribly uncomfortable.'

David thought March's behaviour was peculiar to say the least. He went into the small kitchen and found two champagne glasses already waiting on a tray. It appeared tidy to the point of obsession. What sort of girl *was* March to live like this? David preferred a rawer existence. He didn't like his women squeaky-clean and pomaded. He didn't like homes to be squeaky-clean and smelling of air-freshener either. What was she up to?

Back in the sitting room, he fussed with the ice-bucket but held back from removing the cork until March re-appeared from her bedroom.

March was a-flutter. She'd got David where she wanted him, with the minimum of effort. She was hot with anticipation.

She slipped out of the yellow blazer and pleated skirt she'd worn all day in the office, and slipped into slacks and a kimono jacket with a brilliant red dragon on the back of it. She put on a pair of gold slippers and swathed herself in Opium.

The effect wasn't lost on David. He was stunned when she appeared before him, oozing availability, but he was equally put off by it. The more a woman pushed herself at him, the less he wanted her. Besides, March was too middle-class, too smooth. He liked his women less polished, less acquiescent at first.

'Aren't you going to pop the cork?' March asked him, settling down on the sofa where David couldn't escape joining her.

He was still torn. March was eminently desirable. She looked every bit as radiant as she did on TV, but he wasn't sure he actually wanted her.

In the end, he couldn't resist.

'Come on, through here,' she said. 'Let's do it properly.' And she led him towards a Queen-sized bed that occupied much of her room. There were mirrors in the headboard. What was she thinking of? David was quietly appalled.

March had proved something to herself. She had also confirmed what it was that drew women to David. She was not disappointed.

Even when they'd finished, David remained slightly detached from March's wiles, and spent the night in splendid discomfort while she slept blissfully at his side.

Lynne was walking on air during most of her Tuscan tour with Nikki. They sat in the sun, drank, ate, read paperback thrillers, and went for little drives to Sienna, Pisa, Lucca, and the surrounding countryside.

They adored San Gimignano of the Fine Towers, a fourteenth-century town with just over a dozen tall towers left out of the original seventy-two – a medieval Manhattan in miniature.

And they did wonderful things, like eating *porcini* to the sound of tolling bells.

And they laughed a lot. Lynne managed to throw off some of the depression which she'd accumulated in recent months and felt so light-hearted she wondered whether she could be bothered to return to the grind at N-TV. Nikki proved a delightful companion and never a cross word marred a moment of their time together.

One night they came down from the bedroom where they slept in separate, canopied beds, in order to have the ritual 'camp and sod' before dinner in the Villa San Michele's restaurant. They'd decided to dress up for the occasion. Hardly had they taken a sip when into the long tapestry-covered room came two men.

Lynne immediately recognized one of them and leapt up to greet him.

'Paul,' she cried. 'What a surprise!'

'Oh, hello, Lynne' he answered, a touch hesitantly. 'Staying here, are you?'

'Yes.'

'We've just come up for dinner. We're down at the Excelsior.'

'Join us for a little *aperitivo*,' said Lynne. 'You know Nikki, of course ...'

Paul Whitehall, as one of N-TV's studio directors, didn't really *know* Nikki but he'd seen her many times across a crowded newsroom – and, indeed, tagging along with David Kenway.

His eyes widened, as if intrigued at the thought of Lynne and Nikki holidaying together.

'And this is my friend Trevor,' Paul said, introducing a pretty youth several years younger than himself.

'Hello, Trevor,' Lynne greeted him boldly, equally intrigued at the thought of Paul cruising round Europe with his boyfriend. 'I'd no idea we were all painting Italy red at the same time. What a coincidence.'

The two couples ate separately in the dining room and then joined up again for coffee in the refectory. There was a good deal of N-TV gossip which meant little to young Trevor. He sat and looked out of place, turning to Paul for reassurance from time to time.

The older man touched him frequently, whispered in his ear and behaved so that no one could be in any doubt they were lovers. Paul wasn't shriekingly gay and neither was Trevor, but lookers-on could tell how they took their pleasures.

Lynne tried to draw Trevor into the conversation, and failed. So she had to resort to asking him what he did for a living, if that wasn't too bold a question.

'I'm a dresser at Drury Lane.'

'The theatre, you mean?'

'Yes.'

Lynne said that must be very interesting, but somehow the topic proved difficult to sustain. She went back to rubbishing Patrick Ritchie, David Kenway, David Kenway's wife, and all the customary targets.

It was a jolly encounter and Lynne went to bed positively clucking with the pleasure of it.

'Fancy Paul queening it round Italy with little Trev! He's usually so discreet back home. Thought he wouldn't be spotted out here, I expect. Obviously, one had thought he was probably *that way*, but one didn't have the proof, so to speak.'

'I'd never really thought about it,' said Nikki, truthfully. 'I thought he was a bit camp, but it's so hard to tell, really. He could've just come from up North. Often Northern and camp sound the same, have you noticed?'

Lynne wondered how Paul would take to having his secret revealed. She allowed herself to ponder what Paul would be making of herself and Nikki.

Appearances could be so deceptive.

CHAPTER 36

Still somewhat discomfited by March's seduction, the next day David went through a similar experience, in a more professional sphere. What was more, again his unease was provoked by an extremely attractive woman who might have been expected to excite him.

Charlotte Cordova was very much the Hollywood actress of the moment. *Time* magazine said so. She was of mixed English and Italian-American blood and had been brought up in France and Germany. With such a background her natural habitat might well have been an airport transit lounge. But no. She flourished in international cinema and by the age of twenty-five had notched up five substantial film roles: in *Hell Bender* and *Forest of the Night*, both thrillers; in the sex comedies *Shrug* and *A Pleasure Unemployed*; and earlier in the year she'd been nominated for an Academy Award for her portrayal of an amnesiac in *Tomorrow Can Wait*.

She had now, prematurely perhaps, written her autobiography, *Bright Star*, which was due out in Britain imminently. To the amazement of almost everyone but herself, the book was extraordinarily frank and perceptive about what it was like to be an actress. No one had written about the making of films from the inside like this before, certainly not an actress at the peak of her fame. She hadn't even been helped by a ghost-writer.

Charlotte's British publishers, Acorn, an old-established firm, were nearly bankrupting themselves flying her over for a promotional blitz. She would be trotted around the chat-show circuit on television and radio. She would talk about herself until she was hoarse and there was no reason to suppose she would ever get bored with the task.

Her publicity manager for all this was to be a pleasant but rather soft young man called Robert Fleming. He had the dark hair and ruddy complexion of the classic Scot, tempered by his upbringing in a minor English public school.

Robert was neither good nor bad at his job, though he tended to be more at home promoting the memoirs of elderly politicians.

And he was an absolute whizz at charming the pants off million-aires who'd *paid* to have their memoirs published, even if no one actually bought a copy. Robert buttered up his journalist friends to come and interview the authors, though didn't expect the interviews to materialize in the papers.

He'd sent advance warning of the Cordova blitz to all the customary outlets and, not hoping for very much, had also sent the kit containing her photograph, one or two steamy extracts from the book, and a hard-sell sheet of blurb to the 'News Editor, N-TV'. Robert knew that TV news was rarely interested in a book unless it had won a prize or already stirred up controversy.

What he hadn't reckoned with was Patrick Ritchie taking a personal look through the mass of promotional material arriving at N-TV that week. Most of it normally would have gone straight into the wastepaper basket, but Ritchie hoped he would discover what was being rejected by N-TV that might give its programmes the flavour they needed.

'I say, Alison, dearie, why don't we get David to interview this Cordova bint for tonight's Big News? She's quite a character by all accounts.'

Liz Hastings, swallowing Ritchie's habitual mistake with her name, took a deep breath and told her new boss: 'But it's not exactly *newsy*, is it?'

'Now, don't come the raw prawn with me, dearie. I was a TV producer while you were still in diapers. Of course, I know it's not newsy,' Ritchie went on. 'Not newsy like the Third World Wanking Conferences you're always stuffing into the *Nightly*. Or the economics of East European yoghourt factories. But the story's got colour, glamour, sex and balls, saving the lady's better-known qualities. The trouble with this place is you people can always find reasons why *not* to do items. But you can never find the ones we *ought* to be doing. Now, I like my news to have tits on and Charlotte Cordova's certainly got those.'

Liz Hastings steamed quietly under her Chairman Mao jacket and thought of all the things she should say.

'Can we discuss it at the afternoon meeting?' she suggested cannily, hoping that the weight of opinion from her colleagues would help overturn Ritchie's idea.

'What'd be the point of that? If you're going to have the sheila in tonight's show you've got to move your ass and get it arranged before this afternoon's bloody meeting, now haven't you?'

'I don't know whether David would want to do it ...' Liz countered without much conviction, her resistance crumbling.

'Why shouldn't he? Just because he likes getting shot at in dug-outs and hard-nosing the politicos, that doesn't prevent him having a tête-à-tête with a bit of crackling, does it? If what I hear about our Mr Kenway is correct, he'll be poking his mike over the sex-pot's tits before you've got off your arse and fixed him with a camera crew.'

'But it's not the kind of thing we've ever put in the Big News before. We don't plug books. We're not into soft-toy journalism. We wouldn't have picked up all those awards if ...'

'Now, don't give me that, Alison,' Ritchie shouted back, fixing Liz with his glare and starting to go his usual beetroot colour. 'Whatever happened before I arrived at this place is yesterday's cold potatoes. Don't ever wave your bleeding awards at me, my girl. Just get off your arse and stick your fingers in the phon-io and get some action. I want to see that woman on the show tonight. Without fail. And that's an order.'

'And what if I say no?' Liz reddened, sounding tearful.

'Look, darling, what *is* the matter with you? Is it your time of the month, or what?

Liz did then burst into tears and ran off to the loo. Ritchie looked about him, amazed but unrepentant. Turning to one of the assistant producers, he barked: 'You heard what that was all about. Fix it.' Then he stalked back to his office, slamming the door. Sharon looked up, pulled a face, and went back to reading her *Cosmopolitan*.

David Kenway hated the idea when, having dried her tears, Liz finally tracked him down at March's flat – of all places – and asked him to be a dear and go straight to the Savoy at 11:30 a.m. sharp.

'But I haven't even read the book,' he complained. 'And I purposely avoided the extracts in *The Sunday Times*. What am I being put on this showbiz stuff for, anyway? Can't someone else do it?'

Liz described the scene she'd had with Patrick Ritchie. She said she was worried about the fall-out if it grew into a full-scale incident.

'Why won't she come in and do it live?' David asked. 'What are we trotting after her for?'

'She can't manage it. She's already taping a show at LWT this evening.'

'So we'll just be one among the many. No exclusives?'

'Perhaps you'd like to tell Ritchie that ...'

'Um. Yes. Well ... so we have to join the queue of hacks down at the Savoy? Bloody 'ell. Has it really come to this, Liz?'

Liz could think of no adequate answer. She was still wondering what on earth David was doing in March's flat at ten o'clock in the morning.

Matters were no better when David arrived at the Savoy and met up with the crew from N-TV. Robert Fleming came down and said that Miss Cordova was running an hour behind with her interviews. 'But she's giving good value for money, I'm told.'

'For heaven's sake,' cried David, raising his eyes heavenwards, 'I've got a programme to do tonight, you know. I'd rather not hang around here all day.'

'Yes, I'm very sorry. I understand.'

'I'll be in the bar. Call me when Her Madge deigns to grant us an audience.'

By the time David was ushered into the presence he was almost ready to bite the expensive flock wallpaper. It was half-past one, he'd been kept waiting all morning, and he was desperately hungry.

As for Charlotte Cordova, David felt not the slightest shimmer of excitement at shaking her by the hand. She might look blessed by the camera on the screen but she was awfully small when you met her in the flesh. She'd probably given ninety-nine interviews before this one and David found it hard to get her to answer his questions freshly.

Worst of all, it was apparent that Charlotte Cordova had no idea who David was or what his standing was in British television.

He took against her in a big way.

To begin with, David asked if she'd really written the book herself. She smiled in what might have been a forgiving way, or simply in relief at being bowled a question she could go into on automatic pilot. When she had given her by now well-rehearsed answer, David moved on to his second question, about the identity of a well-known politician with whom, in the book, she claimed to have made love one night on the steps of the Lincoln Memorial.

But Nosmo King, the cameraman, chose that very moment

to announce a technical fault. They had to call a halt, whether David liked it or not.

'Sorry about that,' said Nosmo a moment later. 'It was the tape, I'm afraid. Could I ask you to start again, David?'

'Is that all right, Charlotte? We'll start again from the top. I'll ask you the first question again.'

'No, it's not all right,' the actress shot back with more than a hint of frost. 'I couldn't possibly answer a question for a second time.'

David froze, too, and wondered just how rude he could afford to be. Who the hell did she think she bloody well was? Greta-fucking-Garbo? 'You're just a two-bit piece of ass who happens to have hit the big time and you'll be back humping on the casting couch in a couple of years if you carry on like this, you stuck-up little bitch.'

None of this did David actually say, though it may well have shown on his face.

The publicity man, his mouth dry and his stomach-ulcer throbbing, curled up in squirms of embarrassment and wished he were a thousand miles away.

When Patrick Ritchie saw the interview on the *Nightly News* he was ecstatic. The edginess in the relationship between David Kenway and Charlotte Cordova, the clash of two considerable egos, was palpable and David had made a news interview out of showbiz slush.

The altercations over the re-take had been kept in.

'I thought you were supposed to be a professional,' David was heard saying. 'Why can't you repeat the question? It's just like repeating your lines, for God's sake. You do that every day in films. And who's doing who a favour here? We're plugging your bloody book!'

Charlotte Cordova was seen gradually to awaken from her jet-lagged, mid-Atlantic torpor and realize she wasn't being given an easy ride on this TV show.

'Fantastic!' Ritchie leapt from his executive chair when he saw it. He even apologized to Liz Hastings for his behaviour earlier in the day – apologized with the ease of a man who had been vindicated.

'Sexual chemistry,' he said, jabbing Liz in the shoulder, as though he'd just invented the phrase. 'Pure sexual chemistry. Never seen anything like it. That's what we want to have more of, and don't you forget it.'

Liz was past caring, having been much more concerned with the lead story of the day, an earthquake in Peru. But Ritchie didn't seem terribly interested in that.

'And do you know,' he went on, addressing all within earshot, 'do you know what David did when she refused to do the re-take? He just waited until the end of the interview, rephrased it so she wouldn't recognize it, then put it again! The silly cow then answered without a murmur. Magic!'

David himself, by this stage, was beyond comment.

CHAPTER 37

Jo Lake Kenway had quite forgotten what it was like to be in love – that first heady obsession with David when they couldn't stop touching each other, the desolation when they were apart, the heartache every moment of the day, the complete indifference to every other area of life.

Back in 1975 it had seemed right to get married in those circumstances. David had proposed to Jo in bed. He didn't actually 'ask' her, he finished a paragraph with the words, 'Well, in that case we'll get married then,' and afterwards he could never quite recall the justification which had preceded the statement.

Then, after they were married, and however wobbly their relationship had been most of the time, Jo thought she'd known another type of 'love' – the love that's based on dependency, sharing, simply existing together with another person. Then the second child came along and Jo was locked into the system called 'marriage'. The question of whether or not there was love in it was hardly worth examining. Especially if it meant she might discover there wasn't.

So Jo was taken unawares when, following the sudden rush of positive proof of David's numerous infidelities, which until then she'd been able to half-dismiss as a sort of fantasy, she found herself in love again.

The object of her love was Aaron Rochester and she was astonished at herself for it. Perhaps her husband's little flings had precipitated the fall, but she had always thought she'd be above behaving in such a tit-for-tat fashion.

Besides, Aaron was not exactly the most obvious choice for a lover. He was a fellow-countryman and that counted for a lot; but Aaron was a bachelor of thirty-seven and Jo couldn't help feeling there must be something wrong with anyone who survived to that age without having ever been married.

Their encounter at the Prime Minister's reception occurred at just the right psychological moment for Jo. She was a new woman as a result. The day after, she wondered if it had been just a dream, a moment of intense excitement and release, a one-off, and resolved that it wouldn't be. She desired more than anything to see Aaron again.

213

Jo knew he was based in London but, like David, he was more often than not on the road, abroad. Beyond that she knew next to nothing about him. But she knew that, if she was to see him again, she would have to enter the clandestine world of the affair, of which she knew nothing. There could be no lunching openly in London restaurants, no weekends away. It would have to be conducted with the utmost circumspection, not in the casually open way David seemed to employ for his liaisons.

She devoted herself entirely to plotting how to bring about another meeting. She rang ABC News in Curzon Street. No, he wasn't available, he was in a meeting. Jo didn't leave her number in case he rang back at an awkward time. She kept on ringing until she spoke to him in person.

'Oh, hi, Jo,' Aaron said. Jo's heart sank. He sounded so matter-of-fact. Had he forgotten already? Was she being a bore, calling him like this?

She could imagine him reaching for his stoagy as a prop. 'I meant to ring you,' he replied. 'But I, you know, kinda hesitated ...'

Jo's spirits picked up. So he was interested after all.

'I thought we could have lunch,' she blurted out, nervousness catching in her voice.

'Yep ...' There was a pause. 'That would be nice, but ...'

Jo sagged again.

'... but, I can't think where ...'

'Anywhere ...'

'Hold on, hold on. You're in Islington, right? And I'm in Curzon Street. What's half-way?'

'The Zoo.'

'Well, that's no good. Have to think of some place else. Tell you what, have you heard of the Montcalm? It's a hotel just by Marble Arch. It's, ah, very discreet. Tomorrow?'

'Anything ... but no one must see us.'

'They won't. The Montcalm's a ... different sort of world.'

When Jo hung up, she was shaking with excitement. Making the arrangements for an illicit affair gave her almost more of a *frisson* than she might expect from sex itself. She hadn't felt anything like it for years. The rest of the day and most of the night was spent worrying about what she would wear and how she would conceal any transformation from David.

He had returned late from N-TV after an exasperating day, in which the Charlotte Cordova interview was only a small part. He gave Jo a ritual hug and kiss before rolling over and falling asleep. Jo didn't mind. She wanted to save herself for Aaron the next day, though the ache was hard to bear.

When the time came, with one boy at school and the other in the nanny's charge, Jo bathed for a second time that morning, tipping a bottle of fragrance into the water as she did so. She tried on five different sets of clothes before rejecting them all and settling for a red cotton top with a white cotton skirt and a tan belt. A string of pearls, pearl earrings, and a gold wrist-watch, a present from David, completed the get-up. She toyed with her gold wedding ring (from Tiffany's) and wore the Osiris perfume that seemed like a talisman.

Eventually she set off, telling Nanny Jo she was going to shop in the West End.

At the Montcalm, she sat as discreetly as she could amid the plants in the reception area, crossing and re-crossing her legs, trying to be inconspicuous. She tried not to burst as the minutes ticked by.

Aaron was ten minutes late, which wasn't very much but every second of it was cruel to Jo. She mumbled a greeting, hardly able to look at him.

'Rochester,' Aaron announced rather more loudly than Jo would have liked to the reception manager.

'Yes, Mr Rochester. Come this way, please.'

To Jo's surprise, they were taken not to some discreet table behind a pillar in the restaurant, but upstairs.

They were shown into a room decorated in pastels. Light filtered through a large white gauzed window. The ceiling was made to look like that of a tent. Lunch for two was set out already, two bottles of Krug already on the chill.

As soon as the manager had slid away, Jo just stood there and said, 'Wow . . .!' She registered that there was no bed in sight. No bathroom either.

'Aaron, you shouldn't have done this . . .'

'It's the only way we can be alone together, without anyone seeing.'

They still hadn't touched when they fell to eating. Aaron's appetite didn't seem impaired by his lust, even if the lunch mostly consisted of salad and nuts. But he polished off the *paté de foie gras* and the *antipasto misto* in large helpings. He filled Jo with as much champagne as he could, but she couldn't quaff the way he did. A pity, he thought, because it was such a fine Krug, so fine he drank it like water.

'The Cabinet Room in Downing Street was all very well,' Aaron said, enjoying himself. 'But there are *limits* to what a guy can get up to in there.'

Jo smiled at the memory.

'The Beatles smoked joints in the john at Buckingham Palace, you know. I think we beat that, don't you?'

Jo smiled again.

'Who stays at this hotel?' she asked. 'I'd never heard of it.'

'Mick Jagger, I think, used to. Entertainers. Show biz. Charles Aznavour.'

'Very select.'

'And there used to be a lot of Arabs. Hence the decorations. They always seemed to leave the door ajar. You'd go past and see them sitting here with row upon row of wives, having a feast. Sheep's eyes, I expect.'

'Have you been coming here for long?' Jo sounded mournful at the implications of her question.

'I used to stay here until I took a small duplex near Harrods.'

'So you've got an apartment in London?'

'Oh, yes.'

Aaron was taking his time, so – emboldened by the Krug – Jo wiped her lips on the napkin, went over and laid her head in his lap.

He unbuttoned Jo's red top and started kneading her breasts. Then he shifted his weight so that his tongue could reach down and lick and suck her dun-coloured nipples. Jo groaned deeply. Aaron nuzzled her with his moustache. Jo's nipples were hyper-sensitive and she came quietly, almost unnoticeably, under Aaron's persistent attentions.

To find the bedroom, they had to walk up a white spiral iron staircase to the floor above. The bed filled the room completely. It had already been turned down for them, revealing crisp white linen with monograms on the pillowslip.

Both finally sated, they lay quietly together and they talked some more.

'I don't feel as much of a shit as I should, really,' Aaron admitted.

'What's that supposed to mean?' asked Jo.

'David and I are meant to be all buddy-buddy. This is not in the script.'

'I shouldn't bother about it, if I were you. This is separate. This is just for us. Please don't mention him.'

'OK. But what would he say if he knew?'

'I think he'd go through the roof. You know – it's OK for him to fool around, but not me. The usual.'

'Well, let's be careful,' Aaron cautioned. 'Let's be very careful.'

He was very keen they should finish the second bottle of Krug. Which he did.

Jo felt herself well and truly laid. So much so that she took a taxi all the way back to Islington, though she made it stop round the corner from the house so that Nanny Jo wouldn't see it.

Nanny Jo *did* notice that her employer hadn't brought any shopping bags back with her, but that was the least of the oddities she encountered daily in the Kenway household. She also noticed her employer smiling more often, which was a breakthrough. Even David noticed a difference and favoured Jo with his lovemaking that night. He was agreeably surprised at her enthusiastic response, but fell asleep afterwards ignorant of the reason.

CHAPTER 38

David's interview with Charlotte Cordova, however enthralling it might have been to the Editor-in-Chief, came to be looked upon as a watershed of another sort in Patrick Ritchie's relations with the team on the N-TV *Nightly News.*

Ben, who had been presenting the *Nightly News* with David on the evening in question, first of all thought that David was making too much fuss, letting his pride get the better of him. But as the days went by and provided further evidence of the direction in which Ritchie was pushing N-TV, Ben had second thoughts.

He began to see David as a rival, a potential threat to his own pre-eminence on the network. Nowadays, David was the one who got the breaks. No one asked Ben to interview actresses or do quirky little features about beer-drinking chimpanzees or skate-boarding parrots. He almost wished they did. From being a revered figurehead in the organization under Sir Charles's editorship, Ben came to feel ever more an isolated anachronism.

As always, the only person to keep a motherly eye on the newscasters was Vanessa Sinclair.

'How are you getting on with the Führer?' she asked Ben, when she persuaded him into her office to deal with his mail.

'You mean P. Ritchie?'

'Yes.'

'Well, I never thought Charlie Craig's editorship would look like the Golden Age so soon, but it's beginning to, isn't it?'

'Who on earth appointed him? Why do they do these things?'

'That's the Board for you. Worthy but ineffective. I'm sure they were right to bring in an outsider, but I wonder whether they realized just what he'd do?'

'Is it just that he's a shit?' asked Vanessa pointedly. 'Or is it that he's an *Australian* shit?'

Ben laughed loudly and at once seemed more cheerful than he had done for weeks.

'You're right, of course. Australia does seem to breed them. Especially in the media. They come over here and think we're a boring load of old fuddy-duddies and only they know best.'

'He seems to be upsetting a lot of people. It's not a happy ship any more.'

'That's true, Vanessa. But that's not everything, you know. The happiest ships aren't always the best, or the most productive. We shall see ...'

'Patrick, could I have a word?'

With uncharacteristic haste, Ben had gone straight from chatting with Vanessa to the Editor-in-Chief's office.

'Sure, sure. Come on in. Take a pew. Make yourself at home,' said Ritchie, gesturing to the seating area. 'What can I do for you, Ben?' He sounded unusually relaxed and in a good mood.

'Well, Patrick, I thought I'd wait until you'd had time to settle in before broaching the question. Didn't want to make things difficult for you in the early weeks. But, as you may have gathered, a change of Editors hasn't been the only event in our lives over the past few months.'

'Too right. What is it, Ben?' said Ritchie, a trifle suspiciously.

'As you know, I lost my wife recently. I thought that throwing myself back into work would help keep my mind off things, but I'm afraid it hasn't. I feel listless. Can't work up much enthusiasm for the daily grind. That sort of feeling.'

'Yeh, I've noticed you've been a bit off-form,' said Ritchie, brutally.

Ben went on. 'Anyway, I think what I need is a change of scene. Do some different types of programme. Travel.'

'You mean the BBC have made you an offer you can't refuse?'

'The lunch at the White Tower? They made me an offer of sorts, it's true, but I couldn't accept. No, I just want to get out of television news altogether for a while. Would you let me have a sabbatical?'

Without a second's hesitation, Ritchie replied: 'I see no reason why not.'

Then Ritchie jumped up from his desk, shot over and shook Ben by the hand, and cried, 'Glad to oblige. All the best.'

For all the world it was as though he was saying goodbye to Ben forever.

Half a minute later, in the corridor outside, Ben couldn't decide if he'd been dignified or made a fool of. He would have been even more worried had he been able to hear the conversation which took place shortly afterwards between Ritchie and Adam Ravenscroft.

'Now, here's a funny thing,' Ritchie burbled. 'Everything's

219

working out nicely. Old Ben Brock says he wants out for a while so he can do some non-news work elsewhere. Says it's because he feels low after his wife's death.'

'He'll be hard to replace.'

'Nah. Two a penny, people like him. And if he likes it, appearing on quiz shows or whatever he wants to do, I wouldn't care two arsefulls of shit if he stayed out there. We can manage without him. No one's irreplaceable in this business.'

'I'm not so sure about that,' said Adam, uneasily. 'Take care, Pat.'

'Don't worry 'bout me, pal. I know what I'm doing.'

CHAPTER 39

Ritchie next devoted some thought to March. He didn't know what to make of her.

'Is she just the English-rose type,' he asked Adam, 'or has she got iron knickers? Perhaps there's nothing underneath. Perhaps she reads the news with one foot on the floor, if you know what I mean.'

'Hard to tell. I don't know myself. She looks good, she sounds good. That's why Sir Charles took her on, if you'll pardon my mentioning him. She can certainly read the news. They love her out there in viewerland.'

'But why doesn't she ever do any reporting?'

'She's done odds and ends. Mostly women's stuff. Fashion, education, pop stars, Royalty, that sort of thing. But I don't think she *sees* herself as a reporter.'

'That's not what I've heard. I've seen interviews where she's gone on about having been a reporter on some station out in the sticks. Even produced her own programmes, she said.'

'They all say that.'

'Um.' Ritchie restlessly pounded round his office, never staying in one place for more than a few seconds. 'I don't like the idea of pretty faces on TV news – pretty faces that aren't capable of anything more, that is. If we're to have women at all on our shows, they should be proper, dinkum journos, capable of getting their hands dirty as the need arises.'

'Then you're saying that March won't do, because I doubt if she'd be any good at reporting.'

'No, I'm not saying that. What I'd like to see is March having a *try* at reporting, serious reporting, never mind what. Let's see whether she's got it in her. Find her something to do.'

'All right. But it could be a disaster.'

'So? Television thrives on disaster.'

March had had to deal with the police over her 'false imprisonment'. She'd been so exhausted and jittery after her experience that she'd barely taken any notice of them. But she'd sensed that they were a race apart, cut off from others by their calling. She'd found them friendly, sympathetic, optimistic. Perhaps it was just

221

a question of the police being wonderful when they were on your side.

Now she was to have another opportunity to study them at close quarters. And she felt that in her role as a TV reporter she was automatically 'on the other side' as far as the police were concerned. That she was a familiar face from the TV screens would cut little ice with them.

The Zoo Killings had been taking place at nearly two-month intervals for a year now. The police were making no progress and had to resort to displays of themselves working with a computer to sort through the evidence – and the age-old device of dressing up a policewoman in the victim's clothes and parading her about in the hope that it would jog someone's memory.

Victim number eight was found early one morning by a jogger in Regent's Park. Like the previous seven, she was female, she'd been sexually assaulted, then brutally murdered. It took no one in the media very long to realize that in Regent's Park was the London Zoo. This could just have been coincidence except that the police did nothing to deny the connection. They simply withheld a piece of information concerning the way the latest victim had been murdered, which they knew was common to all the Zoo Killings.

By early afternoon, a police incident-caravan had been parked near where the body had been found. White tapes and black screens cordoned off the grassy area beneath the trees where the corpse still lay. Forensic experts went about their tasks. A briefing for press and broadcasting was announced for five o'clock.

'I want March to take that story,' Ritchie rasped at the afternoon meeting. 'Take whoever's on it, off it.'

Penn-Morrison wasn't sure. With March sitting there, he couldn't go into his reservations about her. 'I'm just thinking of March,' he said. 'She's got to present the programme with Ben. If she's got to run around packaging the item, she'll be pretty pushed by the evening.'

'You'd like to do it, wouldn't you, March?' Ritchie asked, ominously.

'Yes,' she replied, sensing that Ritchie was pushing her. She wondered at his motive.

'That's it, then.'

So, not only was the reporter who specialized in crime stories pulled off this one, but he found his potted summaries of the Zoo

Killings to date, complete with video clips of police searches, all passed over to March who'd never covered a murder story in her life.

March wasn't accorded a scriptwriter to hold her hand this time. Penn-Morrison told her to join the camera crew, get along to the police press conference at five, then return and package the item so that it was ready by seven. That would just about give her time to skin through the rest of the script she would have to deliver at eight.

March took a deep breath and regretted she'd not brought more sober clothing with her. She dug out her pristine reporter's notebook and went to join the camera crew in the N-TV car park.

She was momentarily unhappy to see that it was Ralph Collins and Pete Nash. They were both cocky individuals, not much older than herself, and called her 'darlin'', and generally behaved like the Starsky and Hutch of the video world.

'Don't you live near 'ere?' Pete Nash asked as they swung up northwards through the park, heading for the main entrance to the Zoo.

'Used to. Just across the road from the Zoo.'

'Thought so. When you 'ad your spot of bovver they said in the paper you lived 'ereabouts.'

Ralph Collins, not to be outdone, added: 'You got away wiv it a bit better than this little darlin', di'n'tcha?'

'Must 'ave bin on the gime, if you ask me,' said Pete as he steered the N-TV saloon up to a policeman. ''Ere's Old Bill, larger than life. Mind if we park 'ere, guv? Got some 'eavy equipment we need to unload.'

'Who are you?' the constable asked, bending down to look in the car. Seeing March, he brightened. 'Oh, hello. News, is it? You can park here. I'll keep an eye on it for you.'

'Ta, muchly.'

March walked over to where a group of other TV people and newspapermen was already being addressed by Detective Chief Superintendent Marshall of the Metropolitan Police. Basically, he was saying he hadn't a clue. BBC and ITN were represented by their foot-in-door crime reporters, burly men who could have excluded March with a slight shove of their elbows.

Fortunately, she found them inclined to be chivalrous to such an obvious rooky, and she wasn't going to play down her looks and her air of little girl lost, if it would help her get what she wanted.

March found that, whereas the others had to share a quick interview with the Detective Chief Superintendent, she was accorded an interview all on her own.

Marshall remembered March's recent role as a victim and so was more accommodating than usual. After the short tight-lipped interview, he relaxed.

'I used to have a flat near here,' March told him. 'Bit worrying, isn't it, what's happened?'

'Yes. Local girl, too, she was. Maybe you knew her.'

'Until you say who she is, I can't tell ...'

'We'll be releasing the name in just a few minutes. Had to trace the next of kin. They're local.'

'I don't envy the person who has to break the news to them.'

'Now, March, I can't say anything at the moment. Wait a few minutes until I get the all-clear.'

This March duly did. When Marshall received his signal, he called the reporters into a huddle and announced:

'Right. Victim's name. Carol Locksleigh. Carol without an "e". Locksleigh – L-O-C-K-S-L-E-I-G-H. Age: twenty-six. Occupation: typist. Not married.'

'How did you know it was her?' a reporter asked.

'Can't say of now. But it was, er, straightforward.'

Ralph Collins whispered to March, 'Ask 'im what 'er address was.'

'Why?'

'So you can nip round and get a picture of the girl.'

'Oh.'

Another reporter was just asking Marshall, 'Have you got a picture of the girl?'

'This is being processed and will be available from about eight o'clock.'

'Nice and handy for the first edition,' the reporter muttered ironically.

'Impossible for us,' March murmured to Pete Nash. 'We're on the air then.'

'C'mon, March, luv. You can do better than that. Where's the nearest phone box?'

Having failed to find a phone box and, more specifically, a phone box with the L-R volume of the London directory still in it, Pete

Nash said, 'Silly me', and used his car phone to call up N-TV.

'What are you doing?' March asked.

'Finding out where the Locksleigh relatives live. They're local, aren't they?'

'Yes, but ...'

'Well, it's no use ringing up directory inquiries, 'cos they won't give you addresses, only numbers.'

'But there may be lots of Locksleighs around here.'

'Wouldn't bank on it.'

Indeed, when Pete got through to base, they turned up the name of only one Locksleigh who could be said to be 'local' to the Zoo.

'Come on, then,' said Ralph Collins. 'Let's get round there, and get a snap out of 'em. Might give you a bit of talkie-talkie, too.'

'Hold on,' said March. 'You mean we're going to call on the relatives of the dead girl?'

Mr and Mrs Locksleigh lived over the railway not far from the Round House in Camden Town. About half a mile from March's old flat as the crow flew.

'Uh-oh, they got 'ere before us ...' Ralph exclaimed as they turned into the road and saw a police vehicle parked outside the house. 'Go on, March. Out you get and sweet-talk your way to a picky. If they'll give you an interview, give us a shout.'

'Oh, shit ...' cried March and stumbled up to the front door of the modest semi, not knowing quite what she'd say.

Tentatively, she rang the doorbell. After a second or two, she heard footsteps. A policewoman opened the door.

As if in answer to a prayer, March recognized the WPC who'd interviewed her after the abduction.

'What do you want?' the WPC asked in a whisper.

'I was wondering whether ... oh, this is terrible ... I desperately need a picture of ... you know, the girl. It won't be coming from the Yard in time for our programme.'

'Hmm. I doubt you'll get one here. Mrs Locksleigh's in a fine old state, as you can guess. Shouldn't imagine she'd want the Press bothering her.'

'Oh, please ask her. Do me a favour. Would it help if you told her what it was for? Mention my name.'

'I'll see,' said the correct, unsmiling WPC and closed the door.

March stood on the step, then walked to the gate and gave a helpless shrug to the crew in the car.

After another minute, the policewoman opened the door again.

'She says you can come in.'

In the back parlour, March noticed the huge TV set before she took in the woman who sat next to it. The TV set had pride of place.

Mrs Locksleigh was about sixty and red-eyed, as might have been expected. She had a curious kind of stillness, as though she was already coming to terms with the awful blow dealt to her.

'The woman from the television,' the WPC announced flatly.

'Hello, my dear, how are you?'

March was surprised to be greeted like this by a woman who'd just lost her daughter.

Mrs Locksleigh veered between reason and tears, reminiscing about her daughter, then wiping her eyes, then sobbing deeply again. March doubted whether she would ever be in a fit state to be interviewed. Then suddenly she looked at March and took her hand.

'Meeting you has really made my day,' she said.

March couldn't believe her ears.

'Come and sit you down. Let's have some tea.'

'Shall I put the kettle on?' said the WPC, who by now felt she'd seen everything.

'Yes. That'd be kind.' Then turning to March again, Mrs Locksleigh told her, 'I always watch your news. Best thing on the telly. And you, my dear, are a princess. Lovely, dear, really lovely.'

March tried to think what to make of this reception. But she knew she must keep calm. She looked at her watch.

'You're taking all this very bravely, Mrs Locksleigh ...'

'I always warned her. And her Dad, he said the same. But there you are. There's no telling them, is there? I just hope they catch the fellah, though. I'm a Christian but if they left me in a room alone with him, I'd soon show him what the rest of us thought of him ...'

'Yes. Your husband is not ...'

'Drowning his sorrows at the pub, I expect. Nothing new about that, either ... Remind me, dear, to ask for your autograph before you go.'

When the WPC brought the tea, March was sufficiently

recovered from the bizarre nature of the occasion to broach the purpose of her visit.

'Could you possibly let us borrow a picture of . . . Carol. I know the police have one, but we need another one urgently. I'd look after it personally and make sure you got it back.'

'Of course, my dear. Or may I call you March? We've only got the two snaps of Carol. She never liked having her picture took. Odd that, isn't it? And if you could send me a picture of yourself at the same time, that'd be lovely.'

March swallowed and realized she had managed, quite in spite of herself, to get to first base.

She went on to conduct a short interview with Mrs Locksleigh which Ralph and Pete quickly recorded in the kitchen.

It went into the package on the Zoo Killings which March introduced on the *Nightly News* less than two hours later.

Patrick Ritchie was jubilant. Never mind how she'd gone about it, she'd made a success of her first assignment.

After the *Nightly News* was over, Ritchie asked March to pop into his office for a word.

'Like something to drink?' he asked, gesturing at his well-stocked hospitality cabinet.

'White wine, if you have it?' March answered, feeling she deserved a small celebration.

Ritchie handed her a plastic beaker-full and opened a can of Castlemaine XXXX for himself.

'Sit yourself down.'

March sat, and found Ritchie sitting next to her, so their legs touched.

'You did a real beaut job on that murder. I just wanted to congratulate you.'

'Thank you.'

'I'd like to see you do much more of that sort of thing – if you want to, that is.'

'Oh, yes, I do. People just want me to be a pretty face, but I really want to get out there on the job.'

Ritchie didn't smile. 'Good, good. That's what I've been telling everybody. "We must get March out of the studio," that's what I've been saying. "She's got a lot to offer."'

'Thank you.' March was interested to learn they'd been discussing her.

The conversation continued on its uneasy way, with March not quite sure why Ritchie had taken the trouble to single her out for praise.

When she found out, it wasn't very pleasant.

In addition to having aligned his small, chubby thighs with hers, Ritchie put his arm round her, leaning on the back of the sofa, but without quite touching her.

Eventually, March twigged. Ritchie was exerting what he no doubt saw as the boss's prerogative of cuddling up to the most attractive female member of his staff.

She made an unsuccessful attempt to switch the conversation to unarousing matters such as the ratings. But to Ritchie even they were part of his masculine ego-trip, so the ploy back-fired. March tried politics, unemployment, South Africa, but none of these topics would deflect Ritchie from his apparent goal.

March had to throw him somehow. 'You've said a lot about me, and thank you. But what about Lynne? She's terribly good, you know. Why is she in the doldrums?'

That did the trick. Ritchie stood up and walked around his desk, picking at odd tapes and papers he found there.

'Now, Lynne's a problem. She's a liability. That's why you don't find me singing her praises. Haven't you noticed how quiet and peaceful life's been since she went on holiday?'

'That's unfair, surely,' March spoke up bravely.

'She's incompetent, she's unreliable, she's a boozer, and she's unattractive. So what's unfair about that?'

March saw which way the wind was blowing. 'But the whole point about Lynne is ... however dotty she might be, that's *her*. It's what people expect.'

'So you agree she's dotty?'

'Well, I'd like to think she's a chum, as well as a colleague, so I don't think I should ...'

'Take care, March. Don't get too involved with her. She'll drag you down to her level.'

March stood up, abruptly. 'I must be going, Patrick, it's been a long day ...'

'Naw, sit you down, dear. I didn't mean to upset you. Let's not talk about unpleasant things. Come on.'

He crossed over and put his arm around her.

'You're a very attractive young woman. You know that? I was hoping we could get better acquainted ...'

March could hardly believe the obviousness of his approach ... But he was her boss, so she'd have to play it carefully. If she put a foot wrong, she'd end up on his blacklist, like Lynne. She even wondered whether he'd tried anything with Lynne to give rise to such dislike of the older woman.

March carried it off very well. She went up to him, kissed his cheek, and said beguilingly:

'You never know your luck, Patrick. But not tonight.'

She left the Editor's office with him rejected but not defeated.

It had been as simple as that. He finished his beer alone, in a better mood than he'd been in all week.

CHAPTER 40

Next night it was back to problems. Prime Minister Ross, after the customary speculation, had unveiled his first Government reshuffle since the Election. It was chiefly remarkable for his promotion of Sally Gerald from Education to the Foreign Office, making her Britain's first woman Foreign Secretary.

Mrs Gerald had been a backbencher, overlooked for years (not least by Britain's first woman Prime Minister) until she became Trevor Ross's campaign manager in his bid for the Conservative Party leadership. Her help was rewarded by a Cabinet place when Ross became Prime Minister. She was plump, bespectacled, had a deep, gushing voice, and a poor public manner. In addition to these disadvantages, she'd been cited in a messy divorce case three years before which, at the time, had seemed to rule out high office. And her performance in committee was haphazard. A Labour MP had called her a 'liar of the worst sort' when, as Education Secretary, she'd been caught fudging statistics for her department.

Mrs Gerald talked to David Kenway for the *Nightly News*. It was an unremarkable bread-and-butter interview but David's dislike of the new Foreign Secretary was plain. It was as though he were attempting to relive his triumph over Charlotte Cordova. She responded with a mumbling, non-committal performance.

This in itself was not enough to upset anybody, but what upset and annoyed Colin Lyon, who caught the interview on a rare evening at home with his wife, was the context in which it had been set.

'I've never known anything like it,' he bristled. 'Instead of talking about the reshuffle with the usual pundits, which is just about bearable – if people are really that interested – they concentrate solely on Sally and drag up every bit of dirt they can about her. On and on, for fifteen minutes. They call themselves "The Newsmakers" – "News Manufacturers" would be nearer the mark.'

Karen Lyon pushed her fork into the Marks & Spencer fish pancake (which she'd managed to overcook) and told her husband, 'You're only saying that because you weren't mentioned. You should be jolly glad you were left where you were in the reshuffle.'

'That's not true, Karen,' he protested, self-righteously. 'I *was* mentioned. That Kenway fellow said I was obviously considered a success in my job which is why I hadn't been moved. I'm not that petty. But I think it's outrageous that an outfit like N-TV can slag off a minister, and a woman at that, with all that irrelevant guff about her private life. I thought we'd come on a bit since the days when those matters counted for anything in the public life of this country.'

Lyon found a fish bone in his pancake. 'Why do they have to leave these bits in?' he said irritably. 'Just to prove there's real fish in here somewhere, I suppose. When are you going to learn to cook, anyway?'

'You said we could have a cook.'

'Can't afford it and that's that.'

Karen relapsed into sullen silence.

Lyon still thought he lacked the wealth to keep himself in the manner to which his political eminence entitled him. He feared for the inevitable day when he would be out of office. Had he feathered his nest sufficiently? Would the company directorships come his way? Would his flamboyant and free-spending wife stick with him if he failed?

The Home Secretary went on: 'The whole report was a loaded attack, not only on Sally but on the Government as a whole. Completely unjustified. Talk about balance! There was none of it.'

'What are you going to do about it, then? Complain, the way you do about everything?'

Lyon chose not to rise to his wife's bait. 'Not in so many words, no. I had thought with Patrick in at the top of N-TV, matters might improve. Apparently not.'

Karen Lyon looked at her watch and saw that it was time to put the *boeuf bourguignon* (with noodles) into the microwave.

While she was out of the room, Lyon took the opportunity to track down the Political Editor of *The Times* and give him an unattributable blast down the phone about David's interview.

'What are you going to do about it?' the journalist asked, just as Karen had done.

'I can tell you, though again don't quote me on this, that it signals a start to my very real attempts to sort out that bunch of hornets. Something must be done about N-TV, and I'm the man who's going to have to do it.'

'I understand,' said the man at *The Times*.

Next day, to Lyon's even greater annoyance, he could find not so much as a sentence about his gripe anywhere in the paper. Nothing attributed to a 'Senior Cabinet Minister', nor even a 'Whitehall source'. Still, he consoled himself with one of his favourite phrases: he had 'put down a personal marker'.

A few days later, N-TV gave him further evidence of bias. This time it was because of a factual error, an error more important than the odd, casual slips that creep into most news reports.

A vote had been due to take place in the House of Commons, just after ten, on the issue of defence spending. After prolonged debate in the Commons and Lords, a key provision of the Budget was still awaiting parliamentary approval. It allowed for sixty million pounds to be spent on research for a new portable battlefield communications system known as PTX.

In itself, the system was not revolutionary, nor an emotional issue like welfare benefits or pensions. However, the Opposition had seized on it as a means of embarrassing the Government – which even with its good majority was becoming more vulnerable to militant activity by its own backbenchers.

Such a head of steam had been built up over the PTX system – which the media played for all it was worth – that if one was to believe what had been written in the previous Sunday's papers, there was a good chance of the Government being defeated on the vote. The Government wouldn't fall if this happened, but it would be a significant victory for its opponents.

By ten o'clock on the night, excitement was high at N-TV as George Lee, the Home News Editor, waited to see whether the outcome of the vote would arrive in time for the end of the bulletin at 10:20 (or 10:18:35, to be precise, allowing for commercials to follow). If there was any delay in getting the news onto the screen it would mean that ITN, whose *News at Ten* ran on until 10:29, would be able to put it out first.

All his twenty years in the news business, George Lee had worried about such moments. Just as he worried what he should do if the IRA rang up with a bomb-warning and gave the correct code-word, which he was privy to.

He had risen to the post of Home News Editor at N-TV after spells as a senior sub-editor in Fleet Street, and as a news editor in commercial radio. He was reasonably well liked, as bastards go, and generally thought to be efficient. He usually worked from noon to midnight. A colleague would work from midnight to noon. It was punishing and, like many of those who worked 'unsocial hours', he felt that his whole body mechanism was distorted. He had difficulty in telling what time of day it was. The newsroom at N-TV was so full of partitions and humming computer equipment that he couldn't even *see* whether it was night or day. The pressure was continuous. So George drank. He drank many pints of beer at N-TV's club bar and took frequent slugs of Bell's whisky from a bottle he kept in a drawer at the side of his desk. His drinking habits were no secret. But this was the man who effectively decided what N-TV should do when a newsworthy item came up.

At 10:17:34, the result of the Commons vote was made known in the House. George reacted quickly. The Government had been defeated by three votes. He pressed the talkback key to the studio control room and shouted. 'They've lost. Lost by three votes. The flash is there.'

He soon heard the newscaster, Delia Steele, smoothly reading out the words: 'And news just in from Westminster. The Government has been defeated by three votes following the debate on the PTX defence system. More news and analysis of that in our next hourly news at eleven.'

N-TV was disappointed at not having been able to do the item justice, but at least they'd put over the news before their rivals. There was a sudden air of relaxation as the commercials played.

The phone rang on George Lee's desk. He picked it up.

'You fuck-wit ... what the bloody hell did you do that for?'

George was fuddled and felt a sudden stab in his chest.

It was N-TV's Political Correspondent at Westminster.

'You got it the wrong way round. The Government *won* by three votes. Bloody hell ...!'

A quick look at the Press Association's print-out confirmed George's mistake. The programme editor tried to get a live correction put out after the commercials, but the tape of the next segment had already started to roll. A newsflash caption was put at the bottom of the screen just as soon as a suitable moment presented itself.

George Lee vacated his desk at once. It was observed he was not altogether steady on his feet.

As soon as Patrick Ritchie arrived in the office the following morning, he was told of the mistakes of the night. He looked at a recording of the cock-up.

'How did it happen?' he asked Adam Ravenscroft.

'George'd had the usual too many and fucked it up. It was bound to happen, sooner or later.'

'Yes, well ...' Ritchie seemed none too concerned.

Adam knew how Sir Charles would have dealt with the situation. Lee would have been summoned, from his bed if necessary, and quietly and coldly fired.

'I suppose I'd better give him a kick up the jacksie,' Ritchie ventured, after a little thought.

'No more than that?'

'Well, we all like a drink. Just a pity he had to pick on *that* mistake to make. The Tories'll see it as another example of N-TV's anti-Government bias ...'

'I'd say it was a dismissal offence.'

'Would you now?'

'Yes. There are procedures to be followed, of course. Otherwise we'll have the union on our backs. Even so ...'

'But we all make mistakes, Adam ... Why the fuss over this one?'

'I still think, as an example ...'

'Ah, come on, you talk like this is a Scout troop. Why get rid of a seasoned, well-trained journalist, just because he makes *one* mistake?'

'It's not the first.'

'Well, I'll have to think about it. I can't see that being pissed on the job is an offence in itself. Or that even two or three mistakes justify that kind of action. Hell, if it was, how come that Kimberley woman's still on the payroll?'

Adam Ravenscroft chose not to rise to this particular bait.

'I'd better see George,' Ritchie sighed reluctantly. 'As soon as he comes in this afternoon ...'

CHAPTER 41

David was at Vanessa's again – rather to his own surprise – but she'd suggested a nightcap and it seemed too much trouble to refuse.

'You're very good at getting rid of your flatmates when I come round here,' he said, stroking the nape of her neck as he prepared to unbutton Vanessa's blouse.

'I'm a born organizer, aren't I?' She gave a little laugh. 'No, Ros has a boy friend she more or less lives with and only comes here to do her laundry. And Caroline's away at the moment. Just coincidence.'

'Have you ever been had on the hearth-rug?'

'No, but I have a feeling I soon will be. Come on. Get stuck in, I'm getting desperate.'

David did as he was told and didn't much enjoy it. The touch of the headmistress was not a turn-on.

Afterwards, David pulled himself up and sat staring into the empty fireplace, while Vanessa scrabbled in her handbag for tissues.

Vanessa attempted to snuggle up to him, complimented him on his sexual equipment and pretended she'd had an orgasm.

Not quite able to decide on her moment, she waited a minute or two, and then blurted it out anyway:

'I've missed my period. I think we may be harry-preggers.'

'Christ!' said David, suddenly aware of his nakedness. A pause, and ruminations on both sides.

'Slept with anyone else recently?' David asked.

'No, I haven't!'

'So, if you are, it was me?'

'Correct.'

'Oh. Time I called for a taxi.'

It was the excuse he'd been looking for and he moved quickly.

'Now, David, you're putting me in a tricky situation.'

Patrick Ritchie swung to left and right in his executive chair, snapping a rubber band between his fingers. He rummaged among the papers until he found a small box, took out a capsule and swallowed it.

235

David sat across the desk and waited. Ritchie leaned on his intercom. 'Sharon, two coffees, pronto.' David crossed his jeans-clad legs and then uncrossed them.

'You see, I need you where you are. The fact that you're fit enough to go on the road again is beside the point. But the Board has just agreed that Ben Brock can take six months' sabbatical. It may extend beyond that. He may go altogether. That leaves a big hole.'

'I can't be all that indispensable. I'm not even any good at it.'

'Balls and balls! Stop fishing for compliments, Dave. News-casters are *not* two-a-penny, over-rated though they may be. Not everyone can do it. And you're growing into it, Dave. You really are. I've seen an impressive development in you since I got here.'

'But I'm a journalist, Patrick. It's no job reading the bloody autocue all the time and being let out to do the odd interview.'

'Sally Gerald?' Ritchie grinned at him, then pulled a face. 'We haven't heard the last of that. I've been getting shit in sacks from Central Office.'

'The interview was OK. It was the package they objected to. And I didn't even write that. It was Lynne's stuff.'

'It would've seemed even more bloody bitchy coming from that old cow. But that's beside the point. We all went a notch too far on that one.'

'I can't cope with that type of set-up,' said David firmly. 'At least when I'm out in the field they're my words I'm using and they're my impressions. Besides, Westminster politics stink as far as I'm concerned. I've always been much more interested in foreign news.'

Sharon waddled in with the coffee, wearing striped pants that emphasized her rump. She flirted with David, almost made a pass, but he wasn't in the right frame of mind. He'd had most of the desire strained out of him the previous night by Vanessa and it would be some days before he felt like it again.

They sipped their coffee more or less in silence. Ritchie became absorbed in papers in front of him and only when David stood up did he remember he was still there.

'Oh, well, leave it with me, will you? But don't expect to hear anything just yet. Too many messes to sort out first.'

Later in the day, the Editor-in-Chief appeared more resolute when talking to Adam Ravenscroft.

'George is going on unpaid leave for a month. He's been told to get medical attention for his drink problem.'

'You mean he's being *sent* on unpaid leave for a month?'

'Yes, if you like. I've also decided to get David back on the road. He's nbg in the studio. He'll never be another Ben Brock, so we'd best get shot of him and start poaching some good newscasters from elsewhere.'

'It won't be easy.'

'Wake up, you whingeing pom. Everything's possible. No wonder your bloody empire's crumbled.'

CHAPTER 42

Earlier in the summer, Vanessa had asked March to do her 'a very special favour'.

'I promise I'll never ask you to do it again.'

It was unusual of Vanessa to ask anything of anyone, but March had listened to what she'd had to say.

'This is known as taking advantage of my position ...'

'Go on,' March had said. 'What are you driving at?'

'Well, you know my parents live in Gloucestershire? The vicar of the village church asked my father if I would ask you if you'd please open his bazaar on the twenty-fourth of July?'

'Oh ...'

'Last year they managed to get Derek Nimmo and the year before, Richard Briers. It's held out of doors on the village green and they usually raise £1,000, if the weather holds. You know, the ladies of the church run about thirty tables selling all kinds of crafts, games, pottery, cakes, refreshments. "If wet in church hall." I've got Daddy's letter here. He says, "If I can tell the *Gazette* that March Stevens is coming then lots of people will turn up! It would be a great thrill for us if she could be with us, if only for a brief visit." What do you think?'

'Heavens, I'd be hopeless,' March had said. 'I've never opened anything in my life.'

'It's not much of an inducement, but you could make a weekend of it. Stay with my parents, they're not too bad. Have a romp in the countryside. It's heavenly down there, when the weather holds.'

So March had reluctantly agreed and worried about it far more than anything she had to do for the *Nightly News* these days. Now it was time to deliver her promise.

Saturday July 24 started cloudy but when Vanessa called for March at her flat around ten in the morning, it was already brightening. March popped her weekend bag in the back of Vanessa's Mini and prepared to be driven – all part of the deal – the hundred or so miles to Gloucestershire. She wore pink pants and a loose cotton top to travel in but, as for TV, she carried a special bag containing her appearance clothes.

238

By the time they reached Hawkesgrove, the sun was shining warm and bright. All along the lanes were pink and green handbills proclaiming 'Summer Bazaar' and in even larger letters, 'To Be Opened By Well-Known TV Personality March Stevens'.

Finally the road fell away down a wooded slope into a village nestling in the hillside. March was entranced. Above the cluster of old houses, a red-and-white flag flapped in the breeze on the crenellated church tower. Below, box hedges grew among the gravestones. The rectory was just a short walk away. In a field opposite the church, the ladies of the parish were already out preparing their tables for the bazaar.

Vanessa turned her Mini into the gravel drive of a house called simply Hawkesgrove, like the village. A pair of Dalmatians loped up to sniff and see who had arrived.

'Well, here we are,' Vanessa said. 'Back in the bosom of the family.' Her father, a Brigadier with a port-coloured face and military moustache, tweed suit and orange-brown suede shoes, was the first to appear and looked as though he'd come straight off the croquet lawn. He kissed his daughter and reverently shook March by the hand.

'And you must be Miss Stevens?' March couldn't tell whether he really knew who she was or not. 'Let me take your bag. I'm so glad you could stay with us.'

Mrs Sinclair, a tall woman on the verge of arthritis, had laid on a 'cold collation', as she called it – ham and salad, a piece of cheese. March accepted a glass of dry white wine in an attempt to stave off the ordeal ahead.

'So what precisely is it that you do?' Mrs Sinclair asked March.

'Oh, Mother!' Vanessa jumped on her. 'You *know* what March does. You've seen her doing it.'

March didn't mind. She was getting used to it. The worst you could do was assume that *anybody* knew who you were. Mrs Sinclair hadn't meant the remark unkindly.

'Pretty exciting sort of stuff,' interposed the Brigadier. 'Am I right? Met some of those BBC johnnies in Berlin, you know, in the 'fifties. Seemed to know what they were doing.'

This, March could tell, was a top compliment in the Brigadier's vocabulary.

'And how is Eric?' Mrs Sinclair inquired of Vanessa. 'We haven't seen him for such a long time. Is he going to visit us again soon?'

239

Vanessa looked at March, not sure if she was totally aware of the role Eric was supposed to play in Vanessa's life. But March twigged that, whether or not he was a serious boyfriend, Eric's was a name Vanessa invoked to keep parental marital inquiries at bay.

'Haven't seen him for a while,' she replied vaguely. 'You know how it is.'

The Brigadier put a pickle on his plate.

His wife remarked wistfully, 'Such a nice man, I thought.'

March sensed the tension. She often went through these scenes with her own parents. She realized there was an unbridgeable gulf between the world of parents and the world their children inhabited, between home and work.

But that was the way things were. Children of Vanessa's and March's generation were free to move to new environments, to move between worlds, in a way their parents had rarely done.

Mrs Sinclair, straight-backed, started to organize her daughter and, through her, March. 'The rector will be coming over at two-thirty and he'll take you over to the field. Thank goodness the weather held. Three o'clock sharp, he says, the bazaar must be opened. I expect you do lots of these fêtes?'

March, caught unawares by this remark, stumbled, 'No, no. This is my first.'

'How exciting!' Vanessa's mother piped, and March felt the words float past her as though they had no meaning.

The rector, a quaint Victorian figure carrying a pipe and tin of tobacco, arrived just on two-thirty, as promised. His yellowing summer jacket was stained in one or two places and he wore a straw hat which had seen better days.

March was now in her bazaar-opening clothes: a silk, safari-style skirt, split to the thigh at both sides, and a matching blouse with a mandarin collar. It was the colour of fuchsia and she looked ravishing.

Promptly at three, the rector introduced March from the small platform, decked with bunting. He didn't seem a hundred per cent certain of her surname or her TV company. But the amateur-ishness of the moment was, in its way, delightful.

March kept her speech short, encouraged the small crowd to spent its money, won a few laughs, and was much admired before declaring the bazaar open.

Vanessa chaperoned her, like a Royal lady-in-waiting, as they did a quick tour of the stalls. Then March had to sit for twenty minutes signing autographs for twenty pence a throw, and have her picture taken for the *Gazette*.

'We'll soon be able to slip away,' Vanessa whispered to her around four o'clock. 'You've done magnificently. But you must just meet someone I think you'll rather like. Do you see him over there, by the second-hand book-stall?'

'Mm, yes. Who on earth is he?'

'He's a bit of all right, isn't he? He's the squire.'

'Do they still have such things?'

'Round here they do. It means nothing, but it doesn't half give him an air. He could leave his boots under my bed any time.'

'Well, why doesn't he?'

'I'm hardly ever here. It's the first time I've been back since Christmas.'

'What's he called?'

'Mark Rippingale. He farms. Pots of money.'

'Wife?'

'He was married, but she was killed in a car crash about three years ago.'

Vanessa made the introductions. March wondered whether it was more for Vanessa's benefit than her own, but she was glad to have a closer look at this dashing man. Tall, aristocratic, and with an odd abrupt charm.

'Good little speech you m-made there,' he complimented March, with the slightest of stutters. 'Not easy. Can't stand getting up on me hind legs, m-meself.'

'March is staying the weekend with us at Hawkesgrove,' Vanessa told him.

'Mmmm. How d'you two know each other?' Mark asked.

'We both work at N-TV,' Vanessa explained patiently.

'Oh, do you now?' For all the significance the initials appeared to hold for him, they might have stood for a political party.

'Television, you know,' Vanessa added helpfully.

'Ah, that rat-race, eh?' Mark said to March, slightly distracted.

'Of course,' Vanessa exploded. 'That's why she's here today, to open the bazaar ...!'

'Never watch it m-meself,' said Mark, firmly but kindly. 'Don't possess a set.'

'Very wise,' said March. 'Much better off without it.'

Vanessa seemed a touch put out by the way her introduction had misfired ever so slightly.

'Well ...' said Mark. 'M-Must be off. Done my duty for another year.'

Then, in what might have seemed an after thought, solely intended to be polite, he said: 'Like to pop over for a glass before lunch tomorrow?'

'Yes,' said Vanessa for the two of them. 'We'd be delighted wouldn't we?'

March nodded and smiled fetchingly.

Dinner that night at Hawkesgrove was a stilted affair. Vanessa tried to organize her parents as best she could but they were slowing down, cutting corners, and the meal they served was not entirely edible.

March, nibbling rabbit-like, was not a glutton at the best of times and found it easy to say no to second helpings when she'd barely touched the first. She relaxed in the light of the candles in their silver sticks, she warmed to the musty sense of age that the house embodied, and she delighted in the complete silence of the country night and the smell of country air wafting in through the open window.

Brigadier and Mrs Sinclair soon announced that it was time for them to be turning in.

'We'll do the washing up,' Vanessa told them. 'Don't worry about a thing.'

'There's some good port and cigars if you want them, in the drawing room,' the Brigadier announced, as though to his fellow officers in the mess.

'Oh, thank you, Daddy,' Vanessa said, giving him a peck. 'That's just what we like ...' She winked at March.

The drawing room was in fact the library, full of leather-bound volumes and fine high-backed chairs. It was just that the Brigadier was not a bookish man and thought that calling it a library would be pretentious.

The girls went in and sat down. Vanessa set the port before them and even examined the cigars.

'Have a drop, March. Go on.'

'All right. Just a teensie one.'

'Cigars only make me sick, though. How about you? I don't know how that Nikki Brennan manages.'

'She doesn't smoke cigars, does she?'

'Well, cheroots, Gauloises, that sort of thing. I suppose she thinks they go with the image, the whole Parisian Left Bank bit.'

'I hear she went to Italy with Lynne,' commented March. 'Nice for them.'

'They bumped into Paul Whitehall and his boyfriend. Very curious.'

'You're not suggesting there's anything between them – Lynne and Nikki, I mean?'

'You can never really tell, can you? I don't know about Lynne, but I'm sure there's nothing funny about Nikki. Serena in Make-Up was saying Nikki had it off with one of the cameramen on the studio floor.'

March felt uncomfortable. 'Heavens, they're all at it, aren't they? Did I tell you about my encounter with P. Ritchie?'

'No. Go on.'

'After the show one night, he invited me up to his office, to look at his ratings, I suppose. He made a pass at me. I mean, I ask you! I know he's Australian, but even so ...'

Vanessa didn't comment for a moment. Then she leant forward, poured out another glass of port for herself, and took a deep breath.

'I think you ought to know, March. I'm preggers.'

March gasped.

'But who ...?'

'David.'

'*David*! No. How could you ...?'

''Fraid so. You know what he's like. Push, push, push. So I let him. Bloody silly of me. There you are ...'

'But, Van ... that's terrible. What are you going to do?'

'Haven't thought. Well, I have. But I haven't come to any conclusion.'

'Does he know?'

'Yes.'

'How did he take it?'

'He didn't.' Vanessa gave an embarrassed little laugh.

'No wonder he's talking of going abroad again.'

'He's not is he?'

'Oh, Van ...' March wondered whether Vanessa had contrived this whole weekend in order to give her the news. But what could March do? What did she know about what really happened at N-TV? The place really stinks, was all she could think.

'It's selfish, I know,' said March, 'but you know what my reaction is ... to your news and all the rest that's been going on recently? It's to get out. It seemed such a happy place when I joined it. Now we don't seem able to put a foot right.'

'I know,' Vanessa agreed quietly. 'We seem to have been walloped by fate.'

'Will you have the baby, or ...?'

'I expect so. Can't face an abortion. Or can't face Mummy and Daddy finding out. They'd be awfully *disappointed* and it would confirm all their worst fears about London and working in telly.'

March took a very big swig of port and coughed over it. She might almost have tried a cigar at that stage.

One thing March decided against was telling Vanessa how she'd inveigled David into her own bed.

Sunday morning at noon. March and Vanessa, both nursing their secrets, went up to Hall Farm for drinks with Mark Rippingale. The squire was nowhere to be seen when they first arrived, both wearing the skimpiest of summer dresses, but eventually he emerged from underneath one of two ancient Alvises which stood gleaming in the yard.

'Beautiful beasts, aren't they?' he remarked. March could see they were his pride and joy and wanted to ride in one instantly, with her hair blowing in the breeze.

'Let me get this grease off m-my hands and I'll be right with you.'

Mark disappeared into the house while March and Vanessa poked about the farmyard. They found a carthorse, two ponies, three peacocks, an eagle owl, two dogs, three cats, and cages full of exotic birds. And those were just Mark's pets.

Their owner returned briskly, suddenly smart, wearing a dark-blue blazer and white slacks, and smelling faintly of spices.

'Come through the house and we can sit on the lawn.'

Inside, March was surprised to find it wasn't like a farm at all. It was an elegant country house.

'Georgian, Grade II listed, actually,' Mark informed her. 'It's beautiful, isn't it?'

March was lost for words. The house was neat, well kept and comfortable. She felt she would love to see it in winter when real fires would roar in the grates and keep out the bitter cold. Now, golden sunlight broke through the partly-shuttered windows and fell on the oil paintings of people and landscapes covering the walls.

Just before they stepped out again into the garden, they came to a long white room with pillars and a stone floor. Mark went behind a door in the corner and, a few seconds later, the most beautiful music filled the room and spilled out into the garden. Mark appeared again bearing three tall glasses and a bottle of wine in an ice-bucket. March inspected the label and found it was from an English vineyard – St George's Müller-Thurgau.

'But what is the music, Mark?'

'M-Mozart, of course.'

Of course, thought March.

'Piano Concerto No 20 in D Minor.'

March took her glass and sat on a rug on the lawn, saying nothing while Mark and Vanessa murmured platitudes in the heat. She let the sun brush her face and the music tinkle in her ears. She had never encountered the likes of Mark before. He seemed interested in everything. Except perhaps her. And television news.

What would she have to do to meet him again? And on her own?

CHAPTER 43

'ENTERTAINERS. 1/273. Take 1.' The clapper-board snapped and, after a pause, Ben Brock started walking slowly towards the camera.

'Mann's Chinese Theatre on Hollywood Boulevard, Los Angeles. This was the cinema they came to in Hollywood's Golden Age, in the 1920s and 30s, when film premieres were real film premieres. Sleek white limousines would draw up at the kerb here. The stars would dismount and exchange a few pleasantries with the radio commentator who stood just there. Meanwhile, overhead, searchlights raked the sky.

'It doesn't happen any more. Movies still have premieres, of course. But they're not what they were. And the reason is obvious. Television is now the main medium of popular entertainment.

'You can see that change of taste and habit reflected here on the pavement, all along Hollywood Boulevard, in the Walk of Fame.'

Ben bent down and the camera tilted to follow his pointing finger.

'Each of these bronze stars has on it an actor's name – there are two thousand five hundred of them – Mary Pickford, the Marx Brothers, Rita Hayworth, Fred Astaire. But look who they honour now – Lucille Ball, Johnny Carson, Bill Cosby – the stars of the television age. Another chapter in the evolving story of entertainment . . .'

Ben stopped. 'And, cut!' said the director.

'Perfect, Ben,' said the director. 'We'll just do some close-ups, then it's a wrap.'

Ben smiled. He was enjoying being a pro, especially in Hollywood. The crew from the BBC were somewhat in awe of him, what with his reputation as one of Britain's TV 'greats', but there was no doubting he deserved the title. His pieces to camera were always delivered impeccably and seldom required a second take. He was as urbane and unflappable as everyone had always said.

Hollywood was but one of the California locations for a twelve-part series of sixty-minute documentaries with the title *The Entertainers* which Ben had been snapped up to introduce

246

when the original choice, an American film star, suddenly upped his fee-requirement. Ben had made it known around the business that he was available for offers during his sabbatical six months. The offer from the BBC had fallen in his lap. The producer, a young man named Peter Herriot, had managed to arrange interviews with a number of key figures in entertainment history, including Bob Hope and – to everyone's astonishment – Frank Sinatra, who hadn't given an interview to anyone for as long as could be remembered.

Ben was enthusiastic. It was a new world for him and he took to it like a boy with a new hobby.

He enjoyed meeting the stars. They made a change from Cabinet Ministers and trade union leaders and pundits on Third World affairs, even if they anecdotalized everything and analysed nothing.

Oddly enough, Ben might have been in Los Angeles at that time, even if he'd not left N-TV, for the Democratic Convention. The large field of Presidential hopefuls had been reduced to six after the final round of primaries, held at the beginning of June.

Youthful Senator Gerry Iver was still in the lead. Former Governor Winston Mann was sixth.

Ben followed the Convention as best he could. He would quite happily have watched the TV coverage all day but was secretly quite relieved not to have to keep turning his thoughts into words by reporting the event.

On the off-chance of being able to get through to his old friend, Ben called up the Winston Mann team and left a message. But nothing happened. Then, the next night, about 9:0 p.m., he was returning to his room in the Biltmore Hotel when he saw a crowd of excited people in the lobby, moving like a swarm of ants.

Being taller than most, Ben could see over their heads and spied in the mêlée his friend's familiar mop of thick grey hair.

Ben felt this was too good an opportunity to miss and waded into the crowd until he was standing just behind his old friend. Despite the huddle of security men, Ben managed to tap Winston on the shoulder and shouted very loudly in his ear, 'British television, Governor, I wonder if I could ask you a few questions ...?'

Winston broke off the interview he was giving in the middle of the scrum and turned to face Ben.

'*Ben Brock*, what are you doing here?'

'I'm on a sort of holiday. I tried to get in touch with you yesterday.'

'Beat it, beat it, go away,' Winston shouted at several importunate reporters. 'Can't you see I'm talking to an old friend?'

Indeed, Winston seemed so pleased to see Ben that he told his back-up team to leave them alone. It was not as easy as that. The two men had to fight their way up elevators and along corridors full of thrusting, jostling, shoving reporters and gofers.

Eventually, apart from Winston's wife, Lorraine, two security men, and five members of his team sprawled over telephones or jotting things down on yellow legal pads, they were as alone as they were going to be.

'I have to tell you, Ben, I was devastated to hear about Natalie,' the candidate began. 'I know you warned me when we met in February, but still ...'

'Yes, that's why I felt like a change of air. We've had a lot of other upheavals at N-TV as well and I wanted out, as you say. This "coffee-table" TV series I'm doing is rather enjoyable, though. It's so different from the daily grind of newsgathering. I hope I'll be able to go back infinitely refreshed, if not a new man, at the beginning of next year.'

'You're not the only guy who's hoping to go some place and do that,' said Winston, sinking a bottle of Classic Cola with one swig.

'You really think you have a chance?' asked Ben, doubtfully.

'It's up in the air. Just because I'm bottom of the polls doesn't mean I'm finished, y'know.'

'You amaze me, Winston.'

'Yep. I tell you, I've been on a high ever since the day I declared. Haven't touched a drop – 'cept Coke – since then. So you can *tell* how high I've been.'

Ben was astonished at the resilience of his old friend. But there had been a price to pay. Under the tan, the permanent TV make-up and the feisty, hand-pumping manner of the candidate, there was a deeply-exhausted man.

'Tomorrow's your big day,' Ben said.

'Correction, Ben. Tomorrow is *a* big day. That's when the nomination gets buttoned up. Then there's the question of the ticket. Then there's the acceptance speeches. You ain't seen nothin' yet.'

Ben thought Winston either a mad optimist or a fool. He lingered for a long while, lapping up the atmosphere of hope and hype that Winston was currently swimming in. He wished that some of it could rub off on him. He always felt enthused by his visits to the United States. There was a feeling of infinite possibility in the air. There was no British reserve, no cries of 'Sorry, old boy, it can't be done.'

Two days later, Ben and the film crew were preparing to fly on to New York, the next location for *The Entertainers*. They were able to hear, as the limos took them to Los Angeles International Airport, that Senator Gerry Iver had not only won the Democratic nomination, as everyone expected, but he'd chosen former Governor Winston Mann of Ohio as his Vice-Presidential running-mate.

CHAPTER 44

The benefits of Lynne's Italian holiday had long since worn off. Soon her spirits had sunk again. And with good reason.

'I've said it before and I'll say it again,' Ritchie announced. 'She's too old for this network. Have to shoot her through gauze to make her look half-way presentable. I want Delia Steele to take her slot on the *Nightly News*. She's a fresh-faced little thing. You can't see the crow's feet on the march like you can with Lynne. I'm taking Lynne off newscasting. If she's such a beaut at reporting as people always tell me she is, then let's see it.'

Adam Ravenscroft, to whom these remarks were addressed, thought Ritchie was on dangerous ground.

'I'm not sure how Lynne'll take it,' he said to his chief.

'I've looked at her contract and she hasn't got a leg to stand on,' said Ritchie abruptly. 'She's simply employed here as a "special correspondent". No duties specified. We don't even have to put her on the air! It's as open as that.'

'Just wait until she starts throwing contractual talk about "realistic expectations" at you. I don't fancy getting into a situation over that. If we're not careful, she'll have the unions out, and be on to the Equal Opportunities Commission, and everybody.'

'I don't give a toss if she takes us to the Race Relations Board, the Monopolies Commission or the bloody House of Lords. Management's job is to manage, and what I say, goes ...'

'But, Pat ...'

'Look, Adam, you seem to be very much on Miss Kimberley's wavelength, so I'll give you the job.'

Adam looked at Ritchie suspiciously and asked, 'What job?'

'You tell her what I've decided – but not *why* – and make sure she agrees to it. OK? Now git ...'

Adam had, to date, managed magnificently to tone down Ritchie's excesses and to act as buffer between staff and boss. Now he really was on the spot.

'OK, Cap'n, you know best ...'

'Good afternoon, can I speak to Miss March Stevens, please?'

The N-TV switchboard operator was alert to anyone asking for that name in particular.

'Who's calling, please?'

'M-My name is Rippingale. It's personal.'

'Oh, yes, Mr Rippingale. I can't put you through direct, but would you like to speak to her secretary?'

'All right, then.'

In a second or two, Mark Rippingale found himself talking to Vanessa.

'Who's calling?' she asked.

'M-Mark Rippingale.'

'Mark! It's Vanessa, here. Vanessa Sinclair.'

'Oh, hello ...' He sounded fractionally put out. 'I wanted to speak to March. I don't begin to understand this television business. It took me ages to find the number. Getting past the switchboard wasn't easy, either.'

'You have to realize she's a protected species. We have to look after her *very* carefully.'

'Can I speak to her? Or do I have to put it in writing?'

'She's in a meeting just now. Really. Can I get her to ring you?'

Mark wondered whether March would return the call, but he had no alternative but to leave his number.

'See you down here soon, I trust?' he said, a touch formally, to end the call.

As Vanessa replaced the receiver, she realized, forlornly, that March was the one he wanted to see down in the country.

The interview March had given to Geraldine Botolph now finally appeared in the pages of *Woman*. Vanessa handed her a copy with the words, 'I don't expect you'll like it.'

March didn't. In one way, it was typical of most of the interviews she'd given since coming to N-TV. The journalist had drawn attention to her tight-lipped revelations about nothing very much, how she drew a veil over every aspect of her private life, never said a critical word about any of her colleagues, and was generally little Miss Perfect.

In another way, Geraldine Botoloph had lifted the curtain on March ever so slightly:

Perhaps there are no skeletons in this newsgirl's cupboard, perhaps no boyfriends either. After reading the news with her accustomed professionalism, March goes home to a solitary cup of cocoa. 'I'd never marry anyone in television,' she avers. 'It wouldn't last and they're not my kind of people. I'd much rather marry a man who did something completely different. Besides, almost every marriage you care to mention at N-TV is on the rocks. News is bad news for marriages.'

March's knuckles whitened when she read this. She could remember discussing marriage with the journalist, but these didn't sound like her words. And as for saying specifically critical words about her N-TV colleagues, she was sure she'd done nothing of the kind.

There was worse to come:

'Newscasting is a terrible treadmill,' says March, looking suddenly older than her twenty-six years. 'It's a chore, frankly. Hardly what you'd call creative. I'll soon be looking for opportunities to spread my wings elsewhere in TV.'

A breakfast show, a chat programme, her own documentary series? Or flashing her (reputedly) fabulous legs on a showbiz spectacular? March was not prepared to reveal.

Surely, she hadn't said all these things? And, as for her '(reputedly) fabulous legs', that was pure fiction. The last straw was when she read what she'd 'said' about David Kenway:

'He's marvellous. A really great reporter – and so good-looking! If he wasn't married already, I'd be right round there,' said March with stars in her eyes.

Keep an eye open for the sexual chemistry when next you see them together on the screen.

Not for the first time after reading a newspaper or magazine piece about herself, March felt quite sick. Why did she never learn?

'There's nothing new about it,' Vanessa consoled her. 'It's hopeless trying to get them to correct anything afterwards. And a letter to the editor just looks petty. I'm afraid you've just got to grin and bear it. Hope people here don't read it and, if they do, don't believe it. Laugh it off. It's only drivel.'

'But I didn't *say* that about David ...'

'No, but perhaps you looked it.'

Vanessa asked March whether she'd returned Mark Rippingale's call.

'Not yet,' she replied, exchanging one embarrassment for another.

'He's obviously keen on you.'

'Why do you say that? He probably wants me to open a new cowshed for him, or whatever squires are supposed to do.'

'What squires are *really* supposed to do is probably exactly what *he's* after. It must have taken great courage for him to ring you up here, what with him not knowing what a TV set looks like and his stammer and all. He must've rung every commercial TV station in the country before he found the right one. And then he found himself talking to me! You could almost hear him blushing.'

'Oh, Van! You're probably quite wrong. Totally innocent, I expect.'

'Innocent, my fanny. But I'm very happy for you.'

'I just hope he doesn't read bloody *Woman*, that's all ...'

'A straight diet of *Horse and Hound* and *Country Life* for him, I expect. Anyway, you seemed to be saying that the men round here are a load of creeps, so that should be music to his ears.'

'Oh, Van, don't take it like that. I know *some* men round here are creeps, but not every one. What about David?'

'He's started going abroad again. He's off to Brussels for some EEC summit or other. Then he's going with the PM to Russia.'

'But what about you?'

'I don't really know what to do.'

'Why not ask Lynne? She's a wise old bird. I bet she's been through all this sort of thing before.'

'But she's not got any children.'

'Well, you could at least ask her.'

'I'll see.'

'Have you told anyone else? Do people *know*?'

'I've just told you. And David.'

News of a pregnancy at N-TV *did* soon reach a wider audience. A story in one of the Sunday tabloids stated, without equivocation, that March was pregnant.

This was said to explain the quiet, Mona Lisa smile that had been observed playing about her lips on the *Nightly News*.

Although she'd said in a recent magazine interview that she would never consider marrying a TV person, it was generally assumed that the father was none other than fellow newsman,

David Kenway. He, meanwhile, remained married to feisty, New-York-born, mother-of-two ...

The N-TV press office put out a firm denial: the story was completely without foundation. But who had put two and two together and made five?

The *TV Times* astrologer when asked *his* opinion said he was certain March wasn't pregnant – 'at the moment', he added, just to keep the ball rolling – and, for good measure, added that he'd cast a horoscope for N-TV as a whole, based on its 'birth date' in November 1984. There were turbulent times ahead for the station, he said. But they would provide excellent opportunities. All contracts should be looked at very closely, however, before being signed.

Adam Ravenscroft handled Lynne brilliantly. He told her almost everything that Patrick Ritchie had said, dissociated himself from most of it, but said she didn't have much option but to go along with it. For a while at least.

Lynne, who had anticipated a move back to reporting from the first moment she set eyes on Ritchie, declined to give Adam a hard time in return. Playfully, she called him her 'man in a suit', Ritchie's 'hatchet man' and 'the Godfather's gofer'.

Adam took it in good part. 'Trust me, Lynne,' he told her. 'I'll make sure you're all right. You won't get hurt.'

'Trust you? Which gangster film are you quoting from now? How can I trust a megalomaniac's side-kick?' But she said it with a smile.

'You know what it's like, Lynne. We've both been in this business long enough to know that what's decided one day is likely to be forgotten the next. No one lasts very long. Meanwhile, you're still on the payroll. Life goes on.'

Lynne wasn't so sanguine, but she was reassured by the trouble Adam had taken in breaking the news to her.

'I can't say I *like* your Australian friend,' she told him. 'Doesn't exactly inspire confidence in a woman.'

'You mustn't be too hard on him, Lynne. He's only a visitor to our shores.'

'Like Hitler was to Poland?'

Adam smiled and rounded off the conversation. 'Take you out to lunch?'

Lynne, vulnerable to treats, said she'd love to accept. They had a very agreeable lunch together at Walton's and Lynne discovered that though she'd associated Adam with all that she disliked about Ritchie, he bore some resemblance with all that she disliked about Ritchie, he bore some resemblance to a free spirit.

The way she was being treated, it occurred to her, was like a police interrogation: one fellow doing all the rough stuff, the other playing Mr Nice Guy and offering the cigarettes. Adam was the nice guy and Lynne was susceptible to his charm.

In fact, she found it irresistible. So much so that after presenting what would be her last *Nightly News* the following night, she invited Adam home for a drink and ended up inviting him into her bed.

It was a sticky, close, August night. Lynne's large Irish wolfhound poked around with its snout as they fell to it, which was a new experience for Adam.

Unfortunately, he couldn't stay over, as his wife and five children in Orpington expected him to sleep in his own bed at nights.

CHAPTER 45

The story that March was having David's baby was greeted with derision at N-TV. Nothing could be more far-fetched, people thought. Liz Hastings remembered the morning she'd found David in March's flat at an early hour but, to most people, March seemed positively virginal and David was almost continually abroad. If it hadn't happened before, any connection between them would now be difficult to achieve. But speculation continued that *someone* was dramatically pregnant at N-TV and March did show signs that she was somehow 'different' these days.

The cause was Mark Rippingale. As had been anticipated, he knew nothing of March's views according to *Woman*. Nor had he the remotest idea of the tittle-tattle in the tabloids. That all happened in a world other than Hawkesgrove.

March hadn't been totally bowled over by him on that sunny July day. Mark seemed a touch remote, upper class. His manner was polite but shy. He had a strain of sadness, too, inevitable perhaps from losing his wife the way he had. Or that was what March reasoned. He was also, at forty-one, fifteen years her senior.

But she'd been touched when he plucked up the nerve to ring her. Who wouldn't be flattered by such attentions? He even managed to issue an invitation to visit him again which seemed to contain no innuendo, no hidden motive. It was a throwback to an earlier type of courtship.

In a phrase, Mark was old-fashioned. His clothes, his manners, his haircut. And such is life's way, she instantly overcame all her unstated prejudices when the call came.

The first weekend they spent alone confirmed her expectations. Mark seemed keen to demonstrate his world and his indifference to hers. The few people who drifted in and out of Hall Farm didn't seem to know who she was either. They treated her as a distant relative from the town.

On the Saturday night, they dined alone in the pillared room, waiting on themselves from the array of delicious dishes Mark's

256

housekeeper had left on the sideboard. Afterwards, March accepted a brandy, complaining of the slight chill of the late summer night in the big house.

'We'd better m-make tracks, then,' Mark said, quietly. 'I m-mean – we'd better keep each other warm.'

'Yes. I rather think we better had,' replied March, surprised at how easily they'd slipped into it.

Mark shut the kitchen door, to keep all the animals out of the rest of the house, took March by the hand and led her upstairs.

Moonlight streamed down from a glass dome at the top of the stairwell. The only sounds they could hear were those of peace and beauty.

Mark turned a switch by the side of the bed, and March again recognized the twentieth Mozart piano concerto. By the time they were between the sheets, the disturbing strains of the *Allegro* had given way to the *Romance*, to which they made love.

'Mark, there's something I want to ask you,' she said to him, just before driving back to London on the Sunday night.

They had spent the day walking in the long grass and having a picnic in the late summer fields where combine harvesters droned continuously.

'Have you ever seen me on television? Have you any idea what I do?'

'Erm, I'm a late developer,' he smiled in that rather serious way he had. 'But the other night, I did contrive to see you, yes. I'd called on the rector to pick up some jam his wife had m-made. He had his old set on. And there you were. You looked very nice and terribly professional. Interviewing some AIDS victim, I understood ...'

'Oh, that, yes ... so you have a *little* idea?'

'Yes, I do ... but not really very much. I live a rather m-medieval life in the country. Reading books. Running the farm, all that. It doesn't leave a great deal of time for watching TV, even if I had one. I get all the news I want from a newspaper. I hope that isn't impolite?'

'No, I love it,' March laughed. 'I'm just so pleased that you don't ... *like* me because of the publicity.'

'No, I like you for what I can see and what I can sense. I'd rather not know the rest.'

'You really are wonderfully ignorant about me, aren't you?'

'Why? Is there m-much to know? Are there dark secrets?'

'I sometimes make mistakes ... I'll tell you about them one day.'

Mark smiled. He bent over to pick small tufts of moss from the crazy paving. At times, he could look terribly lonely and sad, but when challenged he flatly denied it.

'Promise me one thing, then,' March said very positively.

'What's that, M-March?'

'You'll never buy a TV.'

'Hardly a difficult promise to keep.'

March edged near, put her arms round him, kissed him on the side of the forehead, and announced she'd have to be setting off home.

As she drove across country, the Cirencester and Oxford route, she noticed the first, small hint of autumn in the air. She lowered the car window and let the breeze brush back her hair. It made her a touch anxious, this hint of the coming season.

It reminded her of new beginnings at school. The smell of new pencils, new exercise books. She felt deliciously nervous but didn't know quite what about.

CHAPTER 46

Godfrey Manchester was a British businessman who'd been charged with spying by the Russians and given a long prison sentence. The word around N-TV was that he clearly *was* a spy, but the official line – which Manchester himself put forcibly at his 'trial' in Moscow – was that he was not.

Whatever the case, he was in luck, because his conviction happened to coincide with the first visit to the Soviet Union by Prime Minister Ross. It was always felt that, on such rare occasions, British Prime Ministers shouldn't spend *all* their time being photographed in Red Square or downing too many lethal vodkas at Kremlin receptions.

And so, a job-lot of minor irritations was drawn up by the Foreign Office so that, in a spirit of international friendship, soothing balm could be publicly applied. Among the job-lot was the freeing of Godfrey Manchester.

In time, word filtered through that Manchester would be arriving from Moscow on a British Airways flight, reaching Heathrow at 7:05 in the evening.

'That's tight for the Big News, isn't it?' the duty editor mused. 'If we send someone down there, by the time he's through immigration and customs, it'll be 7:35 at the earliest.'

Lynne was wearing a Burberry, so she looked quite the reporter as she found herself being driven out to the airport by Jelly Bean and Nosmo King just after six. They reached the terminal just as the news on the car-radio pipped seven o'clock. Should they have a hand-held camera to catch Manchester coming out of the Arrivals area – or just set up in the press conference suite?

'I think we'd better have hand-held,' Lynne said, taking one look at the rival crews from BBC and ITN. 'They're all ready to grab him as he comes out. We'd better not risk it.'

A man from the Civil Aviation Authority, recognizing Lynne, came across and told her, 'Everything'll be all right. Mr Manchester is being met off the plane. We'll take him straight to the conference room, so there's nothing to worry about.'

'Well, this is better organized than some,' she remarked to the BBC reporter.

'I wouldn't bank on it,' he replied. 'Not if our Fleet Street friends have anything to do with it.'

'Why?'

'See those two over there, looking like used-car salesmen?'

'Yes.'

'They're from the *News of the World*. Say they've bought him up. Exclusive.'

'Manchester?'

'Yes. So they'll be none too keen for him to say anything to us.'

And so they all stood together. Four television crews and about ten newspapermen, waiting for this man – who might or might not have been a spy, and whom they might or might not be allowed to interview – to pop through the gates.

'I wonder what he looks like,' Lynne wondered. 'Almost impossible to tell from the photos we had of him at the trial.'

'You won't miss him,' said Nosmo, the cameraman. 'He'll be the one with snow on his boots.'

The Arrival doors slid back and a man of medium height, with shaved head and pasty complexion, was bundled out. On one side of him was a small, plain-suited official from the airport, whose job it was to steer him towards the press conference. On the other, there was a taller man whom Lynne instantly recognized as a *News of the World* reporter.

The crews moved forward. Microphones, Lynne holding one of them, were thrust forward. Extra lights were switched on and held up. A small area of theatre was created in the Arrivals hall.

'Now, please, please – to the conference room, everyone,' the liaison official cried out feebly.

The whole group moved slowly in that direction, taping as it went. When they had elbowed their way through the automatic sliding doors and any number of innocent travellers, the party came to a standstill in the roadway between the terminal and the Queen Elizabeth building.

'Now, please ...' The official did his best to make sure there was no hold-up.

Manchester had been told that his wife and mother were waiting for him in a nearby airport hotel, courtesy of the newspaper, and he decided that he must have his emotional reunion *before* his press conference. A row broke out with TV and other newspaper reporters calling the *News of the World* heavies every name they could think of, with the upshot that everyone ground to a halt in the middle of the setting-down zone used by departing passengers.

Cameramen elbowed their colleagues aside to get the best shot of at least part of Manchester's face. Microphones were inserted in the general direction of his mouth, through any available gap. Questions were shouted out of the 'How badly did they treat you in prison?' and 'What does it feel like to be home?' variety.

Finally, the prisoner was released from media bondage and allowed to drive off to his hotel reunion. Lynne, who had hardly managed to get a word in, took the tape and handed it to the despatch rider. He roared off back to London with it at 7:45, fifteen minutes before the *Nightly News* would be starting.

In the third segment of the *Nightly News*, March introduced a part of Lynne's airport 'report'. The tape had arrived back at N-TV at eight-thirty. A quick look at it by one of the producers confirmed that it wsa a mess but there was a 50-second run which could be shown without editing.

The tape was marked up and handed in at the VTR room.

When Ritchie saw it going out on air he let rip at Adam Ravenscroft.

'What the hell does that woman think she's playing at?' he barked. 'All I can see is the back of Lynne-fucking-Kimberley's head and the bloke's nose. The only face I recognize in the whole fucking stew is the BBC guy! What do we want *him* for? She'll have to go, you know ...'

Lynne was wondering how to salvage matters. Briskly efficient, she told Jelly and Nosmo to jump in their car and drive, as discreetly as possible, to the Post House Hotel a mile away. 'I've a hunch,' she said.

It was hunch that proved correct. The *News of the World* had indeed put Manchester's wife up there. Not only was the N-TV team able to tape the actual moment of reunion, but Lynne persisted and won a proper interview with the couple. None of the other news teams had thought to do the same.

It was Lynne's hard luck that it was now past nine o'clock, the *Nightly News* was off the air, and her exclusive would be relegated to the hourly bulletins.

When Lynne returned from the airport, feeling half-triumphant, half-wretched, she sought solace from whoever was available.

Adam had gone home straight after the show. March had disappeared back to her flat in the chauffeur-driven car, so Lynne had to settle for Paul Whitehall.

'You poor love,' he said, taking her across the road to Greeley's for a drink. 'That was a cock-up and a half, from what I could see.'

Paul had been directing the show at the studio end and was just coming down off his own particular ceiling. But he could see how disappointed Lynne was about the airport incident.

'Honestly, Paul, there was nothing I could do about it. The whole agreement fell apart. No press conference. Just a rugby scrum in the middle of the airport. Even if I was some hefty foot-in-door man, I couldn't have done any better, could I? Except, I got it in the end ...'

'When it was too lat for the Big One ... Showed you could pull it off, but that's hardly the point, is it? If it's any consolation, your face *was* plastered all over the BBC report. On the *Nine O'Clock News*! Lovely big close-up of you!'

'Oh, don't, Paul. It's too embarrassing. I'm just not cut out for that sort of muscular journalism. Leave that to the David Kenways of this world, say I.'

'You're so *good* in the studio, too. I've no idea why they took you off it.'

'Oh, that's Patrick Ritchie for you. I could strangle him.'

'Come back, Sir Charles ...'

'Oh, don't say *that*, Paul. It's too misery-making.'

Lynne crumbled and had to have another gin.

'It's a long way from the Villa San Michele, that's for sure,' said Paul, to cheer her up. 'That was nice, wasn't it? The older I get the more I live for my little trips. Don't you find that? When I'm abroad I could run down the street, swing round the lamp-posts, just like Gene Kelly.'

'Does your Trevor like all that? Musicals, I mean.'

'What's that about *my* Trevor, love? What are you incinerating?'

'Well, I thought, seeing as how ...'

'Yes, I know. A bit bold, but you have to take your pleasures where you find them, don't you?'

'You're usually so discreet, Paul.'

'Aw, come on. I'm not the whole hog, you know. Just gay-ish. I've knocked the odd nail in, you know, in my time.'

'I'll remember you, whenever I'm in need of it ...'

'Chance'd be a fine thing! What about you and Nikki ...?'

'Come off it, Paul. Just because we go on holiday together, doesn't mean we're a couple of dykes. I won't speak for myself, but Nikki is as hetero as all get out. So don't go spreading that one about.'

'Mmm. I expect you're right. A little bird told me that Nikki got up to something very naughty with Charlie Black, the cameraman, one night. On the studio floor, they said.'

'You're so indiscreet, Paul, I wouldn't dream of telling you the true facts of the case.'

'Which are ...?'

'It wasn't Charlie Black. It was David K. And it wasn't on the floor, it was on the newscasters' desk.'

'Gawd! Design department would throw a fit if they knew.'

'They won't ever find out, Paul. That's an order.'

'OK. So I won't tell you what *I* heard about David Kenway.'

'Oh, come on. Fair's fair. Even up the score.'

'Might I just drop in your shell-like ear the name of Vanessa Sinclair?'

'No!'

'Yes.'

'Do you know something, Paul? The South Africans really botched it when they failed to blow up David Kenway.'

'That's the spirit, Lynne. Feeling better now? Like to slag off anyone else?'

'How about March? She gets far too much fuss made of her.'

'Now, now, Lynne, sour grapes do not become you ...'

'Why the hell not. They're about all I've got left ...'

CHAPTER 47

March was looking particularly poised and relaxed when she came in early to the studios one morning at Adam Ravenscroft's request.

'We're doing some newscaster auditions,' he'd told her, 'and we thought it would be nice for them if they had someone established, like yourself, to do their bits and pieces with. Do you mind? We can also see how you'd look working side by side.'

'Why auditions?' March asked, apparently unconcerned about her own position.

'Ben's away, as you know. David and Lynne are on reporting again. We're a bit short ...'

'Anybody I know?'

'Mostly they're from outside. One or two from BBC and ITN, with bags over their heads. We've looked at their videotapes, of course, but we want to put them through their paces in the studio. And there's one candidate from the newsroom.'

'Who's that?'

'Mike Feather. He put himself forward. Might work.'

'Oh.'

She patiently helped all the candidates with their auditions. When it came to Mike Feather's turn, March felt obliged to be especially helpful. After all, it was the least she could do.

They had to read news stories together, interview each other, and chat ad lib. Paul Whitehall was directing and Adam Ravenscroft went through all the tricks. He tried to throw Mike Feather with various disasters: stopping the teleprompter in mid-sentence so he had to scrabble on the desk for his script, and sending the studio manager on hands and knees across the floor when Mike was interviewing March, with a note saying she was being too cooperative and would she please clam up.

'Very promising,' said Adam, a shade equivocally, as he came into the studio at the end of Mike's time. 'You still need to relax more, though.'

'Yes,' Paul chimed in. 'And you're sitting all wrong. Get your bottom further forward on the seat. Get your bottom right and everything else follows.'

'So I've heard,' Mike replied, with a knowing look in Paul's direction.

There was real urgency behind N-TV's search for new faces on its *Nightly News* and hourly bulletins. The evidence that now stared Patrick Ritchie in the face was potentially disastrous.

Advertising traditionally fell off during the summer months – it was the same for all TV companies – but the word from N-TV's Sales Department about the autumn was deeply disturbing. Forward bookings for the remainder of September and through to the expected Christmas peak were twenty or thirty per cent down on the previous year.

Patrick Ritchie, though putting his usual bombastic face on it, was secretly alarmed. He was reluctant to accept that any of the blame for the downturn in N-TV's fortunes should be laid at his door.

'The programming's basically the same as last year, isn't it, Adam?' he asked his deputy. 'I've moved one or two people around and pepped up the content, but nothing too fundamental.'

'I don't know what it is, either,' Adam said, soothingly. 'It may just be cyclical. We were flavour of the month at the beginning of the year, winning all the awards. Now we're not. Fickle old public, fickle old advertisers. We bat on a narrow wicket, any way, dealing solely in news. Viewers come and go according to what's *in* the news. We're running into the party conference season which is a big turn-off. What we need is some bloody good running stories.'

'What we need is a bloody miracle, frankly.'

'Advertisers are as hysterical as the Stock Exchange. Slightest hint of difficulty and they demand new programmes, sacrificial lambs.'

'Yep, well, if they want my head, they can't have it!'

In the background hung the possibility of a worse fate for the company. If cashflow got bad, there might have to be an infusion of funds from outside. Maybe a takeover. There was no shortage of predators.

'I've had an idea and I don't know how it'll strike you,' Ritchie said to Adam, quietly and more conspiratorially than usual. 'Have you ever heard of Guy Treacy?'

'No, can't say that I – oh, hold on, wasn't he once with Ted Turner in the States?'

'He worked for Cable News for a while, yes. He's also worked for about twenty or thirty city stations in the States, pepping up their news coverage.'

'You mean, he's a "news consultant"? We need one of *those*?'

'Yes, Adam. It's never been done here, has it? You're all too buttoned up. Well, I'm going to give him a try. See what he can do. Guy Treacy has worked miracles in his time. Like a dose of salts when he gets to work.'

'Is he expensive?'

''Course he's expensive. But you got to spend a buck to make a buck. You know that. I imagine he'd probably do a deal with us on the basis of a flat fee plus a bonus on results.'

'If he puts the ratings up, he gets more loot?'

'That's for sure.'

'Are you going to refer this to the Board? They might not like it.'

'No. I'm not going to refer it to that bunch of stuffed-shirts. I'm quite within my rights to take on whatever consultants I like.'

'Be it on your head, then, Pat.'

The first proposal to come out of the consultancy agreement Guy Treacy signed with N-TV was greeted with laughter from one end of the company to another. It was simple. Some would say simple-minded. The name of the *Nightly News* should be changed to the *Big News*.

Treacy, a small, balding man with a bow-tie and spectacles that seemed to cover most of his face, was unrepentant. Ritchie backed him to the hilt.

'I agree with Guy. It has a confident ring to it. A good number of news shows are called that in the States. And I don't care if a lot of stuck-up Brits don't like it. At least it'll get us noticed, and that's what matters.'

'We'd get noticed if we called it the *Mickey Mouse News*,' Liz Hastings pointed out cynically.

The idea was quietly dropped.

CHAPTER 48

Jo Lake Kenway was finding that her secret affair with Aaron Rochester, for all its excitement, was running into one of the same obstacles as her marriage to David. It was just her luck to have fallen for a man in the same profession who had to travel so much.

David had been to Moscow with the Prime Minister, also to Nicosia and Tripoli, Brussels and Benidorm – all within the space of a month. Aaron, for his network, had been on the Nicosia and Tripoli stories, too, but also to West Berlin, Dublin and Stockholm.

One September afternoon, as they lay in bed in Aaron's *pied-à-terre* near Harrods, Jo ventured to find out how much contact there had been between her lover and her husband on their recent assignments.

'Do you think David *knows* about us?' Jo asked.

'No. I don't think he suspects a thing. Tunnel vision. He only has eyes for one thing when he's abroad. Sorry, two things: his work and his girlfriends.'

'And you don't let on about *us* ...'

'No, Jo, I don't. I am a master of dissimulation. I'd have made a wonderful spy if I hadn't ended up in this godforsaken job. There are people who believe I am a spook, of course. Working for the CIA. But it doesn't happen to be true.'

'How do I believe you, since you're a master of dissimulation?'

'There's no answer to that. But to answer your original question, if you can take it, your name doesn't readily come up between us.'

'I can take it ...'

'And I'm not the sort of guy to play with fire by introducing it. I don't want to run the risk of losing you.'

Aaron kissed her on the nose and held her tighter to him.

Ben Brock had returned from the United States after an exhausting six-week schedule of interviews and to-camera pieces for *The Entertainers*.

Then it hit him. He was terribly alone.

Filming in the States had merely distracted him from the void left by Natalie's death. The young team he had worked with had been great fun. Every day had been crammed with interesting activity and there had been scores of stimulating people to meet.

Now all was quiet again. He missed being part of a team. So it was with relief that he received a dinner-party invitation.

'Do come – and I promise I'll not pair you off with anyone, Ben. I don't see the need to have an even number round the dinner table, anyway. So much more lively if people aren't trying to seduce one another. They've got time to join in the general cut and thrust.'

The speaker was Yvonne Hamilton – Lady Hamilton, as it happens, and thus the inspiration for a number of ribald jokes. Her remarks to Ben about not pairing off her guests were undoubtedly sincere. But she omitted to mention that, as the hostess herself was a widow and unattached, there was still scope for pairing off single men at her frequent social gatherings.

Yvonne Hamilton was striking rather than beautiful, people would say. She had a vast mane of blonde hair, her make-up was lavishly but expertly applied, her frocks were of the very best, and there were few parts of her body which didn't seem to be draped in the most expensive jewellery. In other words, she did not hide her wealth. Indeed, Ben had been heard to liken her to a Christmas tree. She had a full figure, she glittered and shone. She also talked volubly in a mezzo-soprano voice.

Ben parked the Rolls in the pathway of the substantial Hamilton house in Avenue Road, St John's Wood. He made a mental note that it was time to switch to a smaller vehicle now that parking had become such a problem. A manservant greeted Ben and took him up to the first-floor reception room which was already quite full. The other guests were politicians, publishers, businessmen, even a pair of minor Royals notorious for their pushy manners.

Ben made a beeline for Richard Dobson, a junior minister at the Foreign Office, knowing who he was and not wanting to go through the tedious business of pumping a fellow guest for information about himself. Dobson's wife, Susan, was with him.

'Haven't seen you on the box much recently,' Dobson commented.

'Yes, well, I'm having a bit of a break from the news just now. In fact, I'm working on a series for the BBC about something completely different ...'

'How interesting!' exclaimed Susan Dobson, without asking Ben what it was.

'It's a history of popular entertainment. Quite brought me up with a jerk it has. Thought I knew it all. I now find myself having to read endless books, trying to pin down facts and dates. Alas, it's almost impossible with show-business biographies. No better than fan-fodder most of them. No historical sense at all.'

'Dear, dear,' said Dobson, not totally absorbed. 'Still, it explains why we haven't seen you for so long.'

'Yes, I suppose so.'

'I imagine they'll be glad to have you back at N-TV. By all accounts they're going through a sticky patch.'

'Really? I'm rather out of touch.'

'You'll have heard at least we've got a new Foreign Secretary?'

'I have, indeed. Sally Gerald. Interesting appointment.'

'Well, we're very pleased at the FO. But there was a spot of bother even over that. N-TV did a very loaded piece about Sally when she was appointed, lots of dirt and innuendo. Didn't go down at all well, I can tell you.'

Ben tried to find a way out of the conversation. He didn't wish to spend the evening discussing N-TV's supposed perfidy. Relief, of a sort, was to hand when he spotted the portly form of Derek Jordan, an outrageously camp actor, hovering not far away, very much on his own. Ben half-knew him and waved him across, always glad to be able to jumble worlds together. He introduced the actor to the Dobsons. They were friendly but at arm's length.

'I suppose people think you're resting, Derek, if they see you out and about in the evenings,' Ben prompted him. 'It's the same with me now. People think I'm unemployed if I'm free for dinner.'

'Actually, I *am* resting,' said Derek, confidentially, with a small flutter of his hands. 'But I've got a lovely part in a film coming up. Eight weeks in Cyprus during November. It'll be heaven, so I should worry.'

'Wonderful,' said Ben, beaming, as though he was genuinely happy for the actor. 'Lucky for some. I hope you'll behave yourself with the locals.'

At dinner, Ben found himself seated next to his hostess. They tried very hard to out-beam each other. Both had considerable charm. Enough in fact to light up a whole neighbourhood. Their fellow diners noticed how well they looked together and how entertainingly they talked.

It was not long before Yvonne touched on Ben's widower status. 'You'll get used to it one day, dear. I felt like half a person for *years* after Desmond died. But little by little feeling returns.'

Ben knew she was exaggerating. Sir Desmond Hamilton, the industrialist, must have been dead for a good five years now and Yvonne had hardly blinked when he died at the age of sixty-eight. True, there had been a spot of bother over the will. With £4.5 millions at stake, this was only to be anticipated. But an ex-wife and a phoney illegitimate daughter had been successfully fought off and Yvonne, twenty-five years her husband's junior, came into the lot.

'I'm trying not to rush things,' Ben said. 'That would be easy in my position. I've already chucked in my work at N-TV. But, fortunately, I can always go back. Everything else, though, is stalled. I wonder about selling my house in town and commuting from the farm in Oxfordshire, but then I think I would go barmy out there on my own. Then I think of selling the farm, but it means so much to me and, I think, to the children, too. So I don't know whether I'm coming or going. Mind you, when I arrived here this evening, I did seriously wonder about getting rid of the Roller. It's such a job parking in town.'

'Oh, I should, Ben. Much too ostentatious for the likes of you. I mean, your style mustn't be too show business, must it?' With a shake of her mane and a flash of several-thousands-pounds' worth of diamonds, Yvonne let out a loud, full-throated laugh.

Yvonne liked to think of herself as a latter-day political hostess, as though her house in St John's Wood might come to resemble a French salon where the great thinkers and men of action of the day might mingle. She was having quite considerable success at it. Few politicians, except the most die-hard Left-wingers, felt able to refuse her invitations and the contacts she had spread out from politics, through the media, to the worlds of entertainment and the arts.

'I consider a day wasted when I haven't introduced one person to another,' she had proclaimed, a little grandly, on one occasion.

'D'you know, Ben,' she now leant towards him, and whispered, 'a little bird told me ...'

'Another of your little birds, Yvonne? You must have a cageful!'

'Yes. But not anyone here tonight, I'll tell you that. This little bird told me that the Cabinet discussed N-TV on Thursday.'

'I suppose it was the usual thing. Ross thinks we're biased. Am I right?'

'Quite right. It seems they'd been banking on the new editor – Richmond, is it?'

'Ritchie.'

'Him, yes – changing the *tone* of N-TV, but they think he's only made matters worse. So Colin Lyon is busy plotting as usual.'

'That man! Smile on the face of the tiger.'

'You ought to get back in there, Ben, and throw your weight about a bit.'

'Dear Yvonne, it's not as *simple* as that. I don't carry much clout. I'm just the fairy on the Christmas tree. There's very little I can do to change the flavour of the output. Besides, I'm not sure I even want to. I see no harm in a TV news organization being *generally* opposed, if not outright hostile, to the government in power. It seems infinitely preferable to the cosy relationship that Ross and his chums seem to have in mind.'

'So you'll not go back?' Yvonne looked almost petulant at her proposal having been squashed, however charmingly, by Ben.

'I've said I'm staying out of the way until the first of February and that's final.'

Derek Jordan attempted to take the small amount of heat out of the disagreement by saying, 'I hear that N-TV's ratings are on the slide. Shows they can't do without you, Ben!'

'It's got nothing to do with me. I'm so out of touch, I don't even know whether the ratings *are* on the blink or not.'

'Yes, they are,' said Derek, confidently. 'Or the advertising's down. One or the other. I read it in the paper.'

'Oh well, it must be true, then!' laughed Ben. 'It sounds as though I'm well out of it.'

Ben dutifully worked his way round the other guests after dinner and ate more brandy truffles with his coffee than he should have done.

'You'll put on weight,' Yvonne teased him. 'In fact, I think you *have* put on weight since I last saw you.'

'It's all that junk food you have to eat in America.'

'More coffee?'

Ben was the first to leave, finding it hard to conceal his yawns. His body-clock had shifted and, whereas when he was regularly on the *Nightly News* he was at his peak between eight and midnight, he now rapidly declined after about ten. It would be a struggle getting back into the routine come February.

Perhaps he wouldn't do it after all.

'Goodbye, Ben, dear,' Yvonne leant forward, indicating that she expected to be kissed on both cheeks. 'We must see each other again soon.'

'That would be lovely, Yvonne.'

'Two lonely people. We must hold each other up!'

What a schemer, thought Ben as he drove home. But impossible to resist. Yvonne was the most glamorous steam-roller he had ever been run over by.

CHAPTER 49

March didn't know whether to laugh or cry.

She was sitting by the window of her flat overlooking Hyde Park. She had done her early-morning exercises, which she did religiously, and was now sipping orange juice, munching an apple, and thumbing through the great wodge of newspapers delivered to her door.

Tim Rathbone, now the editor of the diary column in the *Express,* was stating confidently that David Kenway and Jo were about to split and that David planned to marry March ...

She was still gnawing at the gossip item as she dried herself after her shower and set about drying her hair. As always now, whenever anything appeared about her in the papers, her reaction was, 'I hope Mark doesn't see this'. There was little chance that he would, or that he would be bothered if he did, but March's fear was an indication of just how far she had settled her affections on him.

They had seen each other only three or four times – always in the country, never in London. They rarely talked during the week: Mark was not at his best on the phone. But, never mind, he was *there*. Something of a rock. She knew he would be 'faithful' to her. March was enjoying the slowness of it all, as well as the unlikeliness. The thing that would spoil it would be if it became public knowledge, or even common knowledge round the office. And that depended on Vanessa. Her secretary knew just a little too much about everybody – herself, Lynne, Ben, David ... Ah, yes, David. What a mistake it had been even to try and win him.

At least Adam had the grace not to wait until he'd been to bed again with Lynne before he broke the news to her.

He asked, with some urgency in his voice, if he could call one evening when she wasn't on reporting duty. He duly turned up, looking suitably cowed, carrying a very expensive bottle of malt whisky.

'I'd better come straight out with it,' he said, after giving Lynne a peck on the cheek. 'I've got to give you the concrete handshake.'

273

'Because they know about *us*?'

'No, Lynne, they don't know *anything* about what there may have been between us.'

'"May have been," eh?'

'Has been, is, will be, may be . . .' Lynne quite enjoyed Adam's embarrassment and was not inclined to lessen it. 'So what grave news have you come to impart?'

'We – they – I mean the company – N-TV –'

'You mean Patrick Ritchie . . .'

'Yes, OK. He wants you to go, completely, now. Between you and me, he's doing it for all the wrong reasons and I'm not supposed to tell you what they are . . .'

'Typical, isn't it, he couldn't tell me face to face?'

'I've often spoken up on your behalf before, and I'm not just saying that. So I've been given the dirty work to do.'

Lynne continued cool outwardly, though her pulse was racing.

'And what are the reasons you're not supposed to tell me?' she asked.

'You've got to appreciate, Lynne, that Ritchie is your original Aussie bastard. From the land of the male chauvinist pig. To him sheilas are for one thing, possibly two. But whatever it is he wants them for, he wants them younger than you. He thinks you're too old for the box. He can't see you responding to requests to jazz up your appearance. He doesn't like your on-air image, whether you're reading the news or out reporting. Call it a clash of personalities.'

'You can say that again! I could do him for wrongful dismissal.'

'Ah, well, I'm glad you mentioned that. It's not dismissal, in his language. It's a simple parting of the ways and you'll be paid up to the end of your contract.'

'Big deal. It only has another two months to run . . .'

'Well, perhaps a sweetener could be arranged.'

'I'd better speak to him.'

Adam winced. 'No, Lynne, he plays by different rules. When Ritchie gets rid of people, it's like a trap-door opening. It's instant. No physical traces must remain.'

'So, I'm a non-person *already*?'

'Yes. There's no need for you to return to N-TV. I can pick up your belongings.'

'So, no farewell party, no gold watch?'

'I'm sure something will be arranged – off the premises.'

'I knew it would come to this! As soon as Charlie Craig pulled out, I knew it instantly.'

'I'm sorry, Lynne. That's his management style. He just said one thing: "Ask her not to rock the boat." I suppose he means publicity.'

'Rock the boat! Of course, I'll bloody well rock the boat. Why shouldn't I?'

'Just be careful, Lynne, that's my advice. If you talk to the Press, he could get you over the confidentiality clause in your contract. Then you'd really be dismissed. No talk of sweeteners, then.'

'"I WON'T BE GAGGED, she said." Who the hell does he think he is, Adam? Of *course* I'll talk to the Press. I'm not taking this lying down, I can tell you. I'll jolly well create a stink if I want to. Enjoy it, even if it means losing every penny.'

'Be careful, Lynne.'

'I think you'd better go, Adam.'

It wasn't just Patrick Ritchie who wanted to see the back of Lynne. Guy Treacy had his fingerprints on the dagger, too.

Treacy had been moving through the whole N-TV operation seeing how it functioned, asking questions, taking notes, and thinking how the programmes could be improved. He took the widest possible brief and not all of his conclusions were what Patrick Ritchie had expected.

'Drop the Kimberley woman, yeh,' said Treacy. 'We're agreed on that. She's a write-off. Promote Delia Steele to full-time on the Big News. But she needs some money spent on her. Needs to go to a hair-stylist. Looks like a tramp. She needs help with her clothes, too. She's too freaky. We might run to a nose-job?'

Ritchie nodded, not disagreeing or quibbling over cost but with an inevitable acceptance of whatever Treacy proposed.

'I recommend that Mike Feather be given a *trial* run as a newscaster, say for a month. There's a lot of wrinkles in him need to be smoothed out. But he's gotta make his mistakes on camera. That's the only way to correct them, when he sees them played back afterwards. He may be too flip for a news show, but I reckon he's worth trying.'

'He looked good with March, didn't he, at the audition?'

'Yes, pleasant couple, but perhaps not the ideal mix. Which brings me to my next point. You gotta bring back Ben Brock.'

'Now, Guy, you know what I feel on that subject. Nothing

doing. I don't want him back, thinking he owns the ruddy place
...'

'I'm your news consultant, Patrick. Take my advice, and
pronto. What the Big News lacks now is authority. Someone the
viewers, male and female, can respect. You got that man in Ben
Brock. One in a million. I can't imagine how you let him go.'

'I can't get him back before February now.'

'Are you sure about that? Throw some money at him. Apply all
the levers. But I'm telling ya, get him back.'

Ritchie ungraciously assented. He thought he had made all the
right decisions before Treacy arrived, but they hadn't worked.
There must be something wrong with Britain if its viewers failed
to respond to his bright new approach.

'I'll try. See what can be done.'

'Otherwise, frankly, Pat, I think your head's on the block. The
station will go under. You've got to get back on top by Christmas,
or you'll be on a slow boat back to Australia.'

'OK, OK, OK, I've taken it all on board. I'll do everything you
say. Damn you.'

CHAPTER 50

As well as getting tired earlier in the evening, Ben had taken to waking earlier in the morning. He hated being in his bed alone with no one to murmur to in the half-light. And so he got up as soon as he awoke and pottered down to the kitchen in his dressing gown, at about six o'clock.

Never mind whether Mrs Baldwin would object, he tracked down the machine and made himself a pot of black coffee which he took to his study. With the curtains still drawn against the October cold, he would type away at the manuscript of his book. He found that he was warming to the theme of *The Entertainers*. He was also gratified that the transcripts of his interviews read so well.

At eight o'clock, the housekeeper brought him his normal breakfast – orange juice, croissants, lashings of butter and thick-cut Oxford marmalade, another pot of coffee, and the newspapers. Increasingly, he found the Press described a world with which he'd lost touch. He was starting to miss N-TV, even if it was in a mess. The hustle, the adrenalin, the excitement, the odd spot of glamour. But a dark suspicion lurked in Ben's mind that he might have made a mistake in getting out when he did.

Was the unthinkable possible, that they'd refuse to have him back?

At nine, Ben shuffled into old clothes, shaved, and wrote on. But then the phone started ringing and he cursed himself for not having the will to refuse to answer it.

First, it was Lynne.

'Ritchie's ditched me,' she announced bluntly.

'Oh, Lynne, I *am* sorry. You're not going quietly, I trust?'

'The hell I am. You know me, Ben, I'll take them for every penny I can get.'

'That's the spirit. I hope they've got some pennies left.'

'Will you support me?'

'To the hilt, Lynne. Perhaps I ought to have a word with Charlie Craig. See if he can stir the Board on your behalf.'

'Would you? You'd be a love if you did.'

Ben hadn't done a minute or two more work when the phone warbled again. It was Sharon putting through Patrick Ritchie,

277

the arch-villain himself, who asked politely how Ben was getting on with his BBC series. Then, cutting the cackle even before it had begun, he asked for an early lunch appointment so that they could discuss an important matter. Would tomorrow be in order? At the White Tower?

Ben couldn't refuse. At least it would enable him to find what his own future, if any, with N-TV might be. He lit his first cigar of the day and tried to get back to work. But he couldn't, and so he rang for another mug of coffee.

The phone sprang to life for a third time. Vanessa.

'Oh, Ben, I hate to bother you, but ...'

'Vanessa, how sweet to hear your voice again. I'd almost forgotten what it sounded like.'

'I've got to ask your advice about something.'

'I know what it is and I agree it's terrible.'

'You mean, you know about ... *me*?'

'You haven't been given the sack, too?'

'Not as far as I know. Who has?'

'This is the morning N-TV discovered Old Ben Brock was still alive! I've just had Lynne on. She *has* been sacked.'

'I'd no idea ...'

'Then the Editor asks me to have lunch with him. To discuss some grave matter, no doubt. And now, my darling V, it's you – sounding like a frightened rabbit ...'

'I just wanted to ask a favour, Ben. Not even a favour. Just advice. Can I come to see you?'

Ben pulled a face. 'It sounds urgent. Would you like to come here, have some lunch? We can knock up a salad.'

'You're a lovely man, Ben. At your house? About one o'clock? Bless you.'

Ben knew that work was now out of the question. He would simply have to get up an hour earlier each morning from now on to make up for these diversions.

But the phone hadn't finished yet. This time it was Aaron Rochester of ABC News. Could they possibly have lunch together? He had a proposal to make – on behalf of his organisation. Would the Montcalm, the day after tomorrow, be in order?

'What the hell?' thought Ben to himself. 'Why not? But why am I so popular all of a sudden?'

When Vanessa arrived, she was brisk and matter of fact. She did try to preface her remarks with nice words about how Ben had always been like a father to her and how she'd loved being his companion for the evening when they went to the BAFTA Awards in February ... but Ben cut her off in a kindly way and told her to get to the point.

'There's no one else I can turn to. Nobody at home. Nobody at work. The only person I've told is March and she's – well, she's a bit wrapped up in someone else at the moment and, frankly, I ... hesitate with her ...'

Ben waited patiently. Ignoring the salad he'd mixed, he kept on knifing large helpings of liver pate on to slivers of toast.

'Well, the problem is, and this is why I can't talk to anyone at N-TV, is that it involves somebody else at work.'

'Ah, the plot thickens! Who?'

'David.'

'Ah.' Ben somehow knew that if a woman was in distress at N-TV it was a fair bet that David wouldn't be far from the scene of the crime.

'We had the briefest of fling-ettes, but I'm in the club.'

'And he's not doing the supportive thing, and all that?'

'No. Dropped me like a hot potato and scampered off abroad. He now contrives to be almost permanently away, so I couldn't bend his ear, even if I wanted to.'

'I'm famous for asking the obvious question that ordinary folk want answered, Vanessa. You're going to have the baby, I take it?'

'You bet. I'm not going to be pushed into having an abortion. But I've no one to turn to for advice. My parents would have a fit. It's so outside their experience, living down there in Gloucestershire, reading the *Daily Telegraph* ...'

'I should have thought the *Telegraph* gave an excellent grounding in such matters, but I know what you mean. I speak with all the ignorance of a parent. I'm sure if Heather got into a similar spot, I'd be of no use to her, but other people's parents are always so much easier to talk to than your own.'

'That's why I came to you. The amazing thing is there's a lot of guff in the papers just now about David and March having the hots for each other. It's just not true. They are as different as chalk and cheese. But somehow a mad rumour has got about that he's got *her* pregnant.

'Can I duck it just for now, Vanessa? I'll have to put my thinking cap on. As it happens, I'm having lunch with Ritchie tomorrow. I might have to mention it to him. Would you mind?'

Vanessa shrugged her shoulders. 'If it helps. You're a dear.'

'No, I'm a fool. I was mad ever to leave N-TV. Talk about rats leaving a sinking ship. I left when I was probably most needed. Now I'm not even sure they'll take me back.'

CHAPTER 51

N-TV, obsessed with its own dramas, still found time to report those in the world at large.

An aircraft hijacked by Palestinians was being held at Cairo airport. Five of the American passengers with Jewish names had been bundled out on to the tarmac and shot. There were fears of a new wave of terrorist attacks across the Middle East and Europe.

At home, Godfrey Manchester, the man the Russians had released to scenes of media mayhem at Heathrow, had been found dead, believed to have taken his own life. Lynne worried lest the media fuss had in any way contributed to his death.

A man had been arrested and charged with seven of the eight Zoo Killings. The police had been forced to admit that the zoo element was no more than coincidence.

A travelling team of British hooligans had managed to kill three Dutch football enthusiasts during a 'friendly' match in Amsterdam.

In short, it was one of those periods when viewers hesitated before turning on the TV news. And they were still hesitating in droves before turning to N-TV's *Nightly News* in particular.

David Kenway was about as far from the scene of N-TV's problems and his own domestic crisis as he could possibly get. He tumbled off a Cathay Pacific flight from Hong Kong to Sydney at 10:00 a.m. on that October morning.

It had not been an easy flight. For once, he was not in Cabin Class (or Marco Polo Class, as Cathay Pacific called it) – an indication that all was not well with N-TV's finances – and he'd been forced to travel in a crowded 747.

His problems didn't end either at Kingsford Smith airport. When he arrived unshaven and jet-lagged at the Walmsley Hotel in downtown Sydney, his room wasn't ready for him. Forty-five minutes later, when it was, he found it was the size of a rabbit-hutch and overlooked a brick wall.

He changed rooms only to learn that Sydney was in the grip of a hotel-workers' strike. So there'd be no room service for the duration of his visit and he'd have to make his own bed.

He could sympathize with the American tourist he overheard

arriving at the Walmsley who exploded: 'I've been right the way round the world and haven't once had to carry my own bag, so I'm not going to start now ...

The Australian General Election was less than two weeks away. David was to file at least four reports on the campaign to be used on N-TV bulletins and in its feature slots. He would stay until polling day and be back in London two days later.

The election promised to be a rough and exciting one. The Labour Party had been in power continuously since Bob Hawke defeated Malcolm Fraser in 1985. Hawke had been succeeded by the downbeat Reg Hardy, but the party's decline into scandals and resignations had continued, reminiscent of the bad days Labour went through before Gough Whitlam was ousted as Prime Minister in 1975.

This time, Labour's decline was largely brought about by a sharp drop in the country's mineral wealth. Stringent economy measures had taken a good deal of the shine off Australia's good life. The scene was set for a return to power by the Liberal Party but it could be a close-run contest.

David realized that he didn't know from which branch of Aussie television Patrick Ritchie had come to N-TV. Was it from the Australian Broadcasting Commission or a commercial channel? He thought it would be interesting to find out.

'Never heard of him,' was the first response when he mentioned Ritchie's name to an ABC executive. It was said with such finality that it was obvious the speaker *did* know Patrick but was determined not to get into any discussion of him.

It was only when David had Fred Solar, his cameraman, pinned to the seat next to him on the flight up to Brisbane that he made any progress.

'Why spoil a beautiful day mentioning that alf?' Solar replied to his query.

'So you know him? I can tell from your tone that we're talking about the same guy.'

'Too right. Though, actually, I must be one of the few people in this business who hasn't fallen foul of him. I've only heard about him from people he's shat upon from a great height.'

'Tell me more. You know he's Editor-in-Chief at N-TV now?'

'Serves you right for all those convicts you used to dump on us ...'

'But wasn't he the great shining talent of TV news in Oz? That's the line we were sold.'

'If you want to know, Patrick Ritchie had a gigantic talent for getting up people's noses and staying there. He may have done all the other things TV executives get up to, like employing his wife on his shows, getting caught with his hand in the till, accepting back-handers, and I don't know what, but what I dislike about him is that he's one of those people who move from one golden handshake to another.'

'You mean, he makes a career out of being given the boot?'

'Yeh. It's happened to him half-a-dozen times at least in newspapers, radio and TV. He does a few months' work, has the rest of his contract bought out, makes a packet, lies low for a while and then bounces back.'

'I wonder how N-TV fell for him?'

'The amazing thing,' Solar went on hotly now, 'is that people like him don't actually have to be any good at anything. I think I'm right in saying that Kerry Packer or Rupert Murdoch once made him editor of a paper in Melbourne, and sacked him after *only one day* ... It's unbelievable what they get up to at that level. Sometimes I count my blessings I'm only a humble cameraman ...'

After Brisbane, David and his crew took a flight westwards to Alice Springs in the great Red Centre of Australia. Prime Minister Hardy was due to go walkabout on Saturday morning.

Flies and dust were oppressive in the 31° heat but suddenly there was Reg Hardy striding down Todd Street, almost a caricature of the Australian politician. At one point, he stood up on a truck which had been parked under the trees and addressed a gathering of about fifty people. Two ALP candidates sat on the truck behind him. Hardy was probably doing it for the media exposure – trying to show that he was Prime Minister of *all* Australia, even the remote and underpopulated Northern Territories. There were a few jeers, evoking names from recent government scandals. One or two protesters bore placards denouncing the Prime Minister.

He wasn't to be put off and gave a resilient, literate speech that lasted almost half an hour. David was impressed, not only by the mere fact of it being given at all but because of the way it was delivered.

He was glad they'd made the effort to go there. The footage they now had of Hardy in 'The Alice' would compare nicely with the barnstorming mass rally of his Liberal opponents in Brisbane.

At one point, David introduced himself: 'British television, Mr Hardy. Any chance of a few words?'

'Sure. Be glad to. Where are you boys from? BBC?'

'Not quite, no. N-TV, the all-day news station. Have you heard of us?'

'Indeed, I have. In fact, I'm not sure I ought to be seen talking to you ...'

David looked puzzled, but Hardy laughed.

'Why not, Prime Minister?'

'You've got a renegade Aussie in charge, am I right?'

'Patrick Ritchie.'

'That's the man. We weren't sorry to see him leave our shores, I can tell you. Our gain was your loss.'

David was intrigued by Hardy's combative pose. He wanted to pump him some more.

'Yes, I could tell you a thing or two about Mr Pat Ritchie,' Hardy began, realizing that this rather than the state of the Australian dollar was what had attracted David to further conversation. 'He has a talent for survival, and that's the only talent he has.'

'You mean he's a conman?'

'No, not really. He was adequate in the jobs he held down here with Murdoch, Packer, Fairfax – he moved around pretty fast. But he's more of an operator, if you know what I mean. Good at making the deals, not least for himself, but not so good at carrying them out. I wasn't too surprised he ended up in the old country.'

'Why not?'

'Well, every dog returns to its vomit! He was married to a girl called Karen Longlades – that's a Greek sort of name. She was born in Toorak, in Victoria, a bit of a tuft-hunter, by all accounts. They hadn't been married long when she upped and left him for a lawyer, named Dan Crosbie. I knew him through the ALP in New South Wales. He was quite useful to us. She went with Dan to London and, in time, got divorced from him, too. Never seems to stay long in the same spot. Next thing, I'm talking with Trevor Ross at Downing Street last Christmas, and he ups and says, "My Home Secretary's married to an Aussie!' And it turns out to be that self-same gold-digger, Karen Longlades.'

'So, Karen Lyon used to be Ritchie's wife ...?'

'Yep. That's it.'

'Well, thank you, Prime Minister. I'm rather ashamed I had to come all this way to find the answer to a question, but thank you very much.'

Hardy grinned. 'My pleasure. Time for a beer?'

CHAPTER 52

If Patrick Ritchie was feeling nervous about the current slide in N-TV's fortunes, he at first gave little indication of it when he sat down to lunch with Ben Brock at the White Tower. His chipper manner appeared intact. But he laid his cards on the table swiftly.

'I'll come straight to the point. We want you back. Soonest. I know we left it open that you could return in February but, frankly, it's urgent. February might be too late. It's as bad as that. I want you on the *Nightly News* from next week. Can you do it?'

'No chance.'

Richie looked shocked by Ben's grim-faced answer.

'I still have to finish the book of my BBC series, and there's about a week of dubbing to do in December. Besides, I'm not sure I want to have anything more to do with N-TV.'

'I'll pretend not to hear that, Ben. I want to talk terms and get it buttoned up soonest ... I really need you back next week, with the American Election on Tuesday.'

'Mm. Yes. I'd like to have been in on that. Winston Mann's an old chum, you know. But, as I say, N-TV seems to be so deep in the doldrums, I'm not sure I'd enjoy it any more.'

Ritchie didn't flinch. 'But that's why we need you, to get us out of the doldrums. It's partly because you've not been with us that we've done so badly.'

'That's very kind of you. But the answer's still no.'

'And I'm still not taking no for an answer. What'll your terms be?'

'What *would* my terms be? Let's talk about Lynne Kimberley. I gather you've given her the Big E? She's had her ups and downs, we all know that, but you've made a mistake in dumping her. I see her as part of the N-TV team. She's contributed a lot since we started and still has a lot to give. I think it was what we pommy bastards call a "dashed poor show" that you treated her the way you did.'

'She's been on to you, huh?' Ritchie avoided Ben's piercing look and shredded a roll. 'I know how you feel, Ben. Believe me, it's not easy coming into a close-knit organization with established sets of rules and loyalties. But I've only done what I believe was necessary to make a better station. Lynne was wrong for us.

Guy Treacy believes she's wrong for us. Despite all the so-called affection she's supposed to bring us, that's not the same as ratings points.'

'I don't give a damn what Guy Treacy thinks, but I grant you've the right to make that sort of editorial decision. That's your job. But I believe you handled it very crassly, putting the frighteners on her like that. Completely uncalled for. It's *people* you're dealing with, you know.'

'Let's negotiate about something else,' said Ritchie, his pale face beginning to take on its favourite colour. 'I'm not budging on that issue. The editor's decision is final. What else is on your mind?'

'It may be none of my business ...' Ben sounded as if he was wavering. Was his on-screen presence the only power he wielded at N-TV? 'But I'm actually rather concerned about the environment I work in ...'

'Sure, sure,' nodded Ritchie, with a speed that made Ben wonder whether he really understood.

'So I like people to be happy,' he went on. 'I know the happiest ship is not always the most productive or the most creative, but frankly I don't care as much as I once did about that side of things. I have enough "up yours" money in the bank, if you know what I'm referring to?'

'What can you be leading up to, Ben?'

'What I mean is: I like to be with people who are happy as themselves. Lynne, despite her behaviour, was basically happy, I think. But you've got rid of her. So that's that, you're telling me. March, I'm entirely pleased with. She came through her ordeal well enough and is shaping up very nicely. But, of the newscasters, that leaves David ...'

'Pardon me, Ben, but I don't see David as a newscaster any more. That was just a temporary status he had after his South African experience. He's a correspondent first and foremost. And a very good one, too, no doubt about it.'

'Quite, quite, but I always feel he's after my job and I don't like that. So I wouldn't want him breathing down my neck.'

'No problem, Ben. Now we're negotiating.'

'No, we're not ... If we were, I'd tell you to get rid of that news consultant you've brought in. Quite preposterous. That sort of witch-doctoring may work in the States, or where you come from, but it's absolutely useless in Britain. I'd want to see the back of him before I returned to N-TV.'

'There you are, Ben, I knew you really wanted to be back. N-TV is where you belong. It's where you made your name. It's what you're all about. How about money?'

'I'd need to be taken up to two fifty grand, that's for sure.'

'Maybe ...'

'Editorial control. A seat on the Board ...'

'You name it, we'll give it to you.'

'No, no, I really don't want to do it.'

'I reckon you're melting ...'

'No, I'm not ...'

'Come on, let's have another bottle.'

Ben was quite relieved he hadn't burned his boats. It looked as if they really wanted him back after all.

CHAPTER 53

Lynne's sacking was orchestrated by the tabloid press as though she were a monarch who'd been deposed. Or a soap-opera star who'd finally been written out of the script.

Readers were encouraged to deluge N-TV with their letters of protest. An opinion poll was contrived to show she was the most popular, and sexiest, female newscaster on TV. It seemed only a matter of time before questions would be asked about her in Parliament or a national petition mounted for her return.

Far from being embarrassed by all the fuss, Lynne lapped it up. She was so incensed at the way she'd been dumped that she roundly ignored Ritchie's request not to rock the boat.

Instead, she chose to pull out the plug and all but scupper it.

Just after the storm broke, she accepted an invitation to appear on the BBC's *Derrick Bream Show*. Bream, a former quizmaster and, before that, former comedian, had just been given a new late-night chat-show.

As is always the case with new chat-shows, it started out with the declared aim of attracting topical, newsworthy guests while avoiding the customary circuit of show-offs and pluggers.

So having Lynne on was certainly topical and also gave the BBC an opportunity to enjoy the discomfort of a rival network.

It was unfortunate that the *Derrick Bream Show* had to go out 'live' so late in the evening. This meant that Lynne would have to be lavishly wined and dined beforehand.

Bream's producers and researchers were not unduly worried by Lynne's condition when she arrived at the Television Centre just after ten o'clock. They offered Lynne the run of the hospital-ity room – which meant chicken legs and canapés, if she was still peckish, and the drinks trolley.

She had expected to meet Bream for a short chat before the programme began at eleven but soon realized she'd meet him for the first time, literally, when she walked before the cameras.

To be sure, a bright young female researcher had been round to chat to her the day before and prepare a brief for Derrick Bream. But this only increased the likelihood that any points she wished to make, and any points she didn't wish to make, would get garbled in transmission.

*   *   *

Lynne's appearance was wedged between an interview with a 'professional personality' – who seemed only to appear as a warm-up act on chat-shows and whose real reason for living was difficult to pinpoint – and a song sung by a black American girl who seemed excessively disturbed by an incident in her private life.

When Lynne walked on, wearing a navy, spotted silk dress, she betrayed a slight unsteadiness. This was due as much to the strangeness of the situation as to her alcohol intake. Padding down the thick carpet towards Derrick Bream, who stood waiting for her with outstretched arms, she was surprised to hear the small band tootling a version of the *Nightly News* signature tune. Show business was not what she was used to, she realized. On TV, she liked to be sitting down, well-protected by a newsdesk.

'My, oh my, so here you are, then,' Bream greeted her, implanting a large kiss on her cheek as if they were the oldest of friends, 'and looking so well ...'

Lynne lowered herself into the oddly uncomfortable but artistic armchair and tried to relax in the contrived warmth of the small studio. She was particularly interested in Derrick Bream's features at close quarters. He was heavily made-up, to give the appearance of an all-the-year-round tan. His hair was either not entirely his own or had been cut in an artificial way and then stuck in place with Elnett spray. His body seemed all suit, but the suit hardly looked his own and probably wasn't.

The questions he asked were *definitely* not his own. Lynne found it disconcerting when his eyes looked past her while she was talking, and she had to make a conscious effort to avoid following his gaze to the idiot boards. She also noticed his eyes glaze over if he had to listen to her say more than two consecutive sentences.

'Now, tell me, Lynne, it was suggested by one of the TV writers in the papers, Gabriel Monk I think it was, that you fell victim to the "new broom" at N-TV, one Patrick Ritchie from Australia, I believe ...?'

Lynne swallowed hard. 'You believe correctly...' Then a small voice whispered in her ear, 'Don't rock the boat!' But it was hard to answer the question without doing so. She floundered. 'Well, I – I – don't know, you know. I mean, I worked there for four years under one editor. Then a new one came along and I was out on my ear. I suppose that speaks for itself.'

'Did they tell you why they wanted you to go?'

'Not in so many words – not even in so *few* words – no. It was just made abundantly clear to me that my face and skills no longer "fitted their plans".'

'So what are you going to do, Lynne?'

'Haven't a clue. If all else fails, I can always go on the streets.'

At this remark, the studio audience erupted into uncontrollable but not entirely human laughter.

'Like they used to say, "Don't tell my mother I work at N-TV. She thinks I play the piano in a whore-house ..."'

Lynne was taken back by the reaction. It was a remark she had quite often tossed off casually before. But immediately now she felt she'd made a mistake. She blushed blotchily about the neck and said weakly, 'It's not original ...'

Bream made as much as he could of it and rolled around, almost on the floor, as though Lynne had just said the funniest thing he'd heard in his entire life.

Lynne saw the need to stop the riot and be more constructive. 'No, no. I'm sure I'll find something. I'm a journalist and have been for many years so, you know, I have that skill to fall back on. I might write a book.'

'I'd love to read it!' said Bream, eyes popping.

'But really it's just one of those things. You don't get on with a particular organization and that's that.'

'Talking of which,' Bream said, his eyes gliding to one side again, 'I see that you were quoted as saying – in the *Mirror* I think it was – that you "hate" your former employers. "I hate N-TV," it said. You feel that strongly about them?'

'No, well, I'm glad you asked me that, er, Derrick,' (she had remembered that it was a chat-show), 'because it enables me to put the record straight. I was talking to a journalist – a journalist from a newspaper which shall be nameless – ' (another roar of ecstatic laughter from the audience) ' – and what he wrote was "I HATE N-TV." But what I really said was, "I hate N-TV – you know the way lots of people have love-hate relationships with where they work, but ..." – and it was an important "*but*" – "it's the only place I can do the work I like doing, in the way it should be done".'

'Really!' exclaimed Bream. 'That was what you really said!'

'So, you see, it was the old trick of only printing half the sentence and leaving out the important qualification.'

'So, journalists aren't your best friends at the moment?'

'I wouldn't say that ...'

'Ha, ha!' The audience laughed again, enormously.

Lynne was puzzled by these responses. Was there something odd about the way she said things? Was her slip showing? Had she left the price-sticker on the sole of her shoe? What was it? She thought what she'd said made sense. Everyone else seemed to think it was hysterically funny.

'Tell me, Lynne,' Bream ploughed on, 'you've never been married, have you ...?'

Now Lynne's feeling of unreality was complete. How had he got that idea?

She hesitated and stumbled. 'Er ... well, that's not quite true, you know. I've been married twice before. I was divorced from my first husband, and my second ... died ... some years ago.'

'Oh, dear, Lynne, so you're saying you *have* been married before. Am I right?'

Lynne nodded. Bream feigned penitence.

'Just hand me that rifle,' said the host, without much humour, 'and I'll shoot the entire research staff!'

The audience laughed uproariously. Lynne squirmed.

Obviously concluding that Lynne was more trouble than she was worth, Bream wound up the interview.

While the audience applauded, the band played and Bream told Lynne how wonderful she was and would she return next time to continue their 'truly fascinating conversation'? Then he introduced the black American singer with her little ditty and Lynne was spirited off the set as the lights dimmed.

Bream's chief researcher grabbed her by the hand, mumbling apologetically, 'Of course, he knew you'd been married before – he's like that, I'm afraid. An ace at passing the buck ... but there you are ...'

'No,' said Lynne, 'there I'm not.' She would leave her make-up on, thank you. No, she didn't want a drink. Yes, she'd have a car home straightaway, please.

If there was to be a life after N-TV, this hadn't been the most auspicious start to it.

'He didn't really mean that about my coming back next week, did he?' she asked, finally.

'Oh, no,' replied the researcher. 'He always says that ...'

'Did you see Lynne on Derrick Bream last night?' Adam Ravenscroft gently broached the subject with the Editor-in-Chief.

'I read about it in the papers. Then I looked at the video. She sat upon us pretty hard but I don't suppose people take her seriously, do they? She's an embittered old bag making the ritual whine of the redundant.'

Adam, who hadn't yet abandoned his role as Lynne's representative on the editorial floor of N-TV, was curious to find out Ritchie's real view of her performance. 'I'll give her credit, she didn't rock the boat too much,' he said. 'She could have been much more personal and abusive about all of us, had she wished.'

'She was half-cut,' snapped Ritchie. 'That much was obvious. She could hardly string two words together, not even "piss" and "off".'

'I don't know why she should've been so drunk. *If* she was. She'd been behaving herself very well until she left here. Perhaps that's what's pushed her over the edge again?'

'Wouldn't be surprised. And I suppose I'm to blame for it?'

Sharon came on the inter-com and announced that Gabriel Monk had arrived.

'Monk, from the *Post*!' exclaimed Adam. 'What do you want him for?'

'D'you mind leaving, Adam, there's a little personal matter I have to discuss with him.'

Ritchie had decided to tell Monk precisely why he'd sacked Lynne Kimberley. Monk could hardly believe his ears and made sure that everything spoken was on the record.

'Publish and be sued,' concluded Ritchie.

Prophetically, as it turned out.

CHAPTER 54

Richard Luard wore a dark grey suit with a pink shirt and bow-tie. His hair was exceptionally white. If he hadn't had such a lot of it, his face would have demanded an eighteenth-century wig to go on top. He was seated in a high-backed, winged leather chair. March noticed the neat little teeth which went rather well, she thought, with his small, neat, hairless hands.

'I've been watching you with interest for some time now,' Luard told her warmly, or as warmly as a bank manager might ask a person to open a new account, 'so that is why I made an *approach*. Frankly, I was surprised, and delighted, when you responded. I took it for granted that you'd already have an agent, but that is why one occasionally makes these *approaches* ...'

He dwelt again on the word as if he enjoyed its vagueness.

'In the hope of striking gold' was how March would have finished his sentence but, having come this far, she had to hear him out.

'The problem with being a television presenter in the news field these days,' Luard went on, 'is that you're very vulnerable to editors. You're in a very high-profile position. But should somebody take against you, there are so few alternative outlets for your talents. One has only to think of poor Lynne Kimberley and what has happened to her ...'

March looked down at her hands. It was not a subject she cared to think about.

'And so,' Luard went on, sounding more and more like an insurance salesman advising on the benefits of policies and pensions, 'one would advise a client, and I very much hope that we may get together on this, to make sure she had other options, other irons in the fire.'

'But what else is there?' March asked pointedly. 'I'm not allowed to do commercials, I can't even be a guest on quizzes and chat-shows, except on radio, where it doesn't seem to matter. There's just no time for more major productions and N-TV has me under an exclusivity clause.'

'Hmm.' Luard grasped his lips between his fingers and twisted them. 'You're getting about thirty grand now, I imagine.'

'Thirty-five.'

'That's very nice. But if you were more established we'd be thinking nearer seventy or eighty. As for Ben Brock, have you any idea how much he earns?'

'I've never really thought about it.'

'In the region of two hundred, two fifty.'

'But I'm not in that league. He's twice my age ...'

'One has to look ahead, March. In fact, it's my belief you've got to think beyond news. With your talent, you could front break-fast shows, chat-shows, magazine shows, anything within reason. And once you're away from news, a whole new world will be open to you – industrial videos, presentations, personal appearances, endorsements, even ads. The world will be your oyster. You could earn more than Ben Brock, even. That's the sort of prospect before you.'

March remained composed, resolutely unexcited by the lures Richard Luard was dangling before her. In her short career to date she knew she'd been lucky. She realized, in her heart of hearts, that she wasn't really a journalist, so to mention her in the same breath as Ben Brock was preposterous. Did she have what it took to push on as Luard was encouraging her to do?

Unlike some she could think of, March knew self-doubt. She didn't believe herself the kipper's knickers.

'I want to think it over first. Talk it over with a friend.'

'You have a friend?' asked Luard, considerately. He had once been an actor but now reserved his performances for the office and for negotiating on behalf of clients. His slamming-down-the-phone routine, when a management made a derisory offer, was one of his great set-pieces. Curiously, it seldom failed.

'Yes, I have a friend,' March replied, with a meaningful look.

'Well ... I hope he gives you good advice. Is your friend in the business?'

'No, quite the reverse. He wouldn't recognize the business if it hit him over the head.'

At Hawkesgrove the following weekend, March was dressed for the country at last. Her check riding jacket, pale blue woollen jumper, jodhpurs and riding boots were exceptionally clean and new.

Mark Rippingale was duly consulted about her future in the big city. 'You m-must do as you wish,' was his unpromising first response.

'Come on, Mark, you can do better than that.'

'My view would only be selfish. I don't really understand what you get up to during the week. It's beyond me. I simply want you to be happy.'

'But I *am* happy. I've got my job and ... I've got you at weekends. I like that arrangement.'

'Then you should do nothing to change your life ... unless, of course, you're worried it won't last.'

'My work? It might all stop tomorrow, of course. I could fall out of favour. Go out of fashion. Get *older*, too – worst sin of all if you're a woman.'

'No, I m-meant your real life. The one I share a little corner of.'

March hesitated. Was he hinting that wouldn't last either?

Mark went into the stables. He was dressed as ever in green corduroy trousers, blue striped shirt and his old navy blue pullover. For the first time March noticed a slight trace of grey hair above his ears.

He patted the pony that March had been for a nominal ride on, then he came to her rescue. 'The trouble is, I don't think we should get m-married ...'

March blushed.

'I mean *not yet*. I've been married before, and I'm over forty, and counting ... But you're, surely, too young to take the plunge just yet?'

'Is twenty-six too young?'

'No, but it might be if you want to establish your career. Do you want to be a big TV lady?'

'I'm not sure. I didn't know I had to make a choice.'

Mark took her arm, led her out of the stable block and walked slowly round the garden with her in the fading late October light. There was the intoxicating smell of a bonfire of leaves coming from the kitchen garden over the red-brick wall. The watery sun was almost gone beyond the Severn estuary.

'It all seems very remote when I'm with you, down here,' said March. 'It's hard to believe it really counts, all that London thing. Then when I drive back on Sunday nights, as I see London looming at me, I feel an excitement, an expectation. It just depends where I am as to how I feel.'

'Do you m-miss me during the week?' Mark asked wistfully.

'Yes and no. Oh, Mark, that sounds terrible. What I mean is, I don't mind that you're not with me. I'd worry more if you *were*, with your tweedy suit and woolly socks and corduroys. So, no, I don't mind. But, sometimes when I'm going into Make-Up, sometimes when I'm even on the air, I think of you. Dear old Mark, what'll he be doing now? Sitting by the fire, patting the dog, worrying about the geese ...'

'It's funny that you call me "old Mark" ...'

'Let's go in. I'll make some tea.'

They turned round and the warm glow of Hall Farm beckoned. It was wonderful, thought March, to have the best of both worlds. She didn't want to have to choose between them.

CHAPTER 55

On the first Tuesday of November, the people of the United States went to the polls. Would the present incumbent of the White House, President Carson, survive for another term? Or would he be unseated by the youthful Democratic challenger, Senator Gerry Iver?

Professionally, Ben Brock had to keep his preference to himself. Personally, he was rooting for Iver. If nothing else, it would mean that his friend, Winston Mann, would have the consolation of the Vice-Presidency.

On the morning of the first Thursday of November, Ben added to his responsibilities by hosting a US Election Special from London, introducing coverage from America and interviewing pundits in the N-TV studio.

At lunchtime that Thursday, he found himself *being* interviewed by Aaron Rochester of ABC News. It had been a close-run thing but Henry Carson had lost the White House. He'd made a graceful speech, conceding defeat and, as was remarked at the time, looked glad at being released from the burdens of office, if only it meant he could go back to sleep.

Gerry Iver, the new young President-elect, was at forty-six only four years older than John F. Kennedy had been when he'd gone to the White House. Spirits rose all round. Winston Mann prepared to sink quietly into the obscurity of the Vice-Presidency, a job described by a previous incumbent as 'about as worthless as a pitcher of warm spit' but which Winston, characteristically, saw as being like that of 'the understudy who never gets to play the king'.

Ben reminisced for American TV about their time at college together, and recycled, with some editing, the things they'd said to one another at Oxford earlier in the year.

Afterwards, Aaron suggested they adjourn for that lunch at the Montcalm which had had to be cancelled because of Ben's sudden return to N-TV.

Aaron enjoyed the opportunity of taking a close look at 'the most trusted man in Britain', as Ben had been called again recently. His return to N-TV had occasioned an outpouring of profiles and interviews in the papers, and this was the phrase most frequently trotted out.

'I was surprised, like everybody, that you rode back to save N-TV from the jaws of defeat,' remarked Aaron with something akin to admiration in his eyes.

'Well, they made me an attractive offer and I realized how foolish I'd been to pull out in the first place. But I'd been confused by my wife's death, you know. There's plenty of risk attached. It'll be a long time before we're out of the woods.'

Ben, in turn, was curious about the young American of whom he had also heard much. It wasn't long before they got round to talking of a mutual acquaintance.

'David Kenway's been in Australia – did you know that? – on the election,' said Ben. 'Odd that Reg Hardy got the boot, wasn't it? I rather liked what I heard of him. But it seems to be all change at the moment, all round the world.'

'Is David still there?' asked Aaron, with a close interest that was lost on Ben.

'On his way back, I think. He's always on the move. Unlike me – I stay put.'

'I wonder what David's wife makes of all this ...?'

Ben, happily unaware of the loaded question, simply replied: 'No idea. Never met her. But I hear she gives as good as she gets. She slapped Lynne Kimberley in the face once, or should I now say "the late Lynne Kimberley"? She's also rumoured to have thrown a TV at David. Do you know her?'

'Not really what you'd call "know her", no,' lied Aaron, and drew upon his stoagy.

'Well, here's to the new President and Vice-President of the United States,' cried Ben, seizing his glass.

'The President-elect and the Vice-President-elect,' replied Aaron, rather pedantically.

Back from Australia, David took his bags home by taxi, had a long warm bath, and went to bed. The blankets were warm and delicious and gently enfolded him just as Jo came in to sit on the side of the bed.

'So, what's this I hear about you and Vanessa Sinclair?' she began boldly.

'Oh, not that already,' thought David, as he sank into half-sleep. 'How do you know about that?'

'There's always someone to tell you bad news, you know. After all, that's your job.'

'Please, Jo. Let me get some kip. I can hardly think. Why is it you always want to argue when I'm tired?'

'What are you going to do about it?'

David was torn between sleep and wakefulness. He decided not to say anything.

'Why don't you do the decent thing, then? Marry her. You might as well. I'm not sticking around ...'

Divorce was the last thought David had before he fell down the spiral into the black depths of sleep. It was the first time it had seriously been mentioned by either of them.

'Oh, you're impossible to deal with like this ...' Jo realized she was acting a tantrum and felt strangely guilty as she left her husband to his slumbers.

'Now, don't you start on me, too, Ben ...'

It was lunchtime two days later at the Savile Club. Ben had invited David for a chat: 'There's such a lot to catch up on.'

'And there's a lot I've got to tell *you*, now you're back on board,' said David.

So when they'd sunk the first bottle of claret, Ben broached the Vanessa topic, as he felt duty-bound to do.

'It may not be any of my business,' Ben explained with one of his smiles, 'but gossip will out, David. It's not a conspiracy, I assure you. All I'm saying is, you need to talk to Vanessa. Just now you're behaving like a character in a third-rate TV play.'

'Life often *is* like a third-rate TV play ...'

'Promise me you'll talk to her and sort it out.'

'OK, I will. Now don't lecture me ...'

Bread pudding arrived, sprinkled with orange rind, just the way Ben liked it. The two men fell to it like schoolboys. Later, David even accepted one of Ben's cigars – remarkable, given his view of smokers. They moved on to the port. Ben was on the *Nightly News* that night, but he would sober up, or so he claimed.

'Will N-TV survive?' Ben asked airily.

'Now you're back, why not?'

'Trouble is, there's no effective counterweight to Guy Treacle, or whatever he's called. Patrick Ritchie's from another culture, if not another planet. I'd love to see the back of both of them.'

'Ah, well, thereby hangs a tale, Ben.'

'Come into the smoking room,' the older man gestured. 'Let's finish our coffee there.' When they'd passed through and settled into the dark leather armchairs, David told him of the encounter he'd had with the now former Australian Prime Minister.

'He was surprisingly forthcoming about our Lord and Master, Mr Ritchie. Quite some old wound festering there, I'd say. Anyway, he came up with this extraordinary link – Ritchie's ex-wife is that flashy piece Colin Lyon's married to.'

'What? Karen Lyon was once Mrs Ritchie?'

'Yes. And Karen-something-else in between. I'd never twigged she was Australian, had you? It turns out she's Greek-Australian, which might explain it. The Mediterranean look.'

'And you think there's more to it than that? They're all buddy-buddy together?'

'Yes. But I'm not sure what it amounts to.'

'You know,' said Ben, 'when the BBC were lunching me, trying to get me to defect, just after Ritchie had arrived, I remember I saw him lunching with Lyon ...'

: 'Which might confirm what Reg Hardy hinted: that Karen Lyon still keeps cosily in touch with her various ex's, including Ritchie.'

'Hmm. Cosy? So why is it we're still getting flak from the Government if there's this relationship between Ritchie and Lyon?'

David had no answer to Ben's question. But either way it was pretty rum. Despite the rosier view of the world engendered by the claret, the port and the cigars, and a good school dinner, both men sensed that out of the rum situation might be plucked something not altogether to their disadvantage.

CHAPTER 56

Lunchtime at Greeley's wine bar. Paul Whitehall had just directed five headline bulletins on the trot and felt like nothing more than working his way through a packet of Marlboros and half a bottle of Vino Nobile di Montepulciano. He knew little about wine, but he loved the sound of the name.

As he pushed forward to the crowded bar he met Vanessa fighting her way out with a plate of quiche and shrivelled lettuce.

'You're supposed to have a drink if you buy food,' he told her mock-bossily. 'They'll kill you if they find out.'

'Left my glass of Perrier on the counter. I'm going back for it ...'

Paul said he'd fetch it for her and when he'd laid on the wine for himself, together with paté and toast, he sat down with Vanessa.

'Like a cigarette? I'm desperate. A morning of Mike Feather messing the headlines about is more than I can take, frankly.'

'No, I'm not smoking at the moment,' said Vanessa. 'What's the matter with Mike?'

'Still very wet behind the ears. I don't think he's really got what it takes. He emphasizes all the wrong words and looks as though he's facing a firing squad. But there you are. They'll probably get the car-park supervisor to read the news soon, if this lot carry on the way they're doing.'

Vanessa didn't want to join in any criticism of 'her' newscasters and quietly began to attack the quiche.

'So what's with the no-smoking, no-drinking, then, Van?'

'Just being careful,' replied Vanessa, primly.

'Anyone would think you were pregnant.'

Vanessa didn't reply. Paul knew at once that he'd hit upon the answer.

'Oh, my poor love ... I don't know why I say "poor love" ... Anyone we know?'

Vanessa could have hit him. Thinking better of it, she quietened down. 'I can't talk about it.'

'Oh, come on. I'd no idea. It just sort of occurred to me that was what it was ...'

'It's silly to get worked up about it ...'

''Course it's not. I quite understand.'

Vanessa gradually spilled the beans to Paul. All of them. He had a gift for sympathy. As a programme director he needed it. He had to hold people's hands to get the best out of them.

Goodness, she thought, how *nice* Paul was being to her. But wasn't that true of many gays? Happier in the company of women. Particularly the unobtainable ones.

Despite, or maybe because of, her uncertain appearance on the *Derrick Bream Show*, Lynne wasn't without offers of work. After the initial fuss had died down, it was revived when Lynne's memoirs were run over three Sundays in one of the tabloids. She was 'helped' by a ghost-writer from the paper and the end-product bore about as much resemblance to her actual life as any other such serialization. But she received £45,000 for it and even when the agent who'd cobbled together the deal had taken his fifteen per cent, it was still a tidy sum to carry forward.

In addition to the memoirs, she was invited to take part in TV quizzes, make after-dinner speeches, and open things. All in all, it seemed, notoriety paid ... even if she had to pay a chauffeur to drive her to and from the various engagements ... even if she didn't always take to the people she had to rub shoulders with in viewerland ... even if she had to put up with their innuendo-laden remarks.

Lynne was just getting used to this slightly artificial form of living, being a 'professional personality', when she saw a way to make an even bigger killing. The opportunity was created for her, ironically, by Patrick Ritchie.

From a quick read of the Gabriel Monk interview, it was apparent to Lynne that whereas she had largely adhered to Ritchie's request not to 'rock the boat', Ritchie himself had had no such scruples.

In fact, he'd overturned the boat and danced a tango on the keel.

In Monk's article purporting to profile the Editor as 'The General at the Front in the News Wars', Ritchie was quoted as saying that Lynne had lost her job because she was 'over the hill and half-way down the other side'. She was 'really terrible at reading the news'. She was 'losing her looks and refused to accept remedial treatment'. She was always pushing her 'feminist viewpoints'. Her off-camera behaviour had become a 'sheer embarrassment to N-TV'. She was so 'unprofessional' she risked the ultimate sin of having to present stories about herself on the bulletins.

The stinging phrases leapt out at Lynne as she read the piece. They leapt out at Adam, too.

'I think you may have landed yourself in a little difficulty,' he told the Editor. 'It looks actionable.'

'Nah,' replied Ritchie. 'She'd never dare. It'd all come out. Make her look worse than ever.'

'You never know. "Hell hath no fury", and all that. If it went to court, a jury might well feel sorry for her. Kicking a woman when she's down. She might go for unfair dismissal into the bargain...'

'It won't happen, Adam.'

But Lynne wasn't going to take it lying down. She took legal advice and a letter from her solicitors was soon on its way to the studios of N-TV.

While the News Wars, the Sex Scandals, and the Personality Clashes were bubbling away, it was remarkable that anyone at N-TV had enough energy left to produce the twenty-four hours of programming the company had a daily duty to provide. But somehow the service was maintained, though uneven and not so bright or authoritative as in the station's heyday, the Golden Age of a mere nine months before.

When Ben Brock presented the *Nightly News* the station regained some of its old authority and verve. But even he couldn't appear seven nights a week.

So, the changes were rung: Ben found himself being paired with Delia Steele rather than March, while March often had to play big sister to Mike Feather.

March even let Mike take her out one evening. Over dinner she told him: 'I've taken the plunge, you know.'

'What?' asked Mike, horrified. 'Not – ?'

'I've got an agent. Richard Luard. He was very insistent and offered me heaven and earth, so I finally caved in.'

'But why give him ten per cent of yourself?'

'Actually, it's twenty. That's what they take in personal management, you know.'

'And what do you get for that? Flowers at the airport?'

'It's more like having a manager. He talked of drawing up a life-plan for me.'

'Christ! But he's not taking twenty per cent of what you earn at the moment, is he?'

'No. But he's negotiating my new contract. It was due at the start of this month. And he'll handle anything else that comes up.'

'So, I expect you'll be off soon. March Stevens Superstar. Ah, well...'

He looked hard at her. It was striking the change that had come over her in the year since she'd first arrived at N-TV. She was still incredibly attractive. The golden hair still shone. But the rough edges had been smoothed. She was more substantial. And, yes, it had to be said, she was tougher. Was that just the job? Or the Beni Patel business?

Mike took the plunge: 'Have you got a bloke?'

March actually had the grace to colour and lower her eyes. 'Yes', she answered quietly, knowing how Mike would be disappointed. 'There *is* somebody.'

'Anybody we know?'

'Nobody you know, no. Nobody at N-TV. In fact, nobody from TV. He comes from another world.'

'Oh – Martian, eh?'

'No, he's a farmer from Gloucestershire. I met him through Vanessa. He lives in the next village to her parents.'

'So, you're going to get hitched to this Farmer Giles character?'

'Only time will tell,' March said, teasingly.

'What does he think about your agent, then?'

'He has no views on the matter.'

Mike stared into his wine glass and thought for a moment. 'You know,' he said profoundly, 'I think if I'm really going to crack this newscasting, I'll have to get my teeth fixed ...'

March smiled at his self-absorption.

'I tell you what,' she said, relaxing and sparkling, 'I'll give you a tip. When you have your teeth done, you can claim fifty per cent off tax.'

'You're kidding ...'

'No, they call it cosmetic dentistry.'

'Amazing. I don't suppose you know a good dentist, do you?'

Vanessa's pregnancy and the identity of the father were matters soon known around N-TV. But her parents down in Gloucestershire pottered about their musty house in happy ignorance. And the national newspapers were apparently not interested. After all,

Vanessa was hardly a 'name' in their terms, and perhaps in these days of mass philanderings even those of a TV newsman had ceased to be red-hot news.

As for Aaron and Jo's affair, not a word of it had reached the gossip columns either. They'd been remarkably successful in keeping it to themselves.

Until Lady Hamilton got to know about it.

Yvonne had kept her word about not letting the lonely pine and was always finding excuses to ring up Ben. There were charities to be supported, friends to be advised, dinners to be eaten.

'I met a lovely man in your line of business at Plummond Almley's the other night,' she informed him. 'Aaron Rochester. He's from an American TV company. Such a nice man and very charming and knowledgeable.'

'I know him,' said Ben. 'I interviewed him about the American Election. Then he interviewed me. It's all very incestuous.'

'Well, here's a juicy titbit for you. The very next day I was by the side entrance of Harrods waiting for Rodriguez to bring the Rolls round when I saw him with a woman. They were coming out of a block of flats. He had his arm round her. He pretended not to see me. But I knew it was him. I mean, I could hardly fail, could I? *And* I recognized her. She's married to that nice David Kenway. I met them at dinner once.'

'Heavens, I wish you wouldn't tell me these things, Yvonne. I'd rather not know ...'

'Ben, don't be like that! It was written all over them. Nooky.'

Yvonne was probably right. But it was no business of Ben's and it only shed more lurid light on life *chez* Kenway.

'She's American, you know,' Yvonne rattled on. 'Perhaps that's the link with Aaron Rochester ...'

'Yvonne, you're a dreadful old gossip. In the old days they'd have cut your tongue out.'

'You may mock, Ben, but I have the best sources and my information is always spot-on. How about another titbit, then? More up your street, this one ... *and* it involves you.'

'No more scandals, please ...'

She told Ben she'd heard the Government was far from pleased at his return to N-TV.

'Now, Yvonne, I know you know *everybody* but when you use the word "Government", who exactly do you mean? It covers a multitude of sinners.'

'I mean the members of the Government who look upon N-TV as a Communist plot, that's who.'

'But why would they be upset at my coming back – nice old, middle-of-the-road Ben?'

'Because they want N-TV to fail, idiot! They know you're tremendously popular. You'll help the ratings, and that won't do at all.'

Ben didn't know whether to believe Yvonne's little story. 'Well, if they're trying to make N-TV fail, they should leave us to our own devices. The way we're going, we'll sink without trace, anyway ...'

'Poor Ben. I wonder who's *really* against you? Is it Ross himself, d'you think?'

'More likely Colin Lyon. By the way, here's some gossip for you, for a change.'

'Oh, lovely. Tell me.'

'What's the connection between Lyon's wife and the editor of N-TV?'

'They're both Australians.'

'So you know that!'

'Yes. You'd be surprised what I know.'

'There's more to it than that. She used to be married to him ...'

'Goodness. The Koala Mafia is formidable, isn't it?'

Intrigued by the connections, Yvonne thought it would be a good idea to bring them all together under her roof. She'd give a big dinner party. She'd invite the Lyons and she'd dangle an invitation before the Editor-in-Chief of N-TV (when she could remember his name). Perhaps Ben would be free to join them after his programme? Such fun it would be. It would have to be one night in the run-up to Christmas.

CHAPTER 57

At the Kenway house in Islington, it was a familiar scene. Jo was trying to write an article on her battered electric typewriter. Bill and Harry were being given their supper in the kitchen by Nanny Jo. David was upstairs packing his bags for an early-morning departure.

As Trevor Ross was about to make his first visit to Israel since becoming Prime Minister, David was going ahead to do a number of reports on the West Bank, the economy, the country's nuclear capability, and so on.

Since returning from Australia, David had been permanently restless. The Vanessa business and the talkings-to he had been given by one and all had irritated him. But he'd done his bit by Vanessa. He'd promised to support the baby and even agreed to help her answer the fan-mail which had been piling up for him.

After supper, the boys came up and watched him finish his packing.

'Where are you going to, Daddy?' asked Harry.

'Israel.'

'Is that where Jesus comes from?'

'Yes. More or less.'

'Will you go to Bethlehem?'

'I'm not sure I'll have time.'

'Will you bring me a present from Bethlehem?' asked Billy.

'I'll try very hard, and I'll bring it back in time for Christmas.'

'Good. You'd better.' So said Harry, every bit as forceful as his father. 'Does Jesus still live there?'

David sighed. It was going to be another of *those* conversations. He loved his sons dearly but two were quite enough. Perhaps that was why he'd only briefly considered moving in with Vanessa before she had their baby.

That step could well have been on the cards, given Jo's mounting demands for a divorce. She never left off the subject. But he was the one who was digging his heels in, refusing to contemplate the idea.

Over supper, they started again.

'You're always going away,' said Jo. 'It's impossible to make any progress with either our divorce or our marriage if you won't

308

stay still for longer than five seconds. I warn you, David, one day you'll come home and find I've taken the boys and gone. And the next you'll know is the divorce papers coming through the letter-box.'

'But that's ridiculous,' David told her. 'Where will you take the boys? What'll you do for money?'

'You'd be surprised at how resourceful I can be. I don't need you for everything, you know.'

Unable to claim that he was sleepy, his usual way out of confrontation, David tried another ploy:

'So, who's the other bloke, then?'

'What?'

'There must be another bloke. Otherwise you'd never have the guts to pull out. Who is it?'

Jo performed magnificently. 'I suppose you can't believe a mere woman could get her act together without another *man* to help. Typical ...'

David noted her evasiveness. She hadn't actually denied it. Yes, perhaps there *was* another man. That might explain every-thing. He'd have to leave it, though, until he returned from Israel.

They were no longer sleeping together, so early next morning he rang for a taxi and slipped off to Heathrow without saying goodbye to her, though he did pop in to see the boys. He was picking up a crew in Jerusalem, so all he had to do now was fight his way on board the El Al jet.

The airline's own body and baggage searches would, as usual, not have disgraced the Spanish Inquisition. Every toothbrush, every sock was held up for examination. Then he was asked about his movements over the previous twenty-four hours. Who had he talked to? Had his luggage been out of sight since he packed it?

At last, the security woman looked at David and said flatly, 'You understand why we have to ask these questions?'

'Yes, I do, don't worry.'

He was waved through and had to walk to the most distant departure gate. That was for security reasons, too. If he'd walked another few yards, it occurred to him, he'd have been in Tel Aviv without needing to catch the plane.

Every time he flew into Lod airport, David remembered that this had been the scene of one of the worst massacres in modern times.

David showed his well-worn, much-stamped passport at the immigration desk and succeeded in not having it franked with an

Israeli stamp (it would save so much trouble if he wanted to visit an Arab country in the future). He went to reclaim his bag.

Risking an enormous fare, he took a taxi all the way to Jerusalem. The driver talked at him incessantly as they drove up to the holy city in the Judaean hills. David felt he was being brainwashed, nudged, cajoled, blanket-bathed in order to accept the Israeli world-view. It was impossible to argue with the driver. The emotional power behind the viewpoint was overwhelming.

He remembered again what an English Arabist had once said to him about the Middle East: 'Spend a week with the Arabs and you're ready to embrace the Israeli point of view. Spend a week with the Israelis and you know the Arabs have a point.'

When the taxi drew up outside the King David Hotel, David was glad that he'd brought his thick overcoat with him. It was bitterly cold in Jerusalem in December. The hills were already dusted with snow.

'Jesus!' he exclaimed softly to himself as he felt the nip in the air, and he didn't mean to be ironic.

Inside the entrance hall, he again thought back to an earlier time, to when the British had occupied Palestine. In 1946, the Stern gang planted a bomb in the King David and killed several top British officials.

There was really no getting away from the past in this land. And yet David was also moved to be in Jerusalem once more. He himself had no religious belief to speak of but the very fact of Christians, Jews and Moslems all claiming Jerusalem as a holy city stirred him. He was touched by the strength of faith in others.

David made his phone calls, turned up the heating in his room, and went to sleep, resolutely alone and unusually apprehensive.

CHAPTER 58

Scorned by Ben, reviled by everyone else at N-TV, and finally abandoned even by Patrick Ritchie, Guy Treacy was packing his bags.

The American news consultant had submitted his final memorandum on ways to turn round the audience slump and restore advertising revenue. He would collect his fee before flying back to New York, hoping that his bonus for producing results would soon follow. There were plenty who felt that N-TV was committing professional suicide successfully enough to make that prospect unlikely.

The basis of Treacy's recommendations had been what he called his 'entertainment news' concept. 'News is entertainment,' he declared. 'The people you need to present it are like disc-jockeys. Call them "news-jockeys", if you will ...'

Where there was entertainment, surely there must follow sex. One of his more controversial recommendations to improve N-TV's performance concerned the Honey Factor.

'Let me tell you about the Honey Factor. You've heard of "honey shots"? No? It's a phrase we use in sports coverage for cut-away shots of girls in the crowd at football matches. One cameraman is given the job of raking the stands to find them. Sometimes you have to get the talent coordinator to plant cheer-leaders and models, so they can be spotted in this way. It all adds juice to the coverage.'

Long before Treacy arrived at N-TV, it had been customary for journalists to talk about 'sexy' news when they meant items that were shocking or exciting. Treacy added a more literal inter-pretation of the phrase. He wanted to see sexier presenters. He wanted people in the news to look sexy, too. There was a limit to what you could do to make the new Foreign Secretary look like a film-star but at least Sally Gerald could be interviewed or introduced by someone who'd set pulses racing.

A report on the Honey Factor was one of several that Treacy filed. They were discreetly worded lest they be leaked to Women in Media or *The Guardian*, leading to a feminist uprising on N-TV territory. But the thrust was obvious. Tits and bums were to be

311

added to N-TV's presentational appeal, probably stopping short at March Stevens appearing topless on the *Nightly News*.

Patrick Ritchie accepted the Honey Factor notion without demur and Adam Ravenscroft, as ever, made no direct objections. He merely questioned how it was to be implemented. 'You try telling Liz Hastings or Annie Friedman to put a bit more leg on the Big News and see how they react.'

Apart from more stories involving female entertainers and frequent objections to female pundits on the grounds they resembled the back of a bus, the only clear instructions were given to the programme directors. They were told to 'honey up' the look of programmes. Given Paul Whitehall's preferences this could have resulted in the Prime Minister being intercut with angelic boy trebles.

A kind of crunch looked imminent in early December when Michael Penn-Morrison was walking through the N-TV foyer one morning. He noticed a half-familiar face. It belonged to – well, he wasn't sure who she was, but she looked glamorous in a rather obvious way. It was only when he'd gone up to the newsroom that it clicked.

George Lee was still Home News Editor despite his misdemeanour in the summer. He was said to be a reformed man, which meant that he stuck to beer and no longer meddled with spirits. That morning, he was seated at his desk, plucking at his beard and skimming the newspapers.

'George,' said Michael, 'what's that beauty queen doing in reception?'

'What beauty queen?'

'Anne somebody. Or is it Carole? Is she in for an interview?'

'Nothing to do with me, squire.' George Lee went back to cutting out stories from the papers and scratching himself.

Penn-Morrison forgot about the girl until lunchtime when he found himself sitting next to Liz Hastings in the canteen.

'And what are you toiling over today, me old beauty?' he asked.

'Bloody newscaster auditions again,' she replied.

'Anyone of interest?'

'Not bloody likely. Lot of actors looking like hairdressers. A lot of escapees from the Beeb, looking like policewomen. And a couple of beauty queens.'

'So that's what she was here for, the one I saw in reception – Anne somebody.'

'Anne Sackville. Absolutely spastic, but nobody ever takes any notice of what I think round here.'

Oh dear, concluded Penn-Morrison, the writing's *really* on the wall . . .

CHAPTER 59

David was driven over to get his accreditation fixed by an army officer at the Israeli government's Press Centre. Then he went with his freelance camera team to the Allenby Bridge over the River Jordan. There were few Biblical echoes. At this point, the river was no wider than a green, slimy stream, thick with reeds.

He watched as Jordanians wishing to cross the border were subjected to body-searches even more stringent than El Al's. They had to remove their clothes. Their money, rings and keys were put in plastic bags which they had to hold while they went through the checks. This was to save the Israelis facing accusations of theft. Their shoes were loaded into boxes to go through an X-ray machine. Their luggage was turned inside out. Children cried. It was as unlikely that terrorist weapons or explosives could be smuggled through this checkpoint as for a camel to pass through the proverbial needle's eye.

For lunch, David had been persuaded by the ever-zealous Israeli authorities to visit the Arab mayor of a small town, Baqa El Gharbiya, which was in the part of Israel known as 'The Triangle'. As such, he was something of a freak: an Arab who had accepted the fact of Israel and who thus tended to be shown off to visitors as an example of peaceful coexistence.

Zafer Mansir was much the same age as David and welcomed him into his smartly modern home. Outside in the farmyard, nevertheless, were his parents, wearing traditional Arab robes, tokens of an ancient lifestyle now on the wane.

David was struck by Zafer's air of melancholy, as if he expected fate to exact revenge at any minute. He was an agricultural engineer by trade but seemed to spend most of his time on municipal business. Lunch was provided by Nuhar, his dark-haired, wide-eyed, nineteen-year-old wife who, although she liked to consider herself a liberated woman, resolutely stayed in the kitchen while the men ate their rice and kebabs.

Not for the first time on a visit to Israel, David felt he was being got at, pressurized into seeing only positive achievements. They took black, muddy coffee in small cups and chatted on. At two o'clock Nuhar came in and spoke quietly to her husband in Arabic. His expression hardly changed.

'Mr Kenway,' he said. 'I think you would wish to know. There is trouble in Jerusalem. A bomb attack. My wife heard it on the radio.'

David thanked the Mayor for his hospitality and dug the crew out of a small restaurant two streets away.

'We'd better get back to Jerusalem,' he said, ignoring their half-finished bottle of wine. 'I don't know what it is. But we ought to take a look.'

Forty minutes later, they were back in the city, trying to get close to the area where they were told the bomb had gone off. There was an unusual amount of panic, David thought. Surely they were used to this sort of thing? The city had witnessed every kind of horror known to man.

How had it happened? If it had been caused by Palestinians, as must be the case, how had they obtained the explosives? Would it interfere with Trevor Ross's visit? The Prime Minister was due to stay at the Embassy in Tel Aviv but he was coming up to Jerusalem in three days' time.

Above all, how could David find out what was really going on?

There was no alternative but to turn on the portable radio that Chaim, the cameraman, carried with him. Chaim was a softly-spoken Yemeni Jew who subtly conveyed the fact that he'd seen it all before. The announcer was jabbering away in Hebrew. 'Isn't there an English service?' Chaim retuned the radio without a word.

It appeared that a bomb had exploded in one of the narrow streets of Old Jerusalem, near where the Via Dolorosa skirts the Moslem Quarter on one side and the Temple Mount on the other before zig-zagging towards the Church of the Holy Sepulchre. It was thought that five or six people, mostly tourists, had been killed. The terrorists had been cornered by soldiers. They had taken two hostages and were holed up inside an old house a short distance from the tourist shops on the Via Dolorosa. The area had been sealed off.

David could see the story was going to be a tough nut to crack. There was no getting near the house where the hostages were being held.

The only slight comfort he had was that 'Kenway's luck' had held again. He had the knack of being in the right place at the right time.

'You stay here,' he told Chaim. 'And if they let you any nearer, go along with them. I'll catch up.' Four other TV crews had arrived and were standing around idly, waiting. 'I'll pop back to the King David and make a few phone calls. OK?'

David was put through to the Foreign Desk. 'It's David in Jerusalem. Is Jack there?'

The Foreign News Editor came out of a meeting and took the call. 'David, we were trying to get you but they said you were on the West Bank or somewhere. We've only had an AP snap so far. How does it look?'

David gave him the information he'd taken from the radio. Then he added: 'The army'll smoke them out, I should think. The odd thing is that it should have happened at all ...'

'Can you give us a one-minute sit rep for the tea-time hourlies? And two to two-and-a-half for the *Nightly*?'

'OK. The tape has to go from Tel Aviv?'

'Yes. Satellite at five, GMT.'

If there was one type of story David disliked it was a siege. Any occasion when you had to sit outside somewhere, waiting for hour after hour with the possibility of nothing to show for it at the end, was anathema to him. It was especially difficult when you were on foreign soil, when security was tight, and it was hard to exercise any ingenuity ... when you couldn't bribe anybody to let you go where you weren't supposed to go.

David thought hard about what he could do, then curled up and went to sleep in the back of Chaim's Mercedes.

Back in London, Lynne Kimberley too was waiting. Waiting for the due process of law. A libel writ had been issued against Patrick Ritchie. Her solicitors had advised her not to press the unfair-dismissal charge until the first case had been resolved, as they were so closely linked.

Then a great deal of nothing happened. Lynne continued her junketings round the country, speaking to women's luncheon clubs about her experiences as a newsgatherer and newsmaker, and taking part in PR events. She felt like a defrocked clergyman who'd been turned into a sideshow. She only hoped she wouldn't meet the same fate as the renowned Rector of Stiffkey, eaten by lions in his cage at Blackpool Zoo.

She featured quite frequently in the gossip columns on account of her eccentric behaviour. Once she'd got a few lunchtime drinks inside her, incidents tended to happen and they were inevitably reported.

She wasn't happy. She missed the contact with her colleagues at N-TV. It was as if she were a non-person now, had never worked there. Her efforts to find new employment had failed. She had been to see Richard Luard but he had turned her down as he felt he should only have one female newscaster on his books and that one was March.

Lynne wasn't exactly starving, as she sat on a considerable sum of money from the sale of her memoirs and from her personal appearances. But she knew that memoirs were not something you could trade on too often. The time would surely come when she must bite on meatier matters. For the moment, though, the right sort of offers were not forthcoming. Her telephone did not ring.

When the papers reported that a former Miss United Kingdom, Anne Sackville, was to join N-TV as a newscaster, Lynne hit the roof. How could they do such a thing? It was the last straw. No one would ever take N-TV seriously again if they put a woman on screen who lacked 'bottom', whatever she may have had on top.

On the other hand, perhaps it was just as well that Lynne was out of that madhouse.

When she calmed down, she painstakingly cut out the reports and photographs of Anne Sackville from the papers. It was just the ammunition she needed for her libel action. It proved, surely, what N-TV's thinking was on the subject of women newscasters and why they'd got rid of her. Yes, it was a gift, this latest appointment – the evidence to clinch the case against Ritchie.

Lynne poured herself another gin and tonic and only wished she had someone to share it with.

'Who's Yvonne Hamilton when she's at home?' Ritchie asked.

'"At Home" being the operative phrase,' replied Adam. 'Is she after you now?'

'Yes. Invite to dinner. Embossed card and all. Says, "To meet the Rt Hon Colin Lyon PC MP." What do I want to do that for? I've met him already.'

Adam explained. 'She thinks she's the great political hostess of our day. Widow of an old fart who left her pots and pots of money. I think Ben's a buddy of hers.'

Ritchie wasn't sure what to make of the invitation. 'Should I go, Adam? Does it mean I've *arrived* in London Society when the embossed invitations start to thud through the letter-box?'

'Can't do any harm, Patrick. You could do with an evening off anyway. You've been working all day and all night since you got here. It'll soon be Christmas. Enjoy!'

'But why me?'

'She probably thinks you're a man of great importance and influence. Ask Ben.'

Ben turned to the camera and read:

In Jerusalem, the authorities now say they believe that *four* Palestinians are holding *six* people hostage in the Old City. Earlier it had been thought that only two gunmen and two hostages were involved. The gunmen are thought to have been responsible for an explosion which earlier killed six people. The siege, which has now entered its second day, has been described by the Israeli Prime Minister as 'a merciless assault on our land'. N-TV's special correspondent, David Kenway, sends this report from Jerusalem ...'

David spoke over general shots of the city:

At least two of the hostages are American tourists. They failed to return to their hotel after a sightseeing trip which took them to the Wailing Wall and the Dome of the Rock. It's not known who the other four people are, though it is thought they're probably Israelis. They may include a husband and wife who run a shop for tourists in the Via Dolorosa. The army hasn't so far been able to establish contact with the gunmen. Nor has any Palestinian faction yet claimed responsibility for the attack ...

When David's report had ended, Ben added: 'Mr Ross, the Prime Minister, who's due to visit Jerusalem during a two-day visit to Israel starting on Thursday is expected to leave as scheduled.'

'It's a shade more interesting now we know the Americans are in there,' David said to Chaim with the callousness of the professional newsman. 'I suppose our friends from the networks will be along shortly. Yanks are only interested if their own people are involved.'

Chaim grunted. He'd heard the same said about the British by

American reporters. He spat, and politely kicked sand over the result.

'Oh, my God – no sooner said ...'

David pointed to a truck which was pulling up at the army barrier. A familiar stocky figure, cigar held aloft, jumped out, for all the world as if he was the adanace party for the US Cavalry.

'It's that bastard Aaron Rochester.'

David watched Aaron go about his business and noticed the ebullient manner gradually subside as the soldiers firmly told him he couldn't get any nearer to the siege. He'd just have to wait, like all the other reporters and TV crews.

Aaron turned and spotted David. He appeared a touch embarrassed and David assumed this was because he'd been beaten to it on this occasion.

'Dr Livingstone, I presume?' said Aaron. 'How long have you been here?'

'Since Day One. It's not exactly a whizz-bang show, I'm afraid.'

'I was in Athens. When New York heard Americans were in there, I was told to get my ass on over here. I *hate* sieges ...'

'Join the club.'

By the late afternoon, David had done his piece for the satellite and was spending most of the time standing by a brazier which the military press officer had thoughtfully installed for the frozen media.

They were still being kept outside Sha'ar HaArayot, the Lions' Gate in the Old City walls, unable to get near the scene of the action. David half-listened as Aaron did his piece to camera and sent it off down to Tel Aviv for onward transmission.

The two reporters decided to set up headquarters in a restaurant, the Falafel, about a hundred yards from the police barrier. They went through their rituals. They mentioned their 'bet' and made approving noises every time they spotted Israeli women soldiers in khaki (stunning as always). They chatted about the new US President, to be inaugurated early the following month. Aaron spoke of going home to New York for Christmas with his family. David told him of the upheavals at N-TV and even revealed his own spot of bother over Vanessa.

Aaron was not exactly surprised by this piece of information, but David saw no significance in that, only that there was a certain edginess between them.

'How long do you think this'll last, then? Care to bet on it?'

'No,' David answered. 'It's a tricky one. As far as one can tell, it's a very poky little place they're in. Even the SAS would think twice about swinging into action. I suppose they've moved up their Eilat Force, one's not to know. I expect there'll be a big bang in the small hours one morning and all we'll get to see will be the bodies coming out.'

'Will it be over by Christmas, that's the question?'

'God, I hope so. I'm freezing to death. Trevor Ross arrives tomorrow and I'm supposed to be running round after him.'

'Perhaps we should cover each other, Dave. Take it in turns. Get some shut-eye. Where are you staying?'

'The King David. You?'

'Hilton.'

'OK. It's a deal.'

Aaron was the first to start calling it the 'Christmas Siege'. He used the phrase in one of his reports and quickly every television and newspaper journalist took it up.

News came through that Yasser Arafat's PLO and a Syrian-based faction, the Democratic Front for the Liberation of Palestine, were claiming responsibility for the bombing. It also listed the demands: the freeing of fifty prisoners from Atlit gaol and free passage for them – and the gunmen – out of Israel.

What wasn't clear was what the gunmen themselves were thinking, or whether indeed they belonged to the DFLP faction as claimed. As they had no link with the outside world, they couldn't have been in touch with Damascus or anywhere else.

'I wonder if they've given them a communications set-up?' David asked. In Britain, it was standard procedure to put in a phone, so that police or army could maintain a dialogue with the terrorists.

'I wonder if they've given them any food,' wondered Aaron, 'or whether they're trying to starve the buggers out?'

'Wouldn't put it past the Israelis. They're bollocky as anyone. No concessions. No nothing.'

'God, I'm bored. If there's one thing I can never forgive the Palestinians for, it's giving me such a sore arse and such screaming boredom on so many bloody occasions.'

'Just as well you're not a hostage, then. I shouldn't think they're exactly playing charades in there.'

*   *   *

Trevor Ross duly arrived on the Thursday and came up to Jerusalem, where he paid visits to the Israeli Parliament in the Knesset and to Yad Vashem, the memorial to Jews killed in the Holocaust.

Like everyone, he shed a tear at this. And, like everyone, he had to resist the emotional force of the visit lest it cloud his view of modern Israel.

David pulled out of the siege and attended Ross's press conference, staying behind to interview the Prime Minister. Ross asked David how he was and recalled their discussion of the South African business at the Downing Street reception. 'I hope that's all finished with now,' he said.

Ross also muttered that because of the siege he wouldn't be able to visit the Old City as originally planned. 'Trouble is, in Israel, politicians like to deal with sieges themselves. It's hard to make them concentrate on what I've come to tell them ... Still, I'm going to Bethlehem tomorrow. Rather seasonal, don't you think?'

David remembered he was supposed to be getting a present for Billy, but there was going to be no time for that excursion now.

'Then I have to get out before the Sabbath starts tomorrow night. They won't let my plane take off while that's on.'

'Ah yes.' The siege would go on, Sabbath or no Sabbath.

That night, David declined to go to the dinner the British Ambassador was giving for Ross and members of the Israeli Cabinet. He needed to monitor the siege, though once more he spent most of the evening in the Falafel restaurant with Aaron, keeping just on the right side of sobriety lest their runner came over to tell them that something had happened.

David was still feeling sullen and unsettled and, after they'd exhausted every other topic, he finally started to confide in Aaron his feelings about Jo.

'You know what she threatened just before I left? That I'd go home one day and find she'd taken the boys.'

Aaron looked at David warily, and lit another cigar.

'It's obvious we've hit rock bottom, isn't it?' David went on. 'I should never have got married. I'm not the sort to stick with one woman. And even if I was, who'd put up with a man who spent half his life sitting about waiting for terrorists to blow people up? I'd have been better off like you, the bachelor boy.'

Aaron stared into his wine glass and wondered. After a pause, he said cautiously, 'So, d'you think that you and ... Jo ... will split?'

'Yes, I do. I'd put up with a lot for the sake of the kids, but being married to her is like sawing my leg off without an anaesthetic.'

Aaron occupied himself conspicuously with his cigar. 'So you wouldn't consider making an honest woman of this Vanessa you knocked up?'

'You don't marry people just because they're pregnant. I made that clear to her and everyone else who's been sticking their noses in.'

Then Aaron braced himself. He'd have to say it one day. Why not now?

'David, what would you say if I told you Jo and I'd been seeing each other for several months? Ever since the Prime Minister's reception.'

David's expression hardly changed. But his mind was racing, putting this curious question through various tests, setting it against other pieces of knowledge, seeing what bearing it would have on present plans and future policies.

'I wouldn't believe you,' he replied simply. 'I mean, I know you knew her, and all that, before we got married. But I hadn't really thought...'

'So, you wouldn't get all emotional about it?'

'Why should I? You could take her off my hands ...'

'Oh, no, you don't. That would be just too neat, very convenient. Why should I release you from guilt and obligation? I've met your type before, divorced husbands desperately trying to find someone to take on their ex's so they won't get crippled by the alimony.'

'I don't believe you, anyway, as I say. It's not true, is it?'

'You'd better ask Jo, hadn't you?'

Yvonne Hamilton smoothed down the sides of her sheeny, emerald-green dress. 'I believe you know each other,' she said to her guests.

'Oh yes, Lady H,' said Patrick Ritchie and leant forward to kiss his ex-wife, Karen.

Safely over that one, thought Yvonne. 'And I wouldn't be at all surprised if you know Colin Lyon, too?'

'G'day, Colin. How are you keeping?'

Goodness, what an odd trio they made. Yvonne waved the drinks tray in their direction. Still living out of one another's pockets, by the look of it.

In fact, even she had no idea of the full extent of the connections between the guests at her pre-Christmas supper. She was the only person not related through business or marriage to one of the others there.

She was disappointed that Ben had been unable to come but he was on the *Nightly News* and had promised to look in for coffee if he felt up to it.

Wherever she turned, Yvonne thought she saw collusion. Lord Almley monopolized Colin Lyon for what seemed like half the evening. Karen Lyon chatted to Patrick Ritchie as though she were still married to him – though, come to think of it, if they'd still been married, they would probably have ignored one another.

The hostess felt quite isolated from the main flow of conversation which seemed to be exclusively about N-TV.

'What are you talking about that's so important?' she asked, barging in on Ritchie's and Karen's tête-à-tête.

'I'm supposed to be quaking in my boots,' explained Ritchie. 'Karen's just told me that the Government, of which her husband is such a distinguished member, is declaring total war. A boycott, no less.'

'That's right,' Karen said, flashing Yvonne a sideways smile. 'There's going to be a policy of non-cooperation at all levels.' She sounded like an official hand-out. 'No interviews with anybody. It came into force yesterday.'

'You could have fooled me,' Yvonne remarked, demurely. 'On last night's news I distinctly saw Trevor Ross being interviewed in Israel.'

'Ah well,' said Colin Lyon, joining in, 'the PM always was a bit of a rebel. I expect that one slipped under the net.'

'As you can see,' Ritchie grinned pugnaciously, 'I'm quite *devastated* by the blow. In fact, we'll be pretty strapped digging up enough old wind-bags to make up for this sad loss.'

'I think it's all rather petty,' said Yvonne. 'Surely the Government's big enough to be called a few names by N-TV?'

'No, forgive me, it's not petty, Yvonne,' Lyon replied. 'N-TV has been consistently biased against us. And that's not a criticism of Patrick because it was the case long before he came along. We don't see why we should play along with it. There are four other

TV channels in this country and we'll put our message across through them until N-TV cleans up its act.'

The odd thing, Yvonne noted, was that Colin said this with a smile on his face. She couldn't begin to understand the polite responses from both sides in what was supposed to be an acrimonious dispute. Why was Patrick Ritchie taking it so calmly? Why was Colin Lyin being so buddy-buddy with Patrick? If there was supposed to be a change in editorial attitude, surely Patrick was the one who should be bringing it about?

'I think there's more to this than meets the eye,' Plummond Almley winked at her over coffee. Yvonne wondered whether he, too, was mixed up in it. She would find it hard to trust any man with side-whiskers like that.

If only Ben would hurry up and arrive. He'd be able to make sense of it all for her. Gradually she was coming to rely more and more on his judgement and good sense.

But Ben had taken the coward's way out. He hadn't fancied being at the same table as Lyon and Ritchie, the way things were going, so he'd gone straight home after the programme. He put on the record-player and fell asleep in front of the fire.

'Ben?'

It was Lynne on the phone next morning.

'Something rather odd's just happened.'

'What is it, Lynne? Surviving all right, are you?'

'Sure, sure. But I've just had this phone call – and I'm in need of a few phone calls these days, I can tell you. It was from someone called Mervyn Baxter. Have you ever heard of him? Said it was all very hush-hush ...'

'Which is why you're ringing to tell me all about it, of course ...'

'Yes, Ben. He asked would I be interested in joining a new news consortium that's going to apply for the N-TV franchise.'

'But that's ludicrous! We've got another five years to run, at least – unless the IBA throws a wobbly. What do they want from you?'

'To help them win it, I suppose. He also made noises about me getting back on the screen where I truly belonged, etcetera, and giving me editorial status.'

'I wonder who they are? Do they have a name?'

'I think he said something like World News Network.'

'You've heard the Government's blacking us? Refusing all co-operation. Nice little Christmas present, eh? It looks as though Ross is trying to sink us and this lot are hoping to muscle in on our patch. Did you say yes to this Baxter fellow?'

'You bet. Anything to teach those pricks at N-TV a lesson.'

'Good old Lynne! When do you get Patrick Ritchie in the witness box?'

'Oh, not for aeons, dear. You know the Law ...'

CHAPTER 60

The approach of Christmas was marked in deepest Gloucestershire by two festive announcements.

Vanessa told her parents she was pregnant. The Brigadier and
his wife affected to take the news calmly, though they were
naturally disappointed that their daughter wouldn't tell them
who the father was, that she wouldn't be marrying him, or,
indeed, anyone at all.

But there was no escaping the fact she was pregnant. There she
was, standing on the rug in front of the miserable fire, with the
bulge to prove it.

'It's not what your father and I would have wished for you,'
said Mrs Sinclair, 'but these days anything goes, doesn't it?'

The Brigadier wiped his eyes, but he always did that anyway.

Vanessa had been pushed into making her condition known to
her parents as March had very much wanted her to be in
Gloucestershire when the second announcement was made. She
had finally made up her mind. Mark Rippingale had been
popping the question every weekend for two months. What
probably settled the matter was reading Patrick Ritchie's libel-
lous remarks about Lynne in the *Post*.

'Isn't that unforgivable?' March had said, showing Mark the
article. 'I don't think I can keep on working for a company where
that goes on, do you?'

'Does seem extreme,' Mark told her. 'But you've got to be
tough to survive in those parts, eh?'

'I'd rather live a quiet life down here with you, if you have to
put up with that to survive in London.'

'Then you'd better marry me.'

'All right. I will.'

It had been as simple as that. Then Mark had second thoughts. He
worried that March had been pressured into saying yes by her
dislike of what was happening at N-TV. He insisted she have two
weeks to think it over before they went hard and told anyone.

During those two weeks, March thought of all the impedi-
ments. For the first time she told Mark about her ordeal with
Beni Patel. How she'd finally had sex with him though she hadn't
told the police.

'It isn't rape if you consent, I don't suppose. From what you say, you weren't *forced* to do it. You could have refused him, just about.'

'But what if he started boasting about it and word got round?'

'There'll always be that possibility. You'd have to laugh it off. It doesn't bother me if it doesn't bother you.'

And then there was her seduction, if that was the word, of David Kenway. She admitted how calculatedly she'd gone about it and how foolish she still felt.

Mark was blithely indifferent. 'We all do things we later regret. All's fair in love and war, but – m-more to the point – what's past is past. I'm sure David Kenway doesn't give it a m-moment's thought. That sort of thing has no bearing on *our* future happiness ...'

March was concerned that Mark was being a little *too* saintly, but by admitting all now she felt purged.

Mark saw his opportunity and proposed to her afresh, properly, romantically, in front of the fire in the pillared room of Hall Farm.

Then he carried her up the big staircase and they sealed the knot in the appropriate manner.

So, on the Saturday before Christmas, *The Times* revealed that Miss March Stevens had become engaged to Mr Mark Rippingale. The rest of the Press latched on and hied it down to Hawkesgrove where the happy couple posed for photographs standing in the gateway to Hall Farm, well-wrapped against the cold.

'IT'S MARCH AND MARK', concluded the *Sunday Express*.

'HERE IS THE NEWS – WE'LL WED, SAYS MARCH', was *The Sunday Times*'s contribution.

'THE SQUIRE AND HIS LADY-TO-BE' noted the *News of the World*.

Underneath the headlines were various allegations about Mark never watching his future wife on the *Nightly News*. 'Too busy milking the cows,' he was reported, none too accurately, as saying.

The Observer noted drily that the Government was most unlikely to be offering Miss Stevens its congratulations. The recently-declared boycott of N-TV would prevent it.

CHAPTER 61

After five days, everyone agreed that the siege must end soon. The gunmen had shot dead one of the Israeli hostages. Washington was applying pressure for an end to the confrontation in the hope that no American lives would be lost. Tempers among the Israeli security forces handling the siege were frayed. Aaron and David were increasingly irritable at the vigil they had to keep.

But the days of inactivity ended abruptly.

After a fumbling start, the Palestinians behind the Christmas Siege made it clear that what they had in mind was a horror spectacular.

The Israelis had been able to hold out against this prospect so far because of a stroke of luck. The hostages were being held in in a place to which access, visual or otherwise, was denied to the media. The media had to camp outside, out of sight and earshot. This fact hadn't escaped the masterminds in Damascus, even though the actual gunmen on the spot were probably unaware of the precise situation. As far as the Israelis knew, the gunmen had no radio or television, so wouldn't be conscious of the extent to which the world was following the siege.

The Israelis were wrong in their assumption. Shortly before he'd been captured, one of the American tourist hostages had purchased an FM portable radio with the words 'A Present from Jerusalem – Shalom' stamped on it. The gunmen listened to the news on this set. They could barely follow the English bulletins from Israeli radio so they tuned in mostly to what was coming in loud and clear from Jordan. Until the batteries ran down, that is.

But in this way, they heard the surprising news that the leadership in Damascus was saying they would execute a hostage a day until the Israelis complied with their demands.

One of the demands was that the media should be allowed to cover their departure and be made to broadcast a statement on the aims of the Palestinian faction.

General Av Bador was the Israeli security chief in charge of the siege. His initial reaction was to dismiss this demand as briskly as all the previous ones. 'We don't make deals with madmen,' he told reporters. 'We don't answer their demands for publicity.'

Nevertheless, as the hours and days rolled by and the siege

showed no sign of lifting (it had been assumed by now that the gunmen and their hostages had found some source of food), General Bador decided he would try to 'loosen' the situation by allowing a number of media representatives to take a closer look.

'I will allow in four TV crews and four newspaper journalists. The journalists will come from the agencies and from the *Jerusalem Post*. One of the TV crews must be from Israeli TV. You can fight it out among yourselves who else comes. And I'll accept no responsibility for what happens to you.'

After a good deal of earnest debate, the three TV crews were decided upon: one was from an East European agency, Aaron's would represent the US, and David's N-TV team would go in because of its satellite coverage of Western Europe. All agreed that whatever they shot would be available on a pooled basis.

Shortly after breakfast on the Monday before Christmas, they were allowed through the barriers with their equipment and taken down the narrow cobbled streets. The bodies had been removed, but there was still the devastation left by the bomb. Doors off hinges, windows shattered, small shops turned upside down. The roof over a shop that sold earthenware pots had completely caved in.

A hundred yards further down the hill towards the Dome of the Rock, General Bador stopped everyone before going himself, alone, round the next corner.

Here the Israelis had erected huge one-way screens so that they could observe the house without being observed themselves. One by one, the journalists and TV men were waved into the observation post that had been set up. The exterior of the siege house was brightly lit all round the clock by special spotlights.

The body of the dead hostage still lay where it had been thrown from a window three days before.

It was an eerie, unnatural scene. Oddly quiet and oddly lit – like a film set.

When everyone was inside the post, General Bador picked up a loud-hailer and handed it to a rather serious-looking man wearing thick glasses and several pullovers. This man spoke in Arabic. 'Hello. We have a message. We have with us representatives of the media of many countries. Do you wish to address them?'

There was silence; nothing stirred within the house.

Five minutes later, the bespectacled man repeated the message word for word.

Aaron asked, 'Do you think there's anyone there?'

General Bador said, 'Oh yes, they're still there. There's no way they could escape.'

'Perhaps they've died of boredom,' Aaron murmured. The General frowned.

Further minutes passed. The cameramen began to feel the weight of their cameras. Abruptly, one of the shutters on the house flew open and the butt of an AK-47 automatic rifle poked out. A single shot was fired into the air.

Then a long Arabic shout was heard.

The interpreter said, 'They want a TV crew to go in and film the hostages. To show they're all alive.'

Bador frowned again. He was unsure whether he'd made a mistake playing the media card.

'I'll go,' said Aaron.

David thought he must be mad.

'I'll go, too,' he said after a pause.

'No. You've got a wife and kids.'

'What's that got to do with it?'

'What are you trying to prove, David?'

'Nobody's going,' said Bador, firmly. 'It is much too dangerous.'

A reply was sent back to the gunmen. If they wanted to show the hostages were still alive they should parade them in front of a window.

There was another long wait while, presumably, the Palestinians debated among themselves.

Again they made their offer and again the General refused.

And then Bador changed his mind. He turned to Aaron and said, 'You want to go? Just go, film what they have to show you, take a good look at the inside of the house, make no promises, and return.'

'Gee, I'm just a reporter. But that's OK by me.' Turning to his cameraman and recordist, he said, 'OK, fellahs?'

They nodded, less certain.

The interpreter broadcast that one TV crew – from the United States of America was coming over – three men only.

'Send them in. Unarmed. Hands up.'

The cameraman had the hardest job keeping his hands up, so he carried the forty-pound slab of machinery on his head.

At a signal from the General, the three Americans set off slowly to walk to the door of the house. First, the cameraman. Then, five paces behind him, the sound-recordist. Then, five paces behind him, Aaron.

David was quietly furious he'd been scooped.

The door opened, a rifle was glimpsed again, and the three disappeared one by one into the darkness within.

CHAPTER 62

The nail-biting went on. Not a sound from the house.

Twenty minutes passed.

Then the door opened and the sound recordist, looking worried, stumbled out and half-ran, half-walked back to the command post.

'Where are the others?' Bador hissed.

'They're having an argument. It's difficult to understand what they want. Their English isn't good. But ...' – he wiped the beads of sweat from his forehead and David noticed his hands were white and shaking.

'They want us to film them shooting one of our people in there ... Aaron says no.'

'Oh, God in heaven!' cried Bador. 'I shouldn't have let this happen. How did *you* get out?'

'I said I'd left the mike behind. I thought that'd delay things. I'll have to go back though ...'

'You mustn't do that.'

'What about Aaron and Dan? They'll end up taken hostage, too.'

The General spoke Hebrew to the interpreter. The interpreter picked up the loud-hailer and turned in the direction of the house.

'Your demand is impossible. The TV men must return to us. You have broken your agreement. They were only to film the hostages – alive.'

There was a sound of shouting and shuffling from inside. David thought he heard Aaron's voice rise amid the hubbub.

Then a shot was fired.

Silence. Blood froze.

David looked and saw that Chaim, his cameraman, had been turning over all the time, while the sound recordist held his microphone up to catch whatever he could. He'd no idea how long they'd been doing this.

The General shook with anger.

He grabbed the loud-hailer and shouted in English: 'Return the Americans. Free the Americans. That is an order.'

The door opened and Dan, the American cameraman, stumbled out and ran forward with his camera held over his head. He was sobbing, and couldn't say a word when he reached the safety of the command post. He fell to the ground, still wordless and shaking. He dropped his camera and was violently sick all over it.

Then the door was thrown open again and Aaron's body was pushed forward until it slumped in a heap.

David saw, at the same time as everyone else, that Aaron had been shot in the head.

CHAPTER 63

It fell to David to file reports not only to N-TV but also to Aaron's ABC. Just as Aaron had reported on the Oudtshoorn bomb for both networks, so David now had to swallow his own feelings, his stomach-churning contempt for the whole bloody business, and get on with the job of reporting what he had witnessed.

He didn't care what happened to the siege after this. He knew he should stick it out, but he couldn't. He took the tapes down to Tel Aviv. Then he put them on the satellite with instructions that they be copied, not sold, to ABC and offered to all the other networks, free of charge.

Then, finally, he placed a phone call to London.

It took a long time for anyone to reply.

It was Nanny Jo.

'Oh, Mr Kenway, where are you calling from ...?'

'Is Mrs Kenway there? I want to speak to her.'

'No, Mr Kenway. She's gone away with the boys. I don't know where to. I'm about to go home for Christmas.'

David paused. 'Then don't change your plans. Thank you. Happy Christmas.'

He hung up. So that was it.

He remembered Aaron's hypothetical question about how he'd feel if Jo had been having an affair.

All was clear now.

How would Jo react to Aaron's death? She would hear about it, like everyone else, on the TV news.

She'd finally pulled out, too. And taken the boys with her. At Christmas. David rang Jack Somerset again and said he was coming home.

'But what about the Christmas Siege?'

'Fuck the Christmas Siege,' David cried. 'I've had enough. I'm coming home, whatever you say.'

Jo was inconsolable. As a sometime N-TV slogan had put it, 'You heard it first from The Newsmakers'. And that was how Jo learned of Aaron's death, which made it all the more unbearable. She hadn't even known he'd been diverted to Jerusalem, least of all that he was with David.

Then two nights before Christmas she tuned into an N-TV 'hourly'. Her husband was describing someone's horrifying death in a siege. Only bit by bit did it dawn on Jo that the dead body she saw being dumped was that of her lover.

It was the worst Christmas that Jo and David had ever known. Having bolted with the children to give David a shock, Jo had been staying with sympathetic friends near Cambridge when she heard the news. She returned hysterically to London, which was where David found her when he arrived home the next day expecting an empty house.

'It's true, isn't it, about you and Aaron?'

'Did he tell you?'

'Not in so many words, but, yes, I knew.'

'You knew ...?'

'Yes. There was a lot of waiting around during the siege and he just kind of mentioned it. I didn't believe him. I was blind. Did it make you happy?'

'Yes. Incredibly happy. It made up for so much. He was a lovely man. And now ...'

They put on what Christmas show they could for the boys, very much a last-minute effort, and it didn't really work. Jo felt that her last, best hope had been snatched away. David felt terribly, terribly cheated.

'What do you want to do?' he asked bleakly.

'I have no idea, David. Nothing worse could possibly happen.'

David was similarly incapable of thinking straight or seeing into the future. His instinct was to try to get away again – back to work – but the circumstances of his pulling out of Jerusalem gnawed at him and made him despise the job that could land him in such an appalling position.

'At least you've come back,' David said. 'I'm sorry it had to be like this, but if it could bring us together again ...'

'I don't know, David. Now I've known real love, it's hard for me to settle for less. But look after me. You owe me that at least.'

'Yes, I know, I know. I will look after you.'

David cursed fate. He cursed the Palestinians and the Israelis. He cursed N-TV. He cursed Patrick Ritchie, as the man somehow most responsible for all these woes. He cursed himself. But now he spared Jo, and the memory of Aaron Rochester.

CHAPTER 64

It was an unusually cold January. Snow fell in London on the second day and the capital seemed to dig itself in and hibernate. But twenty-four hours of television still had to be filled every day at N-TV. Retrospectives on the previous year couldn't be put out indefinitely.

March Stevens returned, positively glowing from her Christmas engagement. Ben Brock was more his old self, in spite of all. He was to be seen not only on N-TV but presenting *The Entertainers* on the BBC. There were the inevitable mutterings about over-exposure.

Ben was still anxious about the future of N-TV but didn't see how he could help extract it from the mire except by being himself. He tried to make sense of the behind-the-screen politics.

'What's going on? Have *you* heard anything?'

'Yes, I have,' said Sir Charles Craig, beckoning Ben into a quiet corner of the Savile, where they were lunching. 'You see, we're not total fools on the Board.'

'I never suggested anything of the sort,' muttered Ben, shifting so that Sir Charles could the more easily whisper in his ear. 'All I know is that suddenly the ground's moving under our feet, and I'd like to be told why.'

'Well, the Government boycott is outrageous. Pure spite. Very petty. Constitutionally dangerous. Infringing the freedom of the Press and a hundred other things I could bang on about. But there's more to it than bad temper on their part. It's megalomania, too, on the part of one member of the Government. You know who I mean?'

'I could guess at several. Lyon for a start.'

'Lyon's the one. It's deeply foolish of him but we've just heard that he's openly encouraging other parties to put in for our franchise. The IBA selects the TV companies and he's not supposed to have any say in the matter. But he's out to kill us off. It's a flagrant abuse of his position as Home Secretary. How he expects to manipulate the IBA into ditching us and taking on his nominees, I can't begin to figure out. But he's treading a fatal path.'

'What's the Board going to do about it?'

'There's not a lot we can do. Patrick Ritchie has been told to play it very straight as far as the Government is concerned. Coverage as usual, even if they won't play ball with us.'

'And what do you make of his role in all this? Ritchie's, I mean. How do you square the Government's feud with us with his apparent mateyness with Lyon?'

'Simple. Lyon's wife is his ex-wife,' Sir Charles explained.

'So *you* know that, too ...'

'Knew it all the time, Ben. Ever since he was appointed. We did our homework, you know.'

'But how thoroughly did you check him out in Australia? David K said Reg Hardy was unbelievably scathing about Ritchie.'

'Well, he would be, wouldn't he? Look where it's got him. Out on his ear and dumped by his party.'

'My theory is that Lyon engineered Ritchie's appointment all along...'

'So he could sink the ship under him, you mean? That's more Machiavellian than even Lyon could manage ...'

'Maybe so. But it's having that effect, isn't it? Programme standards drop, ratings fall, beauty queens read the news ...'

'Oh that ...' Sir Charles clapped a hand to his forehead.

'Yes, *that*, Charles. What *about* that?'

In the third week of the New Year, Ben flew to New York with David to attend the memorial service for Aaron Rochester. The reporter's murder at the hands of terrorists had caused outrage in the United States. Yet again the exposed position of journalists in the modern world was the subject of indignant editorials.

Between fifteen and twenty inches of snow had fallen on Manhattan the day Ben and David arrived and the blizzard continued. The radio talked of a 'white-out' and the city for a time ground almost to a halt. Sidewalks were cordoned off. Ploughs churned snow from the streets and piled it over hapless vehicles parked at the kerb. Their owners wouldn't be able to retrieve them for weeks.

Aaron's memorial service was attended by his parents and relatives, together with a host of media moguls and public figures whose paths had crossed however fleetingly with his.

Nothing that any clergyman said could make the occasion any the less tragic. It was hard to capture the spirit of the man. There was little tangible that a television reporter could leave behind, unlike a newspaper or magazine journalist. He was of the moment. Now the moment was gone.

His breezy, cigar-waving, confident style was impossible to recall affectionately and vividly in the particular circumstances of his death and amid the cold and gloom of that church service in snow-lapped January.

There was so much, too, that couldn't be said at a memorial service. David could confide in no one, least of all Ben.

'I ought to get back to London straighaway and sort myself out,' David said. 'Sort *everything* out ...'

'I'm sure you don't have to just yet,' Ben advised him. 'Come with me to Washington for the Inauguration. Take your mind off things.'

'No, really, I feel I'm playing truant even coming for this. Whatever I do these days ends up in my having to be given compassionate leave. First it was South Africa, then Jerusalem ...'

'That's not how Patrick Ritchie sees it. He knows you're a valuable foreign reporter who always delivers the goods.'

'How much longer will we last, though?'

'Ah, well. There are cracks in the plaster, certainly. I had a session with Charlie Craig recently. He was talking about the Government boycott and said Colin Lyon had had some say in Ritchie's appointment. Imagine that. A Home Secretary putting in his wife's ex-husband ...'

'Well, that sounds juicy. So who'll pull the plug on him? Can we do it, or do we tip off a paper?'

'Depends how brave you feel. Why don't you go back to London and do a spot of digging? It could be the first big story of the year for you, and on our own front-doorstep.'

'What's Charlie Craig up to?' David asked, warming to the task. 'How does the board feel about Ritchie?'

'There's some feeling that Lyon had a plan to foist Ritchie on N-TV so that he'd destroy it from within. Bit far-fetched, if you ask me. Did I tell you that Lynne's been approached by a new consortium? They're all kitting themselves out ready for N-TV to take a tumble.'

'I'd find it hard to believe in any consortium that thought *she* had any credibility ...'

'Come now, David. Lynne's still got a lot to give. She was just badly handled towards the end of her time at N-TV. Nothing could excuse what Ritchie said about her.'

'Maybe. That's a good idea, though. We're pretty bad at covering stories on our own patch ...'

'If you don't want to come to Washington for the Iver show, that's what I suggest you do. Get to the bottom of this business once and for all.'

'Have a good time in Washington. Will you get to commiserate with Mann on only getting the Vice-Presidency?'

'I doubt it. I'm just doing the commentary on the Inauguration. I'm not even sure I'll get to speak to Winston. He's already been cocooned in aides and security men and all the paraphernalia.'

'Bloody boring job. I don't envy him.'

'Neither do I. But knowing Winston he'll find the silver lining if anybody can.'

Installed in his Washington hotel with icicles crashing down past his window, Ben did his homework for the next day's Inaugural parade and swearing-in. Washington was full for the festivities marking the start of a new presidency. There was a zip in the air and renewed optimism occasioned by the departure of the lacklustre Carson and the ascendancy of dashing young President-to-be, Gerry Iver.

Ben tried to reflect this in the short sentences he was scribbling on index cards, sentences he would drop into his commentary the next day. He was quite pleased with his preparations. He dined alone in his room and slept well.

Next morning, he appeared on N-TV, being interviewed from London by March.

He then did his commentary on the Inaugural ceremonies, following a feed from one of the American networks. He was not at the Capitol but in a warm studio, rather more to his taste than the sub-zero temperatures outside.

On his screen, he saw the Presidential limousine driving along Pennsylvania Avenue from the White House. Gerry Iver had been to have coffee with President Carson and now they were riding along together. In the next limousine came the in-coming and out-going Vice-Presidents. They drew up at the steps of the Capitol to the sound of ruffles and flourishes.

President Carson looked remarkably contented for a man who

had been kicked out of the White House, '... though perhaps,' mused Ben in his commentary, 'he's looking forward to a retirement full of quiet contemplation and deep sleep ... and the unhurried writing of his memoirs.'

Iver, sprightly and vigorous, leapt out of the limo as though eager to get his hands on the ultimate prize, and to read the Inaugural speech over which he had laboured long with a team of speechwriters and advisers.

The two men went into the Capitol for a moment, then re-emerged where all the guests had already gathered in the freezing cold, facing the podium. A yellowy sun lit the scene, supplemented by the cosier glow of TV lights.

Senator Gerry Iver, almost unrecognizable in black club coat and striped trousers, put one hand on an old family Bible and raised his right hand. The Chief Justice of the Supreme Court asked him to repeat the oath:

'I, Gerald Ronson Iver, do solemnly swear that I will faithfully execute the office of the President of the United States and will, to the best of my ability, preserve, protect and defend the Constitution of the United States. So help me God.'

Next, Winston Mann stepped forward to take the Vice-Presidential oath. Ben glowed with pleasure as his old friend held the Bible in his right hand. There was a small lump in Ben's throat.

But Winston never completed the oath.

He was not aware what was happening behind him, as he stood facing the Chief Justice with his right hand still raised. But he noticed a look of horror on the face of the Chief Justice who abruptly stopped feeding Winston the phrases to repeat after him.

Watching on television, Ben could tell something was wrong but the camera was in such a tight close-shot of Winston and the Chief Justice that, for a moment, he couldn't explain what it was.

In a matter of seconds, the camera pulled back to reveal an amazing scene.

President Iver had just entered the history books as the shortest-lived President in the history of the United States. He lay in his wife's arms. He had succumbed not to an assassin's bullet but to a heart-attack.

After an hour's delay, during which Ben excelled himself by

talking non-stop in a *tour de force* of instant reporting, the Inauguration went ahead.

Barely able to contain himself and with nerves fluttering around his voice, Ben described the Inauguration of Winston Edward Mann as President of the United States.

The Speaker of the House of Representatives was sworn in as acting Vice-President.

President Mann read the Inaugural Address intended for delivery by his predecessor.

The theatre of action, as George Washington had once described it, was apparently still capable of putting on the highest drama.

CHAPTER 65

Lynne no longer fell upon the papers in the morning or watched other people's news bulletins with quite such attention as once she had.

But the drama in Washington gripped her as it did everybody. It served as a reminder that nothing was certain in this world. Life was a lottery, and Lynne almost regretted not being on the great roller-coaster of newsgathering that day. Fancy not being able to go on the air and say the words, 'The President is dead. Long live the President.' It would have given her a prickly feeling up the spine to do that.

She had not been forgotten by N-TV. Her solicitor, Gerald Murphy, rang to make that plain.

'I have news,' he said, flatly. 'And you have the makings of a small triumph on your hands.'

'Tell me,' said Lynne.

'N-TV will do anything rather than go to court. If I were in their shoes, I must say I'd feel the same. They know that a libel case before a jury can go either way, regardless of its merits. Even if they won the case, they know they'd probably be thinking of over a hundred thousand in legal fees, which they might have to foot themselves.'

'So?'

'So, they've made you an offer. It is couched in ways I won't bother you with, disclaimers that Mr Ritchie ever intended to say anything defamatory and so on but, in brief, they want to make an out of court settlement. They're offering fifty thousand. We might be able to increase that marginally, but I'd urge you to accept in principle. They promise to make a statement withdrawing any suggestion of professional inadequacy on your part. They are also willing to say, as proof of their good intentions, that you can have your job back.'

'Fat chance I'd take it,' said Lynne, with zest.

'So, without wishing to anticipate, may I say, Miss Kimberley, that you appear to have won. Hands down. May I congratulate you . . .'

'You may. Bloody marvellous. Thank you.'

'I wouldn't be too hasty in rejecting the offer of your job back.

For legal reasons, I'd recommend you keep that option open.'

'Listen, the only way I'd ever dream of going back there would be to see Patrick Ritchie walk the plank ...'

'The likelihood of that, I'm afraid, is a subject on which I'm unable to offer an opinion.'

When David returned from New York he made a point of seeing Ritchie immediately.

'I've two problems on my plate. One's professional, the other's domestic.'

'Tell me about them,' said Ritchie, putting on a relaxed air. 'Both of them.'

'I've lost my nerve. After Jerusalem and what happened to Aaron, an old, old friend, I don't think I can face any more bang-bang assignments. I'd like a spot of R and R. Perhaps even a return to newscasting for a week or two. Would that be possible?'

Ritchie, blithely ignoring the conclusions he'd reached a few months back about David's newscasting abilities, didn't hesitate in saying, 'Sure, yes, whatever you like, Dave. Glad to have you back. Now, there's something personal that's bothering you, you say?'

'Yes. My marriage is on the rocks. Being away hasn't exactly helped. I need some time in London so I can reorganize my life.'

David wasn't telling the exact truth, but he genuinely did need to put his life in order now. He exaggerated his plight to provide a further emotional lever in achieving what he wanted: enough time in London, in and around N-TV, to get to the bottom of Ritchie and Lyon's peculiar game.

'OK, sure, you stay in London. I don't mind.'

The more Ritchie tried to sound accommodating and sympathetic, the more David despised him for being so spineless.

The following week, David was back newscasting on the *Nightly News*. Once more this gave him time to terrorize all and sundry around the office.

But, this time, for a purpose.

Vanessa's baby was due in early February. It was her intention to work right up to the birth. Her increasingly huge form was the subject of a good deal of speculation among those at N-TV who were still in ignorance of the father's identity.

As it happened, Nikki Brennan didn't know. She asked Paul Whitehall. He wasn't letting on, not wishing to say anything that might make Vanessa uncomfortable. But he did confide that the father of Vanessa's baby *was* someone at N-TV. 'You'd be surprised if you knew. Quite surprised. But she's not letting on. So there you are.'

'Does she mind?' Nikki asked.

'Having the baby? I don't know,' Paul said. 'I haven't talked to her about it.'

'How will she look after it?'

Paul smiled and told her. 'Vanessa's a very special girl. She immensely capable. She'll manage all right. Husband or no husband.'

'You sound as if you rather like her.' Nikki smiled. 'I didn't know you were interested.'

'You don't know much,' said Paul.

Then Nikki's intuition let her down badly. Why was Paul being so protective? What did he really know about Vanessa's baby? Surely *he* couldn't be the father? But he seemed to know and was hiding something. Perhaps one shouldn't rule him out? The only way would be to ask Vanessa herself. But she was rather a forbidding figure. Still, it was a puzzler, and Nikki was determined to get to the bottom of it, out of sheer curiosity.

CHAPTER 66

Archie Tuke hadn't actually stepped inside the N-TV studios since the memorable evening when he'd taken March out to dinner at L'Escargot. Interviews with the Leader of the Alliance Party had been conducted at Westminster or outside London. Even so, he still found reason to complain that he didn't appear enough on the channel and that N-TV must be biased as much against the Alliance Party as against the Government ...

Tonight he was back and, to his total satisfaction, found himself being interviewed by March on the *Nightly News* about a housing issue.

After the programme, he lingered in the hospitality room but it wasn't March he engaged in conversation – except for hollow protestation at the news of her engagement.

It was David. David had a fairly low estimate of Tuke as a politician but his ears pricked up when Tuke started gossiping about the media and, in particular, about the Government and N-TV.

'It's a very significant mistake they've made, you know, the boycott.' Tuke shifted and stroked his unruly ginger beard while he talked. Even if he hadn't been small in stature he'd still have given the impression of talking up to people. 'I can't help feeling it's a much more dangerous thing for them to attempt than people realize.'

David wasn't sure whether Tuke had anything of substance to say on the subject. He might just be treading water in the hope that somebody would supply *him* with useful information.

'Who's behind it, do you think? Ross or Lyon?'

'There's no doubt that Ross has expressed strong views on N-TV bias, but I feel those were mostly of a ritual nature, intended to warn and not to sting. Lyon seems to be the chief stirrer, and I find that extraordinary – that the minister with responsibility for broadcasting should so blatantly be sticking his nose in.'

Tuke remembered whose hospitality he was imbibing and lowered his voice. He pressed quite close to David who was given the benefit of Tuke's tobacco-laden breath.

'I'll tell you something, though. Have you heard of a set-up called World News Network?'

345

'Yes, as a matter of fact I have,' David replied. 'Lynne Kimberley, formerly of this parish, has been approached by them. Seem to be after our franchise, not that it's up for grabs.'

'Quite. And have you heard of a set-up called Twenty-Four Hour News. Or another called Dateline, London?'

'Neither.'

'They're both the same sort of outfit. A group of money-men and ex- or disgruntled newsmen who've got together – been *encouraged* to get together, one might say – to put the frighteners on N-TV.'

'Encouraged by whom?'

'I would say by Lyon himself, indirectly. It's folly, of course, but it's my belief he doesn't just want to have a TV station that's sympathetic to the Government and to him in particular. It's money he's after. He has that expensive wife who treats him like a doormat. He doesn't have any money of his own. He's a career politician and has had to survive until now on an MP's salary – which, as you know, is woefully inadequate. Even as a Cabinet Minister he just doesn't bring in the sort of money his wife throws around.'

'But, the Home Secretary can't ditch a station. The IBA does that. And he certainly couldn't put one of his own in its place.'

'No,' replied Tuke, 'but a Home Secretary *can* pull various strings, lean on people. The Home Secretary appoints the Chairman of the IBA and members of its council, so he's plenty of scope for packing that, if he wants to. And then again, he's already done very well in destabilizing N-TV. The boycott, the new editor. What's the result? The ratings stay down, the station's future's in jeopardy.'

David was unable to make up his mind why Tuke was telling him this. Was Tuke allowing himself to believe there was a politically-motivated conspiracy? Was he even right in detecting something underhand in the events of the past year?

'You're probably on to something,' David told him. 'Or, to put it another way, your suspicions accord with mine. Between you and me, I'm doing a little digging myself. If I have to, I'll expose the lot of 'em.'

'You'll be lucky,' said Tuke, brusquely. 'You'll be gagged.'

'There *are* ways ...'

'I'll be interested to see them ...'

Vanessa didn't know what to make of it. Was Paul really

homosexual, as everybody said, and if so why was he offering to marry her?

'I know it seems old-fashioned and a bit chivalrous to some,' he explained. 'But that doesn't bother me. It seems like a positive thing I could do to help.'

'Is that a good enough reason to get married, wanting to help me out of a hole? Or are you trying to prove something?'

'I know that's how it'll seem to other people, but I don't care. And people have got married for worse reasons. It's just that I'd like to see you happy. And we could make a life together. Have more children of our own.'

'Why is it that everyone things you're, you know ... funny?'

'Well, we're *all* a bit of one and a bit of the other. You know that.'

'But how would I know you wouldn't go back to your old ways ...'

'You'd have to trust me.'

Vanessa still thought it was a bizarre proposition. Paul was kind and friendly, always had been, but she'd thought that was because he was gay. There was no danger in the relationship. He could be drawn to a forceful woman because nothing would ever come of it. But what now?

There was another objection to the match. She came from the settled upper-middle classes, almost the gentry. As far as she could tell, Paul was from lower-middle-class stock, disguised though it was by the classlessness of show business. It would certainly be a meeting of worlds, if they were to marry. But a marriage to Paul might be the final straw as far as her parents were concerned.

'It's terribly kind of you, Paul, and I do appreciate it. But I decided to have the baby without getting married. So I might as well see it through alone. Besides, how would you feel about being father to another man's child?'

'I can't see that it makes any difference, love. Like a step-child, you might say.'

'You're very sweet, Paul, but I can't say yes ...'

'On the other hand, you haven't said no. So there's a chance, if you think about it some more?'

'Oh, there's always a chance.'

And Vanessa sighed the deepest of sighs, as though she were overwhelmed by the problems fate had saddled her with. She couldn't help blaming N-TV.

'But without N-TV,' Paul reminded her, 'I wouldn't be here making you this offer ...'

'I know, I know ... Just let me think about it. Please.'

'Take as long as you like, love. I can wait.'

Nikki noticed Paul and Vanessa more and more in each other's company.

There was something going on between them.

But if Paul, unlikely as it might seem, was the father of the child, why weren't they getting married?

It was all very perplexing. Would she never have the nerve to ask Vanessa herself?

'So there's no getting rid of Ritchie?' asked David.

'Only if we manage to expose Lyon,' Sir Charles answered, flatly.

'I fully intend to do that, if only I can produce the evidence.'

'And where will you do that?'

'On the *Nightly News*. Why not?'

'But Ritchie won't let you get away with that.'

'Well, if he won't, I'll just have to leak it to the papers.'

'You're playing with fire ...'

'I know, but I'm in the mood for a scrap, so I don't give a shit.'

They were talking at Sir Charles's house at Gerrard's Cross, a late Victorian mansion with grand lawns and wide ponds. Sir Charles had suggested they'd best meet in secret, as far away from N-TV and Westminster as possible. Ben was there, too. The three were determined to put N-TV back on its feet. But Sir Charles was conscious of his position as a Board member. Theoretically, he shouldn't have been having such conversations with members of N-TV staff, but if the Editor-in-Chief was conniving with the Home Secretary, there was no alternative but to resort to the cloak and dagger.

'What we need is *evidence*,' warned Ben. 'Letters, documents, whatever. Evidence that Lyon *has* been exerting improper influence on the IBA, on anybody, to try and scupper N-TV. Once we have that, we can go public with it. But it's got to be rock solid. You know how governments can behave when somebody points a finger at them. They can whitewash everything out of sight.'

'Maybe the evidence doesn't exist,' cautioned Sir Charles. 'Colin Lyon may be a fool, but I doubt he's a careless fool. If he's up to arm-twisting, I don't suppose he advertises it.'

'But is there anything to stop me getting a list of IBA executives and working through it, asking them?' David asked.

'I don't expect they'd admit to anything, even if you did. They'd bounce back, reveal what you're up to, and you'd be out on your ear.'

'There *is* that risk,' Ben agreed. 'It takes a different sort of courage to get at the facts when your job's at stake.'

'I know,' said David, 'but how many times do I have to tell you, I don't really care.'

Both Sir Charles and Ben knew he meant it. They also vaguely understood the position David found himself in and why, perhaps, he could afford to be so reckless.

'I'm seeing a lawyer in the morning,' Jo told David. 'I've decided it's what's best for both of us. But I'll stay on in England. For the boys. I hope you'll be cooperative.'

David had been expecting the announcement for some time but, now it had come, he felt ambivalent, curiously reluctant for his marriage to end.

'OK, but think about it again, will you? I have a feeling you're doing the wrong thing. Until last month, I'd have agreed. But now, maybe we need each other rather a lot. Perhaps we've always needed each other, most of all when you were hurling TV sets at me ...'

In both their faces the strain of the past few months showed.

'When are you off again?' asked Jo, wondering how easy it would be to hammer out a settlement.

'Definitely not for a while. I'm working on something nearer home.'

'And may I ask what it is?'

'Of course you may ask, Jo. You are still my wife. It's nothing less than the future of N-TV itself.'

'How dramatic! I didn't know N-TV had got a future.'

'That's what I am trying to find out.'

She gave him a familiar look. 'Playing with fire again? Really, David, will you never learn?'

'I don't expect so.'

Jo looked at him again but didn't smile. Him and his obsessions.

CHAPTER 67

It was not what he would say that was important: it was the mere fact that he would say it at all.

Ben returned to Washington DC in February to interview Winston Mann. It was the President's first interview since taking office. Inevitably, there had been rumblings from the American networks about the honour being given to a British interviewer. For a while, too, it looked as though Ben might have to share his opportunity with a panel from other European stations. But, in the end, he made it alone.

'This is one campaign promise I intend to keep,' the President had told his advisers. 'This guy Brock is an old, old friend. And when there was about as much chance of my sitting in this chair as of a mule going to the moon, he had faith in me. That's when I made the promise and I'm going to stick to it.'

Ben flew to Washington on Concorde. It seemed the right thing to do. He invited Yvonne to accompany him.

'I'll pay for your seat,' he told her. 'I can't let N-TV do that.'

'Nonsense, Ben, darling. I pay my own way. You know that.'

'It'll be pretty boring for you,' Ben watered down the prospect further. 'I won't be able to take you along to the White House for the interview. You'll be on your own.'

'I don't mind. There's a lot of people I can visit. It's a lovely idea...'

So lovely was the idea that, behind Ben's back, Yvonne found out which hotel they were staying at and changed the reservation from single rooms to a suite. When Ben found out he was secretly amused and pleased at Yvonne's manipulation.

He hardly dropped a beat, either, when he discovered that the President and First Lady were expecting Yvonne to accompany him to lunch after the interview. How had that happened? Ben never received a satisfactory answer: Yvonne just smiled enigmatically.

The White House limo came to pick them up and, in a rare move, the President greeted Ben at the door as though he were a visiting Head of State.

They posed for photographs, then Winston took Ben into the Oval Office.

'You look very much at home, Winston – or should I call you Mr President?'

'Ben, for old times' sake ... you can call me "Mr President"! But, you're right. I do feel settled in. I suppose the surprise actually helped. I didn't have time to work up any anticipation or anxiety. Suddenly – wham! – I was President. Since then I've been so busy, I haven't had time to worry.'

'Well, it's very kind of you to spare me the ...'

'Bullshit, Ben. I wanted to do this and I was very, very glad when you reminded me. Unlike most men who get this job I don't have all sorts of debts of honour to pay off. Just a few million in campaign debts! In fact, this is about the only debt of honour I owe ... So it's a real pleasure.'

The interview began.

'Mr President ...'

Ben looked his subject in the eye. It wasn't always easier interviewing people you knew well. But this time it *was* easy. They just talked.

'You became President in the most tragic and, one might say, most unlikely circumstances in the entire history of the United States. I won't ask you how you felt at that moment because I imagine it'd be indescribable. When did it come home to you what had actually happened?'

Winston looked serious and Ben wondered what was going on behind the deep, dark eyes.

'I can tell you,' he began eventually. 'Not till next day. I read out President Iver's Inaugural Address, I have to tell you, barely taking in a word. I'd only been shown it in draft form, but I think it came out fine. It was a wonderful piece of work and I take no credit for that. But the rest of the day passed in a dream. Then next morning – I hate to admit this – I was watching one of our breakfast shows, I won't say which one, and the anchor mentioned "President Mann" and it suddenly hit me he was talking about me ...'

Ben decided to scrap the questions he'd painstakingly prepared. He would simply ask the obvious ones.

The interview ran for more than the allotted thirty minutes. Winston talked openly and frankly. Ben barely had to ask questions, but that wasn't to disguise the fact he guided their talk along skilfully.

351

When it was over, the tape was sent by satellite to London and played several times on N-TV, in whole or in part. It was picked up by other broadcasting networks, not least by the American ones. It was the first time the President had spoken informally since taking office. For the first time, people all over the world felt they knew him.

Viewers all over the world were impressed, too, by Ben's handling of the interview and were intrigued by the long friendship that had led up to it. It bestowed on Ben an international fame which had hitherto eluded him. He was to look upon it as the high point of his career as a broadcaster.

Over lunch in the President's private dining room on the second floor of the White House, Winston was behaving roguishly towards Yvonne.

'So you're the woman Ben travels with, are you?' he asked with a nudge.

'You could say that,' Yvonne replied and had a fit of the giggles.

'When Franklin and Eleanor Roosevelt invited people here they were very careful what they put on the invitations. They made no mention of spouses, in case that was inappropriate. So they used to put, "the person who travels with you" ...'

'Perfect!' exclaimed Yvonne.

'Mind you, there's a limit to how far Presidents should connive at that sort of thing. So the next time you come, I expect you to have made it legal.'

Ben said nothing but simply beamed as he always did when either embarrassed or pleased or both. He was, in fact, most pleased by Winston's indiscreet advancing of Yvonne's cause. It was almost as though he'd been put up to it.

The President asked about N-TV. He seemed to be setting the agenda for the small-talk. 'Still riding high, I trust?'

'Er, no. Rather the reverse,' Ben reported honestly. 'Wracked with internal strife, and boycotted by the Government.'

'Boycotted? Tell me more.'

'Ministers refuse to be interviewed because of our supposed bias. It's marvellous most of the time. We don't have to listen to their boring old platitudes.'

'I must keep that weapon in my armoury for when things get hot around here. I can see it's a double-edged weapon, though.'

'Seriously,' Ben went on, 'we do have a problem. It looks as though the Ross Government is out to sink us ... for rather complicated reasons. We've been going through a bad patch.'

'You mean I've just given an interview to a lame-duck?!'

'Exactly. But you might have doubled our ratings overnight ...'

'Want me to say anything to Ross? He's going to be over soon.'

'No, Mr President, if I may give you an order ... *Don't mention it!*'

'Fair enough. Point taken.'

Winston turned again to Yvonne, pleased beyond measure that Ben seemed to have found happiness with another partner so soon after losing Natalie. He thought she might even prove a more suitable wife for Ben. She was more of his world. And her calculation and *joie-de-vivre* were just what Ben needed to stop him becoming morose.

Then Winston quickly rose and announced, 'You must excuse me, both of you. I've got a lot of work to do. I've got to go and be Presidential. It's been a real joy to see you. Do come back. Do keep in touch, Ben ... and Lady Hamilton. It's not enough for friends to be *there* when you need them. Sometimes they've gotta be *here*!'

With a wave, the President slipped away under the chandeliers and through the door. It was closed for him – a very final gesture – and, for all Winston's protestations, Ben couldn't help feeling a chapter in both their lives had ended. If there had been unfinished business between them, it was over now.

Silently, Lorraine Mann led them down the Grand Staircase and bid them goodbye

While they were waiting for the limo to draw up, Ben asked Yvonne, 'I wonder how many proposals of marriage have been made under the White House roof?'

Yvonne took his arm, said nothing, and climbed in the limo beside him.

CHAPTER 68

They went through all the invitations and requests before March dumped them back in Vanessa's lap.

'I wonder what'll happen when Mark and I get married? Do you think the proposals will fall off?'

'Go up, more like. There's a lot of it about ...'

March wasn't sure what Vanessa meant.

'Actually,' Vanessa spoke up, boldly, 'I'm only telling you this because we're, you know, friends ... I've had a proposal, too!'

'Vanessa! Who from? Not ...'

'Not David, no, of course not. No, from the least likely man in the world.'

'Um ... Patrick Ritchie?'

'For heaven's sake, spare me that ...'

'Give up. Who?'

'Now you mustn't tell anyone ... because I haven't decided *what* to do about it yet ...'

'Who is it?'

'Paul Whitehall.'

'But that's amazing, really amazing – Nikki Brennan cornered me two nights ago and started on about her intuition. She said she thought Paul wanted to marry you. I thought she was fishing for tittle-tattle from me. So I told her it was out of the question ...'

'D'you think Paul's been putting it around?'

'I don't know. What's your reaction? It's nice of him even if he's a bit ... well ... you know ...'

'Oh, I don't think he *really* is,' Vanessa answered sharply. 'I haven't ruled him out ...'

March took the hint.

'Lynne Kimberley, please.'

'Speaking.'

'Ah, Ms Kimberley, I can't tell you who I am. But I've a proposition I'd like to discuss with you, in connection with television news...'

Here we go again, thought Lynne. 'I suppose you're setting up a consortium and you were wondering if ...?'

354

'Have you been approached by someone else?' the voice asked, audibly taken aback.

'Yes. The more the merrier, say I, and I'll take lunch from whoever's buying it.'

'Actually, we hadn't thought of lunch, rather more of a chat. We might be able to lay on some coffee ...'

'I can see you must be ex-BBC! But I'll talk.'

'Dateline, London' was no more than the working title for a consortium. If it sounded vaguely like a lonely-hearts club, it had also been the title of a venerable ITN programme of long ago. Whatever the company would eventually be called, temporary offices had been found for it above a bank in the City.

Lynne duly presented herself. She felt strange in the City environment, far from the media area she was used to. On the hat-stand in the reception area she noticed that all the men's overcoats were a uniform dark blue, though some had Edwardian velvet collars.

She had to wait until whoever it was she was about to meet returned from trying to raise funds for the new TV company. There was a stirring of people entering through a back door and then she was shown into an office, carpeted, furnished, but completely unlived in, no books on the shelves, no family photos on the desk, completely lacking in any personality.

Inside were half a dozen men. One rose to greet her. It was Adam Ravenscroft.

'You ...'

'Yes, me, Lynne ... and I think you may also know Lord Almley...'

'Plum, too! Of course, yes, hello.'

'But probably not Max Eastermann who's our financial adviser ...'

'No. How do you do.'

Adam proceeded to introduce the others, but Lynne was never very good at catching names first time round.

'I'll have to ask you first, Lynne, to respect the fact that my, our, participation in this, er, project is, at the moment, under wraps. I'm still Deputy Editor at N-TV. It happens to be my morning off. There would, of course, be the question of a clash of interest, to say the least, if it became known beyond these four walls that I was here.'

Lynne thought this took the biscuit. It wasn't just that Adam seemed to be having it both ways, but she was terribly conscious that here was a man who'd once slept with her. It was always odd to encounter old flames.

'As you'll know, perhaps better than anybody, N-TV's been going through a sticky patch. We've been given to believe that the sticky patch might be terminal if the Government has its way. And so we're in the process of raising money in the City to put together a challenge. It's a big undertaking, but we think we're in with a chance.'

Lynne's first reaction was that it was doomed. But she merely asked, 'Where do I fit in? You want me for the letterhead ...?'

Adam allowed himself a rare smile: 'Not just yet. But, in a sense, yes, we'd like to have a commitment from you that you'd join us as a principal member of the team once we got the go-ahead.'

'*If* you get the go-ahead ...'

'All right, *if*. You've been approached by other consortiums, I believe?'

'I had a call from Worldwide News, but I haven't followed it up, yet ... And, as you may know, I now, technically, have an offer of my job back at N-TV. Not that I'd dream of going back until a certain somebody's chair becomes vacant. But, there's an important aspect I don't understand. Why are you going to all this trouble? Who's tipped you the wink that it's worth your while?'

Adam leant back from the desk and turned to Lord Almley. 'Plum, you tell her.'

'I've a small confession to make to you, Lynne,' he began. 'You remember when we had that agreeable lunch at the House last year, I made a prediction? Charles Craig had just announced he was relinquishing the Editorship and you asked me who would succeed him.'

'I remember.'

'And I teased you a little, I'm afraid. I said that it wouldn't be someone from inside the organization. It would be someone from outside, a foreigner.'

'Yes. And you were right. You must have known all along about that shit Ritchie.'

Almley smiled diplomatically. 'Yes, I did know.'

'From whom?'

'Lynne, you don't have to prove to us that you're good at interviewing!'

'Sorry.'

'I'm not without my contacts in the Government and I can tell you that Patrick Ritchie was personally *inserted* – the right word in the circumstances, I think – by the Home Secretary himself.'

'Colin Lyon?'

'The very same. Things didn't work out the way Lyon hoped, of course. He was looking forward to having someone favourable to the Government, and to him, in the hot seat. He'd taken the gamble that this man he'd heard of through his wife would be his pawn. But, as you know – and as Adam especially knows – he just wasn't up to the job. Got up everyone's noses, not least your own, and the present sorry state of the company is the result.'

'So?'

'So, Lyon changed tack and decided to destroy N-TV instead. The Government boycott was his idea, and pretty pointless, too, if I may say so. But it accords with the hysterical feelings all governments have about the media. If a broadcaster so much as utters the smallest word of criticism, they have him driven off the air, get the IBA to rescind the franchise. And that's where *we* come in.'

Lord Almley sat back and Adam took up the tale. Eastermann looked on, wordlessly, from behind silver-rimmed spectacles, his hands clasped in front of him.

'That's why a number of consortiums, consortia, however you like to put it, are organizing themselves, waiting for the peach to drop off the tree. That's why we want to sign you up, Lynne. You're not, of course, the only person we're interested in. You'll know some of the others. But unless they're very indiscreet or very foolish, they won't let on. So how about it?'

There seemed a remarkable lack of substance to the proposal. Anyone could hire an office and pretend to be bidding for a big prize.

'I'm not sure,' Lynne answered quietly, 'and thank you for thinking of me, by the way. I may appear to be rolling in it after the libel case but I haven't got the money yet. It could go against me on appeal, and the lawyers take their slice. So I'm very interested, frankly, in any work I can get ... but ... well, I find this hard to put, Adam, because of your continuing involvement with N-TV ...'

'Go ahead. *Please* say what's on your mind.'

'There are several people at N-TV who are already on to what's behind the upheavals. It seems much more likely that what you'll have at the end of the day is not a new franchise, but a new Home Secretary.'

Lord Almley spoke next. 'Ministers rarely fall unless they're pushed. It would depend on whether Lyon lost the PM's support.'

'In that case,' said Lynne, 'the pressure would have to come from the outside. The evidence of Lyon's complicity would have to be overwhelming.'

'And who's going to follow it up and do the dirty deed?'

'You might be surprised,' said Lynne.

CHAPTER 69

Nikki went along to the door marked 'Newscasters', knocked and went in.

The room was empty. It was a medium-sized office-cum-Green Room which the newscasters used as a base when not in the studio or at their desks in the newsroom.

Through the room you reached a smaller office where Vanessa presided. Filing cabinets contained the notepaper and photographs that helped keep the flame of fame brightly lit. Scores of boxes contained fan mail, and pestering mail, which had already been dealt with.

'Hello,' said Vanessa looking up from her typewriter. 'What brings you to these parts? Looking for someone?'

She could look pretty intimidating, thought Nikki. What a pity she didn't use a softer make-up. Her mulberry-coloured smock from Laura Ashley with its crisp white cotton collar and big black bow did little to distract attention from the large bulge beneath.

'I – I was just passing, so ...'

'March tells me you're very concerned for my welfare.'

Oh, thought Nikki, she's come right out with it. At least I won't have to broach the subject.

'Er, well, not just your welfare, darling. Actually, it was Paul Whitehall I was talking to ...'

'Well, what is it then?'

Nikki wasn't very proud of her performance, but she said it anyway. 'I just think you should know that Paul is very fond of you. Really, you know, *keen* ...'

Vanessa looked at Nikki and wondered where this was leading.

'I think you should appreciate what ... a very nice person he is ... and not listen to what people say about him.'

'I'm listening to *you*, Nikki, aren't I?'

'Well, yes, but ... what I'm saying is ...'

Vanessa looked at her most severely. 'I should warn you not to say anything you might regret about Paul. What you've said already, though no doubt well-intentioned, comes, I'm afraid, too late ...'

'No! How ...?'

'I mean, I've already decided that I'm going to marry Paul ...'

Nikki was so surprised that all she could think of asking was, 'Does he know?'

'Of course he knows, you ninny-pot!'

'That's all right then.'

'Yes. Isn't it marvellous? I'm very, very happy.'

Still bemused, Nikki stuttered, 'There's nowt so queer as folk ...'

'And we'll have no more cracks like that, if you don't mind.'

A discreet ceremony took place one Saturday morning very soon after, at Fulham Registry Office. Brigadier and Mrs Sinclair travelled up from Gloucestershire, slightly baffled by the whole business, and Paul Whitehall's parents, a homely couple from Rochdale, also took the trouble to attend. March and Paul's brother were the witnesses.

The Brigadier commented to his wife, 'Well, it was very nice, but it wasn't exactly what we had in mind, was it, dear?'

The baby, a bouncy, blond little fellow, was born ten days later. He had a wonderful head of curly hair. There were some who detected a resemblance to the father. But they didn't confide this thought to Paul.

David and Lynne had never had much time for each other, but now they were united against a common enemy. They arranged to talk at a distance from the customary media watering-holes.

The Dragon was a cosy, waterside pub in Little Venice. That lunchtime in March it was just about warm enough to sit outside, with Lynne in her second-best fur coat and David wearing his reporter's raincoat over his jeans. There was the faintest hint of spring in the air. Something more cheerful seemed only round the corner.

'You live here, do you?' David asked.

'Not far away, in Maida Vale.'

'Hmm. Bloody difficult parking the Volvo. Mind you, I don't expect I'll have it much longer ...'

'Meaning?'

'"TV MAN'S DIVORCE SETTLEMENT LOOMS ..."'

'You're lucky to have a car. There are some of us they still won't let loose on the Queen's highway. Only another month, though, thank God.'

'I'd forgotten. Your spot of bother with the boys in blue?'

Lynne reached for the orange juice she had ostentatiously

ordered. 'So, you've not been having too smooth a ride yourself then? How *are* things?'

'On a scale of miserable to appalling? I'm now enjoying the experience of getting divorced. It's a laugh-a-minute, I can tell you.'

'I met your wife once,' said Lynne. 'In fact, she hit me.'

'She made quite a habit of it.'

'Ah, well. You'll enjoy the single life. "It's more airy once you get over the shame of it." I should know. Since my Number Two died, I've had nothing but airiness ...'

David changed the subject. 'Ben says you've been approached by a new-fangled consortium. He wouldn't tell me any more. You know what he's like. Doesn't want to get mixed up in any dirty business. When you talk with presidents you tend to lose the common touch ...'

'That's unkind, David. Ben's a marvel. He hasn't been messed about by Ritchie the way I have, but then he's Ben. He's unique. Good luck to him if he's clever enough to survive.'

Lynne went on to tell David about her meeting with the 'Dateline, London' people and what Plummond Almley had revealed of Lyon's plot.

'I'm not sure I'm supposed to tell you any of this,' she broke off with the gossip's leer, 'but, for all I know, they've approached you, too ...'

'No, they haven't. Nobody has. And people ask why I'm bitter ...!'

'There's one thing I haven't told you,' said Lynne, 'and I'm bloody well going to, and that's who was there. Plum Almley's an old mate – or, rather, he likes to flirt with me. Invites me to the Lords and metaphorically feels me up. But I haven't told you who the Chief Exec's going to be. You'll never guess.'

'Who *is* it?'

'Adam Ravenscroft ...'

'Ravenscroft! That arse-licker! Well, thanks for telling me. I could've come a nasty cropper if I hadn't known that scorpion was in the bed.'

'What are you planning to do?'

'Simple. I fully intend to blow Lyon right out of the river.'

'But how?'

'All I need is a tame politician and a good TV director. And I think I've found them both.'

*   *   *

'Have you got a name for him yet?' David asked. 'I must say, I admire you for it. I owe you a lot.'

Paul Whitehall felt a mixture of smugness and discomfort at David's approval. He didn't answer the question.

'I've already said I'll pay towards him,' David went on. 'We must get that organized soon. Chase me, won't you, until I've sorted it out? What are you going to call him?'

'Well, Vanessa thought of it. You'll smile when you hear it. It's Ben.'

'Ben Whitehall ...?'

Paul noticed David's eyes glisten. And he swallowed. What a wonderful idea to call the child after Ben Brock! It was the happiest of names.

David recovered and quickly moved on to the main purpose of his meeting with the man who'd taken on his child.

'You may regard me as an out-and-out shit, Paul, and I expect there are plenty round these parts who'd agree with you, but I desperately need your help. I owe you a lot, you owe me nothing, but ... well, you might find there's something in this for you ...'

Paul looked puzzled.

'It's to do with the mess N-TV is in.'

'Oh, that ...'

'Yes, *that*. We now know without a shadow of doubt who it's all down to. The Home Secretary. Does that surprise you?'

'Not a bit. He's a bastard. Even I can see that.' Paul blushed at his inadvertent choice of word.

'He's out to wreck us and he deserves to get caught. And I'm the one to do it, but he mustn't be allowed to wriggle out of it, or resort to cover-ups.'

'Meaning?'

'I'm going to expose him on the Big News.'

'Ah ... it's some time since anyone called it that ...'

'Maybe ... One of the difficulties, of course, is that Lyon has already infiltrated N-TV, so one's room for manoeuvre is limited. But, tell me, Paul – would you like another drink, by the way – how could I get hold of a little studio time? To record something. Without anybody knowing ...?'

CHAPTER 70

Archie Tuke knew what he had to do. He merely had to ask an innocent question.

'Mr Tuke!'

The Speaker of the House of Commons nodded in his direction. Archie rose clutching the order paper on which he had scribbled a few notes.

Trevor Ross had been prepared on all the obvious topics that might be raised during Prime Minister's Questions. He waited patiently for whatever the Alliance Party leader would throw at him.

The quaint rules of the game were that he must ask the Prime Minister an innocuous question about his plans for the future – then follow that with a hard-hitting supplementary.

'Mr Speaker, would the Right Honourable Gentleman kindly inform the House whether he has any plans to address the nation on television in the near future?'

Ross confidently stood up. 'While grateful for the Right Honourable Gentleman's interest in these matters and concerned as I always am that he should be properly informed of the achievements of Her Majesty's Government, I regret to say I have no plans at present to broadcast ... on any channel.'

Ross's heron-like form folded up onto the green leather seating, a smile of triumph on his lips. Tory backbenchers caught the allusion to the Government's feud with N-TV and brayed with delight.

Heckling broke out on Tuke's side of the House.

'Order! Order!' called the Speaker, with apparent irritation.

The Alliance Party leader rose again.

'Would the Right Honourable Gentlemen care to justify the apparent and some would say incomprehensible instruction he had given to his colleagues not to appear on N-TV?'

Ross, still unperturbed: 'Mr Tuke is mistaken. There has been no such instruction issued either by me or by any of my colleagues.'

The House roared, shouted and marvelled at the reply. It was not a noise heard anywhere else in the world, with the possible exception of the London Zoo, but its message was clear. Some of the MPs didn't believe what the Prime Minister had just said. Others didn't know what to think but knew, at least, they were supposed to be supportive.

Tuke rose again for the third time.

'The Prime Minister's answer will come as a considerable surprise to journalists and editors at N-TV who have been unable to persuade either him or his colleagues to be interviewed on any of their programmes since just before Christmas. While to some this might be considered a boon, does he not have a view as to the constitutional propriety of withholding his persuasive powers of speech from a part of the media? We thought he had an even-handed policy in such matters. Evidently some hands are more even than others ...'

Ross rose again, putting on a theatrical show of weariness as he did so.

'I should have made it clear to the Right Honourable Gentleman that when I said that I had issued no instructions to the effect he mentioned, I was only speaking the truth. Nevertheless, it is possible that individual members of Her Majesty's Government may have decided, on their own account, to adopt the attitude to the television company that he indicated. If that is their view, then I must say I feel they are entitled to it.'

Here the House made another indescribable noise, this time with the element supporting the Prime Minister's thrust predominating.

Tuke didn't rise for a fourth time. He was satisfied. He had done what was necessary. He had drawn attention to the Government's behaviour. He would return to the matter another day.

'Who the hell put him up to it?' Ritchie barked at Adam. 'Interfering busybody! It's no business of his. If we want to complain about the boycott we'll do it our way. We don't need that wonky galah to do it for us.'

His deputy paused before replying. 'Well, no one here, that's for sure.'

'If I find out it *was* somebody here, they'll be out instantly. We don't meddle in politics in this outfit.'

'Oh, no?'

Ritchie shot Adam a glance. 'No, we don't. Now don't you rat on me, Adam, or I'll have your balls for breakfast.'

* * *

David was pleased by the press reaction to Archie Tuke's exchanges with the Prime Minister.

Until now, Fleet Street hadn't paid much heed to the N-TV boycott, always delighted to see a TV company in difficulty. Believing their readers were more concerned with the latest soap-opera developments, papers didn't pursue the matter. Now they slowly began to do so. The word 'gag' crept into headlines. Editorials were written on freedom of speech and the accountability of government to the governed. Some papers used it as an excuse to print more pictures of March Stevens.

A good head of steam was being worked up. Next Prime Minister's Questions would be on Thursday.

David rang Tuke for a chat. He also made sure he was presenting the programme on Thursday evening. Next day he decided which suit, shirt and tie he'd be wearing on the Thursday and took them with him down to Wandsworth. Paul Whitehall was waiting for him at Ewart's TV studio there.

They went in together.

CHAPTER 71

Thursday, 3:30 p.m. Harry Marchant, the Labour Party leader, was attacking the Prime Minister on social-services expenditure. He managed to extend his questions into miniature speeches of a length that wouldn't have disgraced Fidel Castro.

Then it was Archie Tuke's turn. Slightly dishevelled as always, but with a bright look in his eye, he was clasping a piece of paper with exaggerated care.

For his first supplementary question, he returned to the matter of the alleged Government boycott of N-TV. 'The Right Honourable Gentleman assured the House that he had issued no such instructions to his colleagues and I'm sure his words were welcomed by all in the House. I would ask the Right Honourable Gentleman, however, whether he was aware, when he made his statement, that the Home Secretary had circulated a letter advising his colleagues to desist from cooperating with the company in question?'

It was hard to tell whether Ross was surprised or not.

'I would say to Mr Tuke that I was conscious of my Right Honourable Friend's views on the matter, though I was not aware he had given any "advice" on it. Certainly not to me.'

The slight attempt at humour satisfied back-bench MPs on the Government side. To their groans, Tuke shot up again.

'Is the Prime Minister running the administration, or is the Home Secretary? I find it hard to believe that such an important posture was adopted without reference to the Prime Minister. I find it equally hard to believe that he didn't receive a copy of *this memorandum*,' – he waved the paper he had been clutching – 'circulated from the Home Secretary's office on the 18th December last year and containing explicit instructions to the effect already mentioned. After all, I had no difficulty in obtaining a copy ... and it does list the Prime Minister as one of the intended recipients.'

The House erupted once more. Tuke had triumphed. The Prime Minister had fallen neatly into the trap. Trevor Ross sat impassively staring ahead while the House made its noise.

Colin Lyon had been sitting uncomfortably along the

bench from the Prime Minister during the exchanges.

Now, for the first time, he was hearing calls of 'Resign!'

'My God, he's really done it,' exclaimed Ben, leaning out of bed to turn off the radio.

'Like stealing pennies off blind beggars,' said Yvonne, who lay beside him. 'It was so easy!'

'You really are very clever to have got hold of that memo,' said Ben, turning to Yvonne and kissing her on the tip of her well-powdered nose. 'I still don't know how you did it. You're a wicked old schemer.'

'I have my sources,' Yvonne answered, coyly. 'The best. And I'm certainly not going to reveal them to you. You'd only go and give them away.'

'No, I wouldn't, you old trout.'

'Well, I'll give you a clue. He's been to dinner here and his first name begins with a P.'

'Patrick Ritchie? Surely not?'

'No, stupid, think again!'

'Patrick Dobson, that fellow you know at the Foreign Office?'

'No. And he's called Richard, anyway. You're floundering. Not in the Government ...'

'A Civil Servant then?'

'I don't know any Civil Servants – at least, I don't have them to dinner.'

'I've got it: Plummond Almley.'

Yvonne laughed. 'That's it. Obvious, really. And where, Ben, did he get it from?'

'He might have got it from a Civil Servant, I suppose. He doesn't mind *who* he dines with ...'

'Right, he did. A Civil Servant in Downing Street. For heaven's sake, don't ask me any more ...'

'And you gave it to David and he gave it to Tuke. You are a schemer, just like I said.'

'David's going great guns, isn't he?' Yvonne sighed as though she rather fancied having him alongside her.

'Yes. I'd never have had the guts to do what he's done. But he's playing it for all it's worth, and good luck to him. Ritchie'll be furious. He couldn't understand why Tuke was making all the running. He firmly believed no one at N-TV had put him up to it!'

'What happens next?' asked Yvonne.

She rested her blonde mane on the silk pillow and waited.

'Hold on, hold on,' said Ben. 'Haven't quite digested my lunch yet ...'

CHAPTER 72

A few hours later, David and March were fronting the *Nightly News*. Patrick Ritchie had given instructions that the exchanges in the House were to be reported baldly, without comment. Liz Hastings had to be persuaded by David to go and argue the case for showing Lyon's memo on the screen. Tuke had had photocopies made and had given them to all the media.

Ritchie saw that he couldn't prevent the memo being shown if everyone else had it, and gave in. But again, the instruction came down: 'Don't headline it. Don't make a fuss.'

If this order was obeyed, BOYCOTT/MEMO would be but a short item placeable anywhere in the first part of the programme. Ideally, as the story wasn't long enough on its own, Liz Hastings would like to have stuck it on the back of another political or broadcasting one. That way it would seem less isolated.

By the time of the stagger-through at 7:15, the item was still wobbling around the running order, in competition with others about a bomb-attack in Belfast, a motor accident involving Charlotte Cordova in Hollywood, and the trial of the man arrested in connection with the Zoo Killings.

'It's not right at the moment,' Liz told David and March. 'I ought to put BOYCOTT/MEMO higher up. I'll take another look at the murder stuff and see whether that ought to go lower down.'

David said firmly, 'Don't bury the Tuke stuff, for heaven's sake. BBC and ITN are both leading on it. Just because Ritchie doesn't like it ...' He gave Liz a meaningful look through the camera lens. He wondered whether Ritchie was following the rehearsal on the set in his office. 'But don't put it next to a break, whatever you do. '

Liz pressed the switch on her talkback mike and asked David, 'Who's running this show, you or me?'

'You are. So do what you're told.'

When they were on the air, Liz Hastings decided to put ZOO KILLINGS TRIAL, introduced by March, ahead of BOYCOTT/MEMO.

'OK,' said David, nodding. He gestured to the floor manager and added, 'Make sure Paul's got that, will you?'

369

The floor manager nodded and spoke to the director on his intercom.

David led into BOYCOTT/MEMO as planned. He cued in a taped report from N-TV's Political Editor. It included voice-only extracts from Prime Minister's Questions, illustrated with still photos of Ross and Tuke with their mouths open.

'Stand by VT 5,' said Paul.

'What's that?' asked Liz, surprised.

'Quiet, Liz. Going to David, next.'

'No,' said Liz. 'It's March into 1922 COMMITTEE!'

'It's all right, Liz. David wants to back-announce his PM stuff ...'

'How do you know?'

'We fixed it,' he hissed. 'Here we come.'

'Twenty seconds to end of tape,' the production assistant called out.'

'But there isn't time,' shouted Liz. 'We're very tight.'

'Coming to David ...'

'Five-four-three ...'

'Cue David!'

David looked straight into the camera and said: 'The disclosure of the part played by the Home Secretary in the Government ban on N-TV highlights Mr Lyon's role as the minister responsible for broadcasting matters.'

'Roll VT!' said the PA.

'It is a role which is not always understood, even by those in broadcasting, and it is a role Mr Lyon has made uniquely his own.'

'And ... take it,' shouted Paul.

'What is this?' shrieked Liz.

'You'll see, love.'

The tape began with David naming names. Members of the IBA whom Lyon had tried to nobble. Names of the consortiums he had encouraged to compete for the N-TV franchise.

'Paul, where did you get this from? It's dynamite!'

Paul said nothing but prepared to forestall any attempt Liz might make to take the report off the screen. She would only have to press the right button. If she could find it amongst so many.

He checked with the monitor which showed him what was actually being received by viewers from the transmitter. The programme was going out OK.

'Ritchie will go bananas ...!' Liz was beside herself and crouched at the back of the booth.

The phone rang.

It was Ritchie going bananas.

'I don't know what it is,' she told him. 'It's got nothing to do with me. Blame Paul.'

Liz turned to Paul. 'He says to stop David.'

'But we can't stop David. It's on tape!'

'Stop the tape then ...'

'No can do.'

'You mean you won't ...?'

Paul ignored Liz and stared intently at the bank of monitor screens in front of him. On the pre-recorded tape, David continued to mount his devastating attack on the Home Secretary.

Paul would do *anything* to make sure the tape played to the end. They had recorded the item at Ewart's and made it look as though it was from N-TV's own studio. Paul had then arranged with the videotape engineers to play in the tape off a spare machine, the moment he cued in 'VT 5.' It had worked like a dream.

Never mind what hell there would be to pay afterwards, never mind if they fired him, it was the most exciting thing he'd ever done as a director.

The PA was utterly at sea now with the timing.

'There's about a minute left, love,' said Paul, calmly. 'We'll go to the break ... March to link and trail.'

David was concluding his piece:

And so, the Home Secretary is revealed as having influenced, directly, the running of a television company as well as conspiring to deny that company its right of access to Government sources. Surely this abuse of power must mean that Colin Lyon is no longer a fit person to remain one of Her Majesty's Ministers? Furthermore...'

Paul saw the off-air monitor go blank, and cursed. An apology caption popped up. Somebody in Master Control must have thrown the switch that stopped the programme going to the transmitter.

'Shit, who did that?'

'Probably Ritchie – with his own bare hands,' said Liz, defeated.

After a pause, Master Control ran the commercials.

After the break the *Nightly News* was allowed to continue as normal, while all hell prepared to break loose over David and Paul.

CHAPTER 73

It was one of those rare nights when Colin Lyon was tasting his wife's cooking at home. It might have been chicken casserole they were eating, though Lyon wasn't sure. Karen was insisting he spend more time at home and less lingering at the Home Office or in the House.

After what had been revealed in the Commons that afternoon, neither he nor she shrank from watching the *Nightly News*, even if it was from that godless, Trotskyite conspiracy known as N-TV.

So it was that Lyon witnessed David Kenway's forceful and impressive demolition of his career and reputation. 'How the hell did that ever get on ...?' he whispered.

He was particularly stunned by the imputation that his campaign against N-TV was rooted in his pique at the *Nightly News* having once sunk his chances of the Party leadership.

'I only tried to put the squeeze on N-TV because the PM wanted it ...'

'Are you sure that's what he wanted? Perhaps it was like the King and Thomas à Becket – "Who will rid me of this TV channel?"'

'No, I'm sure it wasn't like that at all ...'

'For God's sake get on to Patrick and find out what the hell he thinks he's doing,' urged Karen.

'Oh, Patrick's useless. I should never have got him involved with us. I only did it for you ...'

'God, you're spineless,' Karen yelped. 'Now's the time to be fighting back, not sitting there whimpering.'

The phone rang.

It wasn't the Press. It wasn't the television people, or even Patrick Ritchie.

It was the Prime Minister's principal private secretary. Could Mr Lyon please make himself available to talk to Mr Ross at nine-thirty that evening at Number 10?

When he put down the phone, Colin didn't have to tell his wife what it was. Nor explain that his political career was at an end.

He'd played with fire and been burned to a cinder.
'You can't take that lot on and hope to win.'
'Which lot?'
'Don't you follow anything I say, you silly woman ...?'

CHAPTER 74

Ben and Yvonne had pulled out all the stops. Even as the final credits were rolling on the *Nightly News*, Ben had managed to fight his way through to the studio on the phone. He spoke to David and ordered him to come immediately to Yvonne's house in Avenue Road. 'We'll have a party ...'

David needed no excuse to get out of N-TV House. He wasn't going to face Ritchie or anybody after what he'd just done. He told March, Paul and Vanessa to walk straight out of the building.

He and March still had their make-up on as they left.

By 10:00 p.m., they'd been joined by Lynne Kimberley, Archie Tuke and even Lord Almley – who sensed already that his consortium was no more likely to be successful at taking over the N-TV franchise than any other.

Yvonne excitedly poured drink down everyone. The choice was Dom Perignon or Dom Perignon. Ben kept making speeches, chiefly in praise of David. 'It took a lot of courage. But what television! I've never known it used like that before!'

Vanessa sat holding Paul's hand, telling him he'd been wonderful, too, and worrying about the babysitter.

March had to go and ring Mark at Hawkesgrove and tell him what had happened. He sounded suitably impressed although he hadn't seen the programme go out.

At eleven, the N-TV hourly bulletin gave them the news they'd been waiting for.

Mike Feather came into vision and announced:

Within the past few minutes it has been announced from Downing Street that the Prime Minister has accepted 'with regret' the resignation of Mr Colin Lyon as Home Secretary. Earlier this evening, it was revealed in an exclusive N-TV report that Mr Lyon had abused his position in relation to the N-TV company ...

'The buggers!' David exclaimed, shooting up from the sofa when he heard this.

They were claiming it as *their* exclusive now.

'Never mind,' Ben said soothingly. 'I tell you what, though. We may not have got any awards at BAFTA this year, but if *you* don't get one *next* year, I'll eat my hat.'

David hadn't even considered the possibility.

He looked around the room. It was full of people he had fought with, people he had fought alongside, people he had loved and betrayed.

Ben ... and March ... and Lynne. Did they still make up the 'First Family of TV News'? They had certainly had their ups and downs, like a real family.

There was Vanessa, one of so many women he had used and thrown aside.

There was Paul who'd done a far, far better thing, and picked her up. Paul, who had proved himself a man of strength in that night's TV coup.

There was Yvonne, who had winkled out the vital evidence from Plummond Almley ...

'And where did *you* get it from, Plum, I *must* know now ...? Yvonne perched on the edge of the sofa, next to him.

'From a Civil Servant ...'

'Yes, we know that, but who?'

'In Downing Street. Very close to Trevor Ross.'

'How close to Trevor Ross?'

'About as close as you can get ...'

'You mean ...?'

'I mean that Ross set Lyon up. He encouraged him to tackle N-TV head on, then used his failure as a means of getting rid of him.'

'Because ...' Archie Tuke put in, 'because he knew Lyon would always be plotting to get his hands on the premiership?'

'Precisely,' said Lord Almley, with a measure of satisfaction.

David allowed himself a small measure of satisfaction, too. And a much greater measure of regret at all the pain he had caused.

Someone was missing at the party, though, and finally he found time to call her.

CHAPTER 75

In the jargon of N-TV it was an 'end-pretty'.

End-pretties were shots of tranquil rural scenes, sunsets over rivers, cities by night, over which the closing credits of the *Nightly News* were made to roll. They were supposed to provide a satisfying contrast to the bomb-blasts, wars, murders and strife which had made up most of the foregoing programme.

High summer at Hawkesgrove provided the perfect setting for March's wedding. The old church, next to the rectory and across the fields from Hall Farm, shimmered in the intense heat. The tree-clad hills surrounding the tiny village resounded to the peal of bells as March and Mark came out of the church as man and wife.

The lanes were blocked with the cars of friends and relatives, and of hundreds who were there only because they knew March from the television screen. Even March had never looked more stunning than on her wedding day, her smile never brighter, her hair never more golden. Her husband, handsome and diffident, allowed her all the attention without envy.

The service in the flower-filled church had been heart-burstingly English. They had sung 'Jerusalem', and the stoutest hearts had been unable to avoid shedding a tear:

Bring me my Bow of burning gold!
Bring me my Arrows of desire!
Bring me my Spear! O clouds, unfold!
Bring me my Chariot of fire!

Now, for the reception in a marquee in the grounds of Hall Farm, the guests felt less uneasy in their summer clothes than they had been in church. The rector revealed a rig that wouldn't have seemed out of place in Trollope. A Silver Band from the next village played an arrangement of Elgar's 'Introduction and Allegro' before moving on to 'A Whiter Shade of Pale' and the theme from the *Nightly News*.

Celebrity-spotters had a field day. If they had no difficulty in recognizing Ben Brock, they weren't terribly sure who the grand blonde lady on his arm was. Perhaps it was his wife. Well, she would be, but not quite yet.

They recognized David Kenway, looking bronzed and handsome once more. Was that *his* wife by his side, and his two little boys? Yes, it was. Jo had dropped the divorce. They had decided they were made for each other; they needed each other, and no one else.

Mike Feather was there, sporting contact lenses now, some very new-looking teeth, and an even newer wife: Nikki Brennan, squeezed into a very tight, hot pair of white leather trousers. Perhaps encouraged by March's nuptials, Mike had impulsively proposed to Nikki, saying, 'I know that TV marriages are brittle and all that, but how about being my *first* wife?' She had accepted and they had been married, quickly and quietly, the week before.

Lynne Kimberley. Wasn't she looking gorgeous? So nice to see her back on the news again. They weren't to know she was proudest of having driven herself all the way down to the wedding without hitting anything. Who was the man in the shiny, lightweight suit by her side? Hard to tell. The name of Adam Ravenscroft meant nothing to anyone in the crowd.

Archie Tuke was present with his wife, the frumpish Molly. Fancy him turning up! Some politicians would muscle in on anything.

Paul and Vanessa Whitehall were there. They'd even brought baby Ben, who behaved himself impeccably and was introduced for the first time to his more famous namesake.

Sir Charles Craig and Lady Pam passed unrecognized also. Most people weren't to know that he'd returned temporarily to the post of Editor-in-Chief of N-TV following the departure of Patrick Ritchie.

Ritchie had gone back to Australia, with a substantial golden handshake, from which should have been deducted the libel money N-TV had had to pay over to Lynne Kimberley. Needless to say it hadn't been.

Sir Charles made sure he kept out of the way of the N-TV camera crew which was compiling a short report on the wedding for the Saturday evening bulletins. He didn't believe in editors appearing in their own programmes. He barely approved of the wedding being covered at all.

No one recognized Richard Luard, March's agent. His face perspired freely in the summer heat. He hadn't been able to do a great deal for March except get her more money from N-TV. He couldn't persuade her to spread her wings and take up opportunities elsewhere. She seemed happy at N-TV and, now she was married, he suspected she'd feel even less like becoming the all-round TV star she had the potential for.

Seeing what she was marrying into and where she was going to live, he couldn't altogether blame her. One day, perhaps, she might change her mind ...

March's father stood aside to let Ben Brock make a speech at the reception. To those who could make the comparison, he looked much older than he had on the last occasion he'd made a speech, at the previous year's BAFTA awards. But he looked happy. His buttonhole was bigger and brighter than anyone else's. And he managed to upstage the telegrams read out by the best man by producing a message of good wishes from Trevor and Alison Ross of Downing Street, London SW1, not to mention one from Winston and Lorraine Mann of the White House, 1600 Pennsylvania Avenue, Washington DC.

Where would it end?

Mark Rippingale wondered what else he was embracing by marrying March. Was he also taking on a wider world beyond Hawkesgrove where such happenings were considered normal?

It didn't matter if he was. He loved her, even if he knew he might never be able to have her completely to himself.

The bride and groom departed for their honeymoon.

Ben turned to David and Lynne.

'Well, newsmakers, time to be going. It's good to see the First Family together again ...'

Turning to Yvonne, he asked, breezily, 'Your Rolls or mine?' And Yvonne giggled loudly at his high spirits.

Ben kissed Lynne, then Vanessa, then Nikki. He was in a mood for kissing.

'He's incorrigible,' said Yvonne to David, knowingly. 'But he's a new man since ... well, you know ...'

David nodded, sure that she was right.

Ben shook hands with Sir Charles and Paul and Archie and just about everybody and, finally, with David.

'Take care in South Africa,' Ben told him. 'And, for heaven's sake, let bygones be bygones. Don't let them get at you again.' Then he looked sympathetically at Jo. 'I thought he'd said, "No more wars", anyway ...?'

Jo shrugged her shoulders and smiled.

'I think that was what the Press Office put out,' David said, putting on his rich, brown voice. 'Not me.'

Ben saw that Jo was about to say something. But she bit her lip, continued to smile at her husband, and kept her comment to herself.

Ben turned to leave. 'When do we get your first piece, David?'

'Wednesday night.'

'Ah, good. Well, I'll be behind the desk. And just remember, news isn't everything. If you're not careful, it can be like a drug.'

'I know,' said David. 'But we have to keep on filling the bottomless pit, don't we?'

'I suppose so – if we're addicts. And that's you and me.'

Ben beamed, saw how the sun was beginning to set over the Severn estuary, and turned to drive back to the city where so much more news was about to be made.